4/3/20

8/10

L.A. Sniper

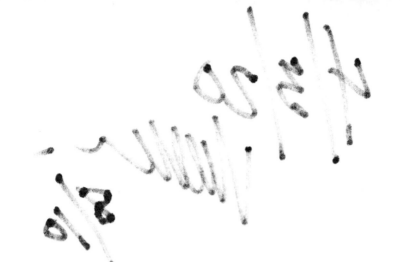

ALSO BY STEVE GANNON

STEPPING STONES

GLOW

A SONG FOR THE ASKING

KANE

ALLISON

INFIDEL

KANE: BLOOD MOON

L.A. SNIPER

◆ ◆ ◆ ◆

Steve Gannon

A
KANE
NOVEL

L.A. Sniper

Library of Congress Cataloging-in-Publication Data
Gannon, Steve.
L.A. Sniper / Steve Gannon.
p.   cm.
ISBN 978-0-9849881-9-8

Printed in the United States of America
10 9 8 7 6 5 4 3 2 1

To the officers of the Los Angeles Police Department killed
in the line of duty,
and to the families and loved ones they left behind

And, as always, for Dex

"Hope" is the thing with feathers
That perches in the soul
And sings the tune without words
And never stops, at all
~ Emily Dickinson

Take hope from the heart of man,
and you make him a beast of prey.
~ Marie Louise de la Ramée

L.A. Sniper

Chapter One

Officer Tony Rios took a swig of stale coffee and squinted out the window of the cruiser. "Hang a left on Venice," he said. "Then go straight. It's a half mile up, just past the library."

Los Angeles Police Department Officer-in-Training Chester "Chet" Grant cut the wheel and swung east onto Venice Boulevard, leaving behind the city of Venice's oceanfront promenade and its carnival atmosphere of artists, performers, food stands, restaurants, and volleyball courts. He checked the GPS map on the squad car's mobile data terminal, then glanced across the seat at his field training officer. "You been to this location before?"

Officer Rios took a final sip of coffee and screwed the metal cup back onto the top of his thermos. "I've been *everywhere* around here before," he sighed, returning the thermos to the glove compartment. Rios was a seasoned P-III patrol officer of nine years, and everything about him said he'd been there, done that, and come back for more.

Chet Grant was in his initial three-month deployment of a one-year probation that all LAPD "boot" officers were required to complete. Officer Rios was a tough, by-the-book mentor, but Chet knew he was lucky to have him as his field training officer. Chet had stayed in contact with a number of his L.A. Police Academy class members, and he knew many of them were undergoing a traditional hazing that most FTOs considered mandatory for their rookie probationers—no short sleeves, no boots, no second handcuff case, no unissued holster, no rookie driving, cleaning the patrol vehicle before roll call, and so on— stemming from a general attitude of "I paid *my* dues when I was a boot; now you're gonna pay *yours*." The only stipulation Rios had enforced was a time-honored "no mustache" tradition for P-I rookies like Chet, and Chet wasn't partial to mustaches anyway.

More important to Chet, however, was that he was being treated like an adult. His six months at the academy had given him a good foundation upon which to build, but a lot of things went down on the street that weren't covered in class, and Chet took being a probationer seriously. You didn't get second chances in the real world, and Chet knew this was the time he would learn the fundamentals that would keep him alive and out of lawsuits when he finally rolled out as a brand-new P-II. A majority of police personnel regularly named their field training officer as the individual who had exerted the most influence on their career, and Chet had a feeling that would prove true for him as well. Academy classes had their place, but it was common knowledge that it was the FTO who ultimately shaped a raw rookie into a cop.

"Put the pedal down, kid," said Rios. "Let's try to get there sometime tonight, okay? And let dispatch know we're on the way."

"I'm on it," said Chet, stomping on the gas and enjoying the instant acceleration of their brand-new Dodge Charger, a recent addition to the Pacific Division's motor pool—part of an LAPD fleet upgrade that had begun a few years back. Shooting past a delivery truck, he grabbed the radio mic and pressed the transmit button. "Fourteen Adam Six responding to location at South Venice and Grand," he said, confirming that they were rolling on a domestic disturbance call that had just come in. A neighbor had reported hearing a woman screaming in an adjacent apartment. According to the call, the woman had sounded like she was being beaten and possibly sexually assaulted.

"Roger, Fourteen Adam Six," came the static-filled reply.

"Getting used to the condensed schedule?" asked Rios, referring to the current LAPD 3/12 patrol watches—twelve-hour patrols for three days in a row, then four days off.

"What's not to like?" Chet replied. He had been working the p.m. watch since beginning his initial deployment, and four days off every week suited him just fine. For one, it provided plenty of time to spend with his new wife, Julie. Actually, it wasn't just the schedule that suited Chet. Not long after starting on the job, he had been surprised to discover that he liked being a member of the LAPD far more than he'd expected. The pay was great, especially for an entry-level salary—almost fifty grand annual

2

starting from day one at the academy. It was money that would come in handy when the baby came. Plus family health and dental plans, paid sick leave, disability benefits, fifteen days vacation, thirteen paid holidays, and even a pension plan.

But there was something about being on the job that Chet considered even more important than the schedule or the money or the perks. He liked hanging with the guys he'd met on the force, at least most of them, and he liked feeling he was doing something worthwhile. Of course working the "watch-3" night shift had its problems, but Chet hoped to get on "watch-2" days as soon as his probationary period was up. After that his goals were to finish college in his spare time, get his degree, make detective in four or five years, and then go for lieutenant. Or maybe enroll in law school if he wanted a change. Whatever. For the moment he was keeping his eyes open, learning as much as he could, and trusting the future to take care of itself.

"Your famous old man still pissed off about your dropping out of UCLA?" Rios asked.

"Not exactly certain on that," Chet answered. "My guess would be yes. We don't talk much these days," he added regretfully, remembering the bitter fight he'd had with his parents when he'd told them Julie was pregnant and they were getting married. Starting a family earlier than planned would be hard, but being married to Julie was worth it. Chet smiled, remembering the feel of Julie's warm body as she'd climbed into bed that afternoon to wake him for his shift. What a sweet wakeup it had been.

"You okay about quitting school?"

Chet shrugged, his smile fading. "Mostly," he answered, long ago having accepted that you don't always get to call the shots. When Chet's movie-star parents had refused to help with expenses after the marriage—in the end not even attending Chet and Julie's wedding—dropping out of school and getting a job had been the only option. "I'll finish when I get a chance," he added. "It's definitely on the list."

"Well, for what it's worth, I admire what you're doing."

Chet feigned surprise. "Me? I thought you said I was a shitty driver."

Rios smiled. "You are. You know what I mean. A lotta guys would have just caved in to Daddy's bankroll. You're trying to do something with your life, and you're doing it on your own terms. I like that."

"Yeah, well . . . I like it, too," Chet said more seriously. And he did. He regretted the recent alienation from his parents, but maybe that was just part of growing up. Given time, his folks would come around. After all, what parents could resist visiting their own grandchild? Life was good, and things were going to come together in the end. He was certain of it.

"That building over there," said Rios, pointing to a four-story apartment complex at the intersection of South Venice and Grand Avenue. Three tiers of elevated exterior walkways faced the building, accessing side-by-side units. "Park in the red, under the streetlight."

"Right. What was the apartment number?"

Rios checked the mobile data terminal, confirming the call address. "Twenty-six B. Second level," he answered. "I hate domestic calls," he added as Chet eased the black-and-white into a no-parking zone.

"Why's that?" asked Chet, shutting off the engine.

"Well, for one thing, on a domestic call you never know what's gonna happen when you knock on that door," said Rios. "Turn your back on a woman who's been getting beat to within an inch of her life, and she sticks a knife in you for arresting her boyfriend. I've seen it happen. By the way, I'm letting you handle this one. Let's see how you do."

"Okay," said Chet, feeling a mix of pride and apprehension. "If you think I'm ready. I promise I won't turn my back on the woman."

"Good. Then I think you're ready," Rios chuckled. "Which reminds me of a story that might relate a bit here."

"I hope it's better than the one you told the other night," Chet said suspiciously, sensing a joke coming on. "You know, the one about the sailor with two—"

"You'll like this one," Rios interrupted. "So this woman calls 911," he began. "'My husband isn't breathing and his eyes are glazed,' she cries. 'I think he's dead! What can I do?' 'Stay calm, ma'am,' says the operator. 'I can help, but first we need to make sure he's really dead.'"

Rios grinned, struggling not to bust up at his own joke. "There's a long silence," he continued, dramatically lowering his voice. "Then a gunshot is heard. Back on the phone, the wife says, 'Okay, now what?'"

"Good one," Chet laughed, realizing that Rios knew he was nervous and was trying to loosen him up. Grateful for the momentary distraction, Chet picked up the radio mic. "Fourteen Adam Six at location, South Venice and Grand."

"Roger, Fourteen Adam Six," came the dispatch response.

Rios shot Chet a nod of approval. Then, all joking forgotten, "Okay, let's do this." Rios grabbed his baton and swung his legs from the cruiser. "You do the knocking."

Chet grabbed his own baton, exited, and started across the apartment parking lot, hurrying to catch up with his training officer. He rejoined Rios at the base of a flight of stairs rising on the left side of the building. One landing up he eased past Rios on the walkway, spotting apartment 26B several doors down. He didn't hear a woman screaming, but he knew the situation might have changed since the 911 call was placed. He also noted that, curiously, the lights in 26B were out.

As Chet started to thumb the doorbell, three puzzling things happened. A hollow thunk sounded behind him, like someone had thumped a melon; a shard of wood flew off the wall, stinging his face; and what felt like a warm splash of liquid spattered his back and neck. An instant later Rios collapsed onto the walkway behind him.

Chet turned. "Tony, you okay?" he asked, shocked by his partner's sudden collapse. Puzzled, he knelt to help him up. Rios wasn't moving. And something was wrong with his head, like it had deflated somehow. Like part of it was *missing*. Blood matted his scalp. More was rapidly spreading across the walkway beneath his face.

"Jesus, Tony," Chet whispered. He took Rios's shoulders and turned him over. He froze, staring in horror. Much of Rios's forehead was gone, exposing a pulpy mass of blood and brain.

Glancing up and down the walkway, Chet drew his service weapon and reached for his shoulder mic. "Officer needs help," he shouted without thinking, saying the words that would immediately bring every available patrol unit to the area.

Trembling with shock, he rose to his feet, close to tears but fighting not to panic.

What happened? Somebody with a gun? I didn't hear a shot. Oh, God, what am I going to do? Go back to the car? Location, give my unit and location, he thought, suddenly remembering his training.

"Officer needs help," he repeated into his shoulder mic, trying to steady his voice. His heart was slamming in his chest. "Fourteen Adam Six, location Venice and Gra—"

At that precise moment, a 240-grain copper-jacketed bullet travelling at 970 feet per second struck Chet in the center of his forehead. As the slug entered his skull, smashing through skin and bone and brain, the copper cladding stripped back from the projectile like petals opening on a flower, exposing a rapidly distorting lead core inside.

An instant later the projectile exited the back of Chet's head, spraying a bloom of red against the wall behind him. LAPD Officer-in-Training Chet Grant dropped like a stone, crumpling to the walkway beside his partner.

Like Officer Rios, he died without knowing what had hit him.

Chapter Two

The Los Angeles Philharmonic's opening night gala has always been an uncomfortable event for me to attend. Tonight's concert, along with the ancillary festivities accompanying the orchestra's annual September extravaganza at Walt Disney Concert Hall, was proving to be no exception.

Not that I don't enjoy the excitement associated with the LA Phil's season kickoff—women in elegant gowns accompanied by balding, overweight men; throngs of concertgoers knocking back cocktails in the lobby; long lines of red-carpet celebrities posing for pictures; tented terraces crammed with dinner tables, banners, and sparkling lights; and everywhere an electric sense of anticipation—I do. I really do. It's just that I always feel a bit out of place.

My three children and I were sitting in the third row of the front orchestra section, just left of stage center, occupying some of the most expensive real estate in the hall. Tickets for tonight's performance had been donated to my wife, Catheryn, by a wealthy patron. The donor had long admired Catheryn's cello playing, and as the woman and her family couldn't attend that evening, she had given her tickets to Catheryn, saying she hoped they could be put to good use. As far as I was concerned, they were. Although I had attended numerous LA Phil performances and been present at every September gala since Disney Hall had opened, this was the closest I had ever sat to the front. Not that there's a bad seat in the house, but this was like being onstage with the musicians.

We were in the middle of a brief intermission while the stage was being reset following a puzzling, at least to me, modern dance interlude—preparing for the final musical presentation of the evening, Haydn's Cello Concerto No. 1 in C Major. Noticing a disturbance brewing to my right, I shot a look of warning at my sixteen-year-old son Nate, who was bored and starting to tease his older sister, Allison. Nate gave me a surly look back, an expression I had lately been seeing more and more.

The youngest of our family, Nate had rocketed up several inches over the past year, and he now stood a solid six feet tall. If he kept growing, I thought absently, he was going to wind up as big as I am. And for better or worse, the resemblance didn't end there. Athletic, stubborn, competitive, his temper fierce and uncontrollable, quick to both laughter and anger, his loyalties unshakable, his moods as transparent as glass, Nate—God help him—was the most like me.

I know being a teenager can be a tough time for kids, but Nate was going through a particularly rough patch, even for a sixteen-year-old. His temper had proved a continuing problem at school, getting him into more than a few fights and eventually resulting in his being kicked off the Samohi Vikings baseball team. Worse, the previous weekend he had been arrested with several of his friends for underage drinking, and Catheryn and I had been called in the middle of the night to pick him up at the Malibu Sheriff's Department. One of the boys with Nate had been caught with weed in his possession, and they were all being charged with that offense, too. Catheryn wanted Nate to see a therapist. Nate refused. I wanted to kill him, but Catheryn insisted that option was out, too—at least for the moment. Seriously, Nate was a good kid, but like most parents facing teenage rebellion, I was finding that my customarily strict discipline didn't seem to be working, and I was at a loss about what to do.

I decided to think about Nate's problems later. Settling back in my seat, I let my eyes roam the interior of Disney Hall, the most recent addition to the Los Angeles Music Center's performing arts venues. It was an imaginative architectural statement that gracefully complemented its sister venues to the north—the Dorothy Chandler Pavilion, the Ahmanson Theatre, and the Mark Taper Forum. The exterior of the building, with its towering steel panels and curved limestone walls, seemed reminiscent of a sailing ship, at least to my eye, and the 2,265-seat performing hall in which we were now seated continued the illusion. Warm interior wood walls, a logjam of concert organ pipes made of Douglas fir, a flooring of oak, and a stage of yellow Alaskan cedar gave one the impression of being inside the hull of a gigantic vessel, with performing artists onstage surrounded by audience on all sides. The effect was one of scope and grandeur, while somehow still seeming inviting and intimate.

"So what do you think of the performance so far?" asked my son Travis, who was sitting to my left. Travis was beginning his second year of graduate studies at Juilliard. Like his mother, he was an accomplished musician. Tall and lean, with an economy of grace and motion definitely not inherited from me, Travis had flown in from New York for tonight's performance and would be returning to school in a few days. I hadn't seen much of him since he'd graduated from USC, and I enjoyed having him home again, if only briefly.

"The performance so far? Not my cup of tea," I answered, lowering my voice. Over the years, in an effort to make its opening-night galas more memorable for patrons and donors, the LA Phil had increasingly presented a potpourri of mixed performances—a single movement of something here, a dance number there, with maybe a visual work of some sort sandwiched in between—and tonight was no exception. Although I usually enjoy experiencing something new, most of the modern works that had been presented so far, especially a musical piece commissioned for tonight's gala, reminded me of the Hans Christian Andersen tale "The Emperor's New Clothes." A lot of flash and show, but not much substance, and I was looking forward to the Haydn concerto for a more traditional conclusion to the evening.

"Trav, you should know better than to ask a police detective's opinion on the arts," advised my daughter, Allison, sitting on my other side. "If an event with this many people present doesn't have goalposts and sweaty men running around in helmets and shoulder pads, Dadzilla's not interested."

I sighed and glanced at Allison, as always struck by the startling resemblance she bore to her mother. Tall and slim, with dark auburn hair and just the remnants of a sprinkle of freckles traversing the bridge of her nose, she had matured over the past few years from a spirited tomboy to a striking young lady. Like her mother, she could look great without much effort. "Not true, Ali," I said. "When it comes to music, I just happen to be more discerning than most."

"Country music, maybe," Allison countered with a grin.

"Nothing wrong with country music," I grumbled. "I like a tune you can remember, especially if it comes with lyrics that say something about the human condition."

"You mean lyrics like 'I'm so miserable without you, it's like you never left?'"

I laughed. "Exactly."

"And when you say 'the human condition,' I'm assuming you're referring to some deep tragedy like your truck won't start, or your girlfriend cheated, or your dog died—or maybe all three."

"Right again. Now quiet down, Ali," I said, wary of matching wits with my daughter, as it usually turned into a losing proposition. "Your mom will be coming out shortly."

As if on cue the hall lights dimmed, signaling concertgoers to return to their seats. Within minutes the hall began refilling with people who had stepped out for a cocktail or a trip to the bathroom. Next, Philharmonic musicians began filing onstage— taking their seats, adjusting scores, and joining in a quick, discordant round of last-minute tuning.

The house lights dimmed a final time, leaving the hall lit solely by a glow from the stage. Seconds passed. I sensed a feeling of anticipation coursing through the audience, spreading from the rows in front to the terrace seats in back, as palpable as an electric current. Then, to a warm round of applause, the Philharmonic's young superstar Venezuelan music director walked onstage accompanied by my wife, Catheryn, who was substituting that evening as the featured soloist. I felt a slight stir of surprise in the audience at Catheryn's appearance, even though a change slip announcing her replacement of the LA Phil's principal cellist, Arthur West, had been included in the program.

For the evening Catheryn was wearing a long red gown that accented her slim figure, making her look almost regal. Though she was smiling, I could tell she was nervous. With her cello and bow held loosely in her left hand, she greeted the concertmaster, briefly taking his hand. She nodded to the other section principals, then glanced at the music director and took her place in a chair near the conductor's podium.

As always when I watched Catheryn perform, I was struck by the realization that she probably could have done a whole lot better than me, matrimonially. We had met in college. I'd been playing football for USC and trying to figure out what to do with my life; she had been enrolled in the prestigious USC School of Music, her heart set on a performing career and a future in music. I had fallen in love with her at first sight. Refusing to take no for an answer, I had pursued her shamelessly until she finally agreed to go out with me.

Despite our differences—she sipped wine, I guzzled beer; she planned a career in music, I wanted a wife who would clean and cook and give me a house full of kids—we had somehow hit it off. We were married shortly after graduation, after which Catheryn had temporarily put her music career on hold with the coming of our first child, Tommy. With a family to support, I joined the LAPD, surprising myself by finding I had a talent for police work, making detective just four years after joining the force. Later, with the births of Travis, Allison, and Nate, Catheryn's temporary career derailment had become permanent—with the exception of her playing with a Wednesday-evening chamber group and giving occasional music lessons to supplement our family income.

Seven years ago, over the course of the same summer that our oldest son, Tommy, had died in a rock-climbing accident, Catheryn had taken a position with the Los Angeles Philharmonic. Since then she had ascended the Philharmonic ranks to the position of assistant principal cello. Lately she had been filling in for Arthur West, who was having health problems and was rumored to be considering retirement. Although Catheryn had performed as a soloist with the orchestra in the past, tonight was a big opportunity, and I knew she wanted to do well.

The music director waited several seconds for the house to settle. A few coughs. Several rustlings as latecomers took their seats. Then silence. The music director raised his hands.

And a moment later they began.

During his life, Joseph Haydn had been described as having "a happy and naturally cheerful temperament," and his Cello Concerto in C Major was an apt example of his generally sunny outlook on life. For me it was also a welcome respite from the twenty-first-century works of the gala's first half. I had listened to Catheryn practicing her solo part over the past months, and I knew the concerto contained extremely demanding technical passages for the soloist. My hands clammy with sweat, I sat nervously through the initial orchestral exposition, waiting for Catheryn to begin, praying she didn't falter. I could feel a sense of expectation in the audience as well, as others waited to hear what the substitute soloist could do.

A minute and a half into the piece, Catheryn's cello finally spoke. Opening with a triumphant chord followed by a lively exchange with the orchestral strings, Catheryn took complete possession of the stage, a possession she never relinquished from that moment on, leaving no doubt that we were listening to a rare performance delivered at the hands of a master.

Haydn's cello concerto, with its rich chords and dizzyingly fast runs, was an ideal vehicle to showcase the ability of a soloist. But in Catheryn's hands, the requisite virtuosity seemed a natural outgrowth of her music. In her hands the piece became more than a technical marvel, transcending virtuosity. For me, it became a wordless poem of emotion.

And as the opening movement progressed, the deep, earthy tones of Catheryn's cello began to tear at something inside me, ripping loose feelings I was unable to express, emotions contrary to the cheery ones usually associated with Haydn's incandescent work. Against my will, my thoughts returned to a darker time of my life, a time of sadness and shame and unutterable regret. Against my will, driven by the heartrending voice of Catheryn's cello, I revisited the anguish that had accompanied the death of my son Tommy, and once more I experienced the sick, hollow emptiness that comes to me in quiet moments and never completely goes away.

* * *

After a second circuit of the block, he pulled to the curb, killed his headlights, and shut off the engine. He waited there several minutes, occasionally glancing at the house, checking for any sign of movement. The windows of the home were dark. The occupants were either asleep or away on a trip, but that didn't matter. An entry light was burning outside the front door, possibly on a timer. Along with illumination from a streetlight on the corner, the front landing was well lit.

And that *did* matter.

Satisfied, he opened the glove compartment and withdrew one of his Walmart prepaid cell phones. Another quick look up and down the street.

Nothing.

Everything seemed perfect. Still, he hesitated. He was nothing if not meticulous. Better safe than sorry, he reminded himself. Patiently, he once again mentally reviewed the details of tonight's shoot, starting at the beginning.

Earlier that day, still high from his kills in Venice, he had visited this, his next field of fire, ensuring that nothing had changed since his last reconnaissance. After that he had checked his firing position, located just below the ridgeline to the east. Then he had spent the rest of the afternoon reviewing his range cards and field sketches, memorizing landmarks, distances to potential target cover, area streets, fallback positions, and exit routes.

Later that evening he had picked up his Ford Expedition, encountering no one at the storage yard who might remember him. As always he had worn a ball cap and sunglasses, as well as carefully avoiding the storage lot's surveillance cameras. The cap and glasses were a preventive measure he routinely employed even after leaving the storage yard, just in case. At any rate, dark glasses improved his night vision, which was an added bonus.

A battery-powered police scanner sat on the seat beside him. He rechecked the radio's settings, turned down the volume, then let his hand travel to a leather pouch fixed to the side of his seat. Concealed in the pouch was a .50 caliber Desert Eagle pistol, cocked and locked. At just over four pounds in weight, the huge pistol was a formidable weapon that could send a half-inch bullet downrange at twice the velocity of a .45 ACP round, at the same time delivering the punch of a round from a .308 Winchester rifle. Although the pistol was a challenge to shoot, after modifying his two-handed grip and adjusting for recoil, he had found it to be surprisingly accurate at long distances. More to the point, it had the power to penetrate class-two body armor, the kind worn by police. Of course, as a self-defense weapon the Deagle was impractical at best, but it was present in the car for one use only—to make certain he would never be taken alive.

After completing his mental review, he glanced into the rear of the Expedition. He had removed the back seat shortly after acquiring the vehicle, and the middle seat was currently folded down, creating a large, flat area partially occupied by his shooting bench, providing a rifle rest to steady his shots. Sandbags stabilized the wooden bench, making his shooting setup easy to reposition and conceal once it had served its purpose.

Beside the bench, concealed beneath a blanket, lay his subsonic rifle, a modified Remington Model 700 Sendero. He had replaced the Sendero's original .233 caliber barrel with a Krieger 1/8 twist, match-grade bull barrel chambered in .300 Whisper. The new Whisper barrel had come threaded for an Advanced Armament Corporation sonic suppressor, the AAC after-market addition making the rifle almost "Hollywood quiet."

Stagger-stacked in the Sendero's magazine were three handloaded .300 Whisper subsonic cartridges, each capable of putting a 240-grain bullet inside a one-inch circle at 200 yards, repeatable every time with a half-minute-of-angle accuracy. A fourth cartridge lay in the chamber, ready to fire. Not that he would need four rounds. Two, or possibly three at most, would suffice. If the job weren't done by then, it was time to leave anyway.

Completing his setup was a Millett 4-16x 50mm tactical scope. Rugged and precise, the scope's optics could bring head hairs into focus at 100 yards. He occasionally felt a twinge of regret for not purchasing a more expensive Leupold he had been considering, but the Millett was a worthy alternative and had yet to let him down.

Everything was ready.

It was time.

Pulse quickening, he lifted the cell phone and punched in the three digits that would bring his targets into range.

Several rings. Then, "911—police, fire, and medical. What is your emergency?"

"Someone's breaking into my house," he whispered.

"Stay on the line, sir. Please confirm your phone number and address so I can send someone as soon as possible."

"I'm at 22893 Las Lomas in Pacific Palisades. Get somebody out here right away. I'm locking myself in the bathroom."

"Sir, please stay on the line. In case we're disconnected, I need to verify your phone—"

He hung up, powered down the cell phone, and tossed it back into the glove box. He could discard the phone later; right now the clock was running.

With a last glance at the house, he started the Expedition and pulled away from the curb, again turning up the volume of his police scanner at the same time. Moments later, amid a background of static, he heard LAPD patrol unit Eight Adam Three responding to a possible four-fifty-nine at 22893 Las Lomas.

He'd have to hurry.

Forcing himself not to speed, he swung left and climbed to a residential street running the crest of the nearby ridge. Several blocks down he pulled to a stop in a cul-de-sac at the end. He glanced at his watch. Two minutes had elapsed since he'd made his call. He cut his headlights. After rolling down the Expedition's windows to vent the percussive blast of his shots, he quietly backed onto a dirt lot overlooking the homes below, parking as close to the edge as possible. Leaving the keys in the ignition, he shut off the engine, removed his ball cap and sunglasses, grabbed his police scanner, and climbed into the back of the vehicle.

Working quickly, he plugged ear buds into the scanner and shoved a bud into his right ear, leaving his left ear open so he could hear anyone approaching. Next he raised the SUV's rear glass hatch, which he had unlatched from outside the vehicle and secured with a strip of duct tape before leaving the storage yard. Trying not to rush, he attached a bungee strap to partially reclose the glass panel, leaving it open just enough to accommodate his shots. Finally he elevated the rear of his shooting bench with a sandbag, angling the front of the bench downward to facilitate his shots into the neighborhood below.

After withdrawing his weapon from beneath the blanket, he removed a neoprene cover protecting the Millett scope, then knelt beside the bench. Although he would have preferred to shoot from a prone position, the downward shot into the canyon required otherwise. He rested the rifle's front swivel on a leather stabilizer fixed atop the bench, then nestled the rear of the rifle stock into a small sandbag that allowed him to make slight vertical adjustments by squeezing with his nonshooting hand.

He made several changes to his setup before he was satisfied. Because of the downward angle of the shot, the business end of the AAC suppressor was now extended well outside the vehicle. Although this made his presence on the ridge less stealthy, at least the sound of his shots inside the Expedition would be extremely manageable—barely enough to necessitate ear protection. Twisting a knob on the left side of the rifle scope, he activated the Millett's reticle illumination. The mil dots and fine lines in the eyepiece sprang to life, glowing a ghostly green. Next he adjusted the focus knob, bringing the front door of the Las Lomas house into crystal-clear view. As expected, ambient illumination at the site was more than adequate.

After a final glance around the outside of the Expedition, he crammed a foam earplug into his left ear, leaving the police-scanner ear bud in his right. One last time he reviewed the shot in his mind. The range to the front door was 230 yards, a distance he had previously measured with an off-the-shelf laser rangefinder. Although a slight breeze was moving up the canyon, the wind was blowing in the direction of his shot and wouldn't require any correction. Not that wind would require much correction at that distance, anyway. Shooting down would slightly decrease the bullet's ballistic drop, but he would take that into consideration. From hundreds of hours on the range compiling his shooting "dope," recording data on his rifle's performance at various distances and conditions, he knew the exact "hold"—a shift in the scope's crosshairs overlaying the target—that would put his subsonic bullet nearly dead-center inside a six-inch circle, the size of a human head.

It was a shot he could make in his sleep.

Now all he had to do was wait.

*   *   *

Allison covered my hand with hers. Like her mother, she often seemed able to sense what I was feeling. In some mysterious manner I've never been able to fathom, sometimes women just know. *How do they do that?* I wondered, a little embarrassed to be so transparent in the eyes of my daughter.

I shot Allison a smile and tried to submerge my dark memories, resolving to stay in the moment. And what a moment it was. All nervousness forgotten, Catheryn had just finished the joyous first movement of the Haydn and was now embarking on the concerto's stately, majestic adagio. In this she joined the orchestra more as a collaborator than as a soloist, at times even accompanying the strings in a transcendent excursion—recurrent themes from the first movement gently taking shape, then growing and swelling, a work of exquisite beauty flowering in the respite between the first and final movements—leaving the audience mesmerized, spellbound, frozen in silence.

And then the concluding movement was upon us. Again the orchestra took the lead, opening with accelerated scales in the strings and an unrelenting bassline driving the work forward. And again Catheryn's cello joined them, taking what was ordinarily a lively concluding orchestral movement into another realm altogether. Pleasure shining in her eyes, Catheryn embarked on a six-minute flourish of breathtaking virtuosic runs and lush, gorgeous chords filled with echoes of themes presented in the first two movements, giving a dazzling demonstration of the versatility and power of a cello played by a master.

As the final triumphant chords died away, the entire audience—from the rows in front to the terraces in back—rose as one, filling the hall with thunderous applause. Feeling a rush of pride, I stood and joined them. Moments later Nate ran to the edge of the stage and gave Catheryn a bouquet of roses I had purchased earlier that day. Seeing the expression of pleasure in her eyes, I grinned like a kid, not for the first time thinking how lucky I was to have her in my life.

Chapter Three

An extensive backstage area surrounds Disney Concert Hall, with various technical facilities that include support offices, practice rooms, lounges, and a rehearsal chamber suitable for small-scale presentations. Musicians even have access to a private garden, in keeping with the architect's stated intention of making performers as comfortable as possible. To encourage free interaction between artists and the public, the backstage area has been designed to be open and welcoming to concertgoers as well. For tonight's fund-raiser, however, I knew that any backstage interaction would be strictly between artists and patrons, donors, and anyone with enough money to buy a sponsor-level table on the terrace.

Avoiding the throng crowding the backstage door, my children and I exited the hall and reentered the building through the artists' entrance on Second and Grand. After I signed in with a guard who knew us from previous visits, we made our way to an impromptu backstage reception being held for the musicians. Upon arriving, I peered across a sea of women in gowns and men in tuxes jamming the room, eventually spotting Catheryn surrounded by a group of admirers including the LA Phil music director, principal cellist Arthur West, and several other people whom I recognized as members of the Philharmonic board.

"Should we go over and rescue Mom?" asked Nate.

"Let's give her a few minutes," I suggested. "Your mom's schmoozing with LA Phil patrons, which is important. Especially on a night like tonight."

"Besides, she doesn't exactly look like she needs *rescuing*, Nate," observed Travis.

"Right," added Allison. "Anyone with a brain can see that the crowd over there loves her."

"A brain, huh? Guess that lets you out," Nate shot back.

Allison sighed theatrically. "Nate, I appreciate the simple things in life. I just don't like having one of them for a brother."

"Knock it off, you two," I warned. "This is a big night for your mom. Don't screw it up."

"Yes, sir," said Allison with a grin, throwing me a sloppy salute.

"Nate?" I said, regarding my youngest. "On your good behavior?"

Nate shrugged. "Whatever."

Just then Catheryn glanced up from her conversation, spotting us across the room. She smiled and waved, motioning us to join her.

It took some jostling to make our way across the room without spilling anyone's champagne. When we arrived, Catheryn took my hand and kissed me on the cheek. "Everyone, I want you to meet my family," she said proudly, drawing us into the circle.

"Dan Kane," I said, shaking hands with the music director and several others nearby. Then, to the rest of the group, "Pleased to meet you all. These are our offspring—Travis, Allison, and Nate," I added, putting an arm around Nate's shoulders.

"Offspring, eh?" laughed Arthur West. "Good to see you here tonight, Detective," he continued, shaking my hand. Arthur and I had not always been on the best of terms, most of that my fault, but over the past several years he had warmed to me— maybe because I had offered him a free swing at me anytime he wanted. Although I deserved it, he had never called in that particular marker.

"Thanks, Arthur," I replied, letting Nate squirm away. "How are you feeling?"

"I've been better."

"Well, I'm glad to see you here tonight," I said, not certain where to go from there. Arthur had always been a handsome, distinguished-looking man, but lately he'd lost a lot of weight, and not in a good way.

"Wasn't Mom terrific tonight?" Allison broke in.

"Yes, she was," said Arthur.

"I'll second that," I added, turning to Catheryn. "Kate, you hit a home run with that concerto of yours. I am so proud of you."

20

"We all are," said the music director. "That was a singular performance, Catheryn. Truly, truly marvelous. I won't soon forget it, nor will our audience."

Catheryn flushed. "Thank you," she said quietly. "I thought the entire concert went well. I think the audience really liked it."

"The audience *loved* it," said an elegantly dressed woman standing nearby, who was wearing what appeared to be a ransom in jewelry. "I think this gala is going to be one of our most successful fund-raisers yet."

"From your lips to God's ears," said the music director.

"Speaking of which, I think it's time we made our way out to the terrace," suggested another well-dressed woman whom I recognized as one of the Philharmonic board members. "Will you be joining us for dinner, Catheryn?"

"Maybe just to say a few hellos," Catheryn answered evasively. "I think Dan has something else planned."

There was no way we would be sitting at one of the sponsor tables—some of which would bring in several hundred thousand dollars that evening. Like most musicians, we weren't in that league. Catheryn, the music director, and the entire ensemble of LA Phil players had donated their performances for the evening, and as far as I was concerned, that was enough. "Something else planned? It just so happens I do," I said. "It's a surprise."

Catheryn raised an eyebrow. "A surprise?"

"We're going to Perch for dinner," said Travis.

"Not a surprise anymore," I grumbled.

"Sorry, Dad," said Travis.

"Perch?" said Catheryn with a smile. "I've been dying to try it out. That's wonderful, Dan. But how did you get reservations on a night like tonight? Every place in town is completely booked."

"I *know* people," I answered. "Besides, I made the reservation months ago."

It was a short distance from the Disney Hall to Perch, so after breaking away from the backstage crowd, Catheryn and I decided to leave our cars in the subterranean parking area and walk to the restaurant. The kids and I waited while Catheryn ducked into a dressing room to drop off the roses and change from her gown into the clothes she had worn to rehearsal earlier that day.

A few minutes later, after exiting the Disney Hall, we skipped making an appearance in the gala tent and headed directly to the restaurant. It was a cool September evening, with a hint of fall already in the air, and the crisp night felt good after being inside. As we walked south on Grand—Travis and Allison out front, Nate dragging up the rear—Catheryn asked, "Anything new on the two officers who were killed last night, Dan? I was so sorry to hear about them on the news this morning."

"Nothing much," I answered, taking Catheryn's hand. "Everyone at the Pacific Division is working overtime, trying to get a handle on things."

"Did you know either of the men who were murdered?"

"One of them. Tony Rios. Good man."

"Well, I hope they find whoever did it."

"Oh, we'll find him," I said grimly. "Count on it." Then, changing the subject, "It was good seeing Arthur tonight, although he's looking a little . . ."

" . . . thin," Catheryn finished. "He's not well, Dan. He talked with me this afternoon. He's definitely going to retire. Maybe we can throw a going-away party for him?"

"Sure. Something at the beach?"

"I was thinking a little more upscale. Maybe the Beverly Hills Hotel?"

"Whatever you say, Kate."

Catheryn hesitated, then continued. "The music director is talking about moving me up to the principal cello position, at least temporarily. Maybe permanently."

"Can you handle the additional work? I mean, I know your medical checkups have been great, but if—"

"I'm fine, Dan," she interrupted firmly.

I thought for a moment before responding. A lot was at stake. Two summers ago Catheryn had been treated for a serious illness that had required a bone marrow transplant. Although everything had eventually gone well, the success rate for her treatment was measured in terms of five-year survivals. I knew that the LA Phil promotion was something Catheryn wanted, and if she wanted it, so did I—but not at the expense of her health. "I know you're fine," I said gently. "But maybe we should see what your doctor has to say before accepting. When's your next appointment?"

"A couple of weeks. Will you come with me?"

"Of course. I'll drive you, like always. What do you say we wait till then to give the Philharmonic an answer?"

"If you want," Catheryn sighed. "Anyway, the Phil may decide to have a competitive audition for the permanent position, in which case I may not even get it." She squeezed my hand and smiled. "But in any case, I'm okay, Dan. I'm fine. Stop worrying."

"I'll try." I took a deep breath and continued, shifting from the subject of her health. "Even if they do have a competitive audition, you're going to get the position. I have no doubt of that. When I said you hit a homer tonight, I meant it. You had the audience absolutely mesmerized. You were . . . I can't describe it."

"Thanks, Dan. I was so nervous, I wasn't certain I'd be able to play. Did you really enjoy it?"

I nodded. "I really did." Still a little embarrassed at how much the first movement had affected me, I added, "Of course, it wasn't country music, but—"

Catheryn laughed and elbowed me in the ribs. "Oh, hush," she said. "How about the kids? Did they like the performance?"

"Ali and Trav ate up the whole concert, including the first half—which wasn't exactly to my taste—and they *loved* you." I glanced back, noting that Nate had fallen even farther behind. "Not too sure about what Nate thought."

"He's having a hard time," said Catheryn.

"Don't I know it." I called back to Nate. "Hey, Nate. Get your butt up here and tell your mom how much you loved her playing."

Nate took his time catching up. When he did, I again put an arm around his shoulders. "You okay, kid?" I asked.

"I'm fine," Nate mumbled. Either my hearing was going, or some teenage-speech gene had recently kicked in, but more and more I found myself having to ask Nate to repeat things.

"What did you think of the performance?" asked Catheryn, taking Nate's hand.

"In particular, did you notice how great your mom was up there?" I added.

Nate surprised me. Instead of the noncommittal shrug we Kanes had become accustomed to, he said, "Your playing was beautiful, Mom."

"Really?"

"Really. It . . . it almost made me cry."

Catheryn stopped and turned. "Why, thank you, honey," she said. "I think that's the nicest compliment I've received all evening."

Nate hesitated, seemingly about to say something else. Then he lowered his gaze and again started walking.

"What is it?" asked Catheryn as we started out once more.

"I'm sorry about the trouble with the sheriff and getting arrested and all," Nate said quietly.

"Your mother and I know you are," I said. "You're a good kid, Nate. We'll get that arrest thing straightened out. I've already met with the Malibu assistant DA, and he sounds willing to give you a break. And I'm going to talk with somebody at your school, too. I want you back playing ball for the Vikings as soon as possible. Your mom and I are behind you 100 percent."

"Thanks, Dad," said Nate, brightening slightly. "Thanks, Mom."

"Hey, what's the holdup back there?" Allison called from a half-block away. She and Travis had paused to wait for us at the intersection of Fifth Street and Grand. They were standing across from the Biltmore Hotel and the Los Angeles Central Library, where I could just make out the library's engraving above the main entrance:

Books Alone Are Liberal and Free: They Give to All Who Ask
They Emancipate All Who Serve Them Faithfully

"Wait up, Ali," I called back, absently trying to recall the last book I'd read, and not at all certain I had been emancipated by the experience. "We need to head over to Hill."

When we arrived at the corner, Allison said, "Dad, while we were waiting for you slowpokes, I thought of some trivia for you to share with your pals on the homicide unit."

"What's that?" I asked warily.

Allison grinned. "How does an LAPD cop go fishing?"

"I don't know. How?"

"He catches a fish. Then he beats it until it tells where the others are hiding."

Travis burst out laughing, as did Nate a moment later.

"Allison, that's not funny," said Catheryn, casting a look of admonishment at her daughter.

"So why is everyone laughing?" Allison asked innocently.

I had been trying not to crack up and further encourage Allison, who is incorrigible once she gets on a roll. There was a brief moment of guilty silence as Nate and Travis and I tried to get ourselves under control. Of course Catheryn's disapproval made that impossible, and an instant later we all dissolved into laughter. Eventually even Catheryn joined in as well. After the stress preceding her performance—not only for her, but for the rest of our family as well—it felt good to let it out.

Perch was located a couple blocks east on Hill Street. Still chuckling at Ali's irreverent shot at the LAPD, we entered a high-rise building on the corner, rode an elevator up thirteen floors, and took a second elevator several floors higher to the rooftop restaurant. Upon exiting the elevator, we found ourselves in a comfortable lounge appointed with plush couches, antique furniture, and detailed woodwork reminiscent of a bohemian French bistro.

The maître d' hurried over to greet us. "Good evening, Detective Kane, Mrs. Kane," he said.

"Good evening to you, Tony," I replied. "How's it going?"

"No complaints, Detective. We have a table reserved for you on the terrace, but we can move you indoors if you would prefer."

Past a procession of tall, arched windows lay an open-air patio with lush landscaping in planters, several ornate outdoor fireplaces, and a breathtaking view of the Los Angeles skyline.

"Outside!" cried Allison and Nate.

I turned to Catheryn. "Are you dressed warm enough, Kate? You can have my coat if you want."

"I'm good," said Catheryn. "I'd love to sit on the terrace under the stars. The view out there is stunning."

"Trav?" I asked.

"Works for me," said Travis.

"Outside it is," I said.

As we followed the maître d' to an intimate table overlooking Pershing Square and the glowing lights of downtown, Catheryn whispered, "Am I just imagining things, or do you know everyone in this town?"

"Only the ones who matter," I answered.

"I can't believe this view," said Allison, gazing past the protective glass rail enclosing the terrace.

"There's another patio one level up," I said, enjoying the scenery but thinking that a lot of ugly things happened down there on the street, things you couldn't see from fifteen stories up. "The view from up there is even better. Go take a look," I added, seating Catheryn at our table and taking a place beside her.

"Can we, Mom?" asked Nate.

"Of course, honey," said Catheryn. "Just don't be too long."

"Don't worry," said Allison. "We'll be back soon. We're starving."

As Allison and Nate departed, Travis joined us at the table. I passed him a menu and began perusing my own.

"It's been great having you home, Trav," said Catheryn. "Thanks for being here to support me tonight."

"Wouldn't have missed it for anything, Mom. I am looking forward to getting back to Juilliard tomorrow, though." He glanced at me. "You're still dropping me at the airport, right?"

I nodded. "Bright and early."

"Thanks, Dad."

"So how's school going?" I asked. "Seems like we haven't had much time to talk since you got home." After graduating from USC, Travis had spent a year on the concert circuit, ultimately concluding from the experience that he wanted more from music than a performance career. Deciding to continue his education, he had enrolled at Juilliard and was now entering his second year of a master's program in composition.

"School's going okay," Travis answered evasively. "I've become friends with Gilbert Ashley, the New York Phil music director. He teaches orchestral conducting at Juilliard. Mr. Ashley likes my compositions and he's sort of taken me under his wing. I've had several opportunities to conduct the Juilliard Conductors' Lab Orchestra, which is our paid student orchestra. It's been a real eye-opener."

"Is conducting something you might want to pursue?" Catheryn asked curiously.

"I don't know, Mom. I'm a little unsure right now about what direction I want to take, so I'm exploring my options."

A waiter arrived with a split of Perrier-Jouet champagne in a silver ice bucket. With a flourish, he set the bucket on a stand beside our table.

"Did we order this?" asked Catheryn, glancing questioningly at me.

"I took the liberty when I spoke to Tony earlier today. I hope it's okay. Seemed like the occasion called for something special."

"It's more than just okay, Dan," said Catheryn with a smile. "It's wonderful. Thank you."

"If by 'special' you mean expensive, you're right on that one, Dad," said Allison, returning with Nate.

"And as this is a family celebration," said Nate, "does that mean I get to have some, too?"

"No!" Catheryn and I said in unison.

"Chill," said Nate. "Just kidding."

"I'd like some," said Travis.

"A Coke for me," said Allison.

I glanced at Allison. Since turning twenty-one she often had wine with dinner, and tonight was a celebration.

Allison shrugged, noticing my gaze. "Don't feel like it. I can be the designated driver."

"Okay, champagne for my wife and Trav, a Coke for Allison," I said to the waiter. "Nate and I will have water. Okay, Nate?"

"I'd rather have a Coke, Dad. On the rocks."

"Okay, make it three Cokes," I corrected, readdressing the waiter. Years ago I had stopped drinking after nearly losing everything because of it—my job, my family, my marriage. Sometimes I missed it. Mostly I didn't.

"Yes, sir," said the waiter. "I'll return with champagne glasses and your Cokes in a moment."

We all fell silent, turning our attention to the menu. The restaurant offered an interesting mix of French cuisine, as well as more conventional fare including steaks, salads, and seafood. "How about if I order appetizers for the table?" I suggested. "They have mussels, baked Brie, steak and shrimp skewers. Plus, I've got my eye on something called Truffle Poutine—French fries, black truffle gravy, cheese, and bacon."

"Bacon?" said Allison, wrinkling her nose. "With French fries? Really?"

"Either you like bacon . . . or you're wrong," I pointed out.

"No appetizer for me, thanks," said Catheryn. "I'm thinking of starting with the beet salad and then having the herb-crusted salmon."

"Bouillabaisse for me," said Travis.

"Leave it to Trav to pick the most expensive entrée on the menu," noted Allison.

"Not true, Ali," Nate chimed in. "I'm going for the filet. That costs even more!"

"Don't worry about the bill," I said. "This is a special night for your mom, so we're pulling out all the stops," I added, inadvertently using the only musical cliché I knew.

By then the waiter had returned with a tray of 1920s-style champagne flutes and three Cokes. Each of the champagne glasses had a blueberry at the bottom. The waiter arranged the glasses around the table, popped the champagne into a napkin, and poured the wine. When everyone had a drink in hand, I raised my Coke.

"Kate, your performance tonight was absolutely breathtaking," I said. "Even after all our years together, you can still amaze me. I know I speak for the entire Kane clan present when I say that you are without a doubt the most gorgeous, talented musician this town has ever seen, and that's no exaggeration. I swear, we are all so proud of you, we could burst," I finished, raising my glass even higher. "Here's to you, Kate."

"Yeah, congratulations, Mom!" said Travis.

"Ditto from me," added Allison. "You were wonderful."

"Thank you," said Catheryn, smiling with pleasure. "Although I think 'the most talented musician this town has ever seen' might be a bit of a push."

"No way, Mom," said Nate. "You were awesome." Taking a sip of Coke, he smacked his lips in a burlesque of appraising its vintage. "Excellent year," he noted sagely.

"Nate, this is a nice restaurant, so try to act a little more intelligent," Allison teased playfully. "Just think of something dumb and then don't say it."

Catheryn intervened before Nate could reply in kind. "Please, Ali. If you and Nate start up, I'm going to blame you."

Allison shrugged. "It won't be my fault if—"

"I didn't say it would be your fault," Catheryn corrected. "I said I was going to blame you."

"Nice, Kate," I laughed. "Now you're beginning to think like me."

"There's a scary thought," Allison grumbled under her breath.

In an effort to change the subject, Catheryn asked, "How is your new job going, Ali?"

Allison had graduated that summer from USC with a degree in journalism. Subsequently, she had resumed a job at Channel 2

News she'd held two years earlier. I have never held much regard for the news media. Putting it mildly, I wasn't enthusiastic about Allison's choice of careers.

Allison glanced guiltily at me, then back at Catheryn. "Actually, it's going fairly well," she answered. "I'm already getting more on-air exposure than I'd hoped. Last week I was even featured on the five o'clock local news with a couple of stories I developed myself. They like me over there," she added proudly, unable to conceal her enthusiasm.

"By 'they,' I'm assuming you mean Lauren Van Owen," Catheryn noted dryly.

"Uh, yeah." Allison shifted uncomfortably. "She *is* the Los Angeles bureau chief, Mom. She's my boss."

"I realize that."

"On the downside, the drive out to Studio City *is* getting a little old," Allison conceded. "Lots of traffic that time of the morning. But leaving straight from Mike's trims the time a little."

I sensed a further frosting in Catheryn at the mention of Allison's boyfriend, Mike Cortese. Lately Allison had been spending most of her nights at Mike's house. I liked Mike and so did Catheryn, but I also knew that Allison's living situation was progressively becoming a source of concern for Catheryn.

"So how's the book thing going?" I asked to steer the conversation in a different direction. In addition to her journalistic bent, Allison was also a talented fiction writer, and the previous September her first novel had been accepted by a major publishing house. Although it had now been over a year, the book still wasn't on the shelves.

"Not yet ready for release," Allison replied with a frown. "They're revising the cover *again*, trying to make it more appealing for the Christmas crowd. In the meantime I just sit and wait. And wait. And wait."

Catheryn shook her head. "Ali, while you're waiting for your book to come out, start writing another. You've always dreamed of being a creative writer. Instead of spending your time at Channel 2, you should be following your dreams."

"I'm tired of following my dreams, Mom," Allison replied. "I think I'll just find out where they're headed and catch up with them later."

Sensing another long-standing disagreement beginning to surface, I started to intervene. As I did, I felt my phone vibrate. I checked the number. West L.A. police dispatch.

I hadn't had a call-out for quite a while. Wondering what was up, I excused myself and walked to a deserted corner of the terrace to take the call. When I returned to the table, my disappointment must have showed.

"You have to leave?" asked Catheryn.

"Afraid so, Kate. Will you be okay taking the kids home?"

"It might be a little tight in the Volvo with my cello and gown, but we'll manage," Catheryn replied.

"Ali can ride on the roof," suggested Nate.

Catheryn silenced Nate with a look. Then, again regarding me, "Are you sure you have to go?"

"Yeah, I'm sure," I answered. "The two police officers who were killed in Venice last night? It's happened again . . . this time in Pacific Palisades."

Chapter Four

For once the westbound lanes of the Santa Monica Freeway weren't jammed with traffic. Pushing the speed limit, I made it across town in just under twenty minutes. From there I took the 405 Freeway north to Sunset and cut west to Pacific Palisades. I had to do a little backtracking to find the crime scene on Las Lomas, but when I arrived there was no doubt I had found the right location.

Police vehicles blocked both ends of the street. I stopped at the nearest barricade. Several hundred yards down the road a cluster of black-and-whites sat angled against the curb, their headlights illuminating the front yard of a ranch-style home. Yellow crime-scene tape had been strung from adjacent properties, also enclosing what I assumed to be the ambushed officers' vehicle on the street. None of the news services had made an appearance yet, but I knew it would be only a matter of time.

"Dan Kane, homicide," I said, rolling down my window and flashing my ID at a young patrol officer manning the barricade.

"Yes, sir," the officer replied, signaling his partner to back up the cruiser and let me through.

I started to drive past, then stopped, again glancing at the residence down the street. "I need you guys to move your barricade around the corner," I said to the young officer. "Have the men at the other end do the same. When our media friends show up, and they will, I don't want them staring over our shoulders. If they squawk, tell them we'll be making a statement later. And if any of them even *thinks* about bringing in a news helicopter, let them know we'll make them wish they hadn't."

The officer nodded. "Yes, sir."

I pulled past and drove slowly down the block, stopping near the crime-scene ribbon. As I stepped from my car and hung my ID on my belt, a blast of static from a police radio sounded to my right. Flashing lightbars of several other vehicles were illuminating the limbs of a nearby sycamore in garish hues of red and blue, lending a carnival sense of unreality to the scene.

Across the street, officers were taking statements from neighbors. Other officers were positioned on the sidewalk in front of the house. Steeling myself, I ducked under the crime-scene ribbon and headed up the walkway toward a young patrolman keeping the crime-scene log—a chronological record of everyone entering and leaving the premises.

I hesitated as I saw the sprawled bodies of two patrol officers—one near the front door, the other by the side of the house. I felt my stomach drop. This wasn't supposed to happen. Not to two of our own.

I took a deep breath and continued toward the young patrolman on the walkway. "Dan Kane, West Los Angeles, homicide," I said when I arrived. I showed him my badge, also making a mental note of his badge number and the name on his plate: Linhart. Officer Linhart recorded my name, badge number, and time of arrival. He nodded somberly, then stepped aside without speaking.

Lieutenant Nelson Long, my boss and ranking officer of the West L.A. Division, was waiting farther up the walkway, hands thrust deep in his pockets. His presence at a crime scene was unusual, and it said a lot. Beside him stood Paul Deluca, another West L.A. homicide detective. Both men looked up as I approached.

Over my years on the force I have seen more than my share of the unthinkable things people can do to one another. Like most who deal with the random horrors of police work, the officers with whom I serve sometimes resort to gallows humor to ease the tension. I knew there would be none of that tonight.

Deluca nodded somberly when I arrived, his face displaying the heavy growth of beard that normally made its appearance around noon, no matter how close he shaved. I nodded back, then addressed Lieutenant Long. "Good evening, Lieutenant."

"Evening, Dan," Long sighed. "Hell of a thing."

Not knowing how to respond, I glanced at the two fallen officers, then back at Long. An African American whose ascent of LAPD ranks had been based on brains, guts, and solid police work, he was one of the few members of the brass whom I trusted. He was a large man, almost as big as I am, but with about twenty pounds of extra girth on his heavy frame. Lately his desk job seemed to be catching up with him. Still, there was plenty of muscle beneath the padding, and if push came to shove, Nelson was someone you wanted guarding your back.

"I knew one of those guys," said Deluca, clearly upset. "Jerry Levinson. That's Jerry by the front door. His partner, Ron Meyer, is the guy over by the side of the house. Jerry was . . . shit, I can't believe this."

"I'm sorry, Paul," I said. "This has to be tough for you."

"Yeah. It is."

Lieutenant Long's cell phone buzzed. He withdrew it from his pocket and checked the screen. "I have to answer this," he said tersely, heading across the lawn for privacy.

Deluca waited until Long was out of earshot. "The lieutenant wants you to take lead on this, with me as second," he said quietly. "You good with that?"

"Yeah, Paul," I replied. "I'm good." As the D-III supervising detective for the West L.A. homicide unit, I could have picked someone else to assist, but I liked working with Deluca. Despite some off-duty womanizing and his distinctly high-school sense of humor, he had a sharp mind and had proved his worth in tight situations more than once.

I glanced around the yard, then at the crime-scene tape strung around the perimeter. "The scene appears to be untouched. Is it?"

"Near as I can tell," Deluca answered.

"Run it down for me. What do we know?"

Deluca shrugged. "Not much. A neighbor saw the squad car's lights and came over to investigate. When he noticed Jerry lying on the front porch, he backed away and called 911. That's the neighbor over there," he added, pointing at an elderly man who was talking with a patrol officer across the street.

"Saw the lights? He didn't hear any shots?"

"Nope. Although his hearing might not be the best," Deluca answered skeptically. "We're checking with other neighbors."

"The guy touch anything?"

"He says not. And from the look on his face when we talked to him, I believe him. Anyway, the responding unit determined that both of our officers were dead and called for backup. Next they knocked on the door. When no one responded, they entered the house with a key provided by another neighbor, making sure there was no one injured inside, or anyone present who might pose a threat, or whatever. They found no one, backed out, and cordoned off the property."

"They touch anything?"

"They say they didn't, except for the doorknob. Everything is about as clean as you could hope for. I called SID as soon as I arrived," Deluca added, referring to the Scientific Investigation Division, which would be responsible for the procurement and cataloguing of trace evidence. "They're on their way."

"Good work, Paul. Give the coroner's office a call, too. See whether Art Walters is available," I added, referring to a coroner's investigator who was one of the best, and a man with whom I had worked on a number of high-profile cases. Although I didn't want to consider it at the moment, there was no doubt that this was going to be headline news, and I wanted someone I could trust to keep his mouth shut.

I thought a moment, then looked again at the murdered patrolmen, puzzled by Officer Meyer's body in the side yard. "I'm assuming they were responding to a disturbance call. Anyone check with dispatch?"

"First thing I did," Deluca answered. "Eight Adam Three was responding to a 911 cell phone report that came in at 10:47 p.m. Supposedly the owner of the house heard someone trying to break in. He said he was going to lock himself in the bathroom to wait for the cops to arrive. Then he hung up. When the 911 operator wasn't able to reestablish a connection, she tried getting through on the house landline. No luck there, either."

"You said the house was empty. If the owner made the call, where is he now?"

"Good question."

Following the murder of two Pacific Division officers the previous evening, I knew we were both thinking the same thing. "Anything new on the shootings in Venice?" I asked.

Deluca shook his head. "Nothing."

I again looked at the bodies, trying to get a feel for things before I started, attempting to picture how it had happened. In the event of a robbery in which an intruder might still be inside, procedure calls for one officer to cover the back of the property, with the other covering the front. When Levinson had been shot at the front door, Meyer could have returned around the side of the house and caught a second bullet himself.

Maybe. Maybe not. In either case, there had to be more.

"Okay, let's get started," I said, turning back to Deluca. "See whether you can organize those guys across the street. Make sure they get names and statements from *everyone* present. And check for anyone who doesn't belong. We also need to get a house-by-house canvass going, starting now. Someone must have seen or heard something. Also look for anyone with a video surveillance system that might have a camera pointed toward the street," I added, trying to remember whether I'd seen any traffic cams on Sunset. "We might get lucky—get a look at the shooter's car, someone on foot, whatever."

"I'm on it," said Deluca, starting across the street.

I saw Lieutenant Long making his way back across the lawn, still talking on his cell. He noticed me watching him and motioned for me to wait. Moments later he finished his call and crossed the final distance to rejoin me. From the look on his face, the call hadn't gone well. "Damn," he grumbled.

"What's up, Lieutenant?"

"I have to leave," he answered. "That was Captain Lincoln. We're meeting downtown with Chief Ingram, Mayor Fitzpatrick, and who knows how many other political flunkies. The mayor wants to get out in front on this thing before a press conference he's holding tomorrow morning."

"Good luck on that."

"Yeah. If this is related to the Venice murders, we're in for a shitstorm like you've never seen."

"Roger that," I agreed.

Long glanced angrily at the body of Officer Levinson on the front porch, then at Officer Meyer's corpse in the side yard. Then, shifting his gaze back to me, "If anyone can find the asshole who did this, it's you," he said, not looking away. "So find him. And do it fast."

I nodded without speaking. I appreciated Long's confidence, but I already had a bad feeling about things. Most homicides on the Westside were the result of domestic violence, armed robbery, drive-by shootings, or drugs. Each of these cases typically had a way to pry it open—looking hard at a boyfriend or husband, shaking down a rival gang, investigating a drug shipment, getting the word on the street. This was going to be different.

Long held my gaze a moment longer. "One more thing, Dan. Be careful. If things go wrong on this, people are going to be looking for a scapegoat. This is the type of case that ends careers, and usually not well."

I gazed at our fallen officers for a long moment, again thinking that this wasn't supposed to happen to two of our own. Four of our own, if the Venice shootings were related. "I don't care about looking good on this, Lieutenant," I said. "I *will* find whoever did it. And I'll do whatever it takes."

"Fine. Like I said, just do it fast." With that, Long turned on his heel and headed for his car.

After Long had left, I pulled out my notebook. Working from memory, I recorded the name of Officer Linhart, who was keeping the crime-scene log, along with his badge number and my time of arrival. I checked the ambient lighting, glanced at my watch, and made several other notations. Although I have a good memory, recordkeeping is an important part of every murder investigation, and these documents routinely wind up in court.

Next I returned to my car and pulled a pair of latex gloves and a flashlight from the glove compartment. After snapping on the gloves, I took a quick look into the murdered officers' vehicle. Although they had turned off the engine, the keys were still in the ignition. Nothing seemed out of order. Deciding to have SID go over the car more thoroughly later, I ducked back under the crime-scene tape and stood for a moment staring at the house, preparing myself for what was to come. For me, the way to deal with the occasional horrors of my job is to disassociate myself, concentrating on the details. It doesn't always work, especially when investigating a particularly horrendous crime like the murder of a child, but it's the best method I have.

The lawn and flowerbeds appeared well tended, but a pile of newspapers on the front porch suggested that the house had been unoccupied for days. Wondering whether the owners were on vacation, I decided to begin my investigation from the outside and work my way in, to ensure that I didn't miss anything important. Starting on the side of the house away from the body of Officer Meyer, I worked my way around the perimeter looking for any sign of a break-in—a forced lock, a broken pane of glass, shoe scuffs on the siding. I found nothing.

When I reached the body of Officer Meyer on the far side, I stopped. Avoiding a spatter of red on the lawn, I knelt beside the still figure. Meyer was sprawled facedown on the grass. He looked young, probably not more than a few years out of the academy. Something about him reminded me of my own son, Tommy. I paused, wondering who this young man's parents were. I wondered how they would be able to accept their loss, having their hopes and dreams for their son snuffed out in a single act of violence. It was a feeling I knew all too well. I also knew that whatever else happened—when the memorial was over and the tears had dried and friends had resumed their lives—their son would still be gone, and they would be left with a loss that would never go away.

Not touching the body, I leaned closer. Meyer's service weapon lay beside his right hand. His left arm was folded beneath his torso at an odd angle. A palm-sized portion of scalp and bone was missing near the back of his head. It looked as if his skull had exploded somehow, exposing a glistening pudding of brain beneath. The lawn had soaked up most of the blood from the bleed-out, but a dark halo was still visible around his face.

I shined my flashlight on the blood spray on the lawn, then back at the wound that had taken Meyer's life. I had to wait for the coroner's investigator to turn the body. When we did, I expected to find a relatively small entry wound on Meyer's face. I had grown up deer hunting with my dad in Texas, and from experience I suspected that the destruction to Meyer's head had most likely been caused by a high-powered rifle, not a handgun.

Ever since my arrival at the crime scene, I had been wondering how two experienced officers—trained police professionals responding to a felony break-in—had been taken unawares, not even firing a shot themselves. Again, I shined my flashlight on the crumpled body. With a chill, I realized this hadn't been a burglary gone wrong.

It had been an ambush.

I rose to my feet and walked to the front of the house. After mounting several steps to a concrete landing, I gazed down at what was left of Officer Jerry Levinson, the other slain patrolman. Levinson's head was turned to the side, exposing a chilling view of blood and bone, his face a remnant of what had once been human. He lay crumpled at the base of the front door in a congealing puddle of blood. A broad smear of red, possibly left by his face as it slid down the wood surface, marked the top panels of the door. At the top of the smear, the red stain was punctuated by a jagged hole about the size of a quarter.

I shook my head, forcing myself to submerge my feelings. Kneeling, I inspected the back of Levinson's head. I could make out a small entry wound on the rear of the skull. I saw no stippling, tissue tears, or powder burns, meaning the shot hadn't been fired from close range—consistent with my suspicion that the murder weapon had been a rifle. I leaned closer. The entry wound was high on the scalp, but the destruction of the middle and lower face caused by the bullet's exit indicated that the projectile had been traveling a downward path.

Puzzled, I turned and squinted into the darkness above the glare of the squad-car headlights, shielding my eyes with a hand as I tried to determine the location from which the bullet had been fired. The descending angle was too steep for it to have come from street level. I scanned the neighboring houses, wondering whether the shot might have come from a second story of one of them.

Remembering that Deluca had mentioned that the responding officers had entered the house, I reached across the body and tried the doorknob. The door was unlocked.

Carefully avoiding the blood puddle, I stepped over Levinson's body and entered the residence, peering into the dark. I flipped on my flashlight and stood for a moment, letting my eyes adjust, then began looking for a light switch. As I did, I noticed Deluca returning from across the street. Deciding that my inspection of the house could wait, I stepped back outside.

When Deluca arrived, he stared down at Levinson's body, getting his first close look at his friend. "Oh, my God, Jerry, " Deluca mumbled. "What happened to you? Oh, Jesus . . ."

I put a hand on Deluca's shoulder. "Paul, you don't have to be here for this. Why don't you go back and help the officers across the street? I can handle things here."

Deluca shook his head, his face pale with shock. "No, I . . . I'm okay," he stammered.

"You sure?"

"Yeah. I need to do this." Deluca took a deep breath and let it out. "I . . . I have half the guys taking statements from the neighbors over there," he continued shakily. He looked away from the body of his friend, making an effort to pull himself together. "The rest are knocking on doors. No strangers in the crowd. How . . . how are things going here?"

"I don't know, Paul. I've been trying to figure out how someone could take down two of our officers like this. One answer is that it wasn't done at close range. I've seen wounds like this before, and they weren't made by a handgun."

"A rifle?"

I nodded. "I think these guys were ambushed. Maybe from across the street; maybe from even farther away. If that's the case, we aren't going to find much in the way of trace evidence here."

"Uh-huh. We need to locate where the shots came from."

"Right. And I have an idea how to do that. Let's step inside."

Although puzzled, Deluca followed me through the front door, avoiding looking at his friend on the way in. Once inside, I flipped on a light switch with the butt of my flashlight.

"What are we looking for?" Deluca asked, glancing around the small entry.

I pointed to the quarter-sized hole in the front door. "The bullet that killed Levinson," I explained. "After it passed through his head, it smashed through the door. Let's find out where it wound up."

"For a ballistics check."

"Yeah, that too," I said, examining a wall opposite the door. Moments later I found a hole in the drywall at about waist height, several feet lower than the hole in the door. "Here."

Deluca bent down and peered at the hole. "Doesn't appear to have gone all the way through. We can have SID dig it out."

"Right. But that's not what I'm looking at. Check the height of the hole in the door, then compare it to the one in the wall."

Deluca glanced at the door, then back at the wall. "Damn," he said, suddenly understanding. "You think we can line them up, get the shooter's location?"

"That's what I'm hoping. Call SID and make sure they're bringing a ballistic alignment laser on the crime wagon. If they're already on the road, have them send someone out with one ASAP." I thought a moment. "We'll need a metal detector, too," I added. "I want to recover the slug in the yard."

"Right," said Deluca, pulling his cell phone from his pocket.

I stepped back outside. Deluca followed, already punching numbers on his phone.

Leaving him on the walkway, I made my way toward the street, searching for Officer Linhart. I found him on the sidewalk talking with another officer. "Officer Linhart," I called.

Linhart broke off his conversation and hurried over. "Detective Kane, one of the guys on the east barricade says to tell you that the news crews have showed up. They want to know when you'll be making a statement."

"Tell our scumbag friends in the media that we'll be talking to them as soon as the officers' families have been notified. Speaking of which—"

"It's being done," Linhart interrupted. "I called my sergeant. Someone at headquarters is making the calls."

"Good work. Let me know when everyone has been reached. In the meantime, make certain the guys on the barricade know that no one gets past without a badge. And I mean no one, *especially* members of the press."

"Yes, sir."

Thinking that Linhart was doing a good job and deciding to make a note of it in my report, I stepped off the curb, finding a spot out of the glare of the cruisers' headlights. Outlined against the night sky, a brush-covered ridge flanked the neighborhood to the east, tracing a jagged course several hundred yards above where I stood. I glanced back at the house, then again at the ridge, judging the angle.

It looked about right.

"I heard from SID," Deluca called from the walkway. "They have a ballistic laser with them. Metal detector, too. You want anything else?"

"Not from SID. I do need something else from you," I answered, motioning for him to join me.

Repocketing his phone, Deluca joined me in the middle of the road. "What?"

I glanced at the ridgeline. "I think the shots may have come from up there."

Deluca squinted into the night sky. "Damn, Kane. It's gotta be 200 yards. Maybe more."

I nodded. "I know. But it's not that far for someone with a rifle."

Deluca looked back at the house, then again at the ridge. "You could be right," he muttered. "The distance might also explain why no one heard a shot."

"Maybe. Anyway, there's a road up there. I see house lights. Go find that road, Paul. Have one of the patrol guys follow you in a cruiser. If I don't miss my guess, there will be an open area up there somewhere—a vacant lot, a house for sale, whatever—someplace with a good view of the neighborhood down here. If there's any evidence to be found, aside from the bullets that killed our men, that's where it will be. When you find that spot, cordon it off and call me."

Deluca looked up at the ridge once more. "Shit, Kane, if you're right about this . . ."

". . . it means we've got someone with a rifle hunting cops," I finished. "Get up there, Paul. Find that spot. And make absolutely certain you aren't followed by any of our pals in the media."

"Right," said Deluca, heading for his car.

The SID crime wagon arrived fifteen minutes later. I spent the following hour supervising the crime team—a criminalist, a latent-prints technician, and an officer from the photo section—determining what trace evidence to gather, what areas of the scene to examine, and what courses of investigation would be best to pursue. Although I was fairly sure we wouldn't find much at the house on Las Lomas, given that the fatal shots had probably been fired from a distance, a careful examination of the entire area had to be done.

As I'd suspected, we didn't find much at the house—no sign of forced entry, no shell casings in the yard, no evidence that anyone else had been present during the shootings, no signs of a struggle. The slain officers' vehicle showed nothing unusual, either. I didn't think the killer had entered the house, but we included that area in our search and evidence recovery as well, just to be certain.

On the positive side, we recovered both bullets involved in the killings. One projectile, the one that had killed Officer Levinson, was dug out of the wall inside the house. Using a metal detector, we recovered another slug buried in the side yard about twelve feet behind Officer Meyer. Both rounds were heavy, copper-jacketed bullets. The projectile recovered from inside the house was too distorted for a ballistic match, but the one we dug up in the yard was in better shape. I had an uneasy feeling that it would match the slugs that had killed our officers in Venice—assuming the bullets found in Venice were in good enough shape for comparison.

Deluca called me just as we were finishing. He had backtracked all the way to Sunset to avoid being followed by members of the media. From there he had made his way to the ridge I'd pointed out, taking a winding road named El Medio that ran along the crest. He found several sites that overlooked the crime scene on Las Lomas, including an unoccupied house and a lot on a cul-de-sac several miles up. Using the bullet hole in the front door and the hole in the wall inside the house for reference, we positioned a ballistic alignment laser to determine whether my hunch was right.

It was. The shooting location turned out to be the vacant lot off the cul-de-sac. Looking down into the canyon from there, Deluca was able to see the red laser beam shining up from the house. We had to modify the laser's angle slightly, but within a ten-yard margin of error, it was close enough for certainty.

I ordered Deluca to secure the site and wait for me. By then Art Walters, the coroner's investigator, had arrived. As the SID team began finishing, I joined Art as together we uncovered, examined, and turned the bodies. Throughout each exam, a photo technician took shots from various angles. Normally one to find humor in even the most gruesome of situations, even Art was silent as he viewed the corpses.

"Large-caliber weapon," he said quietly, regarding the ruin of Officer Levinson's face.

"Probably a rifle," I said.

"Yep."

"You do the shootings in Venice?"

Art shook his head. "I was off last night," he answered. "I did view the bodies."

"And?"

"Similar wounds on both. Headshots. Major bone and soft tissue destruction, just like these two." Art looked away, then back at me. "Definitely the same guy."

By then morgue attendants had arrived and were waiting in a van on the street. Art snapped off his gloves, signaling that he was finished. Officer Linhart informed me the officers' families had been notified, adding that the news crews were still clamoring for a statement. Again deciding to let them wait, I instructed the SID team to follow me to the shooting site on the ridge. As I had told Deluca earlier, if there were any trace evidence left by the shooter, that's where it would be.

I thought for a moment, making certain I hadn't forgotten anything at the house. When there wasn't much to go on, overlooking even the smallest item was unacceptable. Given the situation, I also realized that no matter how thorough our search, all forensic evidence now being gathered would probably be useless until we had a suspect—and the most likely way to obtain one was through an informant or by a confession that could be corroborated by physical evidence. I wasn't optimistic about either of those things happening.

For the second time that evening, I felt the buzz of my cell phone. Realizing I had forgotten to take it off vibrate after leaving the concert, I pulled the phone from my pocket. "Kane."

"Dan, Long here. I have some news, and you're not gonna like it."

"I'm not liking anything about this case, Lieutenant. There's not much that could make it worse."

"We'll see. I just got out of a meeting with the mayor, three police commissioners, the Venice Division's lieutenant, and the chief. Mayor Fitzpatrick will be holding a news conference tomorrow morning. He's going to announce the formation of a joint task force that will be charged with investigating the shooting deaths of our officers in Venice and Pacific Palisades."

"And?"

"And you and Deluca are on it. Be at the Police Administration Building tomorrow morning at seven. Check in at the front desk. Someone will point you in the right direction."

"Okay, I was wrong," I said. "A task force is the one thing that could make this case worse. Listen, Lieutenant—"

"Just be there, Kane. And one more thing. The task force is being headed up by an old friend of yours—just like last time. Lieutenant Snead."

"You've gotta be kidding me. He can't possibly want me to be—"

"Actually, he specifically requested your presence," Long interrupted. "I'll see you there."

Chapter Five

The SID work at the cul-de-sac proceeded quickly. We took impressions of recent tire tracks in the soft dirt, recovered samples of oil drips, and bagged a cigarette butt that looked fairly new. Not much, but it was all we had. We also checked with nearby neighbors, again coming up cold. No one had seen or heard anything. The latter puzzled me. With a high-powered rifle being discharged in a suburban neighborhood, someone should have heard *something*.

I made several calls, setting up a more extensive canvass of the ridgeline neighborhood in the morning. In addition to canvassing the neighborhood where our officers had died, I wanted every house on El Medio checked all the way to Sunset, searching for residents who might have seen or heard anything—especially checking for anyone with a home-security camera pointed at the street. The shooter had probably driven to the dead-end overlook, taken his shots, and left the same way. Maybe someone had caught him on camera.

After returning to the murder scene, I made a statement to a throng of reporters crowding the police barricade, giving a brief summary of the shootings and adding that there would be a news conference at police headquarters later that morning.

It was after 1:00 a.m. when I finished. Deciding to write up the crime report after getting some sleep, I headed home. On the drive back to Malibu, I kept chewing on aspects of the killings that didn't make sense. That two experienced officers had been taken unawares could be explained by their being shot from a distance. But why hadn't anyone heard the shots?

Another thing that didn't make sense was Lieutenant William Snead requesting my presence on his newly formed task force. Snead and I had a long history, most of it not good. When we were both coming up through the ranks, I had broken his jaw. He had been beating a drunken transient with his baton, enraged that the man had accidentally urinated on his leg. When I intervened, Snead had made the mistake of taking a swing at me. Later he'd used his position in Internal Affairs to unsuccessfully go after my badge. More recently I had served on a task force headed by Snead. To say the least, that hadn't ended well, either.

Now he wanted me on his new task force. Why? Whatever the reason, I knew from experience that if the case weren't closed quickly, the investigation would turn into a media circus. And as Lieutenant Long had warned, if that happened, I would need to watch my back.

Twenty minutes later I arrived home at the beach. Instead of stopping, I drove past my house, pulling to the side of Pacific Coast Highway several hundred yards down the road. Over the years I've put away a lot of people, and I knew a number of them would undoubtedly like to get even. One in particular, the subject of Snead's earlier task-force investigation, had found his way to my home several years back. It had nearly cost me everything, and I didn't want a repeat. I knew that in today's world anyone could find out almost anything about anybody, including where someone lived, but I did what I could.

Late-night traffic was light. Nevertheless, I waited for a full minute to make certain no one was following me. Then, timing a break in passing vehicles, I hung a U-turn across four lanes of highway and pulled to a stop in front of my house.

It's a common misconception that everyone living in Malibu is either a movie star or a millionaire, or both. Not that there aren't plenty of those, but there are plenty of the rest of us, too. The original shack built on our beachfront property dated back to the early thirties, but over the intervening years the ramshackle structure had been expanded, bit by bootlegged bit—eventually winding up as a two-story, three-bedroom structure. The beach property had been in Catheryn's family since the mid-forties, and after our marriage Catheryn's mother had deeded it to us as a wedding present. Since then, following the births of our children, a fire, and a subsequent reconstruction, the value of our home had skyrocketed. Nevertheless, thanks to California's long-standing Proposition 13, our taxes were still pegged to the property's original value—preventing us from being taxed out of our home.

I locked my car and entered the house. A light was burning in the entry. Otherwise, the house was dark. Deciding that everyone was probably asleep, I headed for our bedroom, walking quietly so as not to wake Catheryn. When I opened the door, I saw that our bed was empty. Puzzled, I returned to the entry and ducked my head into the kids' rooms. Travis and Nate were both asleep in Nate's room, but the bed in Allison's room was empty, too.

Deciding that Allison must be spending the night at Mike's— undoubtedly irritating her mother—I headed downstairs. The lower floor of our house was located one level down from the street, a few feet above the sand. At street level, with Pacific Coast Highway mere yards from the front door, four lanes of high-speed traffic occasionally made life at the beach seem like living next to a freeway. Downstairs, on the redwood deck outside Catheryn's music room, the ambience was the exact opposite. Highway noise was mostly blocked by the house, and the rhythmic sounds of the ocean hid the rest, making the city seem a thousand miles away.

I found Catheryn asleep on a swing overlooking the deck. She was wearing one of my jackets over her nightgown. Her auburn hair was fanned in disarray around her face, and her long legs were drawn up beneath her on the cushions, partially covered by a light blanket she'd carried down from our bed. Callie, our yellow Labrador retriever, lay asleep on the deck nearby. She raised her head and tail-thumped the redwood planks as I approached. "Hey, girl," I said, bending to scratch her ears. "You out here guarding Mom?"

As if to say *Of course, I wouldn't let her stay down here by herself,* Callie responded with several more tail wags, then reassumed her full curl on the deck. As she did, I noticed her muzzle was beginning to show signs of gray. It wasn't fair, I thought, that man's best friend aged so much more quickly than did we.

"Dan?"

"Sorry, sugar," I said, easing down beside Catheryn on the swing. "Didn't mean to wake you. What are you doing down here?"

"I thought I'd wait out here for you to come home," she answered sleepily, easing up on one elbow. Then she sat up the rest of the way and rubbed her eyes. "Guess I fell asleep." Stifling a yawn, she brushed her hair back from her face and scooted closer. Ducking under my arm, she nestled into my chest.

"I noticed Ali isn't here," I said. "Sleeping at Mike's?"

Catheryn sighed. "It's not that I don't like Mike, Dan, because I do. He's a fine young man. I just wish that he and Ali would—"

"We can't live our kids' lives for them, Kate," I interrupted. "You've told me that more than once. Ali's smart. She'll figure things out."

"I hope so."

"In the meantime, we've got Nate."

"Yes. We have Nate. Which is turning into a full-time job," Catheryn added, shaking her head. "He did seem better tonight, though. More like the old Nate we used to know."

"Yeah, he did. Sixteen is a tough age."

"I hope we survive it."

"Me, too," I laughed. "At least Travis seems on track these days."

Catheryn nodded. "Mostly. He's still finding his way at Juilliard, but he'll get there. Speaking of which, will you still be able to drop him at the airport tomorrow, or should we call a cab?"

"I'll drop him, but we'll need to leave earlier than planned. I have to be downtown at 7:00 a.m. The murders in Venice and those tonight in the Palisades have everyone up in arms, and the brass wants immediate action."

"I heard more about the shootings tonight on the way home. It's all over the news. This has to be hard for you."

"Yeah, it's hard on all of us. The chief is setting up a task force. I'm on it."

Catheryn raised an eyebrow. "Task force? You're okay with that?"

I shrugged. "I don't have much choice. Don't worry, I'll try to behave myself."

"Good. Use it as an opportunity to improve your people skills," Catheryn advised gently.

"Thanks, Kate," I said. "I'll be sure to do that."

"Seriously, Dan, I feel terrible for the families of those poor officers. I hope you catch whoever's doing it."

"Oh, we'll catch him," I said, sounding more sure than I was. "In spite of any task-force interference."

"Dan . . ."

"Kate, the guy is shooting cops. I'll try to stay out of trouble, but I'm going to do whatever's necessary to stop him."

"I know, Dan. I just . . . well, be careful."

"I will. Speaking of which, unless I miss my guess, I'm probably going to be on this full-time, so you may not see much of me for a while." I started to say something else, then let it go, unable to put my feelings into words.

Catheryn regarded me closely, sensing the change. "You okay?"

"Yeah," I answered. Then, with a weary sigh, "Actually, no. The case tonight really threw me."

"Is it something you want to talk about?"

Catheryn rarely asked for details regarding my work, and by tacit agreement, I seldom offered. I gazed out over the ocean without answering, watching the waves rush the shore. A crescent moon had risen over Santa Monica, sending silvery shards of light dancing across the surface of the water. "I don't know," I finally answered.

"What is it, Dan?"

"I don't know," I repeated. "I . . . I guess I'm a little depressed," I went on, realizing that since arriving at the Palisades crime scene, I had been enveloped by a burgeoning sense of loss. "One of the murdered officers reminded me of Tommy."

I felt Catheryn stiffen beside me at the mention of our lost son. Although it had been years, I knew her pain over Tommy's death was still as raw as mine, and I instantly regretted my words.

Catheryn sat up, taking my hands in hers. "I'm so sorry, Dan," she said quietly.

"No, I'm the one who should apologize," I replied, as always struck by her strength. "I didn't mean to lay my troubles on you, especially not on a special night for you like tonight. I swear, Kate, I was so proud watching you up there on the stage," I continued, steering our conversation away from thoughts of Tommy. "I meant it when I said I thought I was going to burst."

"I was so nervous," said Catheryn, also backing away from the precipice. "I'm surprised I was able to play."

"You did more than play, Kate. You were . . . I don't know how to explain it, but you really moved me. And that's saying something coming from a classical-music illiterate like myself."

"Thank you, Dan. I'm glad you can't see me blushing."

"And I regret having to leave the restaurant early."

"I understand. It's your job."

"Yeah. It's my job," I muttered, once more staring out at the ocean. "Sometimes I think . . . ah, hell, I don't know."

"What?"

I paused. "Sometimes I wonder how we make things work," I said at last. "Between you and me. Your career with the LA Phil centers on music and culture and all the finer things in life. Meanwhile I'm getting called out to some of the ugliest things human beings can do to one another. I guess I sometimes just wonder . . ."

" . . . what we're doing together?" Catheryn finished.

"Yeah," I said.

"Dan, you're tired. Things will look different in the morning."

"I know. Still, sometimes I feel like . . ."

Catheryn turned to face me. "Dan, you wonder why we're together? I'm going to tell you something. It's a confession, something you don't know, and I want you to listen without interrupting."

"Have you been sleeping with the pool guy?" I asked in a belated attempt to lighten the mood.

Catheryn smiled. "That would be an example of interrupting. Besides, we don't have a pool. Hence no pool guy."

"Right. Sorry. You're about to confess. Go ahead. I'll shut up."

Catheryn looked away for a moment. Then she gazed at me again, holding my eyes with hers. "I didn't want to fall in love with you, Dan," she said. "When we first met at college, I thought you and I were all wrong for each other. I didn't want to fall in love with you, and I tried my best not to."

"And this is making me feel better how?"

Catheryn smiled. "I tried not to fall in love with you, but it happened anyway. And it kept happening, again and again. And it still does, every day we're together. That's my confession, Dan. I love you, and there is nothing that will ever change that."

Caught off guard by Catheryn's words, I felt a lump rising in my throat, an unaccustomed stinging in my eyes. I drew her to me and held her tightly. "I don't deserve you," I said softly.

"Yes, you do," she replied firmly. "And I deserve you." And then she circled me with her arms and kissed me.

And I kissed her back. Her jacket had come open in front, and I could feel her breasts pressing against me through the flimsy material of her nightgown. Reaching underneath, I ran my hands up the gentle curve of her back, marveling at the smoothness of her slim figure, smelling the sweet fragrance of her skin. Her lips, at first tentative, slowly grew insistent, and I could feel myself responding.

Pushing away for a moment, Catheryn shrugged off her jacket, letting it drop to the deck. Then again pressing her lips to mine, she returned to my arms, her body soft and supple and warm. Lifting her nightgown, I caressed her shoulders and breasts, the feel of her skin silky on my palms, her nipples hardening at my touch. "I want you, Dan," she said, her voice becoming husky with desire.

"Let's go upstairs."

"No. Here," Catheryn replied, her kisses mounting in passion, her tongue now boldly exploring.

Excitement growing, my clothes came off in a tangle, the idea of going upstairs abruptly forgotten. I kissed her breasts, gently teasing her nipples with my tongue and lips. "God, you're beautiful," I murmured.

Feeling the hardness of my need pressing against her, Catheryn took me in her hand and stroked me, her breath hot against my cheek. With a shudder of pleasure, I cupped her hips and pulled her close, caressing her legs and thighs and the hot liquid core at her center. "You are so beautiful," I repeated.

Closing her eyes, Catheryn arched beneath me, her fingers digging into my back. "Now, Dan," she said.

Holding me with her legs, Catheryn cried out softly as I entered her, joining me in a celebration of our union that was as intense and vibrant as the first time we had made love, so many years ago. Hunger building, our rhythm gradually quickened, our passion as unstoppable as an avalanche.

Moments later Catheryn squeezed me tightly, her mouth opening in a gasp of ecstasy. Unable to wait any longer, I closed my eyes and joined her, whispering the words that forever bound us, everything forgotten but the seamless symmetry of the moment, and the presence of the woman who loved me, and an unshakable hope for the future—our embrace enduring proof that despite life's heartbreak and tragedy, living could still be worthwhile.

Afterward we lay entwined on the swing, watching the surface of the ocean shifting in the moonlight. Neither of us spoke, for no words seemed necessary. Callie, who had stood guard during our lovemaking, lay back down on the deck with a sigh, apparently deciding that the curious behavior of her masters was over, at least for the moment.

I knew we had to head upstairs before long; otherwise I would be starting the day with no sleep at all, and it was going to be an extremely busy day. Nevertheless, reluctant to end the singular moment that Catheryn and I had shared, I decided to extend the evening a few minutes more. Lulled by the sound of the ocean, I let my thoughts drift.

And as Catheryn's breathing slowed and became regular beside me, I revisited events of the day, my mind awash with a kaleidoscopic rush of images—the ineffable beauty of Catheryn's performance, the ragged hole in a blood-smeared door, Nate's hopeless shrugs and Trav's bright optimism and Ali's confident grin, the ruin of a young patrolman's face, and my dark, painful thoughts of our lost son, Tommy. And constant throughout it all, threading like a benediction through the fabric of my memories, was the tender look in Catheryn's eyes as she'd made her unexpected declaration of love.

Chapter Six

It was still dark the next morning when I drove Travis to LAX. Although his flight wasn't until 8:30 a.m., I had to drop him off a bit early in order to make the 7:00 a.m. task-force meeting on time. He groused a little when I rousted him from bed at 4:45 a.m., but I reminded him that airlines routinely recommend arriving at least two hours before a flight, so he wasn't going to be checking in *that* early.

We grabbed coffee at a fast-food place on the way in. Although we didn't talk much during the first part of the drive, Travis had perked up by the time we exited the 405 Freeway and headed west on Century Boulevard. "I really appreciate your giving me a ride, Dad," he said, finishing the last of his coffee and placing the empty paper cup in a holder between the seats. "Sorry it took me a while to wake up."

"No problem."

"Will you say good-bye to Mom for me? I didn't want to wake her this morning. We already said our good-byes last night, but . . ."

I smiled. "I'll tell her."

"And you'll call me as soon as you get the results of her checkup?"

"I'll do that, too."

"This is a big one coming up. Two years. If anything serious were going to develop, we'd be likely to see the beginnings of it by now, right? Are you worried?"

I hesitated, caught off guard by Trav's question. I have always tried to be honest with my kids, even if they didn't like it. Nevertheless, I didn't want to raise unnecessary concerns about Catheryn's health, especially if I was worried about it myself. "I've never seen her look better," I answered evasively.

"Dad . . ."

"Okay, of course I'm a little worried," I admitted. There were a lot of things that could go wrong following chemo, radiation, and a bone marrow transplant. I had made the mistake of looking up some of the possible side effects online—liver and kidney problems, heart and blood vessel damage, clots, infection, graft-versus-host disease, even new cancers.

Travis was silent for a long moment. "Is that why you asked her to delay giving the Phil an answer about taking over as principal cello? You're afraid she's going to get sick again?"

"She told you about that?"

"I overheard you guys talking. Is it?"

My conversation with Travis had headed down a highway I hadn't intended. "Look, Trav, I don't want you worrying about Kate. That's my job. Your job is to get back to school and make something of yourself. I'm concerned about your mom's health because if I ever lost her, I truly don't know what I would do. But I meant it when I said she's never seemed better. She's going to be fine," I added firmly.

"I know. But you'll call me with the test results, right?"

"I will," I promised.

By then we had reached the LAX departure level and were approaching the Delta terminal. I glanced at Travis, again realizing how much he had matured over the past several years. I was glad he was looking forward to returning to his life in New York, but I was going to miss him.

Minutes later I snagged a spot in front of the Delta terminal and helped Travis unload his luggage. I've never been much good at good-byes. The two of us stood awkwardly for a moment, preparing to go our separate ways.

"Well, thanks again for the ride," said Travis.

Instead of answering, I put my arms around him and gave him a hug. Then I held him at arm's length and looked into his eyes. "I'm proud of you, Trav," I said. "You know that, right?"

Travis nodded. Then, with a grin, "I love you too, Dad."

Fifteen minutes before the scheduled task-force meeting, I arrived at Los Angeles Police Department headquarters. Better known as the new Police Administration Building, sometimes shortened to PAB, the huge, 500,000-square-foot structure of stone and glass had replaced the aging Parker Center—LAPD's former headquarters—in 2009. To date no one had come up with an appropriate nickname for the new building, at least not one that had stuck. There was talk of renaming PAB after a previous LAPD police chief, Daryl F. Gates, but so far that movement hadn't gained much traction.

Although the Police Administration Building was located mere blocks from Disney Hall where Catheryn had performed the previous evening, to me it seemed anchored in an entirely different world, a world driven by influence and politics and power. Serving as the command post for twenty-one far-flung patrol divisions, PAB took up an entire city block on West First Street. The gigantic complex was surrounded by some of the city's most imposing, iconic architecture, including the *Los Angeles Times* building, the California Department of Transportation headquarters, and Los Angeles City Hall—the latter's proximity to police headquarters more than mere coincidence, as increasingly the administration of the LAPD, through the offices of the mayor, the police commission, and the city council, had become a political football that no politician could afford to ignore.

As I drove past the entrance, I noticed a fleet of news-wagons already setting up outside, undoubtedly preparing for the mayor's 8:00 a.m. briefing. The ramp descending to the building's underground parking was jammed with vehicles, so I circled the block to a nearby parking structure on First, leaving my car on an upper level beside a van sporting a bumper sticker that read: "Jesus loves you. Everyone else thinks you're an asshole."

Thinking there might be some truth to that, I walked back to PAB. On the way to the front entrance I passed several gardens and terraces, a civic plaza, and a large public auditorium just outside PAB's main footprint—design elements that I'd read were intended to offer the public a "nature-based experience," as well as symbolizing the department's new era of openness and connection with the city. I liked the design, but I knew it would take more than modern architecture to change the department. When I walked through PAB's doors, it would be business as usual.

The lobby was flooded with reporters. Upon arriving, I hung my shield on my coat and pushed through a logjam of people to a reception desk at the far end. There, a young duty officer glanced at my ID. "Can I help you, Detective?" she asked.

I glanced over my shoulder. "Members of the media?"

The duty officer, a young Hispanic woman in her early twenties, rolled her eyes. "They've been here all morning."

"No surprise there," I grumbled. "I'm supposed to be at a seven o'clock task-force meeting. I was told to check at the desk."

The young officer again glanced at my ID, then referred to a typewritten roster. Finding my name, she checked it off and handed me a temporary visitor's badge. "Sixth-floor conference room, just past the DB offices," she said, referring to the Detective Bureau administrative center. The Detective Bureau provided line supervision over several commands including Robbery-Homicide, whose Homicide Special Section detectives would normally have handled a cop-killer investigation. As I headed for the elevators, I wondered how the HSS guys felt about having their case preempted, surmising that they probably didn't like it any better than I did. I was certain several Robbery-Homicide HSS detectives would be detailed to the task force, and I expected to hear some grousing from them.

I arrived at the sixth-floor conference room with a few minutes to spare. The atmosphere was somber, with a lot of anger thrown in as well. Both Deluca and Lieutenant Long were already present. Long was standing near a window talking with West L.A. Division Captain Lincoln and another detective whom I recognized from the Pacific Division. Deluca had seated himself near the back of the room. I caught Long's eye and nodded, then dropped into a chair beside Deluca.

"Not like you to be early," Deluca noted. "Get any sleep?"

"A couple hours," I answered. I was about to ask Deluca what the program was for the meeting when Mayor Fitzpatrick and an entourage of political flunkies strode in, quickly followed by Chief Ingram, Lieutenant William Snead, and another man whose twelve-hundred-dollar suit spelled FBI. I groaned inwardly as I realized the bureau was going to be involved—undoubtedly at the request of the mayor, who as usual was doing his best to appear in control of the situation.

Lieutenant Snead, a tall, hatchet-faced man with thin lips and a receding hairline, stepped to the front of the room. "Everyone grab a seat and quiet down," he ordered, raising his hands for attention. As detectives began finding places, Snead's close-set eyes swept the room. He paused when his gaze got to me, his expression hardening.

When everyone was seated, Snead continued. "For those I haven't met, I'm Lieutenant William Snead, Pacific Division detectives' commanding officer. At the request of Chief Ingram, I will be heading this task force. Before we start, both the mayor and the chief have a few words." He turned toward the group behind him. "Mr. Mayor?"

"I can't believe we're working for that hump Snead again," whispered Deluca.

"Join the club," I muttered.

Mayor Fitzpatrick stepped to the front, nodded to Lieutenant Snead, and turned to the detectives seated before him. It had been some time since I had last seen the mayor, and his whiskey-bloomed nose and the network of burst capillaries mottling his cheeks and jowls had grown even more noticeable over the intervening years.

"Good morning," Mayor Fitzpatrick began, making eye contact with several officers in front, then sweeping his gaze across the room in the practiced manner I had seen him employ on other occasions. "I'm not going to sugarcoat things for you," he began. "We've had four officers murdered in the past two days. We need to apprehend whoever did it, and we need to do that before this thing turns into a media nightmare like we had with the Christopher Dorner killings," he added, referring to a rogue cop incident that had taken the lives of a number of LAPD police officers and family members.

"That is *not* going to happen this time," Fitzpatrick stated firmly. "As I look around this room, I see a number of faces from the Candlelight Killer Task Force, the investigative unit that successfully ended the most brutal killings this city has ever seen. I also see a number of top detectives from all four LAPD bureaus. You officers are the best, and as such I will expect the best from you. Later this morning I'm going to announce the formation of an LAPD/FBI interagency task force charged with finding the killer or killers of our officers. I know you won't let me down."

Although no one spoke, I felt an uncomfortable stir sweep the room as the other detectives realized we were going to be working with the FBI. It's not as if the feds don't have good investigators—they do. They are also an insular group, eager to grab the spotlight and not always willing to share. To be fair, that can be true of almost any entrenched organization, including the LAPD. Given the situation, however, I knew there was going to be trouble. The general reaction in the room said that everyone else did, too.

Fitzpatrick paused for effect, then continued. "I have absolute confidence that our two organizations, working under the direction of my office, will work cooperatively to bring the killer or killers to justice," he said, his words clearly taken from the speech he would be delivering to the news media downstairs. "The sniper task force, as I imagine our friends in the press will be calling you, will have the complete cooperation of my office, the office of the Los Angeles District Attorney, and the FBI's Los Angeles field office and resident agencies. You will have the funds, resources, and personnel to close this case quickly. And that's what I expect. Questions?"

Again the room stirred uneasily. No one said anything, including me. I was getting a bad feeling of déjà vu. I'd been present at a similar speech Fitzpatrick had delivered years earlier to the Candlelight Killer Task Force, and at the time my opinion had been the same: throwing money, resources, and personnel at a case didn't necessarily bring results.

Fitzpatrick waited a moment, then nodded to the group. "Good." With that he strode briskly from the room, his retinue of aides trailing close behind.

Again Lieutenant Snead stepped forward. "Thank you, Mayor Fitzpatrick, for those words of encouragement," he said. By then the mayor had already exited, and although I wasn't certain to whom Snead was speaking, I suspected that he had practiced a speech for the occasion and was determined to stick to it.

Snead turned and glanced at the chief. "Chief Ingram, would you like to address the men next?"

Chief Ingram moved forward and cleared his throat. "Yeah, Lieutenant, I would," he said quietly. "First, I'd like to express my condolences to the men and women of the Pacific and West L.A. Divisions who have lost some good officers recently. My heart goes out to the wives and families of the murdered patrolmen, as I know do yours. I feel your pain and I know you're angry. I'm angry, too. We know from the wounds and other forensic details that these two incidents are the work of the same person. Like the mayor said, let's get this asshole off the street, and let's do it quickly." He turned toward Captain Lincoln and Lieutenant Long. "The men we lost last night were two of yours. Do either of you have anything to add?"

When Long and Lincoln both shook their heads, Ingram again addressed the group. "Okay, one more thing. As of now the entire department is on heightened alert. Until this is over, we're adding extra officers to every shift by calling in additional personnel. We are also taking all motorcycle units off the street. All patrol units are to exercise extra caution. And two-man patrol units only—no singles."

Ingram thought a moment, then turned back to Snead. "I guess that's it for now. Bill, it's all yours, except that I want everyone downstairs in the public auditorium later for the mayor's briefing. I'll see you there."

"Yes, sir," said Snead, almost snapping to attention but catching himself in time.

After Chief Ingram had left, accompanied by Lieutenant Long and Captain Lincoln, Snead again took the floor. "Okay, some organizational matters first," he said officiously. "There are two ranking detectives present from each of our four bureaus, as well as the original investigative teams from Venice and West L.A., where the murders took place. We also have four officers from Robbery-Homicide. We will be getting additional staff to help man the hotlines, which are being set up in one of the state-of-the-art communications rooms downstairs. As the mayor said, we have the resources to successfully complete this job. It will be a cooperative effort, and together we will find the killer or killers who did this."

Glancing around the room, I did a quick count. Sixteen detectives—not including the FBI presence. I suspected that before things were over, that number would grow.

Snead turned toward the man I'd noticed earlier wearing the expensive suit. "I'd like to introduce FBI Assistant Director in Charge Alan Shepherd. At the request of the mayor, Assistant Director Shepherd has offered the assistance of the FBI's Los Angeles field office." All eyes turned toward Shepherd, who nodded without speaking, seeming content to let Snead handle the preliminaries.

"Assistant Director Shepherd will be detailing a squad of special agents to our unit," Snead continued. "He has assured me that members of his office will assist in any way possible. In addition, Assistant Director Shepherd has offered to procure a VICAP report and an FBI psychological profile as soon as submission materials are available. Without doubt, these reports will prove invaluable if we don't have this wrapped up by the end of the week."

The Violent Criminal Apprehension Program had been established years back to collect and analyze data on violent crime. At first the nationwide computer center had seemed like a good idea, but over time it had proved only marginally successful as an investigative tool. Like most homicide investigators, I considered a VICAP report a general waste of time. Along the same lines, psychological profiles—or psychological autopsies, as the bureau's behaviorists had begun calling them—were often inaccurate and could even be misleading. In theory, psychological workups also made sense, but in my experience

63

most FBI profiles, like the VICAP program, ultimately were proved worthless.

As far as I was concerned, the task force was already heading in the wrong direction. Instead of hitting the streets during the first twenty-four hours—the most critical time of any investigation, especially a murder investigation—we were sitting in a room discussing operational protocols and bureaucratic oversight. And as far as wrapping things up by the end of the week—unless we got lucky, that just wasn't going to happen.

As if sensing my impatience, Snead turned toward me. "Speaking of reports, did you bring your crime report for last night's shootings, Detective Kane?"

I shook my head.

"Why not?"

"I didn't leave the crime scene until after one, so I haven't had time to write it up. I can run it down verbally, if you want."

Snead scowled. "That won't be necessary. Bring your report with you tomorrow. Detective Jacoby, I'll want your crime report from the Venice shooting, too," he added, glancing at a detective from the Venice Division. "We'll make copies tomorrow so everyone can get up to speed ASAP. By the way, all paperwork must be kept current, including status updates, follow-up reports, and daily supplementals. I will be giving the chief regular updates, so if I look bad because one of you isn't cooperating, the shit will flow downhill. Is that understood?"

When no one spoke, Snead nodded with satisfaction. "Good. Briefings will be held on a daily basis, beginning tomorrow at 7:00 a.m. sharp. Attendance is mandatory. With the exception of court appearances, you are now all on this full-time—six days on, one day off, with alternate days on weekends. You will have the rest of today to reassign pending cases and clear other commitments. We hit the ground running tomorrow morning. There will also be a p.m. shift to man our twenty-four-hour phone and email hotlines, which I'm certain will prove invaluable in cracking this case. I can't stress that point enough. Someone out there knows the killer; we simply have to find him."

Again I felt an uneasy stirring in the room. Like most detectives present, I considered chasing down hotline "static"—worthless rumors, crank calls, false leads, and the like—a general waste of time.

"Now, I realize that the six-day/ten-hour schedule we'll be on is contrary to regulations, so each of you *will* offer to volunteer, and I *will* accept that offer," Snead concluded. "One last thing. All communication with the media will go through me, and me alone. There will be no leaks on this case. If there are, heads will roll. Now, if there's nothing else—"

"I have something," I said.

Snead turned toward me, his eyes narrowing. He glanced at his watch. "What is it, Detective Kane?"

"I hate to say this, Lieutenant, but I have a bad feeling that this guy isn't done shooting cops."

"This investigation isn't going to be run based on your *feelings*, Detective," said Snead. "Or your so-called hunches, either."

"Maybe not, but we can't ignore the possibility that these murders might just be starting," I reasoned.

"The chief has put the entire force on heightened alert," Snead countered. "What else would you suggest?"

"Well, for one, the Palisades shootings were set up by a 911 call. I'm assuming it was the same for the Venice shootings."

Snead nodded. "So?"

"So we must have tapes of those 911 calls, right? Before going on duty, every 911 operator in the city should be listening to those recordings. They might be able to recognize the guy's voice if he calls again. And we need emergency operators to be extra careful on hang-ups or anyone who won't identify themselves, and let dispatch know if something's suspicious."

One of the Robbery-Homicide detectives jumped in. "Kane's got a point. Along those lines, let's get somebody down here from Emergency Services and see whether there are any other ways we can protect our guys."

After several other detectives spoke up in agreement, Snead nodded grudgingly. "I'll set that up."

"Another thing," I continued. "At the Palisades site we used a ballistic alignment laser to determine the origin of the shots. I think the guy used a rifle, not a handgun, and that his shots were fired from a ridgeline about 200 yards east of the house."

"The guy's using a rifle?" interrupted John Madison, a detective I recognized from the Pacific Division. "We didn't consider that. We did think it must have been one helluva big handgun to do that much damage, but we couldn't figure how the guy got close enough to pull the trigger. A rifle would explain it. What it doesn't explain is why no one heard the shots. But if it was a rifle he used, we need to go back and locate the guy's firing position."

"I would," I advised. "In addition to the Palisades neighborhood where our guys were killed, we're canvassing the ridgeline from where we think the rounds were fired. We're also checking for security cameras that might have caught a shot of the sniper, or of his car or van or whatever he was driving. You might do the same."

Madison nodded thoughtfully. "Worth a try."

"You recover any bullets?" I asked.

"Just fragments."

"We dug up a slug in the front yard, another from a wall in the house," I said. "Both were fairly well chewed up, but we should try for a ballistic comparison between the two murder sites. Speaking of which, the report on the Palisade slugs will read that they are 240-grain, copper-jacketed Sierra MatchKing bullets. Because of the unusually heavy weight of the bullets, the lab says they were probably fired from handloaded cartridges rather than manufactured ones."

"I wasn't aware that a ballistic report was available," Snead broke in angrily. "How did you get those details, Kane?"

I shrugged. "I made a call."

Ignoring Snead's outburst, Shepherd spoke for the first time. "The handloading aspect might be something we can use," he said quietly.

Everyone turned in Shepherd's direction. "We can check with local gunsmiths, handloading equipment retailers, online distributors, and so on," he explained. "Current law doesn't require a permit or even an ID to purchase reloading supplies and equipment, so unfortunately there will be Fourth Amendment probable-cause issues to deal with. We'll have to be careful if we start asking for customer names, but at minimum we could generate a list of distributors who sell handloading equipment, smokeless powder, brass cases, and the like. Could be useful if we develop a suspect or suspects," he added. He looked at Snead. "My office has the resources to do that."

"Fine. Go ahead," said Snead, unable to conceal his irritation that things were progressing without his supervision.

"Another thing," I went on. "We should look into the possibility that these murders were motivated by revenge. Maybe all four officers knew each other and were into something they shouldn't have been. Or maybe one of the officers was murdered and the others were killed to cover it up. I'm not suggesting we blame the victims, and I know this is a long shot, but we can't rule it out."

"I can talk with some of the Pacific Division guys about that," said Madison. "Check with patrol sergeants, look at contact lists on the officers' phones and computers, like that. See whether these guys knew each other. We can look for any recent busts that might be related, too. And someone needs to talk with family members. Officer Rios's wife lives in Venice. I'll handle that one."

"Both of our patrolmen lived in North Hollywood," I noted. "I can check with Levinson and Meyer's sergeant in West LA. Maybe somebody else could—"

"I'll talk with the families in North Hollywood," said a detective in the back. "That's my division."

"That leaves officer-in-training Chet Grant," said Madison. "Anyone know where his family lives?"

"His folks live in Pacific Palisades," said someone else. "Chet and his wife had a condo in Santa Monica."

"Okay, I've got those two," I said. Then, glancing at Deluca, "You good to take the autopsies later this morning?" I asked, referring to the postmortem exams on Patrolmen Levinson and

Meyer, which required the presence of a homicide investigator from our unit. Suddenly remembering that Deluca had been friends with Levinson, I quickly backtracked. "Forget that, Paul. I'll take the posts."

"No, I'm good," said Deluca.

"You sure?"

"Yeah. It's something I need to do. I'll head over the County Coroner's Office as soon as we get out of here."

"As soon as you get out of the mayor's briefing downstairs," Snead corrected. "Speaking of which—"

"One last thing," I broke in. "If there are any more shootings, and I hope to hell there aren't, we might consider maintaining case continuity by using the same forensic teams on any future cases—same criminalist, crime-scene technicians, coroner's investigator, pathologist, and so on."

"I'll see what I can do," said Snead, again glancing at his watch. "It's almost eight and we need to get downstairs. Meeting adjourned. I'll see you all here tomorrow at 7:00 a.m."

As men began heading toward the door, Snead added, "Detective Kane, stick around. I want a word with you."

After the room had cleared, Snead sat on the edge of a desk and crossed his arms. "Any idea why you're on this task force, Kane?" he demanded.

"Absolutely none, Bill," I answered truthfully. "It came as a complete surprise to me. After last time, I thought you and I were done."

"That's *Lieutenant* Snead."

"Whatever you say, Lieutenant. Why don't you enlighten me regarding my presence here this morning. I'm all ears."

Snead stared at me for a long moment. "It's no secret that I don't like you, Kane. It's officers like you who make maintaining discipline impossible, and organizational discipline is the backbone of every investigation, *especially* one like this. If it weren't for the fact that you occasionally get results, you would have been drummed off the force a long time ago."

I was beginning to see where Snead was headed, but I remained silent.

"Despite the insubordination you demonstrated when you worked under me on the Candlelight Killer Task Force, I will admit that you were pivotal in breaking the case," Snead continued. "I'm not saying I condone your actions, but like I said, I will grant that you sometimes get results."

"And your point?"

"My point is that somebody's killing cops, Kane. This task force needs to end that ASAP. So I'll tell you what I'm going to do. I have every confidence we will bring the killer or killers to justice, but I'm going to hedge my bets. I'm going to give you some leeway. Stay out of my way—and by that I mean don't screw with me in the meetings—and I'll stay out of yours, within limits. You're my wild card, Kane. I'm going to give you all the rope you need to find this guy, and maybe enough to hang yourself as well. You understand what I'm saying?"

"Yeah, I understand. You want me to make you look good and cut my own throat at the same time."

Snead smiled. "In a perfect world . . . Well, one can only hope. I'll see you tomorrow, Kane. Bring your case file and be on time."

Chapter Seven

Located on a forty-acre parcel in Studio City, CBS Studio Center advertises itself as a full-service production facility that includes eighteen sound stages, 210,000 square feet of office space, 200 dressing rooms, a mill and construction shop, three outdoor filming locations, and a host of other support facilities. In keeping with a film history dating back to the 1928 studios of Mack Sennett, numerous movies had been shot on the lot, along with scores of hit television shows including *Seinfeld*, *3rd Rock from the Sun*, *Entertainment Tonight*, and *Big Brother*.

CBS Studio Center is also home to the Los Angeles bureau of CBS News.

As Allison Kane turned off Ventura Boulevard and passed the Studio Center's main gate on Radford Avenue, she was struck as usual by the sheer size of the entertainment complex that housed CBS's flagship TV station, KCBS-TV, along with its sister station, KCAL-TV. Years back Allison had held an internship position at KCBS Channel 2 News when it had been located at Columbia Square in Hollywood. Since moving to Studio City, the upgraded Channel 2 News studio now enjoyed digitally enhanced facilities—an improvement that made high-definition TV broadcasting possible. After opening their new studio, Channel 2 had even hosted a nationally televised edition of *CBS Evening News*.

Nevertheless, the broadcast center's proximity to the sitcom stages was a constant reminder to Allison of something she had learned on the day she started in the newsroom. Like it or not, TV news was a form of entertainment, pure and simple. Of course there were other, loftier aspects—journalistic integrity, fair and balanced coverage, ethical reporting. But in today's cynical sound-bite world, where ratings were king and corporate accountants held final say, entertainment was the bottom line. And if you couldn't accept that, you didn't belong in the news business.

After crossing the bridge traversing the Los Angeles River— at present a mere trickle running the center of a wide concrete channel—Allison entered the lot's north gate, leaving her car in a parking structure across from the CBS Broadcast Building. As she hurried across Gilligan's Island Road to the news building, Allison smiled to herself, not for the first time thinking the street sign aptly symbolized the unlikely marriage between modern-day entertainment and TV news.

"Morning, Ali," said Lauren Van Owen, the L.A. bureau chief, nodding to Allison as she entered the newsroom. "Drop by my office as soon as you finish your news brief, okay?"

"Sure," Allison replied, heading for her desk. Wondering what Lauren wanted, Allison hung her coat on the back of her chair, checked her makeup, and hurried to a small recording studio off the main newsroom. CBS offered two-minute online news briefs summarizing the lead stories of the day, and Allison had been reading the online spot for the past several months. Although she didn't find doing the webcast particularly rewarding, it did get her face in front of the public, and Lauren was letting Allison develop and present some of her own pieces on the 5:00 p.m. local news as well. There were even hints that management was considering her for an anchor position sometime in the future.

All in all, not bad for just having returned to the station after a two-year hiatus to finish college, Allison thought to herself as she sat at the online news desk. Positioning herself in front of a green-screen background, she took a moment to compose herself, then scanned the stories on the teleprompter. The first item up involved the shooting deaths of two more LAPD police officers, this time in Pacific Palisades. With a chill, Allison suddenly realized why her father had needed to leave the restaurant on such short notice the previous evening.

A moment later the cameraman gave Allison a silent countdown. She looked into the lens and began. "Good morning, Los Angeles. I'm Allison Kane. Here's what's happening in the Southland today . . ."

"So what did you want to see me about?" Allison asked twenty minutes later, seating herself across from Lauren at the bureau chief's desk.

Lauren Van Owen, an attractive blond in her late thirties, regarded Allison for a long moment before replying. Although the bureau chief was still a beautiful woman, in the harsh light of the news studio Allison could make out a number of fine lines on her face that even the work of the best plastic surgeons hadn't been able to erase—remnants of a brutal slashing that had ended Lauren's on-camera career a number of years back.

Lauren finally spoke. "I think you know what I want, Ali," she said. "And if you say no, I'll understand. It won't hurt your chances here at CBS."

"This involves the police officers who were murdered in Pacific Palisades last night, right?"

Lauren nodded. "And the two patrolmen killed in Venice the night before. Network is taking the story national. They're sending Brent Preston out to cover developments, and we need someone local with access to the investigation."

"By access, you mean you want me to get inside information from my father?"

Lauren hesitated. "I'd be lying if I said I didn't, but I know that's not going to happen. Not again, anyway."

Flushing, Allison realized Lauren was referring to a news story that had taken place two years earlier, during a period when Allison had first worked at Channel 2. Allison's father had been the lead investigator on a high-profile investigation involving the murder of a young TV actress, and Allison had crossed the line more than once to get inside information on the story. "You're right when you say that's not going to happen," Allison said firmly. "Anyway, what makes you think my dad is involved in the cop-killing case?"

"Oh, he's involved," said Lauren. "We have reporters at PAB right now, waiting for the mayor to announce the formation of an LAPD/FBI interagency task force. Early this morning your father was seen entering the building. He is definitely involved."

"That may be, but I still don't—"

"Hear me out, Ali," Lauren interrupted. "I know your father can't pass information to you without risking his job, and you're not going to take advantage of being his daughter, either. I just think there might be a way you two could interface without breaking any rules. Will you think about it?"

Allison hesitated. "Interface, huh? I don't want to sound selfish, but if I do this—and I'm just saying *if*—what's in it for me?"

Lauren smiled. "You are a quick study, aren't you? You remind me of myself at your age."

When Allison didn't reply, Lauren sat back and folded her hands. "Network will be calling most of the shots," she said. "Between you and me, they think this is going to be bigger than the Chris Dorner story. If the murders continue, the story might even be bigger than the D.C. Beltway shootings. Bottom line, Network is gearing up for a media blitz, and if the cop killings continue, all hell is going to break loose. If that happens, they want Brent out here covering developments."

Allison rolled her eyes. "Yeah, I figured. It will be *so* nice to see him again."

Ignoring Allison's animus toward Brent, Lauren continued. "So here's the deal: if you come up with anything new on the case, Network will have the exclusive right to break it on *CBS Evening News*."

"But—"

"Hear me out," Lauren repeated. "That first part is nonnegotiable. But here's what I *can* do for you. Although Brent will be Network's L.A. connection, whenever possible I'll do my best to get you some on-air time. You know, 'Here with more from Los Angeles is CBS news correspondent Allison Kane.' You could do follow-ups on the local news at eleven, and again the next day at five and six. Of course this all depends on what you're able to dig up. What do you say?"

Allison considered carefully before answering. Finally she said, "I'll talk with my dad. After last time, I'll need to be up-front with him right from the start. But if he's willing to pass along anything without crossing the line himself, and you can use it, we have a deal."

Chapter Eight

After taking the elevator to the ground floor, I caught up with Deluca outside the Ronald F. Deaton Civic Auditorium, a 450-seat meeting hall at the base of the main building. "What was that with Snead wanting to talk to you after the meeting?" Deluca asked, eyeing me curiously. "He ask you for a date?"

"Not hardly," I chuckled, glancing around at the crowd of reporters jamming the auditorium entrance. "He says he's going to give me some leeway as long as I don't cross him in the meetings. He would like me to come up with results and ruin my career at the same time."

"Sounds like Snead," Deluca laughed. Then, also glancing at the crowd, "Let's head in before all the seats in the back are taken."

Just then my phone buzzed. I glanced at the screen. Allison. "I'm gonna take this," I said. "Save me a place. Wouldn't want to miss a word of the mayor's speech."

"Right," said Deluca. "See you inside."

Thumbing the answer button, I stepped to the side of the building, moving out of the crush of reporters. "Ali? What's up?" I asked.

"Hey, Dad," she said. "I just had an interesting talk with Lauren. Network is sending out Brent Preston from D.C. to cover what they think is going to be the biggest story of the year. Her words were 'If the cop killings continue, all hell is going to break loose.'"

I glanced at the fleet of satellite vans on the street. "Lauren's probably right," I agreed. "The wolves are already circling."

"I have something I want to run by you, but before you say no, just let me speak," Allison continued. "Lauren knows you're working on the case, and she asked whether you and I could get together on things. She suggested that maybe you and I could somehow interface without breaking any rules."

"Interface? Ali—"

"Let me finish, Dad. It won't be like last time. I'll take anything you want to give me, but I won't pry. And anything you want to keep confidential will be kept confidential, I promise. And don't forget, it might prove helpful for you to have an inside connection with the media. You never know."

That last part caught my attention. Snead had warned that he would be the only task-force conduit with the media, but he'd also offered me some leeway . . . whatever that meant. In my experience, manipulating the press in a case like this could sometimes be helpful, as Allison had suggested. It had worked for me more than once. It had also blown up in my face. "I'll think about it, Ali," I said, deciding to leave the door open a crack, at least for the moment. "Don't get your hopes up, but I'll think about it. In the meantime, I have to get inside and listen to our mayor sounding mayoral. We'll talk later."

"Thanks, Dad."

After hanging up, I pushed through the crowd of reporters choking the lobby, joining Deluca inside the auditorium at a seat in the rear. A few minutes later Mayor Fitzpatrick strode to the podium. Again trailing behind was the same entourage that had accompanied him into the task-force briefing—now joined by several members of the police commission.

As I'd expected, Fitzpatrick's media speech turned out to be a rehash of his earlier presentation to the task force, including an extra dose of self-serving rhetoric as well. Near the conclusion he announced a hotline email and phone number, requesting that anyone with information get in touch. After that he introduced the members of our task force, asking us all to stand. Finally the chief spoke briefly, followed by a frenzied question-and-answer period—at which point Deluca and I took the opportunity to slip out unnoticed.

On the walk back to my car, something Allison had said kept running through my mind. Despite the confident assurances made by our mayor that the case would be rolled up quickly, I had my doubts. Nevertheless, judging by the media excitement in the auditorium, I *was* certain of one thing. As Allison had also said, if the cop killings continued, all hell was going to break loose.

Thirty minutes later, following a traffic-congested drive across town, I met with Lieutenant Long at the West Los Angeles Police Station. There, for the next hour, Long and I discussed our open-case reassignments—shifting responsibility for ongoing investigations to other detectives in the squad, many of whom were already overloaded. It was a bad situation, but there was nothing we could do about it. During that time, working from memory, I also gave a complete rundown and status evaluation of our unit's open cases, personnel allocations, and court appearances for the following weeks.

When I had finished, Long looked at me for a moment without speaking. "Damn, Kane," he finally muttered. "That memory of yours. You don't forget much, do you?"

I shrugged.

So far Long had avoided asking me anything about the task-force meeting, and I hadn't volunteered. With our preliminary case-reassignment work completed, Long sat back in his chair. "Is the task-force investigation gonna be the big mess I think it is?" he asked.

"I hope not," I answered. "But I have a bad feeling the killings aren't over, Lieutenant, and so far we don't have a single lead worth mentioning."

Long sighed. "I said this last night, Dan, and I'm saying it again. This is the type of case that ends careers. Be careful."

Following my meeting with Lieutenant Long, I spent another twenty minutes in the squad room tying up case reassignments with John Banowski, the homicide-unit detective who would be shouldering most of the oversight responsibility in my absence. I also placed a call to Deluca. He informed me that when he'd finished at the coroner's office, he planned to drive to Pacific Palisades and supervise a second neighborhood canvass, to which I agreed. We also agreed to meet at the station later that day. Following that, after checking with the day-patrol sergeant, I made several additional phone calls—one to the Malibu assistant

D.A. handling Nate's case; another to Julie Grant, the wife of Chet Grant, the officer-in-training who had been killed in Venice. Although I wasn't able to speak with Mrs. Grant, I did manage to contact Chet's parents and make arrangements to visit them later that afternoon.

Given the circumstances, I knew there was a possibility that Chet's wife Julie simply wasn't answering the phone, so I decided to stop by her Santa Monica condo unannounced and try knocking on the door. As I had pointed out during the task-force meeting, looking hard at the murdered officers for something to explain their deaths was a long shot, but it was something that needed to be done.

Chapter Nine

On the way to Chet and Julie Grant's condo in Santa Monica, I made a quick stop at the Brentwood Country Mart on Twenty-Sixth Street for something to eat. Years back when I had first started working patrol, the mart had been a mostly open-air affair—red-painted picnic tables, green umbrellas with "Country Mart" on the canopies, and plenty of parking. Over time more and more open space had been enclosed, with the mart gradually becoming a warren of shops and passageways, with only a few areas left open to the sky. Worse, parking had been reduced to a few miserly spaces on the periphery. Nevertheless, the mart still had a stall serving my favorite selection—rotisserie chicken in a basket overflowing with fries. The food was as delicious as ever, and I still occasionally found my way there for lunch.

Chicken basket and a large cup of coffee in hand, I made my way to a table beside a large outdoor fire pit—one of the few remnants dating back to the original mart—and dug in. As I ate, I absently began picking over details of the case, especially ones that didn't seem to fit.

Topping the list was why no one had heard the shots in Pacific Palisades, or apparently in Venice, either. A sonic suppressor, or silencer, while legal in many states like Texas, did little to silence the ballistic crack of a supersonic rifle bullet. Contrary to what films portray, a sonic suppressor might significantly reduce muzzle blast, but the sonic crack of a rifle bullet is impossible to mask.

The next logical step would be to look into the use of subsonic ammunition, in which there is no supersonic noise. I didn't know much about subsonic ammo except that it existed. Curious, I pulled out my phone and between bites did some online research. What I found was intriguing. As I had thought, the two main sources of rifle noise were muzzle blast and sonic crack. Using subsonic ammunition could eliminate the latter, but at the expense of reduced range and accuracy. Nevertheless, using a heavy subsonic bullet—somewhere in the 220- to 240-

grain range versus a normal 120- to 180-grain high-velocity round—could produce devastating results out to a distance of several hundred yards. I remembered that the slugs we'd recovered in the Palisades had weighed 240 grains each, considerably more than a conventional high-velocity rifle bullet. Fired from a rifle with a sonic suppressor, a subsonic shot *might* have gone unheard. At least it was an avenue to explore—especially the handloading angle, as Shepherd had suggested. Checking ownership of sonic suppressors might be another.

The second aspect of the Palisades shootings that puzzled me was this: after making his 911 call, how had our shooter managed to find such a perfect firing position so quickly? The ridgeline cul-de-sac from which he'd shot had provided an ideal view of the neighborhood below, not to mention isolation from nearby houses. Simply good luck?

I didn't buy that.

I suddenly realized that I had reversed the order. The shooter had picked his firing position *first*, then selected a kill zone afterward—someplace visible from his shooting site and within his field of fire. Then he had lured police officers to their deaths with a 911 call. It had been an ambush—the shootings planned and executed with precision and expertise. And a preselection of the firing position meant that the killer had scouted the Pacific Palisades area beforehand. The same would probably hold true for the Venice murders. Maybe this was something we could use.

Given the premeditation involved in the shootings, I once more got the feeling that unless the killings were an act of revenge specifically targeting one or possibly all four of our murdered officers, they weren't going to stop.

Following lunch, a short drive down Montana Avenue brought me to Chet and Julie Grant's attractive two-story condo, located in an upscale neighborhood a few blocks off the beach. There was no answer when I knocked, but a neighbor said Julie was staying with Chet's family. Deciding to interview everyone at once, I headed north.

Twenty minutes later I arrived at Jeff and Rita Grant's palatial estate. Their Pacific Palisades home was located on several secluded acres high in the hills, with a long cobbled driveway, towering eucalyptus flanking the main house, and a commanding view of the ocean. I stopped at a ten-foot-high iron gate guarding the property. Not surprisingly, a news van was parked outside. Ignoring it, I rolled down my window and thumbed the intercom button beside the gate.

"Yes?" a woman's voice sounded.

A video camera was mounted over the intercom. I looked into the lens. "Detective Kane to speak with the Grants. I called earlier."

"Yes, Detective Kane. Please drive to the porte-cochère and park in front," said the voice. A moment later the heavy gate began to swing inward.

As I started in, I noticed the news crew taking advantage of the situation by following me close behind. Stopping partway through the gate, I opened my door and stepped out, hanging my shield from my coat pocket as I did.

I walked to the van and signaled the driver to roll down his window. "Nice try, guys," I said to the newsmen inside. "Now back up and give Mr. and Mrs. Grant some privacy." When the driver started to object, I added, "That wasn't a request."

Apparently seeing something in my eyes, the driver gave me a dirty look and backed up. I pulled the rest of the way through the gate and waited on the other side until the barrier had reclosed behind me. Then, following the tree-lined driveway, I drove to the front of the Grants' gigantic ranch-style house, passing tennis courts, a riding stable and corral, several outbuildings, and a detached six-car garage on the way in. When I pulled to a stop beneath a giant porte-cochère shading the front steps, I found an attractive younger woman waiting for me on the entry landing. She was wearing a loose-fitting dress and sweater, and appeared to be about seven or eight months pregnant.

I exited my car and started up the steps. "Julie Grant?" I said, extending my hand.

The young woman nodded, taking my hand without speaking. Although her grip was firm, her hand felt small in mine, and she seemed to be on the verge of tears.

"Dan Kane, LAPD homicide," I continued sympathetically. "I'm so sorry for your loss, Mrs. Grant. I regret having to intrude, but there are some questions I need to ask that may help find the person who killed your husband."

"Yes, of course," she replied, crossing her arms across her chest. "And please call me Julie. Let's go inside."

I followed Julie through an oversized front door, arriving in a spacious entry with a soaring ceiling and an ornate crystal chandelier. Ahead, past a wide hallway leading to the rest of the house, a curving staircase ascended to the upper floors. To the left, an arched portal led into a massive living room with a huge rock fireplace against the far wall.

Julie proceeded into the living room. I followed her, gazing out the room's floor-to-ceiling windows at a panorama of manicured landscape and the Pacific Ocean beyond. Opposite the fireplace, almost lost amid an expanse of furniture and art, was an antique hutch crammed with acting awards. Although not a film buff, in the thicket of less familiar statuettes and cut crystal I recognized a number of familiar objects—two Oscars, a number of Golden Globes, and a handful of Emmys.

Julie perched on the edge of a leather couch near the fireplace. I took a seat across from her, sitting in an armchair. "Are Mr. and Mrs. Grant at home?" I asked.

Julie nodded, glancing toward the entry. "Mr. Grant said he would join us in a minute," she answered dully. "Mrs. Grant is, um . . . not feeling well."

I nodded. From experience I knew what sudden tragedy could do to a family. "Again, I wish I didn't have to be here, as I know how you and Chet's parents must feel." I hesitated, realizing how insensitive my last statement must have sounded, despite the fact that it was true. Before I could apologize, a voice sounded behind me.

"So why *are* you here?"

I turned to see Jeff Grant standing in the doorway, hands clasped behind his back. He was wearing sweats and a T-shirt and looked as if he hadn't shaved for days. Although I recognized him from his films, in person he appeared older.

"We already told the officers from Venice everything we knew when they visited after . . . after Chet was shot."

I rose and extended my hand. "I'm Detective Kane, Mr. Grant," I said.

Ignoring my outstretched hand, Mr. Grant crossed the room and sat at the other end of the couch from Julie. "I know who you are, Detective," he said without acknowledging Julie's presence. "I saw you on TV at the task-force announcement. And as for knowing how we feel, I doubt that's possible," he added angrily. "Ask your questions and let's get this over with. What do you want to know?"

I nodded, deciding not to let Mr. Grant's attitude throw me. "First of all, I'm here because some recent developments have thrown a new light on Chet's murder."

"You mean the killings last night in the Palisades," said Mr. Grant.

"Correct. We think those shootings may have been done by the same person or persons who killed your son. We're trying to determine whether the Venice murders are related in any way to the ones here in the Palisades."

"I don't understand."

"He wants to know whether Chet knew the other officers," Julie interjected. "If there was a reason someone shot them all, right?" she added, glancing at me.

"That's correct," I answered. "I know Chet just graduated from the academy, but I heard he was close to his training officer, Patrolman Rios. Did you ever hear him speak about the other officers who were killed last night, Patrolmen Levinson and Meyer?"

Julie shook her head.

"Mr. Grant?"

Mr. Grant looked down at his hands, seeming embarrassed. "No," he said quietly. "Chet and I hadn't spoken in quite some time. His mother and I didn't approve of some of Chet's life choices, and we . . . well, we really don't know what was going on with him for the past months."

"For the past *year*," Julie corrected.

"Fine, for the past year," Mr. Grant conceded.

"By life choices, do you mean his joining the LAPD?" I asked.

"For one," Mr. Grant said with a glare.

"Marrying me and having a baby, for another," Julie added bitterly.

Mr. Grant glanced at Julie, then looked away. "That's not fair. There was more to it than that, and you know it."

Julie didn't reply.

I sensed movement behind me. I turned to see Mrs. Grant entering the room. Tall, with long auburn hair and startlingly blue eyes, Rita Grant was a beautiful woman, even in her grief. Mr. Grant and I stood as she made her way unsteadily toward the couch. "Darling, you don't have to be here," said Mr. Grant. "I can take care of this."

Ignoring him, Mrs. Grant sat beside Julie, taking her daughter-in-law's hand in hers. "Like you always do, Jeff?" she said, slurring her words. "We've all seen how that works out."

I saw the pain in Mr. Grant's eyes. I looked away to let the moment pass. Then, to Mrs. Grant, "I'm so sorry, Mrs. Grant. I truly am."

Mrs. Grant looked at me, seeming to see me for the first time. "Thank you, Detective," she said. Then she started to cry, not making a sound, simply lowering her head and letting the tears flow, her body trembling with each sob.

Mr. Grant's look of anger turned to one of concern. He slid closer to his wife and circled her protectively with an arm. Then he looked up and again glared at me.

Trying to ignore Mr. Grant's hostility, I turned toward Julie. "Are you certain you don't remember your husband ever mentioning Officers Meyer or Levinson, or that maybe his training officer, Patrolman Rios, might have known them?"

Julie shook her head. "Chet mostly talked about Tony, his T.O. 'Officer Rios this, Officer Rios that.' I never heard him mention the others."

"How about enemies—someone who might have wanted to hurt Chet?"

"No. Nothing like that. Everyone liked Chet."

"It's a long shot, but if there is *any* connection between the two shootings, anything at all, we need to know," I explained, passing her my card. "If you think of something, please let me know. In the meantime, we have Chet's cell phone. We would like to check his contact list and recent calls."

"Whatever you need," Julie replied.

"It would also be helpful if we could have our tech guys go over his computer. I assume he had one at home?"

Julie nodded. "Chet has a laptop." She hesitated, then corrected herself. "He *had* a laptop. It's at the condo."

"Could I have someone drop by today and pick it up? Maybe you could call a neighbor or the condo manager to let them in?"

"If you think it would help, I'll be happy to," Julie replied numbly.

"I have a question for you, Detective," Mr. Grant broke in. "What are you doing to find the man who killed our son?"

It was a fair question, and despite Snead's warning not to discuss the case outside the task force, I tried to answer truthfully. "We're just getting started, Mr. Grant," I said. "The information I'm about to give you is confidential, so please don't share it with anyone. We think that the officers who were killed last night were shot by someone with a rifle. We believe it's the same person who killed your son and his training officer in Venice."

"You think someone hunted Chet with a rifle and shot him like he was some kind of animal?" Mr. Grant asked, his face turning ashen. "But why?"

"That's what we're trying to figure out. A motive would go a long way toward finding who did it. In the meantime, we're canvassing areas at both sites, looking for anyone who might have seen something. We're also searching for anyone with a surveillance camera that might have caught a shot of the killer. We recovered a mostly intact slug at the Palisades site. Something might develop from that, like the type of weapon the shooter used."

Mr. Grant paused, then asked, "The task force the mayor announced this morning—he made it sound as if you guys were going to wrap this up in a few days. Is that true?"

"Believe me, everyone wants to find this guy," I hedged. "It is definitely receiving top priority. We don't like having our men killed. As for wrapping things up quickly, I hope the mayor is right, but . . ."

". . . throwing money and resources at a problem doesn't necessarily bring results," Mr. Grant finished. "Same thing on a movie set."

I caught Mr. Grant's eye and held it. "I can tell you this," I said. "I will do everything in my power to find the person who took your son from you, and I won't stop until I do. No matter what it takes, I *will* find him."

Mr. Grant nodded, then looked again at his wife. "We appreciate that, Detective Kane."

I glanced at my watch, deciding that I had learned all I could from the Grants, at least for the moment. "Thank you for your cooperation," I said, rising to my feet. "I'll keep you in the loop regarding any progress we make."

Mr. Grant looked up and nodded, then focused again on his wife.

With a deepening sense of dejection, wishing I were as certain of myself as I'd sounded, I let myself out.

Chapter Ten

After leaving the Grants' estate, I returned to the West L.A. station and spent several hours there tying up loose ends with Deluca and Banowski. During that time I also wrote up the Palisades crime report, including supplementals, interview summaries, and the preliminary results of our neighborhood canvasses—which Deluca informed me had generally been a bust. No one had seen or heard the shooter, although several neighbors reported having noticed a white or gray van cruising the area on the day of the shootings. Not much, but something.

On another front, a surprising number of homes in the neighborhood had security cameras, although to date none had been found that gave a clear shot of the streets where the killer might have driven. Deluca had scheduled another canvass for tomorrow, checking farther out. I wasn't hopeful, but it was worth a try. You never knew what might turn up. Deluca also informed me that the postmortem exams on Levinson and Meyer hadn't discovered anything unexpected, and that the cause of death on each homicide would be ruled as a gunshot wound to the head.

It was after 9:30 p.m. when I finally returned home. Allison was again staying at Mike's, and Catheryn and Nate had already finished dinner. I found Catheryn in the kitchen, cleaning up. "Hey, Kate," I said, giving her a kiss. "What did I miss?"

Catheryn smiled. "Paprika chicken," she said, glancing at a pot still simmering on the stove. "I saved you some."

"Great. Where's Nate?"

"In his room. Go say hi while I dish you up some leftovers."

I headed down the hall and banged on Nate's door. "Hey, Nate. You decent?"

"Come on in, Dad," came the reply.

I found Nate at his desk, laptop open, apparently doing his homework. He closed his computer as I entered. "What's up?" he asked.

I sat on the edge of his bed, glancing around the room. Unlike his older sister, Nate always kept his bedroom neat and orderly—clothes put away, bed made, desk and closet neat enough to pass military inspection. I don't know where he got that, but certainly not from me.

"What's up? Not much," I answered. "Just thought I'd check in, see how you're doing. You good?"

Nate shrugged.

"I talked with the Malibu assistant district attorney today."

Hearing my words, Nate seemed to shrink. "What did he say?"

"He said he's going to give you a pass on the pot bust, as the weed wasn't in your possession. He's also going to allow diversion on the underage alcohol offense," I added, referring to a California criminal justice program that gave first-time misdemeanor offenders a chance to keep a clean record.

"Diversion. What does that mean?" Nate asked nervously.

"It means that in a few weeks when your case comes up, you're getting a second chance. You won't have to go to trial. Instead you'll be entered in a four-month program, usually with educational videos and counseling, after which all charges will be dismissed."

"So it won't affect my chances of getting into college?"

"Nope."

I could see a look of relief flooding Nate's eyes. "Thanks, Dad," he said quietly.

"Glad I could help. Just don't screw up again."

"I . . . I won't."

"See that you don't. Speaking of which, next week we have a meeting with your counselor at Samohi. We need to get that situation under control, too. I want you back on the ball team playing for the Vikings."

"Yeah, me too."

"Dan, come and eat," Catheryn called from the kitchen.

"Coming," I called back, looking at Nate one last time. He wasn't a kid anymore, but he wasn't a man yet, either. "You going to be able to keep your temper in check at school from now on?"

Nate nodded. "Absolutely. And if anyone thinks I can't," he joked, smacking his fist into his palm, "I'll make them wish they hadn't."

Catheryn had set a place for me in our nook, just off the kitchen. Still smiling after my talk with Nate, I sat at the table, which provided an unobstructed view of the beach below. The moon wasn't up yet and the sand lay in darkness, but a phosphorescent red tide—a bloom of poisonous phytoplankton that glows when disturbed—was lighting the waves as they hit the shore, illuminating the curling tubes with a faint, ghostly glow. I watched for a moment, struck by the contradictory thought that something so beautiful could also be so deadly— especially if you were a fish.

Catheryn joined me with a bowl of ice cream, sitting across the table and watching as I dug into the leftovers she'd served—a mound of rice topped with spicy paprika chicken, a side of steamed broccoli, and a small salad. "Thanks, Kate," I said between bites. "Didn't realize how hungry I was."

"Save room for dessert," she advised, digging into her ice cream.

"I'll pass on dessert. Wouldn't hurt to lose a couple pounds. Besides, sugar keeps me up, and I have to be downtown early tomorrow morning."

"How's that going?"

I shrugged. "So far, pretty much as expected. Bureaucratic oversight, organizational protocols, questionable leadership, zero leads, and a roomful of detectives getting nothing done. We'll see how things shake out tomorrow."

"Your case has already made national news," Catheryn noted. "It was on *CBS Evening News* earlier. They even ran part of Mayor Fitzpatrick's speech. I got to see you stand with the rest of the task force. You looked very, uh, handsome. In a rough sort of way."

"Yeah?" I chuckled. "Well, I hope I'm as good looking when this is over. Then, changing the subject, "How are things in the music world?"

Catheryn's face brightened. "Rehearsal went well today," she answered.

"You like sitting in the principal chair, eh?"

"I do. I hope things work out," she said thoughtfully. "Speaking of that, a number of us have started planning Arthur's retirement party. We're taking up a collection, and it's probably going to be at the Beverly Hills Hotel a week from Sunday. Will you be able to make it?"

"I'll sure try. Like I said, I'm gonna be working weekends till this thing is over, but I can try to get that day off."

"Good. I really want you to be there, Dan."

I took another bite of chicken. "Beverly Hills Hotel, huh? Pretty fancy, but Arthur deserves the best."

"He's actually grown quite fond of you, too," Catheryn said with a smile. "For the life of me, I don't understand why."

"Must be my sophistication and charm," I suggested, playing along. "Although I usually save that particular quality for the ladies."

"Sophistication and charm," Catheryn laughed. Then, her smile fading, "I heard you just now with Nate. Is everything going to be okay with his court appearance?"

I nodded. "I talked with the Malibu assistant D.A. He's going to let Nate skate this time. There had better not be a next."

"Oh, Dan, I'm so relieved. How did Nate react to the news?"

"I think he was relieved, too. I hope this makes an impression on him. I swear, sometimes I don't know what's going on in that kid's head."

"He's a teenager, Dan. There's absolutely nothing going on up there."

"You've got that right," I sighed.

"Are you okay? You seem a little . . . down."

I took a final bite of chicken and pushed away the plate, not surprised that Catheryn had sensed my mood. After years of marriage, there wasn't much I could hide from her. "I guess maybe I am," I admitted. "I talked with the family of one of the murdered patrolmen today." I started to mention that the murdered officer was the son of Jeff and Rita Grant, but given the circumstances, the fact that Chet Grant's parents were actors didn't seem important.

"It must be so hard on them, losing their boy like that."

"It is. I could see it in their eyes—that confused look people get when something so terrible happened to them that it doesn't seem real. But it is, and deep down they know it, even if they can't accept it yet."

Catheryn regarded me for a long moment. Then she moved behind me and began kneading the muscles of my neck and shoulders. "Were you thinking of Tommy when you visited them?"

"Yeah, I was. I tried not to, but I couldn't help it. To see someone else going through the same thing we did . . ."

"It doesn't seem fair," said Catheryn. "Life doesn't seem fair."

"No, it doesn't. I'm glad I have you, Kate. If I didn't—"

"That's not something you have to worry about," Catheryn interrupted. Giving my shoulders a final rub, she leaned down and kissed my neck. "C'mon, let's go to bed. Things are bound to look better in the morning."

*   *   *

Two hundred miles to the north, in the foothills of the Sierra Nevada Mountains, Dr. Luther Cole sat at a workbench in his garage, also considering what the morning might bring. He hoped his upcoming visit to Los Angeles would prove as satisfying as the previous one. Given the care and planning he had spent on his current project, he saw no reason why it shouldn't.

Concentrating, Dr. Cole used a Hornady digital scale to finish weighing the last of his Lapua .223 brass cartridge cases, sorting them in .1-grain variances. The weights of this latest lot were disappointingly inconsistent, varying almost three grains from high to low. Not much in the grand scheme of things, but Dr. Cole believed successful precision handloading to be a matter of trifles. Uniformity was the key to accuracy, and performing each small step with meticulous care was necessary to produce as accurate a cartridge as possible—each an almost perfect duplicate of the one before. In the task at hand, for example, a difference in case weight indicated a discrepancy in brass wall thickness, which could affect case capacity, thereby causing a variance in muzzle velocity and subsequent bullet flight at longer distances. Of the 200 brass cases now sorted and "batched" on the workbench, he would discard almost half, saving only those closest to median weight for use.

Case selection and preparation, primer and powder combinations, and bullet choice were only a few of the reloading elements that he had mastered in his effort to handload the highest-quality match-grade ammunition. Of course brass preparation was the most time consuming—deburring and chamfering, uniforming, neck-turning, reaming, and so on—but in Cole's estimation, creating nearly perfect cases was a critical first step in the handloading process. Without it, no matter what came after—from "throwing" powder charges to spending hours on the range compiling and recording data, or "dope," on rifle and cartridge performance—it simply wasn't possible to consistently hit a target out to 1,000 yards and beyond. And hitting targets out to 1,000 yards and beyond was exactly what he intended to do.

In Dr. Cole's opinion, some people didn't deserve to live.

Chapter Eleven

I didn't sleep well that night. At 5:00 a.m. I slipped quietly from bed, being careful not to wake Catheryn. After pulling on a swimsuit and a pair of sweats, I grabbed a towel and descended to our redwood deck for my customary morning regimen of sit-ups, push-ups, and bar-chins, followed by a twenty-minute ocean swim.

Afterward, shivering from my swim, I rinsed off in an outside shower, toweled dry, and redonned my sweats. By then the sky over Santa Monica was beginning to light with the coming dawn. A gentle offshore breeze had picked up, carrying the smells of the hills higher up. I watched as a flock of brown pelicans progressed majestically up the beach, flying in formation a few feet off the water, barely moving their wings as they rose and fell on currents of air lifting off the waves. I followed the pelicans' flight until they had rounded a rocky point to the west, enjoying a quiet moment before the day began. For a few minutes the beach belonged to me, the sun was rising on a new day, and as Catheryn had suggested, things were already looking better than they had the day before.

I hoped it was a trend that continued.

I climbed the stairs to the kitchen and got a pot of coffee brewing, shaved, and grabbed a cup of coffee for the drive. My watch read a little after 6:00 a.m. when I slid behind the wheel of my car, joining a surprising number of commuters already on the road. It seemed more and more drivers were leaving early to avoid morning rush hour, which simply resulted in an earlier rush hour. Fortunately, Westside traffic into the city wasn't as bad as elsewhere, and I made it downtown with time to spare.

On the short walk to PAB from the First Street parking structure, I noticed that the fleet of news vans was still parked outside police headquarters, and a number of reporters were already taping stand-ups out front—undoubtedly enumerating all the things they still didn't know and hadn't learned since the news conference yesterday.

The sixth-floor conference room was crowded when I arrived, most task-force detectives getting there early to be on time. Deluca nodded as I entered, as did several others whom I recognized from the various divisions. Assistant Director Shepherd was accompanied by a half-dozen special agents being detailed to assist on the hotlines. Lieutenant Snead studiously avoided looking in my direction as I took a seat beside Deluca.

At 7:00 a.m. on the dot, Snead stepped to the front and cleared his throat. "Let's get started," he said. He paused as the room settled. "We have a lot to cover, including a briefing from Captain Don Schwartz of the Metropolitan 911 Dispatch Center," he continued, glancing toward a heavyset man standing to one side. "Plus a number of hotline tips have come in, so we're also going to be delegating investigative teams to get started on those. But before that, let's get some other business out of the way. Detectives Kane and Madison, I assume you brought your crime-scene reports?"

I nodded.

"Yes, sir," said Madison.

"Good," said Snead. He glanced toward a tall Hispanic woman sitting at a desk near the window. "Ms. Stella Hernandez will be helping out with our clerical work. Give your reports to her and she'll have copies available by the end of the meeting. In the meantime, let's hear what you've got. Detective Madison, you want to start?"

Madison stood. Referring to a thick three-ring binder known in LAPD vernacular as a murder book, he spent several minutes outlining the elements of the Venice shootings. I noticed interest in the room picking up when he mentioned returning to the area to look for the site from which the shooter had fired.

"We checked trajectory angles like Kane suggested," Madison said. "The bullets came in on an upward slant. Working our way back from the apartment building, we traced the origin of the shots to a library parking lot about 150 yards south. Unfortunately, our canvass didn't turn up anyone who remembered seeing or hearing anything out of the ordinary."

"I have something that might bear on that," I volunteered.

"We'll get to you next, Kane," said Snead. "Madison, anything else?"

"Not much," Madison answered. "We talked with Rios's wife about the possibility that he might have known the other officers killed in the Palisades. We checked with his sergeant and the guys he hung with at the station, too. We also examined his cell-phone contacts and email. Came up cold on everything. No connection with the other murdered officers. We found no indication this was a revenge thing, either. Rios put away his share of bad guys, but no more than the rest of us. I don't think that was it."

"Thank you, Detective," said Snead. Then, glancing at me, "Kane?"

Working from memory, as I had already passed my files to the task-force secretary, I summarized our Palisades crime-scene findings. At the end I stressed the discovery of the ridgeline firing position, along with my suspicion that the shooter had selected his firing position first and his target zone afterward.

"So how does that help?" Snead demanded impatiently.

"I think the target zones are secondary," I answered. "If we're looking for someone who was cruising the area earlier, we should be concentrating on the neighborhoods from which he fires. That's where he's spending time. He may never even visit the actual kill zones except to make the 911 call."

"Makes sense," said one of the detectives from Robbery-Homicide.

"And you did that in the Palisades," said Snead. "Canvassing houses on the ridge, correct? Any results?"

"Not much," I admitted. "Several people did say they saw a white or gray van in the area on the day of the shootings. We're still looking for a video surveillance camera that might have caught a shot of the guy."

"Same in Venice," Madison added. "No luck yet, but it's still a good approach. Especially if it happens again."

I nodded. "I also visited Officer-in-Training Chet Grant's family," I continued. "They weren't aware of any connection between Chet and the officers killed in Venice. We're still going over Chet's computer and phone, but nothing has turned up so far."

"I talked with Officer Meyer's and Officer Levinson's families," a detective from the Hollywood Division broke in. "Checked with the guys at the station, went through Meyer's and Levinson's computers and phones, and so on. No connection to the Venice murders."

There was a brief silence as everyone came to the same conclusion. If the killings were unrelated and the sniper wasn't targeting specific patrolmen, then his motive for killing cops was simply that: to kill cops, *any* cops. And if that were the case, there could be more shootings.

"So our guy has a hard-on for police officers," said Madison.

"Seems that way," agreed Deluca, speaking for the first time. "Maybe we should take a look at that angle. Interview police academy washouts, officers dismissed for cause, anybody with disciplinary problems, find out who Internal Affairs is investigating—that kind of thing."

"Jesus, now we're combing our own ranks for the killer?" said Detective Jerry Dondero from Robbery-Homicide, looking disgusted.

"Has to be done," said Snead. "Good suggestion, Deluca," he added with a smile. "You and Kane work up a complete list of possible police suspects by the end of the day."

I glanced at Deluca, noticing him slump in his seat as he realized that Snead had tagged us with what would undoubtedly be an extremely unpopular task. Unfortunately, like investigating the murdered officers' personal lives in search of a motive, it needed to be done.

"How about checking California Department of Justice computers for similar shootings?" asked one of the guys in the back. "Maybe try NCIC, too," he added, referring to the FBI's National Crime Information Center database.

"I can handle those inquiries," offered Shepherd.

"Fine. Now if there's nothing else, let's move on," suggested Snead. "The hotline roster—"

"One more thing," I interrupted.

"What is it, Kane?"

"Something about these shootings has been bugging me," I said. "Why hasn't anyone heard the shots?"

A number of detectives nodded.

"I did some research on that," I went on. "A sonic suppressor, or silencer, doesn't do much to muffle a rifle shot—mostly because a rifle bullet travels faster than the speed of sound, which creates a kind of sonic crack when it leaves the barrel. A suppressor can't mask that. Using a subsonic round could get around the problem."

I noticed Shepherd leaning forward.

"You're saying the guy might have used some kind of special bullets?" asked Snead.

"Maybe," I answered. "At least it's something to consider. Along those lines, I read that subsonic rounds can be manufactured by handloading enthusiasts."

"Handloading? That fits in with what we know about the guy so far," Shepherd broke in. "With a subsonic round and a sonic suppressor, the rifle noise might have gone unnoticed."

"Especially if he fired from inside a car or van," I added. "I know suppressors are illegal in California, but he could have bought one in another state. Purchase requires a class III federal weapons permit, correct?"

Shepherd shook his head. "Actually, no. It's a two-hundred-dollar tax stamp issued by ATF, but it does require a fairly complete application—fingerprints, pictures, background check, and so on." He glanced at Snead. "I can generate an ATF list of every sound-suppressor application in the thirty-eight states where they're legal for, say, the past ten years. There will be thousands of names on the list, but like the handloading aspect, it might come in handy if we develop a suspect or suspects."

"Fine," Snead conceded. "Do it."

"Making accurate subsonic shots could involve its own area of expertise, correct?" I continued, still addressing Shepherd. "That might be another angle to consider. Is there someone we could get in here to enlighten us on that?"

"I could have one of our HRT operators come in," Shepherd suggested, referring to the FBI's elite Hostage Rescue Team. "We have a number of snipers onboard, most of whom were originally military-trained SEALs or Army Rangers. One of those guys should be able to answer any questions you have."

"We have sharpshooters on our own SWAT units," said Snead. "But if you think one of your HRT operators might be better . . ."

Shepherd shrugged. "I'd put my money on our 'HuRT' snipers, but whatever you think."

Snead nodded. "Okay, set it up. We can always have one of our own guys talk to us later." He glanced around the room. "Anything else? No? Okay, before we go to hotline assignments, Captain Schwartz, who commands the LAPD Communications Division, has a couple words for us." He turned toward the heavyset man who had been standing patiently on the side of the room. "Captain?"

Carrying what appeared to be a music boom box, Captain Schwartz walked to the front and set his equipment on a desktop. "Good morning, Detectives," he said. "Before I go any further, I' want you to hear this." He pushed a button on the player. A moment later a woman's voice sounded in the room. "911—police, fire, and medical. What is your emergency?"

Then a man's whispered voice: "I think there's a woman getting beat up. Really bad."

"What is the location of the emergency?"

"5710 Grand Ave, in Venice. Apartment 26B."

"Please stay on the line, sir. Someone is on the way. I need your phone number in case we get disconnected."

"Just get someone out here. It sounds like he's killing her!"

"Sir—"

The line went dead.

I glanced around the room. Everyone had frozen, realizing we were listening to the voice of our shooter.

A moment later another emergency call began. This time the dispatch operator was a man.

"911—police, fire, and medical. What is your emergency?"

A muffled male voice answered, speaking softly. "Someone's breaking into my house."

"Stay on the line, sir. Please confirm your phone number and address so I can send someone as soon as possible."

"I'm at 22893 Las Lomas in Pacific Palisades," the caller whispered. "Get somebody out here right away. I'm locking myself in the bathroom."

"Sir, please stay on the line. In case we're disconnected, I need to verify your phone—"

Again the line went dead.

Captain Schwartz hit the stop button on the player. "Both of those calls came in to Metropolitan Dispatch Center downtown. In each case after the caller hung up, our PSR dispatcher tried unsuccessfully to reestablish contact," he said. "Police Service Representative," he added, noticing several questioning looks.

"Same guy on both calls?" someone asked.

"We analyzed the recordings," said Schwartz. "Because of the whispering, comparative results were inconclusive. Not enough data points for a voiceprint."

"Let's move on," Snead suggested. "Maybe you could give us a quick rundown of how the 911 Emergency System works, for those who don't know."

"Sure," said Captain Schwartz. "All 911 service calls originating in Los Angeles, including those for police, fire, and paramedic, come in to one of two central Public Safety Answering Points—Valley Dispatch Center and Metropolitan Dispatch Center—for which the LAPD Communications Division is responsible. We handle police-related calls; all others are handed off to appropriate agencies."

"How many operators do you have answering calls?" I asked.

"We have over 500 PSR operators on staff, but of course the number present at any given time is less. Maybe a quarter to a third of that."

"Would it be possible to have every operator listen to this guy's voice on your recordings before starting their shifts? Maybe they could recognize him if he calls again."

"That's already being done," Schwartz answered. "We started yesterday, right after the mayor's news conference. Each board operator typically answers hundreds of calls per eight-hour shift, so it's hard to pick out a particular voice, especially a whispered voice, but we're trying. Our guys are listening to these recordings after every break, too. We also have operators on alert for any reports in which a male caller hangs up and we can't reestablish contact—most likely meaning he turned off his phone. In those cases dispatch operators are advising responding units to exercise extreme caution."

My opinion of Captain Schwartz shot up several notches. "How about voice identification software?" I asked. "Any way of putting that on incoming lines?"

Schwartz shook his head. "Not at the moment. Too many calls, and a need for that type of screening has never come up before. At present we do have the resources to analyze *selected* calls in real time, once they've been identified by an operator. We're currently working on setting up a more inclusive system."

"When will that be ready?" someone asked.

"We hope to have a voiceprint system up and running sometime next week," Schwartz answered. "The following week at the latest."

"So at the moment, besides having your people be on the lookout for hang-ups and listening for our guy's voice, is there anything else you can do that might help?" I asked.

Schwartz considered a moment. "I wish there were," he answered regretfully. "If you guys come up with anything, please let me know. Anyway, I do have a couple more things about the shooter," he continued. "He made his 911 calls on separate cell phones, after which he probably tossed them, if he was smart. We're watching for those particular numbers, so if he turns on either of those phones again, we'll know where he is. Another thing: using cell tower triangulation and GPS, we were able to confirm that both of his 911 calls were made from the murder site locations."

"So the guy places a 911 call from his target zone, then drives to a nearby overlook and waits for our men to show up so he can shoot them?" growled one of the Robbery-Homicide detectives. "Sick bastard."

"Anything else on the phones?" someone else asked.

"We ran a check on the numbers," Schwartz replied. "Both phones were purchased over six months ago at a Walmart in the Baldwin Hills Crenshaw Plaza. Prepaid minutes—no contract, no activation fee, no credit check, no monthly bills. The phones are virtually untraceable, unless he paid with a credit card, which is unlikely."

"He probably paid cash, but we still need to check," I said, thinking that our shooter's purchasing his phones six months in advance meant he'd been planning this for a long time.

"I've got that," said one of the South Bureau detectives. "Crenshaw's my division."

Snead scribbled something on a pad beside him, then turned to Captain Schwartz. "Anything else, Captain?"

Schwartz thought a moment. "I'm afraid that's all I have," he answered. "At least for now. Like I said, if you come up with anything else we can do, please let me know."

Snead again took the floor. "Thank you, Captain Schwartz. Now, if there are no other suggestions, we have the weekend duty rosters compiled, and Stella has copies for everyone. Pick one up at the end of the meeting, along with copies of Kane's and Madison's crime reports."

Snead waited as Captain Schwartz gathered his equipment and started for the exit. After he had departed, Snead continued. "We'll be dividing up the hotline tips next. There's plenty to do, but as I said before, I want everyone to keep current on their paperwork. Pressure is coming down from the top to close this case, and if one of you isn't carrying his weight, you *will* regret it. I'm certain you all saw that pack of reporters out front. The news stations are already all over this, and it's going to get worse. We need to find our guy. And we need to find him before this case turns into a media circus."

"Screw the media," someone muttered. "We need to find that dirtbag before he shoots any more of our men."

"That, too," said Snead. "Let's get to it."

Chapter Twelve

ON Tuesday morning, following a leisurely three-hour drive to the city, Dr. Luther Cole left his car in long-term parking at the Los Angeles International Airport and rented a car from Avis. From there he checked into a Doubletree Hotel on Centinela Boulevard, booking a room in the same accommodations he had used many times in the past. Years back he had chosen that particular hotel, a franchise member of Hilton Worldwide, for several reasons. One, it was conveniently located in Culver City close to the 405 Freeway, just a few miles from LAX. Second and more important, it was within easy walking distance of a self-storage lot where he had leased a 300-square-foot storage unit, paying cash for several years in advance. As with his rental car and hotel registration, he had leased the storage space using a bogus California driver's license that identified him as William Johnson—ID that a few hours of internet research had made surprisingly easy to acquire.

After checking into his room at the Doubletree, Dr. Cole rode the elevator down to the lounge, where a breakfast buffet was being served. He cooked himself a plate of waffles, which he had with fruit, yogurt, and coffee. As he ate, he watched the local news on one of the TV screens mounted around the room, noting with satisfaction that most of the morning coverage centered on Los Angeles's recent cop killings.

Following a second cup of coffee, he returned to his room and spent several hours reviewing photos and sketches of his next target zone, memorizing landmarks, distances, elevations, street maps, escape routes, and the location of any fallback positions his targets might take in the unlikely event things didn't go as planned. He believed in leaving nothing to chance. If he had learned one thing in the army, it was that preparation was the key to success, in life as well as death.

At noon he left the hotel and retrieved his rental vehicle, a Nissan Altima, from the parking lot outside. It was time to do a final reconnaissance of the kill zone, making certain nothing had changed since he'd last visited. It was doubtful that he would find anything of significance, but one never knew. Attention to detail meant the difference between success and failure.

Wearing a ball cap and sunglasses, he took the 405 Freeway north, exiting on Sunset. There were more direct routes to his destination, but he was in no hurry, and he liked cruising the palm-lined streets of Bel Air and Holmby Hills. When he reached West Hollywood, he turned left on Laurel Canyon Boulevard and drove into the Hollywood Hills. Several miles up the narrow canyon, he entered a residential subdivision known as Mount Olympus.

Following several minutes of climbing, he pulled to a stop near the top of the exclusive subdivision, parking in front of a large vacant lot. A seedy hedge separated the lot from an adjacent home on the right. A "For Sale" sign was crookedly displayed near a home on the left, which still appeared to be under construction.

The view from the dirt lot was breathtaking, encompassing the streets of North Hollywood as well as providing a commanding panorama of homes lower in the canyon—many of them within rifle range.

He shut off the Altima's engine, reached into the glove compartment, and withdrew a map. For the next several minutes he pretended to study it. Actually his attention was focused on the neighborhood, checking for anything that might have changed since his earlier reconnaissance—barking dogs, roadwork, landscaping—and could negatively affect his plans. And as he sat, his thoughts traveled back to an earlier time, revisiting the reason he was there.

Years before, his future had looked promising. After graduating from college and completing a stint of active duty in the army, he had applied to the prestigious USC School of Dentistry, surprising himself by being accepted. And four years later, on the day he completed his state board exams, his future hadn't simply looked promising; it had looked positively stellar. The most demanding part of his training was behind him, he was confident he had passed the difficult state board dental examination, and an associate position was waiting for him in his beautiful hometown of Three Rivers, California. He didn't even mind being ribbed by friends for not being a "real" doctor, merely a DDS. Best of all, he was in love.

He had met Janice during his sophomore year. She was working as a secretary in the prosthetics department, and by their second date he knew she was the one. She wasn't the most beautiful girl he had ever dated, but she was by far the brightest. Plus there was something about her that was unforgettable, at least to him. And to his amazement, in the end she came to love him, too.

They were married shortly after he completed the state board exams, and the following day they had driven to San Francisco for a week-long honeymoon. Looking back, he realized it had been one of the happiest times of his life.

And of course he passed the boards; he knew he would. During the entire four years of USC's dental program he had been at the top of his class, both academically and in the clinic. He had great hands and a talent for putting patients at ease, and although he could have easily established a practice in Westwood or Century City or Brentwood or anywhere he wanted, he chose to return to Three Rivers. It was there he had grown up— spending summers hunting and fishing the high country of the Sierras—and he could think of no better place to live. It was also there that years back his family dentist, Dr. Davis, had promised him an associate position in his busy practice, should he ever go to dental school. It had sounded like one of those childhood dreams that never came true, but this one had.

Janice adored living in the cozy, village atmosphere of Three Rivers. After all, what was there not to love? Billed as the gateway to Sequoia National Park, Three Rivers lay nestled in the foothills of the Sierra Nevada Mountains—close enough to Los Angeles and San Francisco for a weekend getaway, but remote enough that one could enjoy the serenity of nature right out the back door. And it was a back door that never needed locking.

Dr. Davis had retired from practice the following year. Now acting as sole practitioner, Dr. Cole hired an associate and a dental hygienist. He also updated the office equipment, some of which had been in service since Dr. Davis began practice. Along with modernizing the front office and the reception room, Dr. Cole added a number of operatory upgrades, including stereo headphones, nitrous oxide, and TV screens. Before long his patient list doubled, then tripled, with people coming from as far away as Bakersfield, Visalia, and Fresno.

Two years later Janice gave birth to a baby boy. They named him Andrew. Janice had never been happier, and although Dr. Cole wished he were able to spend more time at home and less at his office, he was happy, too. Truly happy. At least that's how he remembered it.

When Andrew was diagnosed with autism, things began to change.

At first, for both Dr. Cole and Janice, there had been periods of guilt and anger and utter disbelief. Had they caused this somehow—a fault in their genes, a vaccination, something they had done to hurt their child? It didn't seem fair. And it wasn't, and all the tears in the world wouldn't change things. But with the eventual acceptance of that sad truth came a fierce, unwavering determination to secure the best possible care for their beautiful, cherished son.

Although most autistic children exhibit a gradual onset of symptoms during the first few years of life, Andrew's childhood development had initially seemed normal. After his second birthday, however, he began to undergo a progressive loss of language. Over the following year significant regression in other areas occurred as well—avoiding eye contact, ritualistic and repetitive behaviors, inappropriate emotional outbursts, and an inability to make social contact with others.

Andrew's diagnosis of autism was confirmed at age three, and treatment began shortly after that. At the time his developmental disorder had simply been called childhood autism; now the condition was included under the umbrella of a more comprehensive category called autism spectrum disorders, or ASD, which encompassed several other neurodevelopmental diseases including Asperger syndrome—all similar, all disabling, all heartbreaking. Nevertheless, although the classification had changed, the basic treatment remained the same: applied behavior analysis, structured teaching, speech and language therapy, and social skills development, with the ideal treatment being tailored to each child's needs.

He and Janice focused on an autism approach that seemed well supported by empirical data: the earlier that treatment was initiated, the better the result. And they wanted the best for their son. Janice located an autism center in Fresno. Three times a week she drove Andrew there to a clinic, where he spent several hours with a therapist undergoing "early intensive behavioral intervention"—a therapy similar to B.F. Skinner's operant conditioning of pigeons and rats, but of course without Skinner's electric shocks. Over time Janice learned as much as she could about applied behavioral analysis and continued Andrew's therapy at home, as did Dr. Cole.

Later Janice joined a support group in Venice. The group met monthly and provided its members a source of new information, current ideas and research on the disease, and treatment options. Janice even enrolled Andrew in a thirty-two-week study at the UCLA Center for Autism Research and Treatment, which required that Janice and Andrew move to West Los Angeles during Andrew's course of treatment.

With therapy, Andrew's speech and cognitive abilities improved, eventually enabling him to attend special education classes in Visalia and Fresno. He even attained the ability and the desire to learn and do well. Nevertheless, by the age of seventeen it was clear that he would never be able to live independently or function on his own.

Having a child with a disability can put a profound strain on any marriage, but like many parents of autistic children, the Coles found that their protective love for Andrew strengthened their marriage, bringing their family closer together rather than driving them apart. Although the victories they experienced with Andrew were sometimes few and seemingly insignificant, at least to the uninformed, to them they were priceless. As Janice once put it, "It's as if everything you ever hoped for, everything you ever wanted for your child, unexpectedly came unraveled. Afterward, when the dust had settled, you found yourself trying to tie together the threads of his life. And when that happens, even a little bit, it's so wonderful you want to cry."

Janice often brought Andrew on her trips to the Venice support group, which continued over the years. On one such trip, a few months before Andrew's nineteenth birthday, he wandered away from the meeting, saying he was bored and wanted to get some air.

Although the Coles would never know for certain what happened that night, the police account was as follows: On April 7 at approximately 9:30 p.m., two LAPD patrol officers attempted to stop Andrew on the street, describing him as walking alone and "looking around and touching something near his waistband." When Andrew did not immediately respond to their orders, they drew their weapons. According to one of the officers, Officer Joseph Strom, at that point Andrew had withdrawn a knife from his waistband.

Fearing for his own safety, Officer Strom shot Andrew through the head and killed him.

The second officer present stated that he never saw Andrew reaching for a knife, although one was later recovered at the scene. Subsequent examination of the knife showed none of Andrew's DNA present, nor were his prints found on the weapon. Nevertheless, after a lengthy LAPD internal investigation, the acting police chief at the time ruled that although grave errors in judgment had occurred, Officer Strom had been justified in using deadly force, acting in what he thought was defense of his life.

Although the police chief had sole disciplinary authority in the case, in a surprise move several months later, the police commission rejected the police chief's ruling, formally stating that Officer Strom was wrong to fatally shoot Andrew. Not that it made any difference—especially to the Coles. A month later Officer Strom was dismissed from the LAPD for lying in another incident involving the use of unnecessary force.

After losing their son, both Janice and Dr. Cole suffered periods of depression. In time, with the help of a therapist, Janice began working through her grief. Outraged at the injustice of his son's death and filled with a poisonous hatred for the man who had killed him, Dr. Cole refused to share his feelings with anyone, even his wife. He stopped working, letting his associate run the dental practice in his absence. And it wasn't until months later, when he finally decided what to do, that things started to get better.

He had kept tabs on the man who murdered his son. He knew that Officer Strom had been fired from the LAPD; he knew that Strom had later secured a security job at a mall in Thousand Oaks; he knew where Strom lived. It was simply a matter of working out the details so he wouldn't be caught. And working out details was something at which Dr. Cole was very, very adept.

During his time in the military, Luther Cole had demonstrated an almost uncanny proficiency on the rifle range, an innate ability far surpassing that of anyone else in his unit, even his instructors—something he attributed to his years spent hunting the Kaweah River canyons during his youth. Building on skills learned in the army, Dr. Cole spent hundreds of additional hours on the range honing his marksmanship, working tirelessly until he was certain he was up to the job.

One year later, on a Thursday evening marking Andrew's twentieth birthday, Dr. Cole lay in wait at the end of a dark, dead-end street in Simi Valley, a residential development in the foothills northwest of Los Angeles. The shadowy outlines of houses under construction flanked him on either side. Farther down the pennant-lined road were a number of newly completed homes, several already occupied. One of them belonged to Joseph Strom.

The neighborhood was quiet. Dr. Cole peered out the open back hatch of the Ford Expedition he'd purchased from a private party in Long Beach, using cash and a fake ID that identified him as William Johnson. Instead of reregistering the Expedition, he had simply swapped plates with another Expedition in a shopping mall, for all intents and purposes making his newly acquired vehicle untraceable.

Time was getting short. After checking his watch, he ran through a mental checklist one last time. He had ranged the shot to Strom's driveway: 176 yards. His suppressed, subsonic .30 caliber rifle lay ready on the shooting bench. The weapon was zeroed at 100 yards, and he knew he could easily adjust for the longer distance. No wind. Streetlight illumination was more than enough to make the shot. Police scanner on, currently providing background static in one of his ear buds. He had memorized streets, landmarks, escape routes.

All that remained was for Officer Strom to show up.

Again Dr. Cole glanced at his watch: 11:25 p.m. Strom was a member of a Thursday-night bowling league in Thousand Oaks, but he should be finished by now.

Fifteen minutes later Strom's late-model Tahoe entered Dr. Cole's field of fire. He watched through the rifle scope as Strom turned into his driveway, stopping briefly as the garage door began to open. Dr. Cole acquired his target in the scope, sighting on Joseph Strom's head. He picked a spot that he estimated was an inch above Strom's left ear.

The garage door was almost open. Strom would move in a moment. After taking a shallow breath, Dr. Cole relaxed and slowly let it out, gently squeezing the trigger during the pause before his next breath.

The side window of Strom's Tahoe exploded, along with his head. After passing through Strom's skull, Dr. Cole's bullet smashed through the opposite side window—spraying glass, blood, and brain throughout the interior of the vehicle and out onto the driveway.

Dr. Cole reacquired his target and held on Strom's slumped body a moment longer.

Somewhere a dog barked.

Otherwise, nothing.

The return to his self-storage garage proved uneventful. After parking his Expedition in the oversized space, Dr. Cole closed the garage door and remained inside to clean his rifle. When he had finished, he placed the weapon back in its hard case and added it to several other rifles stored in the unit.

A short walk brought him back to the Doubletree. After paying cash and checking out, he took a cab to a second hotel near the airport, where he was registered under his own name.

The following morning he attended the final lecture of a three-day dental implant course, signing in at 8 a.m. as he had each day and receiving a continuing-education completion certificate by noon. Later he caught a return flight to Visalia, thirty minutes west of Three Rivers, where Janice picked him up at the airport. His plan was to drive back to L.A. in a few weeks, retrieve his weapons from the storage lot, and abandon the Expedition, leaving it to rust in the storage unit until someone eventually discovered it years later.

That plan had changed.

A week after his return, he was visited by Detective Sergeant Luigi Montone of the Three Rivers Police Department. Detective Montone had been contacted through the Tulare County Sheriff's Department by an LAPD homicide detective named Silva. Montone explained that Detective Silva was investigating incidents relating to the homicide death of ex-LAPD Officer Joseph Strom—incidents that might explain his murder. Incidents like Patrolman Strom shooting Dr. Cole's son.

Dr. Cole assured Detective Montone that he hadn't had anything to do with the murder, adding that although he wouldn't mourn Strom's death, he had been enrolled in a continuing-education course in Los Angeles at the time, and he had remained at his airport hotel for the entire weekend the course was being given. He hadn't even seen the necessity to rent a car— something later exhaustively verified by LAPD investigators. He had saved credit-card receipts for taxi rides to and from the airport, along with hotel registration forms, continuing-education daily sign-in slips, and a course-completion certificate to prove he'd attended all three days. Although something in Detective Montone's questioning sounded an alarm in Dr. Cole's mind, nothing ever came of his visit. Nothing, that is, until several weeks later when he found Janice poking around his things in the garage.

"Where are your rifles?" his wife had asked. And he hadn't been able to answer. He had never intentionally lied to Janice, and he didn't start then. Eventually, with some prodding, he related the entire story. And when he finished, when he had told her everything, he knew from the look on her face that he had made a terrible mistake. Everything had changed between them, irrevocably and for all time.

He had lost her.

Two weeks later Janice took her own life, swallowing an entire bottle of sleeping pills that she'd been given to help her through the nights following Andrew's death. She left a note, which Dr. Cole immediately destroyed upon reading.

For a time he considered taking his own life as well. After all, he now had nothing to live for. Nothing. Andrew and Janice were gone, leaving only a bitter, seething, boundless rage at the injustice of it all.

But slowly, driven by frustration and anger, he formed another plan.

A better plan.

A plan in which those responsible would pay.

It had taken him more than a year to complete his research, assemble all the necessary elements, and raise his shooting proficiency to the highest possible level. The months spent preparing for his Simi Valley encounter with Joseph Strom had made Dr. Cole an expert marksman. To successfully complete the long-range shots he planned required more. Much more. As he had in other aspects of his life, Dr. Cole did what was necessary to make his plan a reality. And he did it well.

That plan was now underway. Although it wasn't a plan that included his survival, it was one that before his death would afford him the satisfaction of seeing those who had wronged him suffer, suffer as he had.

And suffer they would.

With a final glance down the canyon, Dr. Cole restarted his rental car, dropped the shift into drive, and started toward a second shooting destination—an overlook on Mulholland that provided a perfect vantage for a long-range shoot into the hills of Sherman Oaks.

He considered the prospect of taking two pairs of LAPD officers on the same evening. One pair on Mount Olympus, another in Sherman Oaks.

Carefully weighing the pros and cons, he came to a decision.

This weekend, he promised himself.

Maybe Friday.

Saturday or Sunday at the latest.

Soon.

Chapter Thirteen

Later that morning Allison stood at the rear of one of the CBS taping studios, listening as Brent Preston finished recording a lead-story "package"—a report that after being intercut with illustrative B-roll video clips would be aired that night on *CBS Evening News*. Allison felt a trace of envy as she waited for Brent to finish, realizing his report would be introduced by the Network anchor to the entire nation with a lead-in something like, " . . . here with more from Los Angeles is CBS special correspondent Brent Preston."

As much as Allison disliked Brent, she had to admit he was good at his job. Handsome, young, and driven, he was one of several CBS rising stars being groomed for bigger things. Brent knew what he wanted—a Network anchor position—and he was well on his way to getting it. Although Allison admired Brent's drive, she didn't like the cutthroat way he was going about achieving his ambitions. She sighed, listening as Brent neared the end of his on-set piece.

" . . . are searching for a white or gray van, reportedly seen cruising the area on Sunday before the Pacific Palisades murders. To date, investigators have no new leads in the shooting deaths of four LAPD patrol officers last weekend. In the wake of what are now being called the L.A. Sniper shootings, Police Chief Fitzpatrick has placed all members of his department on high alert."

Brent paused before heading into his concluding "story tag," lifting his chin to make certain the studio lights weren't throwing unflattering shadows on his neck and chin. "For now," he finished almost breathlessly, "the city of Los Angeles waits to see whether the sniper killings will continue. This is Brent Preston, CBS News, Los Angeles."

"Great work, Brent," said Lauren Van Owen, who had joined Allison partway through the taping.

"Thanks, chief," said Brent. "I think the last bit about the van added some meat to the piece, don't you?"

"I do," Lauren agreed. "No one else has that yet. I hope it stays that way until we air."

"It will," said Brent. "I got an exclusive on it."

"The police aren't going to be too happy about your revealing that piece of information," Allison noted. "It won't make their job any easier."

Brent shrugged. "It's not our job to make things easier for the cops. We report the news. Period."

"Yes, but—"

"We can debate this later," Lauren broke in. "Brent, drop by my office before you start editing, okay? You too, Ali. There are a few ground rules we need to go over."

Minutes later Allison joined Brent in Lauren's office, taking a seat on a couch across from the bureau chief's desk. Brent remained standing, leaning against a wall by the door.

Lauren folded her hands and regarded Brent and Allison thoughtfully. "These sniper killings have all the earmarks of becoming the biggest story of the year. You both realize that?"

"Of course," Brent replied. "That's why I'm here."

"Ali?"

"Yes, ma'am," said Allison.

"You two have bad blood dating back to the Sharon French abduction," Lauren continued. "I need to know whether you can work together on this."

"I know why *I'm* here," Brent replied. "What I don't understand is why I should have to work with Allison. There must be someone else who can—"

"Does the name Detective Daniel Kane ring a bell, Brent?" Lauren interrupted.

Brent fell silent for a moment, doing the addition. "Oh," he mumbled.

"Hold on, Lauren," said Allison. "When I agreed to talk with my dad about the case, I didn't know I'd be feeding information to Brent. Besides, my dad hasn't agreed to anything."

"I'll repeat my question," said Lauren, her tone hardening. "Will you two be able to work together?"

Brent looked at Allison. "I suppose so," he conceded. "Especially if Allison can pry anything useful out of her Neanderthal father."

"That's not the way it's going to be," Allison replied angrily. "I won't do anything to compromise my dad's case. Not this time, anyway. And watch what you say about my father, Brent. If you think—"

"Quiet, Ali," Lauren ordered. "We don't have time for this. Media coverage is going through the roof, and I need to know where you stand. Can you put aside your differences, act like the professional you are, and work with Brent?"

Allison hesitated a moment more, then nodded. "Yes, ma'am."

"Good," said Lauren. "Brent will be the lead L.A. correspondent for Network. Ali, you can continue to do the webcast briefs, and if this story heats up like I think it will, I can get you some on-set appearances for the local news at five and eleven, as we discussed earlier. Agreed?"

"Agreed," said Allison, brightening.

"Good," Lauren said. "I'm putting you on this fulltime, beginning now. Start by researching similar cases—particularly the D.C. Beltway shootings and the Christopher Dorner case. Maybe we can get a jump on where the story is headed, assuming the killings continue. And you need to talk to your dad."

"All right," said Allison. "I'm supposed to have dinner with him on Friday, so I'll talk to him then. In the meantime, I have a few ideas. I've already started researching sniping cases in California and elsewhere, including the Dorner and D.C. Beltway shootings, as you suggested. There are a surprising number of private sniper schools around, too. I could start checking with them and see what else I can learn. Maybe I could look into the psychology of sniping, too—find out what makes this guy tick."

When Lauren remained silent, Brent spoke up. "I like the psychology aspect. We could do interviews with all kinds of experts—psychiatrists, ex-police officers, FBI behaviorists. Get their opinions, psychological profiles on the killer, stuff like that. People love that crap."

Allison nodded. "Sad but true. Another thing. Apparently the police have been unable to find anyone who has heard the sniper's shots. Maybe he's using some kind of silencer. I could check into that, too. What do you think, Lauren?"

"I think you really are your father's daughter," Lauren replied with a smile. "You think like a cop. So go to it. As I said, I have a feeling this story is just getting started."

Chapter Fourteen

Kane, why don't you and Deluca lead off, tie up a few loose ends," suggested Lieutenant Snead, beginning the Thursday morning briefing. "Did you turn up anything in the ranks?"

Deluca and I had spent a considerable portion of the past two days interviewing police academy washouts. We had also looked into disciplinary actions in the Westside divisions, talking with officers recently dismissed for cause, and checking Internal Affairs investigations that might be related. It had been a thankless job, to say the least.

I glanced at Deluca. "You want to take it?"

Deluca shrugged. "Not much to tell," he said, addressing the room without standing. "We talked with every disgruntled recruit, cop, and washout we could find who might be holding a grudge. We came up with plenty of dirt, but nothing related to the shootings. We put out the word and something might develop, but at this point we've gone down that road about as far as we can. Personally, I don't think it's one of our own."

"At least there's *some* good news there," said Snead. "Another cop like Dorner would give the department a permanent black eye.

"No argument on that," someone in the back muttered.

"We finished our Palisades canvass, too," I added, picking up where Deluca had left off. "Unfortunately, we didn't find anyone with a surveillance camera that caught a shot of the shooter."

Madison spoke up. "Same in Venice," he said, adding, "It's still a good approach if it happens again."

"The last thing we need is for this to happen again," said Snead, glancing around the room. "Who's next? Any of you running down hotline tips come up with anything since yesterday?"

There was an uncomfortable silence. Hundreds of man-hours had already been spent chasing hotline tips. I knew from talking with detectives from other divisions that all those tips had proved worthless. Most of the calls coming in usually went something like "I think my neighbor's the killer. He leaves his truck in my parking space, too. You should arrest him." Or "Is there a reward? My ex-boyfriend might be the guy. He's a real jerk and he loves guns." Everything within reason had to be checked, but if anything of substance actually came in, it would be hard to separate from all the static.

"I got a call from a psychic yesterday," grumbled a detective in the rear. "She said she could help us catch the killer by developing our clairvoyant powers. I told her I could already see the future. Her call was going to be ignored."

A spate of chuckles traveled the room. "Okay, settle down," Snead ordered, clearly irritated by the lack of progress. "Anybody else?"

When no one answered, Assistant Director Shepherd spoke up. "I have a few things," he said. Shepherd, who had been absent for the past several briefings, was accompanied that morning by a compact, hard-looking man with a shock of short-cropped hair and a lined, weathered face. Curious about the stranger, I glanced at Deluca. He lifted his shoulders, indicating he had no idea who the new man was, either.

"First of all," Shepherd continued, "a search of California Department of Justice computers, VICAP, and NCIC databases came up cold. There are currently no open cop-killing cases in California, or in any other western states, either. We do have a short list of open cases involving murdered police officers back East, and we're looking into those. None looks promising, as all were committed with a handgun. Speaking of which, I did some research on handgun versus rifle homicides. The statistics are surprising. Of the approximately 13,000 homicides in the United States last year, over *half* were committed with a handgun. The number committed with a rifle was only around 300."

"How about cops killed with a rifle?" Madison asked hopefully.

"With the exception of the Chris Dorner shootings, none. At least no open cases, like I said."

"Damn," said Madison. "I was hoping there might be a sniper connection there somewhere."

"We were, too," Shepherd sighed. "Anyway, we *have* made some progress compiling a database of handloading equipment distributors. We're also compiling a list of California gunsmiths. Like I said, either one or possibly both of those lists could prove useful when we have a suspect. By the end of the day I should also have an ATF summary of anyone who's applied for a sonic-suppressor tax stamp over the past ten years. Again, although silencers are illegal in California, that might also prove helpful if we develop other leads."

"Any progress on a psychological profile?" asked Snead.

"I sent the submission materials to Quantico yesterday," Shepherd responded. "I asked our Behavioral Analysis Unit to put a rush on it. I was assured that we'll have something by the weekend, or at the latest sometime next week."

I had submitted materials for several FBI psychological profiles in the past, and I knew it to be a tedious, time-consuming process requiring the painstaking assembly of crime-scene reports, victim profiles, photographs, witness statements, autopsy findings, and lab results. Although I was grateful someone else was doing it this time, I didn't have much faith in the final result.

"Good," said Snead, looking pleased. "Okay, we're going to cut short the meeting this morning. I have to be downstairs early for the daily press conference, but before we get to work, Assistant Director Shepherd has asked one of the FBI's Hostage Rescue Team operators to brief us on some sniper profiles and perspectives."

"Correct," said Shepherd, glancing at the stranger beside him. "I'd like to introduce Special Agent Gus Wyatt. Agent Wyatt is a sniper/observer on our Hostage Rescue Team. For those who don't know, HRT is the FBI's counterterrorism unit, which in turn is part of the Tactical Support Branch of CIRG, our Critical Incident Response Group. The team is composed of over ninety full-time operators who offer a tactical option in high-risk scenarios."

Despite Shepherd's alphabet-soup introduction, I felt a chill course through the room as task-force detectives realized what Shepherd meant by "tactical option."

"Before joining the FBI," Shepherd continued, "Wyatt's SEAL background included multiple deployments throughout Iraq and Afghanistan. He flew in from Quantico last night, and he's here to give his impressions on our shooter. Afterward he will try to answer any questions you may have." Again glancing at the quiet man who had accompanied him, he said, "Special Agent Wyatt?"

Agent Wyatt stepped to the front of the room. "Good morning, gentlemen," he said. "As Assistant Director Shepherd noted, I'm Gus Wyatt, and I'm here to assist you in any way I can. I have studied your crime-scene reports and autopsy materials, and I've come up with a few initial thoughts."

I looked around the room, noting that many detectives who normally fidgeted during briefings were sitting stock still, their eyes focused on the soft-spoken FBI agent. I realized that our group's unspoken respect for Agent Wyatt stemmed not only from the knowledge of what it had taken for him to successfully complete his grueling SEAL training—something few men are able to do—but also from the number of operations he must have conducted afterward in two theaters of war. Like most police officers, few detectives in the room had ever needed to draw their service weapon in a law-enforcement situation. Even fewer had needed to fire. And only a very few, of which I was one, had been forced to take a life. For the quiet, unassuming man standing before us, killing as a "tactical option" was part of his job description.

"I think you're on the right track on several lines of your investigation," Agent Wyatt continued. "To begin, whoever suggested that the first thing your sniper is doing is picking his firing positions, or shooting sites, was right."

"Why is that?" asked Snead.

"Several reasons," Wyatt answered, "the most important of which is that given the preparation and care your man has demonstrated so far, I'm certain he knows what he's doing. The selection of a firing position that offers concealment, good fields of observation, and access to emergency escape routes is an essential first step in any sniper operation."

"So our shooter is finding these firing positions of his ahead of time," said Madison. "The target zones are secondary."

"Right," said Wyatt. "Along with preselection of his firing sites, if he were military-trained he might also keep a sniper log that would include a field sketch of the area showing distances, landmarks, possible target cover and fallback positions, and so on. If he decided to go psycho-tactical on you, he might also ID entry and exit routes, lighting, shadows, elevations, wind directions, temps, humidity, and any other factors that could affect his shots."

I wasn't certain what Wyatt meant by "psycho-tactical," but I got the picture, and it wasn't pretty.

"Jesus," someone muttered. "You think our guy is a military sniper?"

Wyatt thought for a moment. "I hope not," he answered. "Military snipers are screened and vetted in their select communities to prevent this sort of thing. SWAT applicants are screened for the same reason. Nevertheless, someone with determination, a lot of natural talent, and plenty of time on the range could attain the skill set necessary to make the shots your man has taken so far. Even if your shooter hasn't had military or police training, it would be prudent to assume he knows what he's doing."

"You said there were several reasons for thinking our guy picks his firing positions first," I said. "What else?"

"Distance," Wyatt answered. "Snipers don't like to work in close. To operate stealthily, a shooter needs to position himself at some distance from his target. In an urban environment, that's usually tricky—buildings, trees, and so on make longer shots difficult unless you find the right spot from which to fire. And that generally means an elevated position."

"Our shooter made 150-yard shots in Venice and 230-yard shots in the Palisades," I noted. "In Venice he shot across a wide traffic corridor, but in the Palisades, where the distance was longer, he fired from just below a ridgeline. If this continues, you're saying we should especially be on the lookout in the hills and canyons—places where our sniper can get enough distance to shoot down on our officers?"

"If this continues, absolutely," said Wyatt. "Especially if he graduates to taking longer shots. Which, by the way, I would expect."

"Because now that we're looking for him, he'll need to shoot from farther out," Deluca reasoned.

"Exactly."

"So the bottom line here is that our guy is driving around finding these firing positions of his," said Dondero.

"That would be my guess," said Wyatt.

"So let's assume that he revisits these sites prior to each shooting, say a few days or so before, making certain nothing has changed," Dondero continued. "Maybe somebody sees him. Like Kane said, we could use that."

Several detectives nodded.

"We should also put out word to the divisions to have their patrols be especially careful in the canyons," Madison suggested.

"I'll do that," said Snead, making an entry in his notebook.

"I read somewhere that the average shot taken by a police sniper is fifty-one yards," I noted. "Is that correct?"

Wyatt nodded. "Sounds about right."

"Our guy is making much longer shots. Are the ones he's taken so far easy or hard? I mean for a trained sniper."

"Both," Wyatt replied. "Which brings me to a second area where I think your task force is on the right track. Subsonic ammunition. I need to give you a little background to explain why I think that, but stop me if you think I'm getting too far afield."

"Go ahead, Agent Wyatt," said Snead, who for once seemed to be paying attention to someone other than himself. "Please continue."

Wyatt paused to collect his thoughts. "Okay, first off," he began, withdrawing a small notebook from his jacket pocket, "I checked some figures this morning before coming in, and I think they will illustrate what I'm trying to say. It's generally accepted in the shooting world that smaller-diameter bullets are better than larger-diameter bullets, and that faster loads are better than slower loads. Put another way, most shooters think that a 140-grain bullet fired at 1,900 feet per second is more accurate and effective than a 220-grain bullet fired at a much slower velocity, say a speed of 1,050 feet per second—just under the speed of sound at sea level. And in most cases, that's true.

"To see why it isn't *always* true, especially at ranges out to several hundred yards, let's check some numbers," Wyatt suggested, referring to his notebook. "When our 140-grain bullet strikes a target at 200 yards, it's now traveling at only around 1,350 feet per second—having lost approximately 30 percent of its original velocity. In a five-mile-per-hour full-value wind—one that's blowing at ninety degrees to the shot—that bullet will have drifted nearly six inches. It will strike with an impulse of around .8 pound-seconds, which is a measure of its ability to knock over a target ram.

"Now let's consider what happens to the heavier 220-grain bullet with an initial subsonic velocity," Wyatt continued. "At 200 yards it will still be traveling at around 980 feet per second, having lost only *6 percent* of its original velocity. In the same wind it will drift only four inches, two inches less than the lighter bullet, and it will strike the target with an impulse force of approximately .9 pound-seconds, delivering over *15 percent* more knockdown power than the lighter, faster projectile."

"Why is that?" asked Madison.

"It's a matter of drag and ballistic coefficient," Wyatt answered. "A supersonic bullet is pushing a wall of compressed air, creating drag that a subsonic bullet doesn't have. Added to that, a longer, heavier bullet has a better ballistic coefficient than a shorter, lighter bullet, allowing it to slice through the air more efficiently."

I glanced around the room, noting that a number of the more mathematically challenged detectives were shifting in their seats, their eyes beginning to glaze. "No offense, Agent Wyatt, but can you cut to the chase?" I interjected. "How does this apply to us?"

"Well, for starters, reading your crime reports suggests to me that your shooter might be using subsonic ammo," Wyatt answered. "Two reasons: first, to date you haven't found anyone at either crime scene who heard the shots, right?"

"That's correct," said Snead. "And we canvassed the areas thoroughly."

"At the distances involved—150 yards in Venice and 230 yards in Pacific Palisades—for no one to have heard those shots would be highly unlikely if your shooter were using high-velocity ammunition," Wyatt continued. "With cartridges normally fired in a high-powered rifle, the bullet breaks the sound barrier as it exits the barrel, creating a distinctive sonic crack that is impossible to hide, even with a sonic suppressor."

"And a subsonic bullet is different," said Deluca.

"Very different," said Wyatt. "A bullet traveling below the speed of sound makes little noise traveling through the air, and the remaining sound of the muzzle blast can be effectively masked with a sonic suppressor. By the way, a suppressor can't completely silence a pistol or rifle—at least not as much as Hollywood would have you believe," he added with a slight smile. "Nevertheless, with subsonic ammo and a good suppressor, you could get off several shots in an urban environment and not attract attention."

"The slugs recovered at the scenes were 240-grain bullets," Dondero noted. "That fits, too."

"Right again," Wyatt agreed. "That's my second reason for thinking subsonic. A heavy bullet is necessary for an efficient subsonic shot."

Wyatt was covering some material that we had already broached in an earlier meeting, but it helped to have confirmation that we were on the right track. "Okay, let's assume our guy is shooting subsonic. Where does he get his ammo?" I asked, hoping to narrow our search parameters.

"Subsonic ammo is available commercially, but most shooters load their own," Wyatt answered. "For that reason, I think the handloading aspect you're working is a good avenue to investigate as well."

"You say you can buy this kind of ammo off the shelf?" said Deluca.

"Yes, you can," Wyatt replied. "There's a commercial market for lighter rounds, but nothing in 240 grains—which means your guy is definitely loading his own."

"What's involved in that?" I asked, hoping for something, *anything*, we could use.

Wyatt rubbed his chin. "Okay, without getting too technical, most shooters load .300 Whispers by expanding the neck of a .221 Remington Fireball case up to .308. Put another way, a Whisper cartridge is basically a 5.56 case with a 7.62 round stuffed into it. There's a bit more involved, like getting the muzzle velocity close to the speed of sound without exceeding it, but that's essentially it."

"So this type of cartridge isn't uncommon," I said, disappointed. We were getting pretty far off course, but I was still hoping there might be something unique to explore.

Wyatt shook his head. "No, it's not uncommon. Exactly the opposite. There are thousands of gun enthusiasts loading Whispers. In fact, there's a whole subculture of Whisper shooters—clubs, forums, blogs—you name it."

"We're currently compiling a database of handloading equipment retailers," Assistant Director Shepherd interjected. "If nothing else, maybe we can narrow our focus by concentrating on the purchase of dies, cases, and other materials necessary to handload subsonic cartridges. Can you get us that info, Agent Wyatt?"

"Yes, sir," said Wyatt. "I'll make up a materials list for you after the meeting."

"What about the type of weapon our guy is using?" I asked. "Anything we might be able to follow up on there?"

"Maybe," Wyatt answered. "He could be shooting one of a number of different weapons—from a bolt-action rifle with a replacement barrel chambered in .30 caliber Whisper, to a semiauto AR-15. There are other ways to go, but you get the idea. In any case, his muzzle would probably be threaded to accept a sonic suppressor. In the case of converting a bolt gun to the proper chambering for a subsonic round, Whisper replacement barrels are commercially available, or you could have a gunsmith chamber and thread a suitable barrel blank. Unless your shooter is a competent gunsmith in his own right, however, he would probably need help doing a conversion. There's a lot more to mounting a new barrel on a bolt gun than just strapping it on. You might think about checking gunsmiths."

"We're doing that already," said Shepherd.

I glanced at Lieutenant Snead. "We could look into Whisper and Blackout barrel purchases," I suggested.

Snead wrote something in his notebook. "For once I agree with you, Kane," he said curtly, glancing at his watch. "You and Deluca run with that."

"Roger. We're on it," I said. Then, again addressing Agent Wyatt, "I'm puzzled by something you said earlier. You said the shots our guy has made so far were both easy and hard. You want to explain that?"

Wyatt nodded. "Sure. A 200-yard shot with high-velocity ammo is relatively easy," he answered. "Add a good scope and it's like shooting at the arcade. With a little practice, my mom could make a shot at that distance. But unless you've done your homework, the same shot with a .300 Whisper is another story."

"Subsonic is different? Why?"

"When we were discussing the advantages of a heavy, subsonic bullet, I left out the downside," Wyatt explained. "Because a subsonic bullet takes longer to arrive on target, it drops more than a high-velocity projectile. Considerably more. At 200 yards, a .300 Whisper drops about a yard, while a high-velocity round drops only a few inches. Farther out, the difference in ballistic drop for a Whisper becomes even more significant. This means that to be able to make long-range subsonic shots, you need to put in a lot of time on the range setting up and recording the performance 'dope' on your rifle."

"So again, our guy knows what he's doing."

"I'm afraid so. There's another thing I didn't mention, something that bears on subsonic ammo. A subsonic 240-grain bullet has about the same knockdown power as a .45 caliber ACP round, which is too slow and too soft to defeat class-two body armor."

"Like the ballistic vests our patrolmen wear," said Dondero. "Hence the headshots."

Wyatt nodded. "Exactly."

There was an extended silence. Finally someone asked, "You military guys work with a spotter, right? Do you think our shooter has someone helping him?"

"I wouldn't rule it out," Wyatt answered. "There were two men involved in the D.C. Beltway shootings. For the shots your sniper has taken so far, however, a spotter wouldn't be necessary."

Snead again glanced at his watch. "Well, our time is about up," he said. "Thank you, Agent Wyatt. If there are no other questions, we need to—"

"I have one last question," I said.

"What is it, Kane?" Snead asked impatiently.

"Agent Wyatt, let me ask you a hypothetical question," I said. "You're a trained sniper. Just for the sake of argument, and I hope you don't take offense, but let's say for some reason you decided to kill as many cops as possible and not get caught. How would you do it?"

"Damn it, Kane!" Snead barked. "What the hell—"

"No, it's okay, Lieutenant," said Wyatt, raising a hand. "I see where Detective Kane is going with this. His question *is* a little out of my comfort zone, but let me try to answer." He thought for a moment and then continued. "First, if I were your shooter, I would carefully pick a number of final firing positions—identifying sites that provided concealment, good fields of observation, and multiple escape routes. As a military sniper, I would also keep a log that would include all my dope and target data.

"Second, working in a suburban or urban environment, I would attempt to blend into the background by shooting from something like a nondescript SUV or van. I would probably use a sonic suppressor to reduce muzzle blast, flash, and report. I would equip my mobile shooting platform with a couple of sandbags to use as a shooting rest, and I'd have some way of concealing my weapons and equipment once I was done.

"Last, at a time of my choosing, I would ID targets in each of my kill zones, take my shots, and be gone. I might start working in close, taking headshots at the beginning, then moving farther out as my targets became aware they were being hunted. And I would make absolutely certain that none of my weapons, ammunition, or equipment could ever be traced back to me. Ever."

"How would you do that?" I asked.

Wyatt shrugged. "There are plenty of ways. Gun shows and private estate sales for weapons, buying supplies online and handloading match-grade ammo, maybe developing the skills to do gunsmith work. Like that. Anyway, as police ramped up their patrol defenses, I would begin working farther out, like I said—maybe out to distances of 1,000 to 1,500 yards—at which point I'd start using a round that can defeat body armor," Wyatt continued. "No more headshots. If it became necessary to shoot even farther out than that, say out to a mile or more, I would switch to an even more powerful and accurate cartridge like a .300 Win Mag, or a .338 Lapua, or maybe even a .50 caliber if I had the money for that kind of weapon."

"If you had the money? How much are we talking?"

"The Barrett sniper rifle I would want runs around eleven thousand new, not counting scope or muzzle attachments."

"Anything else you can add that might help?" I asked.

"A couple things," Wyatt answered after a moment's thought. "I would try to maintain good intelligence on my targets, listening on police frequencies and monitoring developments in the media. Last and possibly most important, I would never succumb to the temptation to talk to the media or to contact authorities, either. And when I was done, I would disappear like a ghost . . . until I felt like doing it again."

Once more an uneasy silence had descended on the room.

"Damn," someone finally grumbled. "You're painting a pretty dismal picture here, Agent Wyatt. Can you help us out a little? For instance, if you were the shooter, what would it take to catch you?"

Wyatt shook his head. "I'm sorry to have to tell you this, Detective. But in response to your question, what it would take to catch me? The answer is simple. You wouldn't."

Chapter Fifteen

Deluca and I spent most of Thursday and all of Friday running down Whisper and Blackout rifle-barrel purchases. It turned out that because sonic suppressors are illegal in California, and because a suppressor is an integral element in making a silenced subsonic shot, most Whisper and Blackout barrel sales were also out of state. We had to draw the line somewhere, so we decided to initially limit our barrel search to the nearby western states that allowed suppressors—Oregon, Washington, Idaho, Montana, Arizona, and Utah—and work our way out from there. We also spent hours contacting gunsmiths in the Southern California area who might have modified a rifle to accept .300 Whisper or Blackout cartridges. We had better success with that, but not much.

To make matters worse, we ran into disclosure issues with both retailers and gunsmiths reluctant to divulge customer names. After explaining the situation, we were sometimes able to skirt the privacy issue, but often we weren't. We didn't have time for search warrants, even if we could get them, and by the end of my shift on Friday I was beginning to think we were heading down another dead-end street.

Upon returning to the beach that evening, I found Catheryn in the kitchen stirring something on the stove. Callie, who was lying in the corner keeping an eye on the food, ambled over to greet me. "How are you doing, girl?" I said softly, bending to stroke her head.

"Just fine, Dan," said Catheryn with a smile, setting down her spoon and turning to place her arms around my neck. "Thanks for asking." Her auburn hair was fastened in a loose ponytail, and she had on a long-sleeved cotton T-shirt, sandals, and a pair of close-fitting jeans. As usual, even without makeup, she looked great.

"Aw, don't be jealous," I said, giving her a kiss. "You know you're the most important female in my life."

"Except for possibly your dog," Catheryn laughed, kissing me back.

"What's for dinner?" I asked, deciding to sidestep that particular issue. I peeked over her shoulder at the stove. "Smells great."

"Beef stroganoff. We're having it with French bread and a green salad. Dinner's almost ready. I thought we could eat outside on the deck, if you want to set the table."

"Consider it done. I'll get one of the kids to help. What are their names again?"

"Travis, Allison, and Nate," Catheryn laughed.

"Oh, yeah. I remember now. Any of 'em home?"

Catheryn nodded. "Mike is shooting on location, so Ali decided to spend the weekend here for a change. She's out on the beach. Nate's in his room. He's, uh, having another bad day. Maybe you could talk to him."

"No problem. Some quality dad-time should brighten his world. Hey, Nate," I called. "Get your butt out here and gimme a hand setting the table."

"That should cheer him up," Catheryn noted dryly. Returning to the stove, she lifted a wineglass from the counter, took a sip, and gave the stroganoff a stir. "Oh, before I forget, I heard from the Philharmonic today," she added. "Arthur's retirement party is set for next Sunday. Can you make sure you're free?"

"I'll try. Right now I'm working Saturdays with Sundays off, so I should be able to make it."

"Good. How's the case going?"

I glanced in the direction of Nate's room. "Let's talk later." Then, again calling down the hallway, "Hey, Nate! What's keeping you?"

"Be there in a sec, Dad," Nate called back. "I'm in the bathroom."

"He's probably taking one of his ninety-minute teenage showers," observed Allison, topping the stairs on her way up from the beach. "Hi, Dad," she added, rounding a corner into the kitchen. "Bust any criminals today?"

"Nope. Fabricate any news stories today?"

"Nope," Allison replied, grinning. "I did talk with Arnie, though. Your ex-partner called earlier and I invited him to breakfast on Sunday. You still cooking?"

I nodded. "Right after church."

My cooking an occasional Sunday-morning family breakfast had become a tradition in the Kane household, and although it had been a while since I had last cooked, I was looking forward to it. I was also looking forward to seeing Arnie. That had been a while as well.

"I told him around ten," said Allison.

"Food should be ready by then," I replied.

"Hi, Dad," said Nate, finally arriving in the kitchen.

"What, you're out of the shower already?" said Allison. "Run out of hot water?"

Nate scowled. Although a playful give-and-take with his older sister had always been part of their relationship, lately he seemed to be taking offense at everything.

"Nate, go downstairs with your dad and help set the table," Catheryn intervened. "Ali, stay up here and keep me company. I opened a bottle of red. Would you like some?"

Allison shook her head. "Maybe later."

Catheryn smiled. "I swear, when you were underage, you couldn't wait to drink. Now that you're twenty-two and legal, you never seem interested."

"C'mon, Nate," I broke in. "Grab some silverware and fill the water pitcher. I'll get the tablecloth, plates, and glasses. Let's go set the table."

Once we were outside on the deck, I turned to Nate. "Your mom said you were having a tough day. Anything you want to talk about?"

Nate set the silverware and water pitcher on the picnic table. "No," he said, not meeting my gaze.

"Is it about school? You haven't been fighting again, have you?"

Nate shook his head, not looking up.

"Then what? Talk to me, kid."

"I'm, uh, flunking English."

I felt a surge of relief but tried not to show it. Of course Nate's schoolwork was important, but there were other things going on with my youngest, things I didn't understand, and at least this seemed to be something we could fix. "So we'll talk about it with your school counselor next week. When is that, exactly?"

"Wednesday, Dad. Four p.m."

"Fine. We'll get things straightened out then. In the meantime, start hitting the books. You're a smart kid, Nate. You've got your mom's brains, so there's no reason you shouldn't be getting straight A's. Is something else wrong?"

"Isn't that enough?" Nate replied, seeming depressed. "I get arrested, kicked off the baseball team, and now I'm screwing up in school. At this rate I'll never get into college."

"We'll get everything straightened out," I repeated firmly. "I'm not exactly sure how, but we will." I thought for a moment, then called upstairs. "Hey, Ali. Come down here for a sec. I need to talk to you."

"Be right there," Allison called back. She stepped out to the deck a minute later, Callie at her heels. "What's up?"

"I just heard your brother here is flunking English," I said. "God knows why, because he's a bright kid, but—"

"I'll help him," Allison interrupted.

"Really?" said Nate.

"Absolutely," said Allison. "We'll start after dinner. I'll be here all weekend. Let's see what we can get done, okay?"

"Uh, okay. Thanks, Ali," Nate said quietly.

"No problem," Allison replied. Then, glancing at me, "Dad, can I have a word with you? Um, in private? It's something about work."

I was both surprised and pleased by Allison's unexpected offer to help her brother without being ordered, which was what I had originally intended. Moments like that made me feel that maybe Catheryn and I were actually doing something right. There were certainly plenty of moments when I felt the opposite. "Okay, Ali," I said. "Let's head out to the beach. Nate, start setting the table. I'll be back in a minute and give you a hand."

Allison followed me down to the beach. The sun was just setting over Point Dume to the west, and an onshore breeze had picked up, carrying the musky scents of the ocean. I noted that the tide was out, exposing a littering of seaweed to the water's edge. Storms that routinely chewed up Las Flores Beach during the winter months had already begun, but there was still plenty of sand remaining, at least for the moment.

"Thanks for offering to help," I said, glancing at Allison as I stepped over the sea wall and dropped to the beach below. "I swear, I don't know what's going on with Nate. I want to help, but I don't know what to do. It's driving me nuts."

"They say mental illness runs in families," Allison replied, jumping down to the sand beside me. "You inherit it from your kids."

"There's some truth there," I agreed with a smile. I sat on the edge of the seawall, letting my legs dangle. "So what do you want to talk about?"

"It's about your sniper case."

"You know I can't discuss that."

"I know. I just want to give you a heads-up on what's happening on *my* end. I had a meeting today with Lauren. CBS is definitely gearing up for this to be the biggest story of the year. I just thought you should know."

"What do you mean, gearing up?"

"Like I told you, Network sent your pal Brent Preston out here to cover the investigation, and I think he's going to be trouble. He just posted a story on *CBS Evening News* about your task force looking for a white or gray van in connection with the shootings."

"Yeah, I heard that," I grumbled. "And he's your pal, not mine."

"Believe me, he's not mine, either," Allison replied. "Anyway, here's the thing. Brent has excellent sources, and he's not above using *anything* he learns—even if it compromises your case."

"No surprise there, either. How do you fit into all this?"

"At the moment Lauren has me preparing for a media blitz by doing background research—reviewing similar stories like the D.C. Beltway shootings and the Chris Dorner case. I'm also checking sniper schools, interviewing forensic psychologists, and so on. She's still letting me do my morning webcasts, with maybe some on-air face time on the local news at five if I come up with anything good. Speaking of which, Brent and Lauren are still pushing me to get information from you."

"And what are you telling them?"

"I'm telling them that isn't going to happen, at least not unless you agree."

I was disturbed by Allison's mention of a media blitz. I knew something like that was always a possibility, especially on a high-profile case like the sniper shootings; I just hadn't expected it to be coming so soon. I also knew from experience that the intense media scrutiny associated with a national news story could generate an insatiable public hunger for information, adding a whole new dimension to any investigation—one that no investigator wanted to face. As far as my cooperating with Allison, I wasn't sure how it could help me, but I once again decided not to slam the door.

"Anyway, things are heating up on our end," Allison continued when I didn't respond. "Brent and Lauren aren't going to hold anything back, even if it makes your job harder. I just thought you should know."

"Thanks, Ali," I said with a sigh. "I appreciate the heads-up. Now let's go eat."

After dinner Catheryn and I decided to take a walk on the beach, leaving the kids to do the cleanup. After admonishing Allison and Nate not to kill each other in our absence, Catheryn joined me on the sand. With Callie leading the way, we headed along the water's edge toward the lights of Santa Monica, not talking, just enjoying each other's company. I hadn't walked on the beach for days, and it felt good to stretch my legs.

"Travis called today," Catheryn finally said, breaking the silence when we had reached the east end of Las Flores cove and turned back toward our house.

"What's new with him?" I asked absently.

"He's excited about a new composition he's writing. And lately he's had the chance to work some more with the Juilliard Conductors' Lab Orchestra."

"Uh-huh. That's great, Kate," I replied.

"You seem preoccupied. Is it about Nate?"

"Maybe a little," I answered. "I talked with him before dinner. On top of everything else, he's flunking English."

Catheryn sighed. "I know."

"I also think he's worried about our meeting with the school counselor next week."

"I think so, too. You'll be able to be there?"

"I'll find a way."

After a few more minutes of silence, Catheryn asked, "You want to talk about the case?"

"Not really," I answered. "Maybe. I don't know."

"Is that what's wrong, Dan? I haven't seen you this preoccupied in a long time. Not since . . ."

Although she didn't finish, I knew she was referring to a series of killings I had investigated several years back. The case had taken a heavy toll on our lives. "Yeah, I know what you mean," I said. "This investigation has the same feel to it. Cops are getting killed, so it's personal, and I'm not sure I want to be involved."

"But you are."

"Yeah, I am. I can't stop thinking about the families of those murdered officers. It's bringing back all the feelings I had when we lost Tommy. I keep thinking that if I can stop the guy who's doing this, it might give everyone some closure."

"And maybe give you some, too?"

"I don't know, Kate. I just know that the last time I was involved in a high-profile case like this . . ." I hesitated, remembering the terrible night that had nearly cost us everything.

"I never want to put you and the kids in jeopardy like that again. That can never, ever happen—"

"Don't, Dan," Catheryn interrupted. "You're just making things harder on yourself. You're a police officer. I accepted that a long time ago, and so did our children."

"But—"

"No, let me finish," Catheryn said firmly. "Being a detective is who you are. It's who you are and what you do, and you do it better than anyone I know. So do it. Find the person who's murdering your officers, Dan. Find him before he shoots anyone else."

Chapter Sixteen

Later that evening Dr. Cole pulled to a stop on Oceanus Drive, high in the North Hollywood subdivision of Mount Olympus. After rolling down the car windows to allow for the concussive blast of the rifle, he turned off his headlights and backed the Expedition onto the vacant lot he had visited earlier in the week.

After shutting off the engine, he sat for several seconds without moving.

Other than the quiet sounds of the sleeping neighborhood, he heard nothing.

He glanced at the house to his left. Apparently the real estate agent had made an appearance since he'd last visited, as the "For Sale" sign had been straightened. Although the residence to his right was hidden behind its bordering hedge, he had noticed the lights were off when he'd passed.

Everything seemed perfect.

He crawled into the rear of the Expedition, tipped up his shooting bench, opened the back glass hatch, and withdrew his rifle from under a blanket. It took several minutes to complete his shooting setup, during which time he monitored police communications on his scanner. Earlier he had heard the dispatch operator contact a North Hollywood patrol unit almost immediately after he'd placed his 911 call. The unit was responding from the intersection of Sunset and Highland Boulevard, so he still had a few minutes before his targets arrived. Nevertheless, he wanted to be ready.

Aware that authorities had undoubtedly initiated protective measures based on his prior shoots, he decided that the time had come to vary his routine. In Venice and Pacific Palisades he had turned off the prepaid cell phones after placing his 911 calls. He knew this was a pattern the police would notice. This time, after making his emergency call from the target property, he had tossed his cell phone into the front yard—leaving it turned on and continuing to transmit a GPS location signal. The police would figure out that trick too, but by then he would have changed his method once more.

Satisfied with his setup, he donned a pair of electronic shooting earmuffs. The surprisingly inexpensive protective headset automatically blocked noise above eighty-two decibels, while still allowing the wearer to hear voices and listen to normal conversation. Or, more to the point in Dr. Cole's case, they muffled the loud clap of a shot and still let him hear anyone approaching his vehicle.

The protective earmuffs had been necessitated by another change in his routine. Making headshots with subsonic rounds had been rewarding, but he realized that the time had come to take his shots from farther out. And for that he needed to use a long-range weapon—which entailed a significant increase in muzzle blast. Also necessary, as headshots at longer ranges became less reliable on moving targets, was a cartridge that could defeat the ballistic armor worn by police.

He had purchased a ballistic vest online and performed some testing of his own. The results had been interesting. Although the ballistic, or "bulletproof," vests normally worn by police were effective at stopping a .38 or .45 caliber round fired from a handgun at close range, they proved almost useless against a high-velocity rifle bullet.

If everything went as planned, tonight's shots on Mount Olympus would be made at 590 yards, followed later in the evening by 720-yard shots in Sherman Oaks. Because Dr. Cole liked to keep his weapons as standardized as possible, his choice for tonight's shoot was a second Remington Model 700 Sendero. The new rifle was similar to his subsonic setup, except this one was chambered in .300 Win Mag—an extremely powerful cartridge that could send a 180-grain bullet downrange at over 3,100 feet per second. The handloaded, match-grade cartridges now loaded in the magazine were sufficiently accurate, when fired by an expert with a good rifle, to take out a target at 1,200 yards.

Dr. Cole was such an expert. And he had an excellent rifle.

In a further effort to standardize his equipment, he had completed his Win Mag setup with a second Millett tactical scope and an Advanced Armament Corporation sonic suppressor—items identical to those on his subsonic Whisper rifle. He realized the AAC suppressor would do little to mask the supersonic crack of the Win Mag, but it would quiet the muzzle blast, hide some flash, and distort the sonic crack of the bullet—making it difficult for someone to determine the direction from which the shot had been fired. Unfortunately, the sound of the shot would still be significant, but every little bit helped.

Kneeling beside the shooting bench, he shouldered his weapon, nestling the butt of the stock into his shoulder. Next he formed a solid cheek-to-stock weld with his lower face pressed against a patch of moleskin fixed to the stock—ensuring proper eye relief from the rear of the scope, as well as establishing a natural line of sight through the eyepiece.

His shooting bench supported most of the weapon's weight, the front swivel resting in the leather stabilizer, the rear of the stock in a small sandbag. He shifted position slightly, making certain he was steadying the weapon using the bones of his arms and shoulders, not his muscles.

Squeezing the sandbag with his nonshooting hand, he next made a slight vertical adjustment, scanning the target zone. Illumination from a street lamp on Olympus Drive was more than adequate. He adjusted a knob on the Millett, bringing the house into razor-sharp focus. Turning a second knob, he activated the scope's reticle illumination. The mil dots and crosshair lines glowed green in the eyepiece, overlaying the front door of the residence. He checked surrounding vegetation for wind. Nothing.

He glanced at his watch. It had been thirteen minutes since he'd made the 911 call. Still no sign of the police. As he waited, he took a moment to mentally review the information he had studied that afternoon—site sketches, elevations, "holds," secondary positions, and emergency escape routes. He remembered it all.

He was ready.

Where were they?

Just as he had decided something was wrong and it was time to abort, a black-and-white patrol car drove slowly into the target neighborhood, easing to a stop in front of the kill zone. The vehicle's exterior spotlight flashed around the yard, stopping on bushes and trees where someone might be hiding.

As with the 911 call he'd placed in the Palisades, for tonight's shoot he had reported a prowler, so he wasn't surprised to see the responding officers proceeding cautiously. He watched through the Millett scope, consciously slowing his breathing and forcing himself to relax.

Leaving the cruiser's headlights burning, a uniformed officer stepped from the driver's side of the vehicle. A moment later his partner exited the other side. Dr. Cole followed them through the scope as they mounted the steps to the front door. The lineup was ideal. They were moving almost directly away from his line of sight. He decided to take the trailing officer as soon as the pair had reached the landing.

And then it was time. The sight picture was perfect. With the forefinger of his shooting hand resting lightly on the stock above the trigger, he grasped the pistol grip with his remaining three fingers. In concert with his left forearm, he exerted a slight rearward pull, solidly placing the rifle stock into the pocket of his shoulder, minimizing the effect of recoil. He let his breath out slowly. Then, placing the tip of his index finger on the trigger, he timed his squeeze to the natural pause in his breathing.

An explosive blast filled the interior of the Expedition. Even with the suppressor and earmuffs, the noise was bright and stunning.

Temporarily losing his sight picture as the rifle discharged, Dr. Cole quickly ejected his spent round, rechambered another cartridge, and acquired his second target. As he did, he noted that his first bullet had struck the trailing officer high on his back, several inches above where he'd been aiming.

The first officer was down, blood already soaking his uniform. Seeing this, Dr. Cole noted with satisfaction that ballistic vests wouldn't be a problem—at least not at intermediate ranges.

His next shot struck the second officer just as he was turning, staring in shock at his partner. This time Dr. Cole made a slight adjustment to his "hold," placing his bullet in the exact center of the second patrolman's chest.

The second officer went down, collapsing in a rapidly expanding pool of blood, his own mixing with his partner's.

Aware that his shots would soon bring a reaction from neighbors, Dr. Cole took one last look through the scope. Then he removed his earmuffs, replaced his rifle under the blanket, tipped the shooting bench onto its side, and climbed into the front seat of the Expedition. Without turning on his headlights, he started the engine and edged quietly onto the street. Driving slowly, he proceeded higher into the suburban neighborhood, resisting the impulse to speed.

A light came on in a residence several houses down, but by then he was well on his way. He rolled up the Expedition's windows, pulled on his ball cap, and redonned his sunglasses before switching on the Expedition's headlights, just in case someone was watching. Or, worse, in case he was caught on one of the surveillance cameras that seemed to be popping up everywhere. He knew that being seen wasn't a significant concern, as his features were indistinguishable with the ball cap and glasses, and the plates on the Expedition were stolen. Still . . . it didn't hurt to take precautions.

Minutes later he began descending the backside of Mount Olympus, threading through a maze of quiet suburban streets on his way to the Hollywood Freeway. Once on the freeway he would drive north, then take the Ventura Freeway east. Within thirty minutes he would exit in Sherman Oaks, where he looked forward to taking a second team of police officers.

It was going to be a satisfying evening.

Chapter Seventeen

The mood was grim at the Sunday morning task-force meeting. I had received word of the North Hollywood shootings in the middle of the night, and I hadn't slept since. Sipping lukewarm coffee from a paper cup, I glanced around the room. From the look of most of the other officers present, few of them had slept after getting their phone calls, either.

Lieutenant Snead looked exhausted as well. I knew the press briefings had recently turned even more hostile, with reporters demanding to know why no progress was being made. The brass were asking the same question, and Snead didn't have an answer, at least not a good one. In positioning himself to take credit when things went right, he had also set himself up to take a fall if things went wrong. And things were definitely going wrong. Somehow I couldn't work up much sympathy.

Despite the overtime involved, Snead had called a full meeting for that morning. There were several new faces in our group—men I assumed to be detectives from the divisions where the most recent shootings had occurred. A quick count of investigators and FBI agents now in the room totaled twenty-three—not counting our secretary and the team of staffers helping to answer hotline calls. If things kept up, I thought glumly, we were going to need larger accommodations.

"Okay, everyone quiet down," Snead snapped. "Let's get started. First of all, two new detective pairs are joining us. Detectives Max Jones and Brian Murphy are here from the Hollywood Division, which patrols the Mount Olympus neighborhood. Detectives Eli Cooper and Kevin Aguilar are here from the Van Nuys Division, where a second shooting took place last night in Sherman Oaks."

Everyone turned to glance at the new members, who were sitting at the rear of the room beside another newcomer—a dark-haired civilian wearing a visitor's badge. From his looks, I quickly concluded that he was probably another addition to our FBI contingent.

"Detectives Jones and Murphy were the investigating officers on the Mount Olympus homicides," Snead went on. "Let's start with them. Their crime report will be available tomorrow, when we'll have copies for everyone. In the meantime, Detectives Murphy and Jones, one of you want to bring us up to speed?"

Detective Murphy glanced at his partner, who indicated with a shrug that he was happy to let someone else do the talking. Detective Jones, a heavyset man with a paunch and a receding hairline, levered himself from his chair and moved to the front of the room. "Good morning," he said when he arrived, withdrawing a notepad from his pocket. "I'm Max Jones from the Hollywood Community Police Station, West Bureau," he began. "I hope I can add something to the investigation, but we don't have much so far."

Referring to his notes, Jones gave a rambling summation of his findings at the Mount Olympus crime scene, beginning with his time of arrival and ending with the discovery of the probable site from which the sniper's shots had been fired. Both of the ambushed Hollywood Division patrol officers, Mike Bennett and Juan Martinez, had died at the scene. Bullets recovered had been sent to ballistics for analysis.

The sniper's M.O. had been similar to the other shoots, with a few changes. A 911 call had drawn the officers to the site, but instead of killing his victims with headshots, the sniper had apparently used high-velocity rounds to penetrate the officers' ballistic vests. Consistent with high-velocity rifle rounds being used, several people in the area had reported hearing shots. A cell phone had been found at the site, still turned on and connected to a puzzled emergency services officer. Dispatchers had been advising patrols to take special care on emergency calls in which the caller hadn't stayed on the line. Because the GPS phone signal matched the emergency address, and because the phone connection had remained active, no such warning had been given.

The recovered phone was being checked for prints and DNA. A neighborhood canvass was underway, but so far no witnesses had been found.

Assuming that the sniper's shots had come from higher in the subdivision, investigators had located a vacant lot on Oceanus Drive with a clear line of sight to the killing ground. Fresh tire tracks in the dirt and reports by neighbors saying they'd heard two loud bangs earlier that evening led officers to believe the sniper had fired from that location. Laser measurements from the Oceanus lot to the crime scene pegged the distance at just under 600 yards.

I recalled the words of the FBI's sniper, Special Agent Wyatt, who had speculated that once we became aware of the sniper's presence, he would move farther out and start shooting through body armor instead of taking silenced headshots. Sensing a stir in the room, I glanced around, realizing that other detectives had come to the same conclusion.

Agent Wyatt's predictions were coming true.

Following Detective Jones, Detective Aguilar from the Van Nuys Division spoke. His report was strikingly similar to the summary given by Detective Jones: Patrol officers had responded to a 911 call, arriving at a residence in Sherman Oaks. As with the shootings in North Hollywood, an operating cell phone had been found in the front yard. Again, because of the live phone onsite, no warnings had been given to responding officers. Both ambushed patrolmen had been shot through their vests. Officer Dave Moses had died at the scene; his partner, Officer Dominic LeBlanc, was in critical condition and currently undergoing surgery at L.A. County/USC Medical Center.

A search in Sherman Oaks had located the probable firing position, a pullout on Mulholland Drive named the Charles and Lotte Melhorn Overlook. The distance from there to the crime scene was lasered at a little over 700 yards. Bullets were recovered at the scene, and possible trace evidence was collected at the overlook. And so on. Nothing, however, that got us any closer to finding the shooter.

There *was* one bright spot: A traffic camera on Mulholland had recorded a green Expedition leaving the area after the shootings. When checked, the plates on the Expedition had turned out to be a match for a set stolen in South Los Angeles six months earlier.

"The traffic cam get a look at the driver?" someone asked.

Detective Aguilar shook his head. "Too dark."

"We have BOLO out on the Expedition," Snead broke in, referring to a "Be on the Lookout" notice to all LAPD patrol units. "We haven't disclosed the connection between the Expedition and the sniper shootings yet. As the Expedition is our first real lead, we don't want it getting picked up by the media—at least not before we can use it. If the Expedition lead does get spilled to the press," he added grimly, "I promise that heads will roll." Then, turning back to Aguilar, "Thank you for your briefing, Detective. You as well, Detective Jones. Both of you have your crime reports available for distribution at tomorrow's meeting."

After Aguilar had retaken his seat, Snead continued. "Now before we move on, I want to stress that we've made real progress with this Expedition lead. With any luck, I'm confident we can have this case wrapped up shortly, and that's what I'm going to report to Chief Ingram when I see him at the news briefing."

Although no one spoke, I knew we were all thinking the same thing. We had lost three additional officers, a fourth was fighting for his life, and we were no closer to finding the guy who did it. Well, maybe a little closer. The green Expedition was something, although there were thousands of green Expeditions in Los Angeles, and somehow I didn't think our shooter was leaving his vehicle parked on the street or driving it to the supermarket, either, so it wasn't going to be easy to find. Which left us waiting for him to venture out on another shoot and hoping we could catch him in the act. I didn't like the odds.

"With all due respect, Lieutenant, I don't think we should be sending out party invitations just yet," I interjected. "Our BOLO may not turn up anything. How about if we discreetly check with neighbors at the earlier sites? See whether anyone remembers seeing a green Expedition. For that matter, sometimes these guys like to revisit their scenes to relive the moment, feel superior, gloat, or whatever. We could have neighbors be on the lookout for a green Expedition and give us a call if one shows up."

"Good idea, Kane," said Dondero.

"The only problem with that would be keeping the Expedition lead quiet," I noted, playing devil's advocate to my own suggestion. "But the press is going to pick it up sooner or later. Probably sooner."

"How about putting surveillance on the previous sites?" Deluca suggested. "Forget talking to neighbors. With surveillance units in place, we could just grab the guy if he shows up, and do it without tipping our hand to the press."

"I'll check with Metro about setting some surveillance," Snead agreed. "Of course I'll have to run it by the brass first," he hedged. "Personally, I'd prefer to keep this under wraps and hope our shooter doesn't change vehicles, but we'll see what my bosses think."

"We should at least have the emergency operators warn our patrols to be on the lookout for the Expedition in high-risk situations," someone else suggested. "Calls in the canyons, for instance. Maybe send out two patrols in those particular cases— one to respond, a second to look for the Expedition."

"I'll check into that, too," said Snead doubtfully, making another entry in his notebook.

"At minimum, we should add an advisory to the BOLO telling anyone stopping a green Expedition to exercise extreme caution," I said.

"Again, I'll have to run that by the brass," Snead said doubtfully. "Anyone else?"

When no one responded, Snead continued. "Okay, before we get to our progress updates, Jim Huffington is here from the FBI's Critical Incident Response Group's Behavioral Analysis Unit. His group has given our situation priority status and assembled a profile of our shooter in record time. I want you to give your full attention to whatever he has to say."

I felt a communal current of doubt sweep the room. Like most cops, I had a healthy distrust of the so-called science of psychological profiling, viewing it as something akin to calling a psychic. Nevertheless, I once more reminded myself to keep an open mind.

Carrying a stack of reports, the dark-haired civilian whom I had noticed earlier stepped forward. "Thanks, Lieutenant," he said to Snead, handing the reports to a detective sitting up front. "Could you pass these around?" he asked politely. Then, addressing the entire group, "Good morning. My name is Jim Huffington. I'm with the FBI's Behavioral Analysis Unit Four—crimes against adults. Assistant Director Shepherd asked me here today in the hope that I might be able to bring something helpful to your case. The copies I'm passing out are our criminal investigative analysis of your shooter or shooters. We're not ruling out the possibility of more than one man being involved, but in this case I don't think so, and for purposes of our study I'll be referring to him in the singular.

"You will note that our analysis examines your shooter's actions from both an investigative and a behavioral aspect," Huffington continued as the reports were being distributed. "In coming up with our results, we reviewed all available crime-scene reports, photos, witness statements, victim profiles, and autopsy reports, as well as conferring extensively with Lieutenant Snead and Assistant Director Shepherd regarding the case. I'm going to quickly summarize the high points, but there's a lot of material in there, so please take the time to study the report later in its entirety."

I flipped through the file I'd been handed. Like most FBI profiles I'd seen in the past, it was divided into several broad categories, including an M.O. or modus operandi section describing the shooter's method of committing his crime, an analysis of the crime scenes and autopsy protocols, a victimology section examining common links among the victims, a section on the sniper's "signature" that discussed idiosyncratic elements of the shooter's behavior, and a psychological criminal profile of the unknown offender—or "unsub" in FBI-speak. The BAU team had also included a short section at the end that provided investigative suggestions based on their criminal profile. I knew

I would give the most attention to this final portion of their report.

"We need to dispense with a couple of basics first," Huffington continued. "To start, your man definitely falls into the 'organized' framework, as opposed to the impulse-type, 'disorganized' killer whose crimes are opportunistic and usually show a lack of planning or any attempt to avoid detection."

"So you think our guy is actually planning these shootings?" someone grumbled. "Yeah, we got that."

Snead shot an irritated glance at the offender but said nothing.

Ignoring the interruption, Huffington continued. "Killers in the 'organized' category usually have adequate social skills, leave little forensic evidence at the scene or scenes, and often engage in a preselection of victims—although in your case that aspect seems to be more a preselection of firing sites."

"The patrol officers were simply targets he drew into his field of fire," Deluca noted. "Nothing personal. Yeah, we got that, too."

"Correct," said Huffington. "Nothing personal. We did briefly consider the possibility that one or more of the officers was specifically targeted, with the other killings being designed to throw investigators off track. Given the ongoing situation, however, I think you're right in concluding that the victims have no connection to one another—with the exception that they were all LAPD patrol officers responding to 911 calls. I think you're also correct in your conclusions regarding the sniper's M.O. He has clearly spent considerable time preselecting his firing positions. He draws targets into his kill zone with a call to emergency services, and then he kills them. And he will probably continue to do so until you catch him."

"When do you think the next shooting will be?" Snead asked nervously.

"The time between the first and second incident was around twenty-four hours, with both occurring on a weekend," Huffington answered. "Then nothing again until last night, an interval of five days. If the killer sticks to that pattern, I would expect another shooting this weekend."

"Maybe that's something we can use," I suggested. "Instead of concentrating on what we *think* might be high-risk 911 calls, let's escalate. Call in extra units this weekend and send out two or even three patrols on *every* 911 call—one unit to respond, the others to cover the area looking for anything suspicious. Like, say, a green Expedition with a rifle hanging out the window."

"We should be so lucky," someone muttered.

"Do you have any idea how many 911 calls come in every day, Kane?" Snead demanded. "Dispatching multiple units on every call is simply not possible."

"Then let's at least do the Westside, where all this has been taking place so far. Especially in the canyons, and especially during the p.m. watch."

"That might be a good idea, Bill," interjected Shepherd, who until now had sat quietly on the far side of the room. "If nothing else, it could make your responders a little less jumpy," he added diplomatically. Everyone there knew he was referring to several embarrassing incidents that had occurred recently. In one, nervous LAPD officers had fired shots at an unoccupied white delivery van on a dead-end street; another had involved a homeless person camped on a hillside in the Palisades. Both incidents had been widely reported in the media. So far no one had been seriously injured, but if things kept up, it would be only a matter of time.

"The overtime will be prohibitive, but I'll see whether I can get it approved," Snead conceded. "In the meantime, please continue, Agent Huffington."

Huffington nodded. "One more comment on your man's M.O. before we get to the profile section. In the shootings last night, your sniper demonstrated a willingness to vary his pattern, confirming our initial impressions. This willingness to vary his M.O., taken together with a preselection of firing sites and the care he's given to leave little or no forensic evidence, indicates that you have a highly intelligent killer who is conscious of his crimes, and who has a strong sense of self-preservation as well."

"So he's not a nut job," one of the Robbery-Homicide detectives observed dryly.

Huffington shook his head. "No, he's not. Quite the contrary. Your sniper clearly has problems, but any psychological examination would undoubtedly classify him as psychopathic rather than psychotic. He's acting without compassion or remorse, but he is fully cognizant of what he's doing."

"Which is killing cops," said Deluca.

"Right," said Huffington. "Which is about as good a summary of his 'signature' as any. To date, at least as far as we know, your sniper has limited his killings to police officers. This leads us to believe that the idiosyncratic psychological need your shooter is fulfilling is simply a desire to kill cops. His rage—and make no mistake, he is raging—is directed toward police officers, and police officers alone."

"Why?" someone asked.

"That's an area in which our analysis might be able to add something," Huffington replied. "In the psychological autopsy section, which is based on our analysis of the preliminary elements just discussed, we list our conclusions regarding your sniper's motivational and psychological makeup."

"That would be in your so-called psychological profile section," said Madison doubtfully.

Huffington hesitated a moment before replying. "I sense many of you consider psychological profiling to be not much different from gazing into a crystal ball," he said. "And much of the time, you might be right. I will be the first to admit that some of what we are about to discuss next is simply educated speculation, but it's speculation based on hundreds of interviews with similar offenders."

"You mean cop killers?" asked someone.

"Actually, no," answered Huffington. "That's where things get complicated. Quite frankly, we haven't encountered this type of situation very often. What is unique about your sniper murders is that from a motivational standpoint they exhibit elements of serial-type killings—a number of homicides occurring over an extended period of time—while also having the earmarks of a mass-murder crime, which is defined as the murder of multiple victims, usually three or more, during the course of a single incident."

"So . . . what are you saying?" Dondero asked.

Huffington thought for a moment. "Okay, here's the problem. We have a lot of profile material on serial killers. We also have good data, although not nearly as much, on mass murderers. Your man lies somewhere between the two. Serial killings are repeat events that are up-close and confrontational, usually committed by men, with motivations including anger, thrill or attention seeking, sexual gratification, and financial gain. In addition, despite the various motivations that can be present, many serial killings involve some sort of sexual contact with the victims. Mass killings, on the other hand, are generally a one-time event and are most often committed out of rage inspired by some actual or perceived wrong done to the killer. He feels victimized, and at some point he decides to get even. You see the problem. Totally different motivations."

"Our shooter sounds a bit like the D.C. Beltway guys," I observed. "Shooting strangers, this time cops, and doing it repeatedly."

"Right," said Huffington. "There were elements of both serial killing and mass murder in that case, too. That's probably the reason our profile on the D.C. case was so far off. We don't want to make the same mistake again. By the way, we learned a lot from the Beltway murders—mostly that we don't really have a good handle on mass killings."

"Why is that?" someone asked.

"Simply because there haven't been enough of them to study," Huffington replied. "As frequent as they may seem, from a research perspective they are actually rare. In our country there are maybe twenty mass killings each year, with about 100 to 150 total victims. That may sound like a lot, but it pales in comparison with the *fifteen thousand* annual single-victim homicides, or the huge number of serial killings we've studied over the years. What we *have* learned is that mass killers follow so many diverse patterns that it's hard to pin down common threads."

"So where does that leave us?" asked Snead.

"The approach we took on your shooter was to generate a 'spree-serial killer' profile using elements that fit both categories, at least whenever possible," Huffington explained. "I'll summarize our conclusions, but again, please take the time to read the entire report. Given the caveat that these are educated guesses based on available data, we think the following traits apply to your sniper: first, statistics show that almost all mass killers are male, something that holds true for most serial killers as well."

"So we're looking for a man," Deluca broke in. "Or men."

"Right. There have been relatively few cases of a female mass killer—Amy Bishop at the University of Alabama in 2010 was one—but because of the sniping aspect of your crimes, we're fairly certain you're looking for a male."

"Fairly certain, huh?" Madison muttered under his breath. "That's helpful."

"Most serial killers are white males in their late twenties to early forties," Huffington continued, ignoring the interruption. "They typically act alone and rarely cross racial boundaries in their choice of victims. Mass killers, on the other hand, vary widely in age and race, and they sometimes act in pairs. Dylan Klebold and Eric Harris, the shooters at the Columbine High School massacre, were white males aged seventeen and eighteen years old, respectively. Seung-Hui Cho, a twenty-three-year-old Korean, killed thirty-two students and teachers at his college in Blacksburg, Virginia. More recently, John Allen Muhammad and Lee Boyd Malvo, the Beltway snipers, were both African American males, aged forty-eight and twenty-nine. Again, you see the problem."

"The descriptors are all over the place," Snead observed.

"Correct," Huffington agreed. "For this reason, even though most serial killers are white, we make no race assessment in our analysis of your shooter. Age is also difficult to pin down. Nevertheless, because of the expertise shown in the shootings, we think that twenty to forty years old is a good age range. As I said earlier, we think your man is acting alone, although we could be wrong. As far as motivation, because of the long-range aspect of the shootings, we feel that sexual gratification is not a factor as it is with many serial killings, although I wouldn't completely rule it out. To the contrary, the mass killings we've studied indicate that your shooter's motivation is most likely a desire for revenge. As I said, he probably feels he has been victimized in some way. Because he is specifically targeting police officers, he is most likely angry about some real or perceived wrong suffered at the hands of the police, and now he wants to get even. Although he may have planned his revenge for some time, as mass killers often do, there is usually a 'stressor' or triggering event that sets him off—being fired from a job, breaking up with his girlfriend, something like that.

"As I said earlier, given the care your shooter has exercised to avoid leaving evidence, we feel he is not clinically psychotic," Huffington continued. "Most mass killers, however, do show serious psychiatric problems, including depression, paranoid delusions, rage, and other acute behavioral or personality disorders."

"No shit," Detective Garrison from Robbery-Homicide grumbled.

"Mass murderers also usually harbor intense feelings of rejection," Huffington continued. "Other common traits are low self-esteem, as opposed to serial killers, who have a sense of their own giftedness and superiority. Like serial killers, mass murderers often come from a background of parental abuse. They also may have engaged in a preadolescent setting of fires, along with demonstrating a sadistic tendency involving the torture of animals."

Huffington paused briefly to refer to his copy of the report. "Okay, just a couple of items left. Your shooter clearly knows the area. We think he lives in Southern California but operates outside the boundaries of a comfort zone—probably killing at some distance from his home. He is able to appear normal to his friends, while inside he's raging. He could be married and even have kids, but in this case we don't think so. He feels victimized and views police officers as ciphers to be obliterated. He is able to compartmentalize his killings and feels justified in his actions. Like most mass killers, he is obsessed with guns. Last, he is undoubtedly watching media coverage of his crimes. That he has yet to contact the press or police—a play for notoriety that usually trips up these types of killers—is indicative of a high level of organization and determination not to be caught."

"You said earlier that you thought our guy was working alone," I noted. "Just now you mentioned that he was probably single. Can you explain?"

"We could be wrong," Huffington replied, "but the late hour of the crimes suggests that the shooter lives alone and doesn't have to account for his whereabouts to anyone. As for working without a partner, the fact that to date no one has contacted the press is telling. Most killers of his ilk crave recognition. It makes them feel powerful, something they need. Keeping a secret like that is almost impossible. You know the saying— 'Three can keep a secret . . . if two of them are dead.'"

The room had again quieted, everyone struck by the seemingly impossible task we were facing.

"To sum up your shooter's attributes," Huffington concluded, "he is probably a loner who is able to conduct himself well in social situations, but inside he's raging. He is highly intelligent, most likely with an above-average education. He is probably between twenty and forty years of age, race unknown. He is familiar with the Los Angeles area, but he is being careful to conduct his killing at some distance from his home. He is obsessed with guns and is an expert marksman—possibly with military or police training. He has already demonstrated a willingness to vary his M.O., and I would not be surprised to see him do so again. If he has ever been treated for a mental illness, the diagnosis would probably have included clinical depression and delusional paranoia. His motive for killing is revenge. Your man feels he has been victimized, ruined in some way by the police. He is angry and depressed and willing to die, but before he does, he wants to get even."

"Is there a bright spot in there somewhere?" muttered Dondero, voicing the question on all our minds.

"A little," Huffington replied. "In the final section of the report we make a few suggestions. Your shooter is undoubtedly following developments in the media. In essence, our unit thinks your best chance of catching him is to get him talking—if not to you, at least to the press. Open a dialogue with him in any way possible. That's the way the D.C. Beltway snipers were eventually caught."

"If our guy is as smart as you think, he knows that too," I pointed out. "In which case he probably won't be calling in on the hotline, sending letters to the press, attending community meetings to discuss the killings, or leaving cryptic notes at the crime scenes."

"I hope you're wrong," Huffington said. "Because if that's the case, you may have to wait until he does it again . . . and hope he makes a mistake."

Chapter Eighteen

Hey, Dad. What's another word for 'thesaurus'?"

After flipping several pancakes on the griddle and stirring the scrambled eggs, I turned from the stove to glance at Allison, who was sitting on a kitchen counter nearby. "Don't bug me, Ali," I ordered, adding some grated cheese to the eggs. "I'm trying to cook here."

"I can see that, Dad. I mistakenly thought you might be able to handle two things at once. Good thing you don't chew gum."

"Right," I said, trying not to smile. Despite all that had gone wrong on the sniper case, it felt great to finally have a day off, and I was in a good mood.

That morning I had risen early, as usual completing my morning workout around the time the sun was coming up. After making a pot of coffee, I had rousted Allison and Nate, and together with Catheryn we had attended 8:00 a.m. Mass at Our Lady of Malibu Catholic Church.

Following the death of Tommy, I had stopped going to Mass. Although I still wasn't certain how I felt about things, I had recently resumed accompanying the family to Sunday services— if for no other reason than to set a good example for the kids. Plus it made Catheryn happy.

"Dan, is the food about ready?" Catheryn called up from the deck below. "Arnie says he's starving. So is Nate."

"Tell my portly ex-partner that chow will be served in five minutes," I called back, turning the bacon one last time. "And send Nate up here to help carry stuff down."

"So how are things going with the case?" Allison asked brightly. "Any new developments?"

"Ali . . ."

"I know, I know," Allison backpedaled. "It's just that I've been spending so much time researching sniper material, I wanted someone to share with."

"So share away," I said, scooping the scrambled eggs onto a heated tray and pouring one last batch of pancake batter on the griddle. "Just don't expect me to share back."

"Fine, but if you change your mind . . ."

". . . I'll let you know," I finished. "Don't hold your breath."

"I won't," Allison laughed. "Anyway, I couldn't believe how many sniper schools there are. Most of them train law enforcement and military personnel, but almost all of them take civilians who can pass a background check. Not to mention the number of military training programs, returning vets, and the like. There are plenty of guys out there with the skills to be your killer."

"Um," I mumbled. I knew the task force had thoroughly investigated the same sniper academies Allison was researching—so far to no avail.

"I even did some reading on the subject," Allison continued. "A retired Special Forces major named Plaster wrote an interesting book called *The Ultimate Sniper*. It was a real eye-opener. I also looked over the army's *Sniper Training Field Manual*. It's available online for free, by the way."

"Learn anything?"

"Yes, I did," said Allison, turning serious. "I learned that if your guy is anywhere near as good as a military sniper, you're going to have your hands full catching him."

"Thanks for the vote of confidence," I grumbled. "Where the hell is Nate? He's supposed to be helping."

"I'll get him. By the way, did your task force find any similar rifle murders? Never mind, I know you can't answer. I did research on that, too. It's amazing how many handgun killings there are compared with rifle homicides. I found hardly any rifle murders at all in our news archives, and only one in the Los Angeles area that involved a police officer."

"An L.A. cop was killed with a rifle?" I asked, recalling that Assistant Director Shepherd had said the FBI considered that approach a dead end. "When was that?"

"A year ago in Simi Valley," Allison replied, sliding off the counter and heading for the stairs. "Actually, the murder victim was an ex-cop. And they caught the guy who did it, so it doesn't really fit."

"What was this ex-cop's name?"

Allison paused at the top of the stairs. "Uh, Strom, I think. Joe Strom. Didn't your task force look into that?"

"Why wouldn't we?" I answered evasively, wondering whether we had. I flipped the last of the pancakes and pulled the bacon off the stove, deciding to inquire about the late Officer Strom at Monday's meeting. As Allison had said, it probably didn't fit. But with the lack of leads so far, I wanted to make sure something hadn't fallen through the cracks.

By the time Allison returned with Nate, I had breakfast served on platters and ready to carry down—a huge stack of pancakes, plenty of bacon and sausage, a bowl of cut melon, a metal pot filled with fried potatoes and onions, a basket of toasted bagels, two pitchers of fresh-squeezed orange juice, a carafe of coffee, and a tray of scrambled eggs mixed with melted cheese, scallions, and chopped red peppers.

"Mmm, smells great, Dad," said Nate. "When do we eat?"

"As soon as you help your sister carry this stuff down," I replied, glad to see Nate in better spirits for a change, not the sulky teen that lately had taken over his body. "What took you so long getting up here?"

"I, uh, was out on the beach with Arnie and Callie. Sorry."

"Arnie and Callie, huh?" I said. "I wondered where the mutt was. She usually hangs in the kitchen when food is getting cooked. I haven't seen her since Arnie showed up."

"She likes Arnie better than the rest of us," Allison offered. "She hasn't let him out of her sight since he arrived."

Callie had a soft spot for Arnie—possibly because he would throw a stick or ball or whatever for her to retrieve until his arm fell off. But I knew there was more to it than that. I've always thought you can tell a lot about someone by how your dog reacts to them. Callie gave Arnie her highest possible canine approval: she considered him part of our pack, and so did I. Arnie had been my training officer when I first came on the force, my partner when I moved up to detective four years later, and my D-III supervisor for most of my time on the homicide unit. He was a mentor, a friend, and one of the few men I trusted with my life.

"Well, Callie has good taste in humans," I said. Then, grabbing one of the trays, I headed for the stairs. "Gimme a hand getting the grub down to the deck. It's time to eat."

Downstairs, Catheryn had set our picnic table for five. When we were all seated, she said grace. Following that we passed the bowls and trays around the table, filled our plates, and dug in. For several minutes the only sounds heard were the clink of silverware and waves breaking on the shoreline.

"Amigo, you outdid yourself this time," Arnie said when the eating had finally slowed down. "I haven't had a breakfast this good since my army days," he added, reaching for seconds with a satisfied smile.

"Army grub? High praise, partner," I said dryly.

"Aw, you know what I mean," Arnie laughed. "Great food, lots of it, and free." Then, turning to Allison, "I've been watching you on the news lately, Ali. You look great on camera. Not to say that you don't look great in person," he added quickly. "What I mean is that you look . . . I don't know, different, lately. Happier."

"I am happier," said Allison, glancing across the table at Catheryn.

"So where *is* Mike this morning?" Arnie asked. "I thought you two were inseparable."

Allison came as close to blushing as I had seen in a long time. "He's on location in Arizona, shooting a feature with his cinematographer friend, Don Sturgess," she answered. "Mike's the second-unit DP—director of photography. He's shooting action sequences with the stunt crew for a sci-fi film scheduled to be released next summer."

"Well, when you see him, give him my best." Arnie paused thoughtfully. Then, turning to me, "I seem to recall hearing you say you knew Mike's dad."

I finished the last of my pancakes and took a sip of coffee. "Frank Cortese. He was in my academy class."

"Frank Cortese. Wasn't he . . ." Arnie's voice trailed off.

"Yeah, he was the one killed in that hostage standoff a number of years back."

"I remember the incident," Arnie said quietly. "Speaking of which, I'm really sorry about the officers you've been losing, Dan. I knew some of those guys. Rios from the Venice Division, and Jerry Levinson from West L.A. Both good men."

I nodded, wishing I had something good to say about the case.

Sensing my plummeting mood, Arnie backed off. "It's times like this I'm glad to be drawing a pension and working security. When are you gonna retire and come work for me, Dan?"

"Maybe sooner than you think," I answered glumly.

"Well, in the meantime, watch your step. Cases like your sniper investigation don't usually end well, pal."

"Lieutenant Long said the same thing," I grumbled. "Don't worry, I know what I'm doing."

"I hope so. You don't have me around anymore to watch your back." Then, turning again to Allison, "Anyway, please say hi to Mike for me. I like that kid."

"I like him, too," Allison said with a smile.

"He's not exactly a kid," Catheryn pointed out. "He's twenty-five, going on twenty-six."

Apparently hearing something in Catheryn's tone, Allison looked up, her smile fading. "What's that supposed to mean?"

"Nothing," said Catheryn. "Just that Mike's not a kid. He's an adult."

"And so am I," Allison shot back.

"I know that. Will Mike be returning home in time for Arthur's party?" asked Catheryn, retreating. I knew the issue smoldering between them—Ali's practically living with Mike without being married—and I was glad Catheryn had decided to let it go, at least for the moment.

Allison nodded. "He's coming back on Saturday. We'll be there."

"How about you, partner?" I asked, attempting to steer the conversation in another direction. "Want to attend an upscale bash for one of the Philharmonic's retiring cellists? Free food."

"Please come, Arnie," said Catheryn. "We're honoring Arthur West for his twenty-plus years with the Philharmonic.

Dinner and dancing at the Beverly Hills Hotel. It should be lovely."

"Okay if I bring Stacy?" Arnie asked, referring to his steady girlfriend of the past six years.

"Of course."

"Then I'd love to come. What's the dress?"

"I'm wearing a tux," I announced.

Arnie grinned. "Then I am, too. Thanks for the invite, Kate."

Nate, who had been eating quietly until then, finally spoke up. "Can me and Ali go to the party, too?"

"Allison and I," Catheryn corrected.

"Huh?"

"Subjective pronoun, Nate," Allison explained with an exaggerated sigh. "Let's get started on your English homework right after breakfast. You and *me* have a lot of work to do."

"'May Allison and I go to the party' is the correct way to ask, Nate," Catheryn said patiently, shooting Allison a look of exasperation. "And your sister meant to say 'You and *I* have a lot of work to do.' I swear, Ali, I'm totally running out of reasons not to put you up for adoption."

"Too late for that," Allison laughed.

"And of course you are going to the party, Nate," Catheryn continued, turning back to her youngest. "We're all going. Now, if you and Allison are finished eating, why don't you both clear the table and do the dishes. There's something Arnie and your dad and I need to discuss."

I poured myself more coffee, watching as Nate and Allison began carrying dishes upstairs, wondering what Catheryn wanted to discuss. I didn't have to wait long to find out.

"Dan, you know I don't normally get involved in your work," Catheryn said as soon as the kids were out of earshot, "but this time I'm worried. When the case began, I told you to find the person who was committing these murders. I still want you to, but . . . I don't know, the news reports have been getting more and more vicious, with no end in sight. I've never seen anything like it. The media coverage has turned positively brutal, with everyone attacking everyone else—the mayor, the chief, the FBI.

People seem to be looking for someone to blame, and your task force is right in the crosshairs. What Arnie said about the sniper investigation ending badly . . . is he right?"

"You bet I'm right," Arnie answered before I could speak.

I remained silent, wondering where Catheryn was headed.

Catheryn thought a moment. "Fine," she said. "I'm not suggesting you quit, Dan. It's too late for that anyway. I just wanted to know what the stakes are. For you, and me, and for our family."

I found both Catheryn and Arnie regarding me expectantly, waiting for me to weigh in. Catheryn was absolutely right in wanting to know the stakes. Unfortunately, she was also right in thinking that it was too late for me to quit. And Arnie was right in warning that the case could blow up in my face. It was my turn to say something right. Or, if not right, at least something wise, or reassuring, or thoughtful.

Much as I wanted to, I couldn't think of a thing.

Chapter Nineteen

Two outdoor staircases descend the steep southeast rim of Santa Monica Canyon. The steps, locally known as the Santa Monica Stairs, are most often used for intense cardiovascular workouts, rather than as a direct route from Canyon Charter School below to the multimillion-dollar ocean-view homes perched above on Adelaide Drive.

The easier of the two staircases to climb is a set of 170 mostly wooden treads rising 109 feet to the canyon rim. Nearby to the south is a second set of 189 concrete steps, generally thought to be a bit harder to negotiate. Both stair sets are often crowded during the day, especially on weekends, when hundreds of sweating climbers create mini-traffic jams on the treads and landings.

By sundown most fitness enthusiasts have returned home to nurse sore quads and down a well-deserved beer, but occasionally some climbers stay later. Lights on the concrete staircase allow dedicated exercisers to continue climbing until all hours. Like tonight. Even at almost midnight, a man and a woman were still completing circuits on the southern stairs. The couple had parked at the top on Adelaide to begin their workout, arriving a few minutes after Dr. Cole had parked his Expedition and begun setting up his shooting bench.

Impatient to proceed, he waited in the rear of the Expedition, occasionally glancing at the glowing numerals on his watch. By then the troublesome climbers had completed seven laps on the staircase and started on an eighth. From past observation, he knew that most people were able to manage only nine or ten laps at most.

It wouldn't be much longer.

Forcing himself to sit quietly, he listened to his radio scanner, monitoring police frequencies as he waited. And as he waited, his thoughts returned to his shooting performance on Friday. He was satisfied with his accuracy at both sites, although he was also disappointed that one officer had survived—possibly saved by his protective vest. He promised himself there would be no survivors tonight.

Even if he had to take follow-up shots to make certain.

In Dr. Cole's estimation, the location he had chosen for tonight's shoot was one of his better finds: an unoccupied Craftsman-style house for sale on Adelaide. The property, clearly a holdover from an earlier era, afforded excellent visibility to the north and west. Mature landscaping shielded the structure from adjacent properties on three sides. Last but not least, the site provided easy access to multiple escape routes into the surrounding beach communities, and to the nearby Santa Monica Freeway as well.

Turning, he checked the area around his car. He had parked at the rear of the home's driveway, almost hidden from the street. In the still night air he could make out an intermittent rush of traffic noise filtering up from Entrada Drive, lower in the canyon. A small plane passed overhead. A siren wailed in the distance. Otherwise, nothing.

He raised his binoculars to study the target area halfway up Rustic Canyon—a suburban enclave connecting Santa Monica Canyon with the city of Pacific Palisades to the north. At just under 1,470 yards, tonight's shoot would be his longest to date. As such, he realized that the ballistic drop of his bullet at target would be huge, and any miscalculation in range would mean the difference between a hit and a miss.

As always, he had measured the line-of-sight distance to his target zone carefully. Because his laser rangefinder was undependable out past 800 yards, he had first ranged the distance with his rifle scope, then rechecked the yardage on his computer using Google Earth's surprisingly accurate built-in software. As a result, he was confident his distance estimate was accurate to within a few yards.

Good enough for a center-mass body shot.

Shortly afterward, the nocturnal climbing couple reappeared at the top of the staircase, winded from their latest circuit. Following several minutes of hands-on-thighs heavy breathing, particularly by the man, they started back to their car, apparently having burned an adequate number of calories for the evening.

He waited until the red of their taillights had disappeared down the street. Then, setting down his binoculars, he pulled aside a blanket spread beside the bench, uncovering a .50 caliber Barrett M107A1 sniper rifle equipped with a Leupold Mark-4 50mm scope.

A recent improvement on the military's .50 caliber Barrett M82, the upgraded M107A1 version was four pounds lighter but just as strong as its predecessor. It also boasted a redesigned bolt-carrier group and a four-port muzzle brake that worked seamlessly with Barrett's quick-attach sonic suppressor. From an aesthetic standpoint, he conceded that the Barrett possessed none of the smooth, flowing lines of a more conventional rifle like one of his Remington Senderos. Instead of the classic sweep of the Sendero's walnut stock and the clean lines of its bolt and upper receiver, the massive Barrett looked almost alien—all rails and ports and hard, utilitarian features that included a vented aluminum extrusion cover and a ten-shot magazine the size of a small phone book. Nevertheless, the Barrett was an extremely accurate, powerful weapon—able to punch holes in an engine block or penetrate a distant masonry wall, and do so with amazing precision. In the hands of a marksman, the weapon was fully capable of completing tonight's task, putting 750-grain bullets on target with unthinkably massive power, striking with enough force to slam through ballistic armor and turn body parts into a red mist.

It was time.

He had already fed four handloaded, match-grade .50 caliber BMG cartridges into the Barrett's magazine. After removing the rifle scope's neoprene cover, he carefully inserted the magazine into the underside of the weapon, hearing a metallic click as it locked into place. With the safety on and the rifle pointed out the rear glass hatch, he pulled back the charging handle as far as it would go and then released it, feeding a cartridge into the chamber.

Safety off.

Car windows down.

He was ready to shoot.

Well, almost. Even with a sonic suppressor, when firing the Barrett he had found it prudent to use double ear protection. With one last look outside his vehicle, he placed an earplug in each ear, then donned his electronic shooting earmuffs. Despite the extra earplugs, he could still hear the police transmissions from his scanner. Not nearly as well, but well enough.

Next he picked up one of his prepaid cell phones. He punched in a number he had memorized that morning—the number of a second cell phone he'd hidden in Rustic Canyon earlier that evening. The second phone was wired to a small explosive device. He hesitated a few seconds to savor the moment, then initiated his call.

An instant later a bright flash lit the yard of the target zone. He began counting, arriving at four just as the sound of the explosion reached him.

He was confident that his improvised noisemaker would bring a police response before long. Lights were already going on in the neighborhood.

Once again, all he had to do was wait.

*   *   *

"Dan. Wake up."

"Huh?"

"Wake up, Dan," Catheryn repeated. "Someone's calling. At this time of night, I'm afraid it's for you."

With a groan, I rolled over and squinted at a clock beside the bed: 1:15 a.m. Raising up on one elbow, I reached for the phone. "Kane," I mumbled, trying to sound alert, and failing.

I listened for almost a minute without speaking. Then, with a despondent sigh, I said, "I'm on my way."

"What is it?" Catheryn asked.

"There's been another shooting," I answered, now fully awake. "Santa Monica Canyon."

"I'm so sorry, Dan. Were more of your officers . . ."

"Yeah," I said quietly. "Two more. Go back to sleep, sugar. I'll check with you in the morning."

Chapter Twenty

D r. Cole allowed himself a brief moment of satisfaction as he proceeded east on Bundy Drive toward his storage unit, as usual wearing his ball cap and sunglasses. With the exception of the late-night stair climbers, his plans had come off without a hitch, his preparations resulting in a nearly ideal shoot. In particular, his explosive device had functioned perfectly— detonating flawlessly, then drawing a patrol car into his field of fire within minutes.

With a few hours of research, constructing his toy bomb had been easy. For one thing, all the parts for the remote-controlled detonator had been available online. After disassembling one of his prepaid cell phones, he had simply wired the phone's vibrator circuit to a three-volt relay, which in turn (when the phone was set to vibrate) completed the circuit from a nine-volt lithium battery to a makeshift initiator—a model-rocket igniter— providing the spark to get things going. The explosive device itself was a small pipe bomb filled with smokeless propellant from his reloading bench. Simple, easy, and—best of all— scalable. All he needed for a bigger explosion was a larger pipe.

And more gunpowder, of course.

Dr. Cole realized that to avoid capture he would need to continue varying his tactics, as he had on Mount Olympus. The police weren't stupid. At least they weren't *that* stupid. As by now they had undoubtedly grown wary of the 911 calls, other methods to attract their attention were necessary. He had prepared several, including the noisemaker he had used tonight. Earlier that month he had tested one of his cell-phone bombs in an isolated field north of Three Rivers—a dress rehearsal that had gone off without a hitch. Of course anything could go wrong on opening night, and there was nothing like the real thing.

Following the initial test of his phone-activated device, he had constructed a larger version of the bomb. A much larger version. It was now attached to the underside of his Expedition, close to the gas tank. He knew he wouldn't be able to continue his activities forever. At some point he would make a mistake, or the police would get lucky, or something. But whatever the case, he would not be taken alive.

Turning his thoughts from any consideration of failure, he reviewed his shooting for the evening, deciding it had been satisfactory. More than satisfactory. There had been no wind, which of course simplified things. Nevertheless, making a 1,470-yard shot was a respectable accomplishment for any shooter, and he had made two such shots within seconds of each other. In fact, he had acquired his second target about the time the sound of his first shot was just reaching the target zone, approximately two seconds after the initial bullet had struck. Both shots had penetrated center mass, killing his targets instantly.

Best of all, his exit from the property on Adelaide had been unobserved, of that he was certain. A few lights had come on in the neighborhood following his shots, but by then he was well on his way. The police would never find him. Not tonight, anyway. Maybe he *could* keep killing cops forever.

As he approached West Pico Boulevard, he glanced in his rearview mirror. His stomach dropped. A black-and-white patrol car was riding his bumper.

A moment later the cruiser's lightbar lit up. He was being pulled over.

Damn!

Why was he being stopped, now of all times? He checked his speedometer. He hadn't been speeding. It must be something else.

What?

Heart pounding, he glanced again in his rearview mirror, this time scanning the back of the Expedition. He had tipped over his shooting bench and covered it and the Barrett with the blanket, so maybe the police wouldn't notice.

No, that was no good. He was driving with stolen plates. That was the first thing they would check, if they hadn't already. And from there things would get worse, especially when they looked into the back of the Expedition.

The chances of outrunning the police were slim. He thought quickly. At that time of night, traffic was light. He was in a residential area with little or no foot traffic, and he was approaching a Santa Monica Freeway underpass. The street lay in shadow beneath the freeway, with a long stretch of landscaping at either end. The concrete underpass might even deaden some sound. All were factors in his favor. Not an ideal situation, but the best he could hope for.

Coming to a decision, he slowed as he approached the underpass, easing to the side of the road beneath the freeway traffic lanes above. He turned off his headlights and killed the engine. As the patrol car pulled to the curb behind him, he removed his dark glasses and dropped a hand to the travel pouch fixed to the side of his seat, making sure to keep his other hand clearly visible on the steering wheel.

The fingers of his right hand curled around the grip of the Desert Eagle pistol concealed in his pouch. As always, the huge pistol was cocked and locked. He flipped up the thumb safety to fire. A .50 AE cartridge was ready in the chamber, with seven more in the magazine.

He kept his eyes on the rearview mirror, studying the two shadowy figures in the front of the patrol car.

He pictured it in his mind, visualizing how it would happen. Then he slipped the pistol from its pouch, opened the door, and stepped from the Expedition. Without hesitation he walked rapidly toward the police car, Desert Eagle held loosely at his side, hidden just behind his thigh.

The officer riding shotgun was talking on the radio. Alarmed by Dr. Cole's sudden approach, he dropped the mic and began exiting the cruiser, reaching for his weapon at the same time. By then the other patrolman had bolted from behind the wheel and was angrily yelling for Dr. Cole to return to his vehicle. He had also reached for his sidearm and cleared it from its holster. He hadn't yet noticed Dr. Cole's gun.

Dr. Cole wasn't nearly as accomplished with a pistol as he was with a rifle. Nevertheless, using a two-handed grip, he was still good enough with the Desert Eagle to put seven rounds inside a four-inch circle at twenty-five yards. Shooting the driver at less than ten yards wasn't even a challenge. Quick as a snake, he raised the Desert Eagle and fired. His first bullet penetrated the officer's body armor an inch above his sternum. An instant later his next shot exploded the officer's head.

The second patrolman ducked behind the other side of the cruiser. His weapon was drawn and he was bringing it into play. Dr. Cole shot him through the windshield before he could fire, striking him in the left shoulder. A second round finished him off.

It was over in seconds.

The noise of the Desert Eagle had been deafening. Dr. Cole's ears were ringing. He had never fired the weapon without ear protection. Absently, he wondered whether he might have damaged his hearing. Deciding to worry about that later, he glanced up and down the street. He spotted a car one block down, turning left on Pico. Otherwise nothing. Maybe his luck would hold.

Noting a video camera on the black-and-white's dashboard, he stepped over the fallen driver and leaned into the cruiser, locating the trunk-release button on the dashboard. Using the muzzle of his pistol, he pushed the button, hearing the trunk-latch click at the rear of the car.

Walking quickly, he moved to the back of the vehicle. A search of the trunk located the video-log hard drive, as described on the LAPD website. Careful not to leave fingerprints, he removed it.

Was he forgetting anything?

Think!

No time. He had to leave.

Dr. Cole gazed at the dead officers, amazed at the destruction he'd inflicted with just a few rounds. The cop who had been talking on the radio lay crumpled against the passenger door, his chest covered with blood, his left arm almost separated from his body by the initial round he'd taken. The cop whom Dr. Cole had headshot was barely recognizable as human.

Another vehicle was approaching, still a block away.

Time to leave.

With one last look at the police cruiser, Dr. Cole climbed into his Expedition, restarted the engine, and drove away. Two blocks farther down Bundy, when he was certain no one was following, he redonned his sunglasses and turned on his headlights.

Seconds later he was gone.

Chapter Twenty-One

I arrived at the Santa Monica Canyon crime scene in just over twenty minutes. By then police vehicles had blocked off both ends of the residential neighborhood, with several more parked in front of a two-story house down the road.

I badged my way past the blockade and signed in with an officer keeping the crime-scene log, who at the moment was also busy stringing yellow Police-Line-Do-Not-Cross tape around the area. Two patrol officers lay sprawled on the sidewalk. One had been nearly cut in half by a bullet strike. The other was almost as bad. A crowd of residents had gathered across the street—some being interviewed by police officers, others simply staring at the mangled bodies.

My initial impression was that both of our officers had been hit with something massive, like an artillery round. Whatever had struck them, the projectiles had passed completely through their upper torsos, blasting through both front and back of their ballistic vests and leaving incredible damage in their wake. Blood had soaked through their uniforms on both sides and was collecting in a growing pool on the sidewalk.

As I was getting an initial report from one of the first officers to respond, other members of the sniper task force began showing up, including Dondero from Robbery-Homicide, Jules Jacoby from Venice, and Lieutenants Long and Snead. I hadn't seen Deluca yet, but I figured he would be arriving shortly.

The mood was one of absolute shock and disbelief. For once, even Lieutenant Snead had nothing irritating to say. Assembling on the sidewalk, we held a quick conference to decide how best to proceed. Although the shootings had occurred in Santa Monica Canyon—technically in Los Angeles County and not West Los Angeles or Santa Monica—it was decided that to maintain continuity on the sniper investigation, I would act as the primary investigator. Assistance would be provided by other task-force members as needed, which suited me fine. At the moment I didn't need any help, so I asked that everyone stay outside the tape, including both lieutenants—diplomatically suggesting that those who wanted to assist could join the patrol officers across the street taking witnesses' statements. Too many cooks, as the saying goes.

I also requested that area residents be moved farther back, in case there was still an unexploded bomb or bombs on the property. The latter suggestion quickly convinced Snead that his talents could best be used elsewhere.

From accounts given by officers on the scene, the sequence of events was as follows: At approximately 12:20 a.m., an explosion in the front yard of the house behind me had roused the neighborhood. Shrapnel had struck nearby homes and a number of vehicles on the street, punching holes in walls and blowing out windshields.

Numerous 911 reports had been phoned in, resulting in a patrol response within eleven minutes of the explosion. Upon arrival the responding officers—Patrolmen John Wolfe and Roger Oliphant—had exited their vehicle and approached a group of residents on the sidewalk. According to witnesses, Officer Oliphant had staggered forward, as if someone had punched him in the back. Blood sprayed from the front of his uniform. Officer Wolfe turned and was struck in the chest. At that point residents heard the sound of a shot. Seconds later the crack of another shot echoed through the canyon. No one was able to localize the origin, except to say that the shots had seemed to come from an easterly direction.

Residents had scattered in panic. More 911 calls had drawn a full LAPD response, including me.

I made a mental note to have our SID team comb the area for shrapnel. The bomb, or what was left of it, might be able to tell us something about the man who had made it.

Before I began my examination of the scene, I took a moment to consider the implication of the several-second sound delay. I glanced across the canyon, concluding that the sniper had probably fired from the southeastern ridge, a distance of possibly a mile. I decided to send units to the ridge to canvass the ridgeline neighborhood and search for the firing position. I would want to recover the bullets too, maybe try to identify the weapon. But whatever weapon the sniper had used, one thing was clear: as Agent Wyatt had predicted, our shooter was upping his game.

My phone vibrated. I checked the caller. Deluca. I thumbed the answer button. "Where are you, Paul?" I asked, surprised he hadn't already arrived.

"West L.A., South Bundy Drive," he answered. "I was on my way to Santa Monica Canyon when I got another call. Two more of our guys caught it up here."

"Are they . . ."

"Yeah. Both of them."

I felt a sinking sensation in the pit of my stomach. I knew both of the officers sprawled on the sidewalk nearby. Back in my drinking days I had downed more than a few beers with Wolfe, and over the years Oliphant and I had talked regarding various cases. Both were good men.

I wondered whether I knew the officers killed on South Bundy Drive. I have always tried to compartmentalize my investigations; in my line of work, you have to. As the sniper case progressed, that was getting harder and harder to do.

"According to dispatch, our guys pulled over a green Expedition," Deluca continued. "The plates matched those on the Expedition we caught on the Mulholland traffic cam after the Sherman Oaks shooting. Apparently our men stumbled onto the killer, and he just blew them away. Neither of our guys got off a shot."

"Witnesses?"

"Not so far. No dash-cam record, either. Our shooter took the video log."

"He opened the trunk and took the hard drive?"

"Yeah. He seems to know something about police work."

I paused a second to let that sink in. "Who, uh . . ."

"Bill Doyle and John Knapp," Deluca answered, anticipating my question. "I knew them both, Dan. Hell, I was an usher at Bill's wedding."

"I knew them, too," I said, again thinking that the case was getting personal. And as a friend had once told me, that's when things go wrong.

"I've got my hands full here," Deluca said. "You have things covered on your end?"

"Yeah. Half the task force showed up, including Snead. I have all the help I need, if you can call it that. I'll . . . I'll see you later at the meeting."

"Right," said Deluca. Hearing something in my voice, he added, "We're going to get this guy, Dan."

After hanging up, I stood for a moment gazing at the glittering lights across the canyon. I tried to imagine the man who had hidden on that distant ridge and ended the lives of two police officers almost a mile away. Why?

I came up with nothing.

Nothing, that is, except the realization that what we were doing to find him wasn't working.

*   *   *

Now that it was over, Dr. Cole took a moment to consider his situation. His careful preparation for the evening had nearly been ruined by a chance traffic stop—which was what the encounter on Bundy must have been. Of course, the cops might have checked his plates and discovered they were stolen, but why would they have been checking his plates in the first place? He hadn't been speeding, or otherwise breaking any laws. Well, not any laws *they* knew about. No, it had to have simply been bad luck. There could be no other explanation.

As usual, he had been wearing his ball cap and sunglasses, once again proving it never hurt to take precautions. He didn't think he had been seen, but one never knew. One thing was certain: he was finished driving the Expedition. The cop on the radio had undoubtedly reported it, and the police would now be on the lookout. He had to get rid of it.

But how?

He had repeatedly backtracked as he neared his storage garage on Centinela, making certain he wasn't being followed. Finally satisfied, he had turned into the storage yard, punched in the gate code, and driven inside. Moments later he had pulled into his oversized storage unit and secured the roll-up door behind him.

What now?

Everything had changed.

On the positive side, he hadn't been caught. He had removed the video log from the police vehicle, so there was no record left for the police to study. He had been wearing dark glasses and a ball cap, making it unlikely that a chance observer could identify him. And the ringing in his ears had finally stopped—although they still felt like they were stuffed with cotton. He hoped that would go away, too. Maybe he hadn't damaged his hearing after all.

On the downside, he needed to get rid of the Expedition. He briefly considered driving it somewhere and setting it on fire, or submerging it in water, or something similar. Unfortunately, that would entail taking the vehicle back out on the street, and that was not an option.

Next he considered wiping down the Expedition and simply abandoning it in the storage space, or possibly even lighting it on fire. Then he had a better idea. Although removing every fingerprint and any other trace evidence from the interior of the car would be almost impossible, thoroughly cleaning the outside of the Expedition *was* feasible. And removing trace evidence from the storage unit itself would be easy, as he had made a point to touch very little in the storage space itself. The explosive device fixed to the frame of his Expedition would take care of the rest.

He had originally installed the bomb as a security measure, ensuring that he would never suffer the indignity of being arrested—at least not while he was driving. The flick of a switch under the dashboard and he would cease to exist. With any luck, he might even take a few more cops with him as well.

Now he had a better use for his bomb.

With some rewiring, he could leave a surprise for the police when they eventually stumbled across his car. An anonymous phone call in a week or so might even help them in their search.

What about his guns?

No, he decided. He still had things to do, things for which he needed his weapons. He would get rid of them when he was finished, not before.

He glanced at his watch, deciding he needed to get started. It was late, and he had to be finished in time to walk back to his motel before dawn.

He had a lot of work to do.

Chapter Twenty-Two

On Monday morning I arrived at the Police Administration Building at 6:45 a.m., driving directly from the Santa Monica Canyon crime scene. Even at that early hour, a fleet of news vans was nearly blocking the First Street entrance. Reporters and camera crews were jamming the sidewalk, as usual taping daily updates with LAPD headquarters in the background. As I waded through the media crowd outside, ignoring shouted questions from all directions, I decided it was time to see whether I could start using the reserved parking facilities beneath the building, rather than leaving my car in the parking structure down the street. Chances were slim, but it wouldn't hurt to ask.

The task-force briefing started on time, as usual. As at the murder site, the atmosphere in the room was one of shock and frustration and anger. Snead began the meeting with a bit of good news: Dom LeBlanc, the officer who had survived the attack in Sherman Oaks, was out of intensive care and expected to live.

From there things went progressively downhill.

At Snead's request, I summarized my findings at the Santa Monica Canyon crime scene. I didn't have much to report, as the sniper had again left little in the way of trace evidence. After covering the basics, I paid special attention to the two areas in which the sniper had varied his pattern—setting off a bomb instead of calling 911, and shooting from a much greater distance than before.

The SID team had recovered fragments of the bomb, which appeared to be a homemade device fashioned from a length of two-inch galvanized pipe, capped at both ends. A field test done on explosive residue at the site showed the presence of nitrocellulose, an ingredient in the smokeless powder commonly used as a propellant in firearm cartridges. In the hope that the explosive might be traceable, the lab was currently using gas chromatography to perform a more accurate test. Fingerprints can occasionally be lifted from bomb remnants, but because of the distorted condition of our recovered fragments, that possibility seemed unlikely. Still, it was being checked.

We had found shards of a cell phone, too, probably part of a detonator used to remotely trigger the explosion. Also recovered were two 750-grain bullets, each of which had passed completely through the murdered officers, the brick facing of a nearby home, and several interior walls before coming to rest.

"Hold on a sec, Kane," said Madison. "The subsonic bullet our sniper used on his earlier shoots weighed 240 grains, and that was considered heavy, right? Now he's using a 750-grain bullet? That's, what—three times heavier? What's he shooting, a bazooka?"

"Just about," I answered. "On the drive in this morning, I made a call to Agent Wyatt. He thinks our sniper has graduated to using a .50 caliber round, most likely something called a .50 BMG. It's a cartridge originally manufactured for a Browning .50 caliber machine gun. It's now being used in long-range sniper weapons as well. A .50 BMG is basically a scaled-up version of a .30-06 rifle cartridge, but five times as powerful. Hornady makes one that shoots a 750-grain bullet. Sierra manufactures a handloading bullet in the same weight, too. Wyatt said that .50 BMGs have been used in Afghanistan with confirmed kills at over 2,500 yards."

Snead made an entry in his notebook.

"Wyatt thinks we should look into .50 caliber rifle sales on this one," I continued. "There aren't that many companies making weapons chambered in .50 BMG—ArmaLite, Barrett, a couple others—so we might have better luck with that particular approach than we've had in the past."

"Did you locate the sniper's firing position?" asked Murphy.

"I did," I answered. "He shot from across the canyon. Parked in the driveway of a house for sale. An initial estimate of the distance is almost a mile. Witnesses didn't even hear the first shot until the second bullet arrived."

"Jesus," someone whispered.

Snead made another entry in his notebook. "Anything else, Kane?"

I thought a moment, then shook my head. Lack of sleep was beginning to catch up with me. "I wish I had more, but that's it for now."

"Fine. Have a copy of your crime report available for distribution at tomorrow's meeting."

Deluca went next, summarizing his findings on South Bundy Drive. His report was even shorter than mine. Per the BOLO notice, Officers Knapp and Doyle had stopped a green Expedition being driven by a Caucasian or Hispanic male—having first determined that the plates didn't match the vehicle. Officer Doyle had been on the radio at the time. According to the dispatch officer with whom Doyle had been talking, seconds after Knapp and Doyle had pulled over the Expedition, it sounded like all hell had broken loose.

Detectives in the room stirred uneasily as Deluca described the grisly results of the shooting, undoubtedly recalling their own patrol days and realizing how easily it could have happened to one of them. In addition, I think many of us were wondering whether an "exercise extreme caution" advisory had ever been added to the Expedition BOLO, as I'd requested. I started to ask but stopped, deciding I already knew the answer.

Deluca wound up his report by noting that the dispatch officer reported hearing four loud explosions, as did area residents. Bullets recovered at the scene were .50 caliber, 300-grain projectiles. Two of the copper-jacketed, hollow-point bullets were suitable for ballistic comparison, if we found the weapon. No one in the area had seen the shooter.

"What about the dash-cam?" asked one of the Robbery-Homicide detectives.

"He took the video log," Deluca answered.

After a moment of silence, someone muttered, "How would he know to do that? Are we talking about a cop here?"

For once Snead said something reasonable. "Let's not go down that road again. We've already covered that possibility. It's common knowledge that our hard drives are stored in the trunk. It's on the LAPD website describing our latest COBAN webcam update, for chrissake."

"Maybe, but still . . ." someone else grumbled, not sounding convinced.

"Anyway, we're still canvassing the neighborhood," Deluca concluded, winding it up. "Someone may have seen our guy, but because the shooting took place in the underpass, we're not hopeful."

"At least now we know there's only one shooter," someone pointed out. "Not a team, like in D.C. That's something."

"And he's white or Hispanic," Detective Aguilar added. "Probably."

"What are the chances he'll keep driving the Expedition?" asked someone else.

"In my opinion, pretty much zero," Deluca answered. "From what we've seen so far, he's too smart for that. He'll get rid of it."

"Get rid of it where?" I asked, realizing the best investigative lead we'd had was now gone, but hoping to salvage something.

"What was that, Kane?" Snead demanded.

"I asked where would he get rid of it," I repeated. "Unless he spent hours eliminating every bit of trace evidence, which is pretty much impossible, he's too smart to just park it under a tree and walk away."

"Kane, we don't have—"

"I think I see where Kane is going," Dondero interrupted. "Let him speak."

Snead shot Dondero a look of irritation. "Fine. Make it fast, Kane."

"Okay, look," I said. "Imagine you're the mutt who's shooting our guys. You boost an Expedition and equip it with guns and stolen plates and whatever. A rolling sniper platform, like Agent Wyatt said. To be safe, you're operating at some distance from your home. Your greatest window of danger, aside from the actual shootings, is when you're driving your sniper vehicle to and from your kill sites. To minimize the risk of being stopped with a sniper rifle in the back, as appears to have happened last night, you need someplace to store your car, someplace closer to your kill sites, so—"

"—you rent a storage garage," Detective Murphy finished.

"This is just guesswork," Snead objected. "Even if you're right, Kane, where would we start looking?"

"He was probably on his way back last night when he got pulled over," I reasoned. "I think his storage yard might be someplace close."

Snead looked doubtful. "I hate to burst your bubble, but I know that area. The shooting on Bundy took place near a Santa Monica Freeway on-ramp. How do we know he wasn't about to get on the freeway and drive another twenty miles?"

"Nothing's for certain, Lieutenant. But if he had wanted to get on the freeway, he could have used the Pacific Coast Highway on-ramp, which is a lot closer to the shooting site. Why would he drive all the way across town to use the one on Bundy?"

"It's still guesswork," Snead said.

"Right now it's all we've got," Dondero pointed out.

"All right, we'll put two teams checking storage yards," Snead said grudgingly. "As we're *assuming* he was driving to this *supposed* storage site, we'll concentrate on the area east of the underpass. Kane and Deluca, you work the southern quadrant; Dondero, you and your partner take the northern section. Now, does anyone else have any suggestions before I go downstairs and attempt some damage control?"

Detective Garrison spoke up. "I've had some experience with storage lot investigations, Lieutenant. Most of them have video surveillance, but there are privacy issues involved. We will probably run into search-warrant problems."

Snead nodded. "We'll have to be careful regarding 'fruit of the poison tree' issues, too," he said, referring to the legal doctrine stating that any evidence gathered as a result of an improper search is itself also inadmissible. "When we get this guy to trial, we don't want trouble with our evidence," he added. "I'll need to check with the D.A."

"This guy ain't getting to trial," someone muttered in the back.

Ignoring the comment, Snead asked, "Anyone else?"

Eli Cooper, one of the detectives from the Van Nuys Division, spoke up. "I've been thinking about what the FBI profile guy said. You know, about establishing a dialogue with our shooter. How about leaking some of the profile? It's not doing us much good as it is, and it might just get the guy talking."

Several detectives nodded in agreement.

"Not an option," said Snead. "We can't appear to have leaks in our investigation. Besides, I didn't see anything in the profile that would get our guy talking."

"Then instead of a leak, how about we *release* part of the profile," Cooper persisted. "Maybe tweak it a little," he added. "Ask the public to be on the lookout for, I don't know . . . whatever."

Snead shook his head. "That's a decision above your pay grade, Cooper. I'll run it by the brass. Anyone else?"

"I have a question," I said, addressing Assistant Director Shepherd, who still occasionally attended our meetings and was present that morning. "Director Shepherd, if I remember correctly, your agency did a search for similar cop shootings. I don't remember any mention in your report of a murder in Simi Valley about a year ago. An ex-cop named Strom."

Shepherd conferred with an agent sitting beside him. "We looked into that incident and rejected it on several counts," he finally replied. "First, Strom was an *ex*-police officer who had not been on active duty since the previous year. Second, he was killed with a pistol, not a rifle. Last and probably most important, the shooter was arrested, convicted, and is presently serving time in Tehachapi State Prison. He couldn't be our man."

By then I had done some research on my own. The *Los Angeles Times* had run a story on the shooting, originally reporting that ex-cop Joseph Strom had been shot in the head with a rifle. Later at trial the prosecution had argued that the murder weapon was actually a Smith & Wesson .44 Magnum Model 29 revolver, although corroborating ballistic evidence was never introduced.

"Nevertheless, it might be worth looking into," I persisted. "I have a feeling there's more to—"

"As I said before, we're not running this investigation based on your *feelings*, Kane," Snead interrupted.

"Lieutenant, I—"

"What part of 'no' didn't you understand?" Snead demanded. "We have plenty of work to do without heading off on a wild-goose chase. Hotline tips have *tripled* since last weekend," he added with disgust, glancing around the room. "I have to go downstairs right now and try to explain to the media why we haven't caught this guy yet. You all know what you're *supposed* to be doing. I suggest you do it."

*   *   *

At that moment in the CBS Studio Center newsroom, Allison Kane was receiving a similar lecture from bureau chief Lauren Van Owen. "Damn it, Allison," Lauren snapped. "I thought we had covered that problem. We're in the news business. We report the news and let the chips fall where they may."

"This is different," Allison countered. "There's a line between responsible reporting and running a story that could get another cop killed. Brent is about to cross that line."

"I disagree," said Brent Preston, who was standing nearby. "Letting people know to be on the lookout for a green Expedition could actually *help* authorities catch the sniper."

"If that were the case, don't you think the police would have already put out the word?" Allison countered.

"I don't pretend to know what the cops are thinking," Brent said smugly. "I just do my job."

"Have you contacted the sniper task force for corroboration?"

Brent shrugged. "Didn't need to. I got corroboration from two other sources. Besides, the task force would have just asked me to kill the story, and that's not going to happen."

"You should at least give them a chance to—"

"I'll give the LAPD a courtesy call prior to airing," Brent interrupted. "If they have a comment, they can make it then."

Allison shook her head. "I don't think that's giving them enough notice, Brent."

"Listen, Ali," Lauren broke in. "Network made the decision on how to handle this. The story will run as scheduled. Anyway, now that the word is out, if we don't report it, someone else will."

"But—"

"No buts. Brent will air the Expedition story on a national newsbreak at noon. In the meantime, I think you have a webcast to do?"

Allison started to object, but something in Lauren's tone made her think better of it. "Yes, ma'am," she said instead, not satisfied with the conversation but uncertain where to go from there.

For the next twenty minutes, as Allison prepared for her morning webcast, she wrestled with her conscience. She had to admit that Lauren had a point. If Brent didn't air the Expedition story, someone else would. Eventually. She also had to admire Brent's connections in the police department, as well as the tenacity he'd displayed in running down the Expedition lead.

On the other hand, Allison had followed enough of her father's cases over the years to know that Brent's revelation could seriously impact the sniper investigation. Bottom line, lives were at stake. If another police officer were killed because of Brent's newscast, could she justify that death by telling herself the public had a right to know?

Coming to a decision, Allison told her producer that she was stepping outside for a few minutes to get some air. When she was well clear of the building, Allison withdrew her cell phone from her purse. She hesitated. What she was about to do would get her fired if her actions were ever discovered.

Still, she had no choice.

Chapter Twenty-Three

Following Monday's task-force meeting, I received a surprise call from my daughter. She advised me that Brent Preston was about to break a story on the green Expedition, adding that we could expect a last-minute confirmation call from CBS prior to the story's airing at noon. After some consideration, I decided the best outcome for the task force would be for me to warn Snead—giving him a chance to do something before the story aired.

I caught up with Snead just as he was walking into the morning news briefing. It took a lot of talking to convince him. Eventually, however, he came to the conclusion that it would be preferable for us to reveal the Expedition story ahead of time, beating CBS to the punch. We would still appear to be in control, and Snead could avoid having to explain a leak to the brass. As an added bonus, I liked the idea of torpedoing Brent's exclusive report.

Despite Snead's orders to the contrary, I then returned to the task-force conference room and did some additional research on ex-cop Joseph Strom, including a call to the LAPD detective who had originally investigated Strom's murder. Afterward I joined Deluca and spent several hours compiling a list of storage yards we planned to visit later that day. Because of the surprisingly large number in the area, we decided to limit our search quadrant to an area south of LAX, reasoning that we could extend our canvass later as necessary.

We made a point of calling as many storage yards as possible, saying we planned to visit later and ask for assistance on a case. I wanted to sidestep the search-warrant issue that Garrison had mentioned in the meeting, and I've found the best way to do that is by avoiding a frontal assault. Most people are willing to help if you approach them correctly. If that didn't work, I'd drop the carrot and try the stick. In either case, police officers were being shot, and we didn't have time for warrants—even if we could get them.

During that time I also talked with a number of other task-force detectives, getting candid updates they weren't willing to share at the 7:00 a.m. meeting. As I'd thought, over half our unit was currently engaged in investigating hotline tips. So far those avenues had all proved to be dead ends. Several detectives were still working the gunsmith and cartridge-reloading angle, and with the FBI's assistance, we were developing extensive lists of names that could prove useful . . . *if* we had a suspect. Several detective pairs were investigating sniper schools, returning veterans, and so on, but everyone was coming up cold. Recently Snead had even requested the loan of several military drones like the ones used in the D.C. Beltway case, which sounded to me like an act of desperation. Bottom line, we didn't have squat.

Deluca and I grabbed lunch downtown, then spent the rest of the afternoon visiting storage facilities in West Los Angeles, Santa Monica, and Culver City. Most of the yard managers with whom we dealt were cooperative, allowing us to view their most recent security tapes and promising copies of earlier recordings, if available.

By the time the day was over, I was exhausted. Not getting much sleep the previous night had taken its toll. Following a quick dinner with Catheryn and Nate, I crawled into bed early and fell into a deep, dreamless sleep.

Later that night I was awakened by the sound of someone knocking on our front door. Catheryn rolled over in bed beside me. "Definitely not for me," she mumbled.

I glanced at the clock: 12:15 a.m. With a groan, I rolled out from under the covers, pulled on a robe, and walked barefoot to the entry. Wondering who could be calling that late, I peered out a side window.

Actor Jeff Grant was standing on our front landing. He looked even worse than he had when I'd visited him at his home.

When I opened the door, Mr. Grant was just starting to leave. He turned back, seeming embarrassed. "I . . . I'm sorry, Detective Kane," he mumbled, slurring his words. "Didn't mean to wake you. I just . . . I wanted to apologize for the other day."

I looked closely at Mr. Grant. He seemed upset, his eyes red-rimmed and swollen. He had definitely been drinking. "Are you okay?" I asked.

"Yeah, I'm fine. I'm sorry to show up on your doorstep like this. I was driving around and I . . . I don't know what I was thinking."

"Come inside for a sec. I'll make you some coffee."

"No," he said quickly, swaying on his feet. "Thanks, but I should be going."

"Please come in," I insisted. "You've had a few, and I'm a cop, remember? You shouldn't be driving. It's either come inside or I'll have to arrest you," I added with a smile, but with an edge to my voice as well.

He hesitated. Then he seemed to deflate. "I'm really sorry about this," he repeated numbly, stepping inside.

"Not a problem," I said, closing the door behind him.

"Dan, who is it?" Catheryn called from the bedroom.

Mr. Grant froze, again seeming embarrassed.

"It's a friend," I called back. Sensing Mr. Grant's discomfort, I took his arm and led him into the kitchen. "Everything's okay, Kate. I'll be in soon," I added, seating Mr. Grant at our kitchen table.

Curious about Mr. Grant's late-night presence, I busied myself making a pot of coffee. It's a misconception that coffee sobers people up; actually, it just makes for a wide-awake drunk. Now that I'd had a good look at Mr. Grant, I could see I'd made the right decision in bringing him inside. He was definitely over the limit.

Mr. Grant sat quietly, staring out the window at the beach. As the smell of coffee began drifting into the kitchen, he took a deep breath, then slowly let it out. "I want to apologize for what I said when you came to our house to ask about Chet. Do you . . . do you remember our conversation?"

I sat across from him at the table. "I told Chet's wife that I knew how you all must feel, and that I sincerely wished I didn't have to be there. You asked why I was there, saying you had told officers from Venice everything you knew when they visited after your son was shot. Next you said you'd seen me on TV at the task-force announcement, and that as for my knowing how you felt, you doubted that was possible. Then you told me to ask my questions and get things over with."

Mr. Grant regarded me curiously. "Sounds almost verbatim."

I shrugged. "I have a good memory."

Mr. Grant lowered his gaze. "After you left, I looked you up online. I read about your son, Tommy. I'm sorry for my rudeness, Detective Kane. And I'm so sorry for your loss. I didn't know. I was wrong to say what I did." He raised his eyes to mine. "You do know how I feel," he said, his voice trembling.

"Yeah, I do," I replied. I thought about getting up and pouring the coffee, giving Mr. Grant a moment to compose himself. But I didn't. At that moment, turning away from him somehow didn't seem . . . honest.

"I know *exactly* how you feel," I said instead, deciding to open up to this man I hardly knew, but with whom I had so much in common. I thought a moment, trying to put my feelings into words. "I know you never thought life could hurt so much," I said. "I know you blame yourself for your son's death. And I know you keep thinking that if only you'd done something differently, your son might still be alive."

I hesitated and then went on, unable to stop now that I had started. "There are times when you can't hear his name or see his picture without feeling your heart is going to break," I said gently. "You wish you could remember the good parts of his life, but all you can think of now is that he's gone. There are so many things you wish you could say to him, now that it's too late to tell him how you feel."

I paused again, then continued softly. "I also know that once in a while you're not certain you want to go on living, and that sometimes, when you're alone, you cry."

Mr. Grant lowered his head. "I'm so sorry," he said.

I stood and put a hand on his shoulder. "I am too, Mr. Grant. More than I can say."

"After all this, please call me Jeff," he mumbled, palming his eyes.

"Fine, Jeff," I said. "I'm Dan to my friends."

He nodded. "Jesus, look at me," he said, wiping his nose on his sleeve. "I'm a mess."

"You want some coffee?" I asked.

Jeff smiled weakly. "Only if it has bourbon in it. Lots of bourbon."

"Take my word for it, booze isn't going to help," I advised, thinking back to my own dark times after losing Tommy.

"Just kidding," Jeff replied. "Sort of. I know I've already had plenty to drink. More than plenty. I will definitely feel like shit tomorrow," he added, glancing at his watch. "Make that later this morning. Anyway, I . . . I should be getting home. Rita is probably wondering where I am."

"I'll drive you," I said. "Someone can pick up your car tomorrow."

"I'll call a cab. Don't worry, Dan. I'm not gonna get behind the wheel like this."

"You mean again," I corrected.

"Right. Again," Jeff said sheepishly.

"I'll drive you," I insisted. "It's not that far. Besides, this late at night it'll take forever to get a cab out here, if one will come at all."

"Okay. I . . . I appreciate it."

"Glad to help." Then, holding his gaze a moment longer, I added, "You're going to be okay. I'm not saying this is something you'll get over, because you won't. But you will be okay. And if you ever want to talk, I'm always available."

Jeff nodded.

"Actually, let's change 'always available' to 'usually available before ten at night,'" I suggested with a smile.

"Fair enough. And Dan?"

"Yeah?"

"Thanks."

Chapter Twenty-Four

So the psychiatrist flips over the next Rorschach inkblot card and says, 'How about this one?'"

Deluca smiled, as usual enjoying his own joke more than the material warranted. "The kid glances over at his dad sitting beside him, then back at the psychiatrist. 'Looks like another naked lady to me,' he says. 'Just like all them other cards you showed me.'"

I cut the wheel and turned into a self-service storage yard just off Centinela, the third we had visited that morning. On the way in I noticed several security cameras—one covering the entrance gate, another pointed down a long row of storage units. More were visible atop a fence circling the lot.

"The psychiatrist turns to the dad and says, 'Sir, I'm afraid your son harbors an abnormal obsession with sex.'" Deluca chuckled, heading into the punch line. "'My *son* is obsessed with sex?' says the father. '*You're* the one showing him all them dirty pictures!'"

"Good one, Paul," I laughed, pulling into a parking space next to an office near the front. "Which reminds me, I need to take off early this afternoon. Kate and I have a meeting with Nate's high-school counselor."

"Everything okay?"

"I don't know," I sighed, killing the engine. "I wish I could say that Nate just has a bad case of teen angst, but Kate thinks it's more than that. Maybe she's right."

"Tough age," Deluca said.

"Yeah. I got in a few scrapes myself in high school. I don't mind the kid sticking up for himself, but he seems to be getting into trouble every time he turns around. Plus his grades are slipping. He's a great kid, but something's wrong. I want to help him so bad it's killing me. I just don't know what to do."

Deluca thought a moment. "Do you think what happened during the break-in at your house has anything to do with it?" he asked gently.

Some years back, two men had broken into our house in Malibu. At the time Catheryn had been rehearsing with the Philharmonic, and I had been unexpectedly called back to the station, leaving Nate and Allison at home alone. In the course of the robbery, Allison had been brutally attacked. In an effort to help his sister, nine-year-old Nate had retrieved my off-duty service weapon from a closet shelf. The intruders hadn't counted on a weapon being in the house, or realized the danger that it posed—even in the hands of a child. One of the men had fled. The other had bled to death with a .38-caliber-sized hole in his femoral artery.

"I don't know," I sighed. "It's a lot for a kid to carry around. Hell, most guys we work with have never fired their weapon in a work situation, let alone taken a life. We got Nate counseling afterward, which seemed to help. At least the nightmares went away. Then he refused to go anymore. He won't talk about it, either."

"Well, I hope he gets back on track," said Deluca. "Nate is a great kid. If there's anything I can do, please keep me in the loop."

"Thanks, Paul."

"At least Ali is doing well," Deluca went on. "Speaking of which, she sure came through with that Expedition tip. We were already looking bad enough in the press without having a major leak like that. Saved Snead's ass, too. Did you get any juice on that one?"

"A little, not that it will make much difference," I answered glumly. "Snead has a short memory. Before long I'll be butting heads with him again about the ex-cop who caught a bullet in Simi Valley."

"That would be the lead he ordered you to drop?"

"That's the one. Joseph Strom, ex-LAPD. I've got a feeling about it, Paul. I called the medical examiner's office and talked with the coroner who did the post. He remembered the case. I had him look it up just to be certain, and he's sending over the autopsy results. Bottom line, Strom died of massive cranial damage, most likely caused by a large-diameter bullet. There was barely enough left of his head to be recognizable as human. Sound familiar?"

"Yeah. They find the bullet?"

"Nope. The prosecution later contended that the shot was fired from a Smith & Wesson .44 Magnum revolver owned by the defendant. Although in his original report the coroner concluded that the shot came from a high-powered rifle, at trial he couldn't rule out a pistol having been used."

"And the jury bought it. You think they made a mistake?"

"I think it's worth looking into," I answered, stepping from the car. "C'mon, let's do this."

"Right." Deluca exited his side of the vehicle, looking pensive.

"What?" I asked.

"Just be careful with Snead," he warned. "I think there's a reason he wanted you on his task force, and it wasn't because of your sunny disposition."

"Yeah, I know. He would love to get me canned. We already had that talk," I grumbled, starting for the office. "Don't worry, I can handle Snead." Then, pointedly changing the subject, I asked, "Is this one of the lots we called yesterday?"

Deluca checked his notebook. "We called. Nobody answered. We left a message."

Most of the storage yards we'd visited during the past several days had twenty-four-hour access, with keypad gates and surveillance cameras comprising their main security measures. Video recording equipment at the yards varied from antiquated VHS tapes to state-of-the-art, motion-based digital recording with multiple hard-drive backups and cloud-based storage. Of those with the former, we usually sat and viewed the tapes, which was tedious, to say the least. The more modern setups enabled some of the yards to send their surveillance feed directly to our task-force computers, making our job a lot easier. Some of the sites saved their recordings for weeks, others just days, and we were progressively working against the clock.

"Let's see whether anyone's home," I suggested, knocking on the front door. No answer. I tried the handle. Locked. "Damn," I grumbled. "Doesn't anybody work in this town?"

"Apparently not," said Deluca. He withdrew a card from his wallet, wrote a note on the back, and stuck it in the doorframe. "Let's try again tomorrow."

On the way back to the car, Deluca got quiet again, which wasn't like him. "What?" I asked again, already knowing the answer.

"I'm worried, Dan," he said. "You've got that look, the one you get when you're gonna do what you're gonna do and the hell with everyone else. I wasn't kidding about Snead. I don't trust him. He could ruin your career, torpedo your pension—"

"I can handle Snead," I repeated.

"I hope so," Deluca sighed. "I truly do."

*   *   *

Later that afternoon I met Catheryn at Nate's high school, arriving a few minutes before our 4:00 p.m. appointment with the school counselor, a Ms. Blackburn. She turned out to be a pleasant woman in her early forties. She introduced herself and ushered us into her office with a smile. Catheryn and I sat across from her at her desk; Nate took a seat nearby. I could tell he was nervous but trying not to show it.

"So what's going on with Nate?" I asked bluntly, deciding to cut to the chase. For some reason I was nervous, too—maybe remembering my own high-school trips to the principal's office.

"My husband and I are both worried about Nate's grades," Catheryn added, shooting me a look that said she wanted to handle things. "Any suggestions you have would be welcome."

Ms. Blackburn referred to an open file on her desk. "We're concerned about Nate's grades, too," she began. "He is clearly capable of much better work than he's been doing, especially in English."

"I thought Ali was going to help you with that," I said, turning to Nate. "What happened?"

Nate didn't reply. He had his arms folded across his chest, looking bored.

"Damn it, Nate," I said, struggling to keep a grip on my temper. "I asked you a question."

"She is helping," he mumbled. "I'm doing better," he added, lifting his shoulders in a careless shrug.

"I'm afraid Nate's grades aren't our only concern," Ms. Blackburn continued.

"You mean the fights he's been getting into?" I asked, again looking at Nate. "I thought we were past that."

"There haven't been any fights *recently*," Ms. Blackburn admitted. "And in Nate's defense, the last instance involved several older boys who were bullying him. It was two against one, but both of the older boys were injured. We don't tolerate bullying, and we are handling that situation. Nevertheless—"

"They asked for it," said Nate.

"That may be, Nate," said Ms. Blackburn. "But fighting on school premises is not allowed. It's not an acceptable way to settle your differences."

"Wait a minute," I interrupted. "Nate didn't start the fight? Who threw the first punch?" For a moment I felt like the dad in Deluca's joke. I didn't want to defend Nate if he was wrong, but on the other hand I've always believed that the best way to handle a bully is to never back down.

"I don't think that's the point, Dan," said Catheryn. "There is more going on here than who threw the first punch."

Ms. Blackburn closed her file, looking uncomfortable. She hesitated, then glanced at Nate. "Nate, could you wait outside, please? I would like to talk to your parents for a few minutes."

Still looking bored, Nate shuffled out of the room, closing the door behind him.

After Nate had left, Ms. Blackburn folded her hands on her desk. "Mr. Kane, you asked what's going on with Nate. I'd like to ask you and your wife the same question."

"What do you mean?" asked Catheryn, seeming puzzled.

"Just that," Ms. Blackburn replied. "I've been a counselor here at the high school for a long time, and I know when

197

something isn't right with one of the students. Has Nate been using drugs?"

"Not that we know of," Catheryn answered. She glanced at me. "He did get in some trouble lately for underage drinking, and one of the boys with him had pot in his possession, but I don't think Nate smoked any."

"Have you had him tested?"

"No, but—"

"That would be a place to start," Ms. Blackburn interrupted. "If Nate has been experimenting with drugs, we definitely need to take that out of the equation."

"If Nate has been fooling around with drugs, I'll take *him* out of the equation," I muttered.

"Hush, Dan," said Catheryn. Then, to Ms. Blackburn, "We'll test Nate for drugs, as you suggest, although I don't think that's the problem."

"Unfortunately, Mrs. Kane, I don't think so, either. I think there is more going on with Nate than drug use. Has he ever seen a therapist, a professional who might be able to help?"

"Several years ago we took him to a psychologist in Westwood," Catheryn answered. "After a few visits he refused to go back."

"Hold on a second," I broke in. "Nate's having a few problems, but you're suggesting that he's, what, mentally disturbed?"

Ms. Blackburn sighed. "I don't know what's going on in your son's head, Mr. Kane," she said. "Being a teenager is tough for lots of youngsters. In Nate's case, I believe it's more than that. Whatever it is, I think he needs help."

Chapter Twenty-Five

Disturbed by our meeting at Nate's school but unsure of how to proceed, I spent Thursday morning visiting self-storage yards with Deluca, generally getting nowhere on that front, either. Skipping lunch, I told Deluca I was taking the afternoon off, advising him not to ask any questions. Giving me a look that said he hoped I knew what I was doing, he dropped me back in town, where I picked up my car from the First Street lot, hit the freeway, and headed north to the California Correctional Institution—otherwise known as Tehachapi State Prison.

Following my unauthorized research regarding the murder of ex-LAPD cop Joseph Strom, two aspects of the shooting had continued to bother me. I had spoken to the investigating officer, Detective Diego Silva, who understandably hadn't been happy to hear from me. No cop likes having someone second-guessing his arrests—especially on a case that has already gone to trial and is currently up on appeal. When I explained that I was doing background research on the L.A. Sniper killings, however, Detective Silva became more forthcoming. The sniper killings were affecting us all.

Detective Silva's summary of the Strom case went like this: On June 10 of the previous year, at approximately 5:30 a.m., a Simi Valley neighbor had discovered Joseph Strom dead in his car. Strom's Tahoe was sitting outside his garage at the time—the garage door open, the car engine still running. The driver's and passenger's windows were blown out. It looked like Strom's head had exploded inside the Tahoe, plastering bone and brain tissue across the dashboard, headliner, and front seat. There were no witnesses to the shooting. Although a bullet was never recovered, the coroner's report had listed the cause of death as massive cerebral tissue destruction, probably caused by a projectile fired from a high-powered rifle.

In searching for someone with a motive, the first line in any murder investigation, Detective Silva had quickly turned up two possible candidates: Albert Winslow, who worked security with

Strom at a Thousand Oaks mall, and Dr. Luther Cole, a retired dentist living in Three Rivers, California. Strom was having an affair with Winslow's wife. No mystery regarding motive there. Dr. Cole's situation was more complicated.

In April of the previous year, then LAPD Officer Strom had been involved in the shooting death of Dr. Cole's eighteen-year-old autistic son, Andrew. Although an LAPD internal review had eventually cleared Strom in the shooting, Andrew's parents had been bitterly vocal in the press, calling for a full investigation. When Strom was later fired for unrelated reasons, it was generally understood that the earlier shooting played a role in his dismissal.

Working with the Tulare County Sheriff's Department and members of the Three Rivers Police Department, Detective Silva had established that Dr. Cole had an airtight alibi for the time of the shooting—an alibi that was later exhaustively confirmed. From there the investigation had focused on the only remaining candidate at the time: Albert Winslow.

Winslow claimed he had been drinking at the time of the murder, a claim no one was able to corroborate. Strike one. Winslow was aware of Strom's affair with his wife, and several co-workers had heard Winslow threatening Strom on the morning of the shooting. Strike two. Winslow owned a Smith & Wesson .44 Magnum revolver, a weapon consistent with the wound to Strom's head. Gunshot residue on Winslow's hands and clothing showed he had recently fired a weapon. A credit-card payment at a Simi Valley gas station proved Winslow had been in the area of Strom's home on the evening of the murder. And at trial, the assistant D.A. prosecuting the case had pushed the coroner to admit that the bullet might have come from a .44 Magnum pistol, not a high-powered rifle as originally stated in his report. Strikes three, four, five, and six.

Not conclusive, as a ballistic match was never made to Winslow's pistol, but enough for a conviction of second-degree murder. End of story for Winslow.

As far as I was concerned, there were two loose ends. One, the lack of a bullet to tie Winslow's weapon to the murder.

Where had the bullet gone? Even a .44 magnum projectile should have slowed down enough after passing through two car windows and Strom's head to wind up someplace nearby. It didn't make sense, unless the bullet had come from a much more powerful weapon—say, a high-powered rifle—and had kept on going.

The second loose end was not as obvious, but it bothered me just as much. Like Strom, Albert Winslow was an ex-police officer. He might not have been the sharpest blade in the drawer, but as an ex-cop he should have at least made *some* attempt to cover his crime—get rid of his clothing, dump the gun, establish an alibi, wash his hands, get rid of his clothes—something. He had done nothing. It didn't add up.

I decided I needed to talk with Winslow.

After Tuesday morning's task-force meeting, I had called the warden's office at CCI, the prison where Winslow was incarcerated. I had identified myself and requested a private visitation booking with Winslow. I could have asked for a compulsory prisoner interrogation, but I didn't want to go that route—at least not if I didn't have to. Instead I asked that Winslow be told I was doing background research on a similar investigation, and that I was aware he had an appeal in progress—adding that there might be a dovetailing of the two cases. I also said that if he wanted, he could have his lawyer present for the interview.

Later that day I got visitation approval and a booking for 3:00 p.m. on Thursday.

All day Wednesday I had debated whether or not to tell Deluca. In the end I decided he would be better off not knowing, just in case things went wrong.

The drive to CCI took a little under two hours. It was located in Cummings Valley, just west of Tehachapi's ranches and wind farms. From past visits I knew CCI was a supermax facility, providing felon incarceration ranging from Level I dormitories with secure perimeters to a Level IV "Security Housing Unit" providing maximum-security incarceration for the most dangerous inmates. Winslow was currently being held in the

Level II facility, which like most of California's prisons was operating at almost three times design capacity.

Upon arrival, I parked my car in a visitors' lot and walked a short distance to the prison processing center. By then regular visiting hours were over, and the processing center was mostly deserted. After showing my ID, filling out a pass, and surrendering my service weapon to the visiting sergeant, I was taken by van to a small conference room a few minutes away. Prisoners known to have police visitors were often suspected by other inmates of being informants—a dangerous situation for any prisoner. For this reason I had asked that my interview with Winslow be held in private, and the warden had complied.

The windowless visiting room was furnished with a small metal table and two chairs. After about ten minutes Albert Winslow was led into the room in handcuffs. One of the correctional officers accompanying him raised his eyebrows and glanced at me. I nodded, indicating that it was okay to remove Winslow's cuffs.

Once his restraints were removed, Winslow sat across from me at the table, rubbing his wrists. Both correctional officers exited the room, one of them making a point to remind me on his way out that they would both be right outside the door.

Winslow was a large man, maybe fifty, fifty-five, with a weightlifter's physique that had turned to fat. His head was shaved, probably a new look since he'd been in lockup.

"No attorney?" I asked.

"Why would I call that douchebag?" Winslow grumbled. "He's the reason I'm in here."

"No argument there," I said, pleased that I wouldn't be dealing with Winslow's lawyer—not that it would make any difference in the long run. There was only one thing I wanted from Winslow, and intentionally or not, he was going to give it to me.

"So according to the warden, you're here to help?" Winslow said sarcastically.

"That depends on you, Albert. Before we start, let's get some ground rules established. First, you're free to leave anytime you want. This is not an interrogation, so I'm not going to Mirandize you," I said, referring to the requirement that someone in custody be advised of his or her right to remain silent, and so on.

"Yeah, yeah, I read that bogus *Howes v. Fields* decision," said Winslow. "Even though I'm in prison, I'm free to walk out of this room anytime, so I'm not technically in custody. What a load of crap."

I studied Winslow for a moment. Over time, necessity turned many prison inmates into jailhouse lawyers, but his knowledge of the controversial Supreme Court decision surprised me. "We're not going to talk about anything unrelated to your conviction," I said. "So it doesn't matter anyway, right?"

Winslow shrugged. "Whatever."

"Whatever? Damn, Albert, you sound like one of my kids."

Winslow shrugged again, staring at me suspiciously. "What exactly is it that you want?"

"Like I told the warden, I'm working on an investigation similar to yours. There are some things about your case that raised some red flags, at least with me."

"Gee, do you think?" he said bitterly.

"I know you have an appeal in the works—improperly admitted evidence, lack of evidence sufficient to support a guilty verdict, like that. Depending on what I hear today, I might be able to help you."

"I seriously doubt that, Kane."

I pointedly looked around the room, then back at Winslow. "What do you have to lose?"

"Okay," said Winslow, for the first time dropping his prison persona. "I'll give you my side. It's simple: I know everyone in here says they didn't do it, but I didn't."

"Fine. You talk; I'll listen. One thing, though. Don't lie to me. I'll know if you're lying, and if that happens, our talk is over."

For the next ten minutes Winslow gave me his version of the case, slowly opening up. According to his account, he had found out about his wife's affair with Strom earlier that week. It had burned a hole in his gut. Things hadn't been right with his wife for months, but her infidelity had caught him off guard. Worse, when confronted with the affair, she had refused to end it, threatening to take half of everything he was worth if he filed for divorce.

The morning of the shooting, Winslow had approached Strom at work. Strom had laughed in Winslow's face, demanding to know what he was going to do about the affair. Winslow had threatened to kill Strom in front of several co-workers, a mistake that had cost him dearly in court. That night he had drunk himself into a stupor and slept in his car. Two days later he had been arrested and charged with Strom's murder.

"What about the GSR exam?" I asked. The gunshot residue test had proved he'd recently fired a weapon, supposedly the Smith & Wesson .44 Magnum.

"What about it?" Winslow demanded. "I shoot targets in the desert all the time. I'd had the gun out the day before—not that anyone believed me."

"And your visit to a gas station near Strom's house on the night of the shooting?"

"That station is over *two miles* from Strom's place," Winslow said angrily. "I always fill up there."

In any police interrogation—which is what this was, despite what I had told Winslow—a police officer is allowed to use all methods at his disposal, including lying. So far I hadn't lied to Winslow. And when I'd told him I would know if he were lying, I was also telling the truth. I don't know how, but somehow I *know* when someone is lying to me. I don't know how; I just do. Sometimes it's a curse—like the way I can't seem to forget anything. But sometimes, like now, it wasn't.

"Let's back up a bit," I said patiently. "I hear what you're saying about being innocent and all, but my gut's telling me different. My gut is telling me you're lying about *something*. What is it?"

"Nothing, I swear," Winslow said, looking away.

The time had come to push. Hard. "I know you're lying," I said, rising from my chair. "I warned you not to bullshit me, Albert. Good luck with your appeal."

"Wait," said Winslow, for the first time completely dropping his mask. "Just . . . wait."

I sat back down. "You have something to tell me?"

Winslow hesitated. "Yeah," he said quietly. "You were right. But I wasn't exactly lying. I just left something out."

I sat without speaking, letting the silence grow between us.

"I left out that I wanted to kill that piece of shit," he said softly. "I swear to God, I wanted to put a bullet in him. And I was going to. I had the gun in the car that night to do it. I even drove out to his house."

"And?"

"And I couldn't," Winslow sighed. "Much as I wanted to, I just couldn't. I chickened out. I wound up getting a bottle instead and drinking myself into a stupor. I slept it off in my car and woke up the next morning with the worst hangover of my life. Two days later I was arrested. And here I am. I didn't even get the satisfaction of killing that bastard."

A chill ran up my spine. It had taken a while to get there, with a few detours along the way, but I had what I'd come for.

Winslow was telling the truth.

It wasn't anything that would stand up in court, but I knew I was right. Which meant that whoever had shot Joseph Strom was still out there.

And it looked like he was doing it again.

Chapter Twenty-Six

Deluca and I spent all of Friday and most of Saturday canvassing self-storage yards. By then we had extended our search area well past LAX, still with no results. Deluca had kept digging at me, too, asking where I'd gone on Thursday. I kept putting him off, but at lunch on Saturday I decided to bring him in—figuring there was nothing Snead could do to him for knowing after the fact about my visit to Tehachapi State Prison.

Deluca listened quietly as I recounted my trip, shaking his head when I finished. He was understandably doubtful that I'd discovered an innocent man in jail, as nearly all prisoners make that claim. Nevertheless, he trusted my instincts, and I finally convinced him that I was right.

"So where do we go from here?" he asked.

"*We* don't go anywhere, Paul," I answered. "At least not yet. No sense in both of us getting canned if Snead gets wind of this. Let me get a little further into it and see what develops."

"What about Albert Winslow?"

I sighed. "Tough situation. He nearly broke down when I told him I believed his story. Said I was the first one. Even his wife and lawyer thought he was guilty. I told him I'd do what I could, but not to get his hopes up."

"So what *are* you going to do?"

I hesitated, again not wanting to jeopardize Deluca's career if things went south. Besides, I wasn't certain myself. I'd asked Detective Silva to send me a copy of the Strom file, and I had reviewed it thoroughly. Afterward my belief was even stronger that the same man who had shot Joseph Strom was now killing LAPD police officers, and that a way to jump-start our investigation might be by looking at the earlier murder. It could have been our sniper's first killing, and maybe he'd been careless—at least more careless than he was being now.

"C'mon, Dan. I've lost friends to this guy, and I want him just as much as you do," Deluca insisted. "Talk."

Finally I relented. "Okay. But if this blows up, I want you in the clear," I said. "You don't know anything about this, understood?"

"Yeah, whatever. Spill it."

"I had the detective who worked Strom's murder send me his files."

"So after all this time, you're gonna reboot the Strom investigation? Did you tell the previous investigator he'd locked up the wrong guy?"

I shook my head. "No point. He'd never believe me. And yeah, I'm going to see where the first case leads—starting by taking a hard look at the other possible suspect in the murder. Some dentist up in Three Rivers."

"A *dentist*? How does that figure?"

"When Strom was on the job in Venice, he shot and killed the dentist's kid," I said. "Sounded like a bad shooting, but Strom walked on it. The kid's parents were understandably outraged. The dentist supposedly had an alibi for the time of the shooting, but I'd like to cross him off the list myself before going any further. By the way, I checked the dentist's name against the databases our FBI pals are assembling—sonic-suppressor purchasers, online handloading supply customers, and so on. Came up cold on all fronts. In any case, I still want to take a look at the guy. If nothing else, it's a place to start."

On Sunday, my single day off from task-force duty, I rose at dawn. Skipping my customary workout on the beach, I kissed Catheryn good-bye, telling her I had to leave for the day, but promising to be back that evening in time for Arthur's party.

After a stop in Santa Monica to pick up a large cup of Starbucks, I hit the 405 Freeway and headed north. Almost four hours later, after missing several turns and backtracking more than once, I arrived in the Sierra Nevada foothill town of Three Rivers, advertised by a roadside sign as "The Gateway to Sequoia National Park." It turned out most of the homes and businesses of Three Rivers followed the *five* forks of the Kaweah River, making me wonder about the town's name.

After talking with Albert Winslow at Tehachapi State Prison, I had contacted the Tulare County Sheriff's Department and spoken with the detective there who had worked the Strom murder. He remembered the investigation and referred me to a Three Rivers police officer named Luigi Montone, who had done most of the legwork on the case. Although Detective Montone had recently retired, he agreed to meet with me that weekend.

A check of the map got me headed in the right direction, and ten minutes later I pulled up in front of a modest single-story structure tucked away at the end of a long wooded driveway. Montone was cooking breakfast, or maybe it was an early lunch. Either way, I could smell bacon, coffee, and a hint of heated maple syrup when he opened the door.

Montone was a short, affable man with piercing blue eyes and an easy smile. "You hungry, Detective Kane?" he asked, leading me into the kitchen. "Pretty long drive up from the city."

I felt my stomach rumble. I hadn't eaten since dinner the night before. "Thanks. Smells great," I said. "And call me Dan."

"Right," he said. "People mostly call me Luigi. We can eat out on the porch. Food should be ready in about twenty minutes," he added, stirring a skillet of eggs. He nodded toward a file sitting on the kitchen table. "Meantime, grab some coffee and take a gander at my case notes. By the way, you can keep those. I have a second set."

I wasn't surprised that Montone had kept a copy of the Strom file. Over the course of a career, most detectives run across cases they don't feel right about and can't forget, and retiring doesn't change that. I poured a cup of coffee, picked up the file, and stepped out to a screened porch off the kitchen. Settling into an armchair there, I proceeded to scan Montone's file.

The information on Dr. Luther Cole, the dentist in question, was well organized. Among other things, the file contained copies of his California dental license, fingerprint cards associated with his controlled-substance prescription privileges, a summary of his criminal record (none), and registration materials for a continuing-education course he'd taken in Los Angeles—

including hotel records, flight reservations, and taxi receipts associated with the course. The latter were among the elements that had helped establish his alibi at the time of the shooting. In addition, there was a section on Dr. Cole's deceased son, Andrew—age, date of birth, medical history and treatment, education, and so on.

Unfortunately, nothing in the file told me what I needed to know.

A few minutes later Montone joined me on the porch. He handed me some silverware and a large plate filled with bacon, scrambled eggs, and pancakes. After setting his own plate on a table, he headed back into the kitchen. "More coffee?" he called over his shoulder.

"That would be great, Luigi," I answered, setting down the file and digging into my late breakfast. It was delicious. I hadn't realized how hungry I was.

Montone returned and poured me more coffee, then sat and started in on his own food. After a few bites he glanced at the file. "What do you think?"

"Good work," I noted around a mouthful of pancake. "Now tell me what's *not* in there."

Montone smiled. "A bit too perfect, huh? Yeah, I thought so at first, too."

When Montone didn't elaborate, I pushed ahead. "So let me see whether I've got this straight. At the time of the murder, Dr. Cole was in Los Angeles taking a three-day continuing-education dental course. He was staying at a hotel near the airport where this course was being given, and he has credit-card receipts for taxi rides to and from the airport and hotel receipts to prove it. Copies of the course sign-in sheets show he was present at the lectures all three days. He didn't rent a car while he was in Los Angeles, something LAPD investigators verified with an extensive search of car-rental companies, along with an examination of his credit-card purchases for the weekend. There are video logs showing Dr. Cole checking in and out of the hotel. Plus a desk clerk remembers his picking up an extra key and heading to his room on the night of the murder. No one saw him leave the hotel the entire weekend. Am I forgetting anything?"

Montone shook his head. "Nope, except that neighbors verified that both of his cars were sitting in his driveway here in Three Rivers for the entire time he was gone."

"What's he drive?" I asked, taking a long shot.

"Silver Toyota," Montone answered. "Highlander, 4Runner, something like that. And a red Chevy Camaro."

"Could he have had a friend help him? Maybe he had someone do it for him?" I asked, taking another long shot.

"It's possible, but I don't think so. That kinda stuff only happens in the movies."

"How about guns? Is Cole a shooter?"

Montone shrugged. "He grew up in Three Rivers. Everybody up here has guns."

"Does he reload his own cartridges?"

"That I wouldn't know. I could ask around."

"Yeah, do that and let me know. Now tell me about Cole. What's he like?"

Montone thought for a moment. "Like I said, he grew up here in town. Quiet kid, from what I hear. Smart, kept mostly to himself. People say he was maybe a little odd. I moved to Three Rivers about fifteen years back, so I didn't know him then."

"What did you mean when you said 'a bit too perfect' earlier?"

"At first I thought everything about the investigation seemed a little too neat and tidy," Montone answered, not the least bit thrown by my scattershot questions. "Like his keeping credit-card slips for his taxi rides. Sure, maybe he needed the receipts for his taxes, but still . . ."

I finished the last of my breakfast and set my plate on a nearby table. "That hit the spot, Luigi. Thanks." I thought a moment, then said, "Tell me more about Dr. Cole."

Montone rubbed his chin. "Well, for one, he had an excellent reputation as a dentist. Very meticulous and precise."

"Had?"

"He quit after his son was killed. Eventually sold his practice to his associate."

"So what kind of person is he?" I asked again.

"Very private. Actually, the most personable thing about the man was his wife, Janice. Everyone loved her. I think she was one of the main reasons his practice did so well. After she died, Dr. Cole sorta dropped out of sight. The last time I saw him was when I questioned him about Strom, and that was over a year ago. He was angry about being questioned. Really angry."

"What happened to his wife?"

Montone looked away. "Janice took her own life. Swallowed a bottle of pills."

"Did she leave a note?"

"At the inquest, Dr. Cole said she did. Said that it had been meant only for him, and that he destroyed it afterward. Wouldn't say what she wrote."

I thought a moment. "When you talked with Dr. Cole about the Strom murder, did you get the impression he was hiding anything? Or if not hiding, maybe not being completely truthful?"

Montone shook his head. "Like I said, he just seemed more angry than anything else. Now let me ask you something, okay?"

"Sure."

"I think I see where you're going by taking another look at the Joseph Strom murder. You're thinking maybe Dr. Cole is the shooter in your Los Angeles cop killings, right? Because if you are, you're on the wrong track."

"Why's that?" I asked.

"Because Dr. Cole didn't shoot Strom. We checked his alibi from every possible angle. It's airtight. It wasn't him."

"You're sure?"

Montone shrugged. "Evidence doesn't lie."

I picked up Montone's file. "Thanks for letting me scan this," I sighed, offering it back.

"Keep it. Like I said, I made a copy for you. And if there's anything else I can do to help, let me know. What's happening to your officers in Los Angeles is something that has to be stopped."

"Thanks, Luigi," I said. "Actually, there is one more thing," I added. It was the main reason I had driven to Three Rivers, and it wasn't for a talk that I could have had over the phone. "Is there a chance we can visit Dr. Cole?"

Montone smiled. "I was wondering when you were going to ask."

Everything in Three Rivers was close. I followed Montone across town in my own vehicle, arriving at the home of Dr. Luther Cole several minutes later. I pulled to a stop behind Montone's Suburban in Dr. Cole's driveway. Montone had assured me that calling ahead would have been a wasted effort, as according to neighbors Dr. Cole rarely left his house, and he never answered his phone.

Dr. Cole's home was a modest, two-story structure with an attached garage. I looked for his vehicles. Not seeing either in the driveway or parked on the street, I figured they were probably both in the garage—assuming Dr. Cole was home. I followed Montone up a flight of steps to a broad landing, noting a security webcam mounted above the entry. I stood to one side as Montone rapped on the door. Moments later I noticed a curtain being drawn back from a side window. Montone noticed it too.

"C'mon, Dr. Cole," Montone called. "It's Officer Montone. I have someone here who would like to talk with you."

The front door swung partway open. Dr. Cole stared at us from the other side, a hand on the doorknob, his face expressionless. He appeared to be an extremely large man, nearly as tall as I am, and a lot heavier. He regarded us impassively, dismissing Montone with a glance, then spending a bit more time examining me. After a long moment he shifted his gaze back to Montone. "I thought you had retired, Luigi," he said, his voice deep and raspy.

On the way to Dr. Cole's front door I had activated my cell phone's voice-record mode, leaving the microphone pickup pointing out of my jacket pocket. I intended to submit Dr. Cole's voice for comparison to the shooter's 911 whispered calls. In the meantime I tried to match his voice to my recollection of Captain Schwartz's recordings.

Following his task-force presentation, Schwartz had forwarded recordings of the subsequent calls made by the shooter in Sherman Oaks and North Hollywood. As in the calls made in Venice and Pacific Palisades, the shooter had whispered, again making a voiceprint analysis of the calls nearly impossible. Nevertheless, confidence was high they had all been made by the same person.

But was that person Dr. Cole?

I couldn't tell.

"I'm assuming you haven't resumed your position with the police department, so what's with the *Officer* Montone?" Dr. Cole continued, staring at Luigi.

"Sorry, Dr. Cole," Montone mumbled. "Just trying to get your attention. This is Detective Kane from the LAPD. He'd like to ask you a few questions. Could we come in for a minute?"

"No," Dr. Cole replied. "You may not. I don't want to talk with you any further about Joseph Strom. I don't regret that he's dead, not one bit, but I had nothing to do with his murder. His killer has been arrested, tried, and convicted. What else could there possibly be to discuss?"

"Actually, it's regarding a similar case," I broke in. "I was hoping you could help."

"I doubt that, Detective Kane," said Dr. Cole. "Now, if there's nothing else, I have things to do."

As he started to close the door, I noticed that he was wearing a large, distinctive ring on the fourth finger of his left hand. "SC?" I asked.

"I beg your pardon?"

"Your ring," I said. "University of Southern California. I have one like it. Played football for USC back in the day," I added, trying to make some sort of connection, loosen him up a little, keep him talking.

"Yes, I attended dental school at USC, as I'm sure you know," Dr. Cole replied. "Back in the day, as you put it. Good-bye, officers. And Detective Kane, good luck with your investigation," he added, ending the conversation by firmly closing the door in our faces.

On the drive back to Los Angeles, I tried to convince myself that the trip hadn't been a total bust. Although I hadn't ruled out Dr. Cole as a possible suspect, it was clear that reinvestigating him would prove extremely difficult, which I suppose was progress of a sort. If other investigating teams had been unable to break Dr. Cole's alibi, it was unlikely that I would find a hole in it—especially considering that the case had been closed for over a year.

Aside from attempting to recognize Dr. Cole's voice—a long shot at best—I had hoped to get a read on him to see whether he was telling the truth, or lying, or possibly just holding something back. His refusal to even let us through the door had effectively ended my chances of that. The recording I had secretly made of his voice might pay off, but as a voiceprint analysis of the whispered 911 calls hadn't even been able to definitively match the first four recordings to each other, the prospect of matching a fifth looked unlikely as well—especially as my recording was spoken, not whispered. I appeared to have struck out on all counts. Bottom line, although Dr. Cole might be a cold fish, that didn't make him a murderer, and I truly understood the anger he felt at losing his son.

The problem was, if Dr. Cole hadn't killed Strom, who had?

One by one, as I drove through the fields and ranchlands of the San Joaquin Valley, I ticked off the things I knew, or at least the things I *thought* I knew, about the case. One: Joseph Strom's murder could very well be tied to our sniper shootings, and the man serving time for killing Strom hadn't done it. Two: Strom's murderer was therefore still out there, and there was a good possibility he could be our sniper. Three: Dr. Luther Cole, the only other named person of interest in the Strom case, appeared to have an airtight alibi for Strom's murder, and I didn't know where to go from there.

I had originally hoped that investigating the earlier murder of Joseph Strom might generate something new. Seemingly, the Strom investigation now back to square one. It's an unfortunate fact that most homicide cases are broken during the first twenty-four hours following a murder, or not at all. After that, witnesses start to disappear, memories fade, trace evidence gets contaminated. The Strom case was now over a year old, with nothing new having been added since Albert Winslow was arrested and convicted. It wasn't simply going to be hard to pick up the threads of that investigation; it was going to be almost impossible—especially considering Snead's lack of cooperation in the matter.

Nevertheless, as I drove, I couldn't shake the feeling that I was missing something.

Finally I gave up and glanced at my watch, surprised to see that it was already late afternoon. Catheryn's party for Arthur West would be starting in a few hours, and I had promised to be on time. Thankful I'd brought my tux in the car, I pulled into the passing lane and stomped on the gas.

If I hurried, I could just make it.

Chapter Twenty-Seven

D r. Cole was stunned. The police had visited his house! How was that possible?

Heart pounding, he reviewed his recent activities in Los Angeles. Where had he gone wrong?

After rigging the explosive and abandoning the Expedition in the self-storage unit, he had walked back to his motel, as always making certain his face wasn't visible on any of the security cameras guarding the storage lot. Had they already found the car? No, if that were the case, he would have heard about the explosion on the news. That couldn't be it.

Think!

He had carried his rifles to the motel in a cardboard box kept at the storage unit for just such an emergency. The Desert Eagle had made the trip to his motel room tucked in his belt at the small of his back, covered by his coat. Of course, someone watching might have thought it odd to see him on the street carrying a bulky package that early in the morning, but the motel wasn't far and he didn't think he'd attracted any attention. Besides, he had registered at the motel under a phony name, paid cash, and left no trace of himself in the room. That couldn't be it, either.

What?

He fought a wave of blinding rage that had begun building inside. He pressed his palms to his temples. He couldn't afford to give vent to his anger. Not yet. He needed to think.

How had they found him?

But had they?

He took a deep breath, attempting to calm himself. The police couldn't know for certain. Otherwise they would have stormed his house and taken him into custody. Or at least tried to. That, of course, wasn't going to happen. He had no illusions about coming out of the game alive. But when the time came to make his exit, he intended to take as many of them with him as possible. And he was far, far from making his exit.

No, he reasoned. They couldn't know. Not yet. Not for certain.

But there was more to it than Detective Montone had let on. Someone had made the connection to the murder of Joseph Strom—the one single incident that could be traced back to him. And that someone who had made the connection certainly wasn't Montone. It must have been the detective from Los Angeles. What was his name?

Kane.

Apparently Detective Kane of the LAPD was looking into the shooting death of Joseph Strom, which in itself was unsettling. The Strom case was closed. Someone had been convicted and was now serving time. Aside from Dr. Cole's motive for murdering Strom, there was nothing to tie him to the crime. Plus he had an unshakable alibi. There had to be something he wasn't seeing. Otherwise, why had Detective Kane showed up on his doorstep?

This wasn't the way things were supposed to go.

Again, he tried to calm himself by recalling the ancient words of Prussian Field Marshal Helmuth von Moltke: "No plan of operations extends with certainty beyond the first encounter with the enemy's main strength." Moltke's words had later been shortened to the pithier "No plan survives contact with the enemy," but the meaning remained the same. This latest development wasn't his fault; it was just the nature of war.

Fortunately, Moltke's military analysis had also included a second, lesser-known axiom: "Strategy is a system of expedients." Dr. Cole understood this to mean that one should adapt and improve any battle plan in accordance with the changing situation. Good, practical advice from a military genius who had lived a century in the past, but advice that still held merit. And advice that he intended to follow.

But first he needed to know more about the enemy, and in particular what the enemy knew about him.

And for that, he needed to know more about Detective Kane.

Chapter Twenty-Eight

Dating back to the turn of the twentieth century, the Beverly Hills Hotel has long been a Los Angeles landmark. Originally built by developer Burton Green in the untouched foothills of the Santa Monica Mountains, the sprawling, Mission Revival-style hotel has undergone a number of upgrades and renovations over the years, while still maintaining its original Hollywood air of glamour, riches, and romance. I smiled as I turned off Sunset Boulevard and headed past the four-story Crescent Wing, its pink stucco walls partially hidden behind a thicket of tropical trees and flowering plants, thinking that something I'd recently read pretty much summed things up: "The Beverly Hills Hotel is better than real life; it's a fantasy fit for a movie."

After driving up the long, meandering driveway, I pulled to a stop beneath an elegant porte-cochère at the hotel entrance. Moments later a tall doorman wearing a black suit with gold trim appeared at my window. "Good evening, Detective Kane," he said, smiling as he glanced at his watch. "I see you're almost on time for the Philharmonic festivities."

Early in my police career I had spent several months on an organized-crime stakeout at the hotel. During that time I had come to know quite a few of the hotel employees, and I had stayed in touch with many of them—including the doorman. "Great to see you, Chris," I replied with a grin. "And yeah, I'm, uh, running a little late. Anyplace around here I can change? I brought my tux in the car."

"I think we can help you on that." Chris waved over a valet in a pink polo shirt. "Larry, show Detective Kane to room 99 so he can change, okay?"

"No problem," said Larry.

"Thanks, Chris," I said. "By the way, I heard you got remarried. Congratulations. I'm happy for you."

"Thanks, Detective. Let's get together sometime. You'll like Louise. And please give my best to your wife. She looks absolutely stunning tonight."

Ten minutes later, after hurriedly changing into my tux in a small room apparently reserved by the hotel for that purpose, I returned to the lobby and headed past the reception desk toward the Polo Lounge. Arthur's retirement dinner was being held in a separate dining room off the main area, the intimate private space aptly named the Polo Private Dining Room. Following several party signs, I exited into the Polo gardens, quickly locating the entrance to the private dining area past one of the upscale garden bungalows.

I glanced around the dining area when I arrived, taking in the room's warm, wood-paneled walls and art deco style. The party was already crowded. It looked like most of the eighty or so guests had already arrived and were having drinks, eating appetizers, and conversing in small groups among the white-linened tables.

I found Catheryn outside on an adjacent terrace. She was talking with Arthur West and our daughter, Allison. For the evening Catheryn was wearing a strapless black gown and a single string of pearls. As my friend Chris had noted, she looked stunning. "Hi, Kate," I said, kissing her cheek. "You look absolutely gorgeous. Sorry I'm late."

Catheryn kissed me back, then held me at arm's length to regard me appraisingly. "Well, at least you made it in time for dinner," she said, adjusting my bow tie. "You look handsome tonight, too," she added with a smile.

"Thanks," I replied. Then, turning to shake Arthur's hand, "Good evening, Arthur. I'm going to miss seeing you up there onstage with Kate. It won't be the same."

Arthur smiled sadly. He seemed to have lost even more weight over the past weeks. "No, Detective Kane, it won't be the same," he agreed.

I held his hand a moment longer than necessary. "If there's anything I can do, anything at all, please let me know," I said quietly.

Arthur regarded me closely, seeming a little surprised. "Thanks, Dan," he said, realizing I was serious. "I appreciate that."

"Hi, Dad," Allison broke in. "Haven't seen you in a tux for a while. Mom's right, you do look great."

I smiled. "Nice of you to notice, Ali. You look very elegant tonight, too."

And she did. Allison had dressed for the evening in a white silk blouse with a matching gray skirt and jacket that made her look like the professional newscaster she was rapidly becoming. She had recently cut her auburn hair to shoulder length as well, in keeping with her job at CBS. But there was more to what I was seeing than simply her appearance. Like Arnie, lately I'd noticed something different about Allison. For the first time in quite a while, she seemed . . . happy. Maybe it was Mike. Whatever it was, I was delighted to see it. It was about time.

"Thanks," said Allison, blushing at my compliment. "Hey, Dad? Before you leave tonight, Mike wants to talk with you, okay?"

"Sure." I glanced around the terrace. "Where is he?"

"Inside with Arnie and Nate, I think," Allison answered. "Probably raiding the appetizer tables."

"Dan, we need to talk, too," said Catheryn. "Arthur just informed me that the Philharmonic has decided to dispense with a competitive audition and offer me the principal cello position. It's a wonderful honor, but they need an answer soon."

I glanced at Arthur, then back at Catheryn. "That's great news, Kate," I said carefully. "When is your checkup scheduled?"

"Next Friday," Catheryn replied. "But if you agree, I want to tell them tonight that I accept—pending a clean bill of health from my doctor," she added, her eyes sparkling with excitement. "Which I'm sure I'll get."

"I am, too," I said firmly, willing it to be true. "Okay, tell them you accept, pending your doctor visit. And congratulations, Kate. I'm really happy for you. You deserve it."

"I agree, Catheryn," said Arthur. "I'm delighted for you as well."

"Thank you, Arthur," said Catheryn. "I just wish it were under different circumstances."

Arthur smiled ruefully. "Don't we all."

I gave Catheryn another kiss on the cheek. "Kate, I'm going to head in and check on my ex-partner before he eats all the hors d'oeuvres," I said, excusing myself. "I'll see you inside for dinner."

As Allison had predicted, Arnie was camped out at one of the appetizer tables, with Mike Cortese and my son Nate close by. "Hey, pard," said Arnie as he saw me approaching, grinning around a mouthful of food. "You try these things yet? Small but good," he added, popping a heart-shaped appetizer into his mouth.

"They *are* serving dinner, Arnie," I said, noticing that Nate had turned his back and was walking away, pretending not to have seen me. Nate had grown even more distant since our meeting with his high-school counselor, and things seemed to be getting worse. "You might want to pace yourself a little, pal," I added, deciding to talk with Nate later. Then, turning to Mike, "How's it going, Cortese? Ali said you wanted to talk to me?"

Mike nodded, seeming a bit flustered. "I do," he said, glancing at Arnie. "It's kind of personal—"

"No problem," said Arnie, taking the hint. "I'm gonna go check out the grub at the next table."

Mike waited until Arnie had moved off, then drew me to the side of the room, finding a quiet eddy in the party. Once there, he took a breath and squared his shoulders. I waited patiently, wondering what was up. I had never seen Mike so nervous.

"Mr. Kane, this may seem kind of old-fashioned, and I guess maybe it is, but I want to get your approval on something," Mike began. "Not that I'm asking permission," he quickly added. "Ali and I are adults, so we can make our own decisions, but I just thought—"

"Spill it, Mike," I interrupted. "What's on your mind?"

"I want to marry your daughter."

"Well, it's about time. Kate's going to be doing backflips when she hears the news."

"Then we have your support? I don't mean financial support," Mike immediately backtracked. "I'm making way more than I expected working in film, and Ali's career is taking off, too. Money will definitely *not* be a problem. I just meant to say that it would mean a lot to Ali and me if our marriage were something you supported. And if that's the case, maybe you could convince Mrs. Kane to support it, too."

"Let me ask you something, Mike. Do you love my daughter?"

I watched him carefully.

"With all my heart," he said.

I nodded, satisfied with his answer. "Then you have my full support," I said, shaking his hand. That didn't seem quite enough under the circumstances, and even though I'm not a big hugger, I gave him one anyway. "And I wouldn't worry about Kate," I added. "Between you and me, she's been waiting to hear this for quite some time."

"Thanks, Mr. Kane," Mike said, looking relieved.

"Let's make it Dan, okay? After all, you're going to be family."

"Right, Mr. Kane—uh, Dan. Speaking of which, could you let Ali be the one to give Mrs. Kane the news? Ali wants to tell her."

"No problem. As long as she does it tonight. That's not the kind of secret I can keep from Kate for long."

"Consider it done."

"And Mike? Thanks for coming to me. I don't think it was old-fashioned at all. And I couldn't be happier for you and Ali. Congratulations."

Mike grinned. "Thanks."

Twenty minutes later Catheryn and I took our places at one of the head tables, joining Arthur, the music director, and several other Philharmonic musicians. I was looking forward to dinner. From past experience I knew the food at the Polo Lounge was unforgettable, as was the service. By then almost everyone was seated and a team of attentive waiters were just completing a preliminary circuit of the room, serving salads and filling glasses.

I had just turned to say something to Catheryn when she surprised me by standing and addressing the room, raising her voice to be heard. "May I please have everyone's attention?" she called several times, finally getting everyone to be quiet.

"I usually let my husband make the toasts on occasions like this," Catheryn began, turning briefly to smile at me. "He's so much better at it than I am, but tonight there are a few personal things I want to say before we all start dinner. First, thank you all for being here to celebrate the career of a very special man, a man who has had an extraordinary career with the Philharmonic. Nietzsche has been quoted as saying that without music, life would be a mistake. I don't know whether 'mistake' is a fair description, but I do know that life without Arthur's music wouldn't have been nearly as wonderful."

Catheryn paused to smile at Arthur, then looked again out over the room. "Arthur West is a true artist who has spent his life sharing his gift with others, and experiencing his music has been a magical journey for us all. He leaves behind a legacy of memories, a history of performances that reaffirm the idea that life can be filled with beauty and meaning, and that life is not a mistake. So I ask you all to stand with me and raise your glasses to a man we all love, a man who has given us so much, and a man who will be missed by all."

As everyone rose in unison, Catheryn lifted her wineglass and turned to Arthur. "To you, Arthur. Thank you for your music. It will never be forgotten."

Later that night, unable to sleep after the excitement of the party, Catheryn and I lay in bed analyzing the evening. It was a warm night, and we had the bedroom windows open to the beach. Shafts of moonlight filtered in, along with the rhythmic sound of waves breaking on the shore.

"All in all, one hell of a party," I noted.

"That it was," said Catheryn, her body warm beside me.

"You know, Kate, I think you were wrong about something."

"Oh?" Catheryn murmured, resting her head on my shoulder. "And what was that?"

"About my being better at toasts than you. Your speech tonight at dinner was perfect. I think Arthur really liked it. You even threw in a Nietzsche quote. Where did you come up with that one?"

"Google," Catheryn laughed. "I knew it from before, but I had to look it up."

"Well, I was impressed. You can still surprise me, Kate."

"Good. And don't you forget it," Catheryn admonished playfully.

"Believe me, I won't."

Catheryn snuggled closer. "I'm so happy for Ali and Mike. That is such great news. Now we can start planning a wedding. Where do you think we should have the reception? Maybe here at the beach? Or maybe the Beverly Hills Hotel? Or—"

"Let's let Ali and Mike pick the spot," I suggested.

"Of course. I just thought we could point them in the right direction. Anyway, it's about time. I wasn't happy with the situation as it stood."

"I told you things would work out if you gave them some time."

"Yes, you did," Catheryn agreed. Then, changing the subject, "Trav called tonight. I told him about Ali and Mike, and about my being offered the principal chair. He was really excited about everything."

"I can imagine," I said. At the mention of Catheryn's new position with the Philharmonic, I started to add something about her medical checkup but stopped, deciding not to spoil the moment. "How's Trav doing?" I asked instead.

"He's still a bit unsure about his music and what he wants to do with it," Catheryn answered. "But he's working hard and optimistic about life. I wish Nate had half his enthusiasm."

"You and me both."

After a long pause, Catheryn asked, "Are you tired?"

"Not really. Although I should be. I got up early enough."

"Where did you go? Something to do with work? I thought Sunday was your day off."

"Yeah, it is."

"So . . . ?"

"So I drove up to a town near Visalia. I talked with a detective up there, trying to figure a way to pry open the sniper case. I came up empty."

"I'm sorry, Dan. I've been following developments on TV. For what it's worth, I think the news people are being totally unfair—especially regarding your task force. Some of the things they're saying are so unnecessarily ugly. I'm even starting to feel sorry for Lieutenant Snead."

"Don't waste your sympathy on him," I said. "He's part of the problem. Unfortunately, there's more to what's wrong with the sniper case than Snead. By the way, if you want to follow the investigation, you'd be better off listening to talk radio. TV coverage of the case has mostly been nonstop psychobabble, self-serving rhetoric, and finger pointing, like you said. At least on the radio most of the discussion centers on ballistics and bullets and which rifle is chambered in what caliber. There are thousands of gun enthusiasts phoning in, and at least *they* know what they're talking about."

"I'll keep that in mind," Catheryn laughed.

"I don't know, Kate," I went on more seriously. "I just can't seem to get a handle on things."

Catheryn lifted up on one elbow and regarded me pensively. "This investigation is getting to you, isn't it?"

"Yeah," I admitted. "It is. Our officers are getting blown away, and we're no closer to finding the shooter than we were two weeks ago. We need to do *something* to break things loose. I just don't know what."

"Let's get some sleep," Catheryn suggested. "Maybe things will look better in the morning."

"I don't know if I *can* sleep. I'm all wound up."

Catheryn kissed me, gently at first, then with growing passion. "You need to relax, Dan," she said softly.

"You have any suggestions?"

With a smile, Catheryn moved even closer. "Something to help you relax? I think I might have some ideas on that."

Chapter Twenty-Nine

With the lack of progress over the past days and weeks, tempers had progressively frayed on the task force. Some were now reaching the breaking point—especially Lieutenant Snead's. Making matters worse, internal tensions were building between LAPD detectives and the FBI special agents working the tip lines, each group harboring little secrets in the hope of closing the case. Increasing everyone's frustration was the knowledge that we were spending a prohibitive number of man-hours running down bogus hotline leads, and the futility of it was wearing on everyone.

After an ill-tempered meeting on Monday and another on Tuesday, followed by an even more argumentative briefing on Wednesday, Deluca and I spent the remainder of Wednesday morning viewing what seemed to be an endless procession of storage-lot surveillance logs. At noon we broke for lunch in town. From there we were scheduled to visit storage yards in Westchester and Inglewood, along with backtracking to Santa Monica and Culver City to revisit places we'd missed earlier in the week.

Instead, I retrieved my car from the First Street parking garage, once more asking Deluca to cover for me. He grumbled a bit, but the fact was it didn't take two of us to visit storage yards, and I had something I needed to do.

Ninety minutes later, after fighting freeway traffic most of the way south to Orange County, I pulled to a stop in the parking lot fronting the UCI Neuropsychiatric Center. After jamming a fistful of quarters into a parking meter, I crossed the lot and entered the three-story psychiatric building. Ignoring the receptionist inside, I proceeded down a hallway on the right leading to an outpatient waiting room. I had visited the center on an earlier occasion, and I still remembered my way around.

I tapped on a glass partition in the waiting room and flashed my badge at a nurse on the other side. "Detective Kane to see Dr. Berns," I said. "I called earlier."

Dr. Sidney Berns was a forensic psychiatrist who worked at the Department of Psychiatry and Human Behavior at the California College of Medicine. He also regularly served as an expert witness for the Orange County District Attorney's office. Most police officers, including me, harbor long-standing feelings of mistrust for the psychiatric profession—usually having run into more than one shrink testifying in court as to why his or her poor client wasn't responsible for his actions. Nevertheless, I had met Dr. Berns while working another case, and I had learned to trust his opinion.

The woman on the other side of the glass nodded and spoke briefly into a phone, then slid open the partition. "He'll be right with you, Detective," she said.

I remained standing as I waited, idly watching a suckerfish clean algae from the side of the waiting-room aquarium. Five minutes later a tall man with pale eyes and a gray-streaked ponytail opened a door into the room. "Dan," he said, stepping through and shaking my hand. "Good to see you. I was surprised to hear from you after so long."

"Good to see you too, Sid," I said. "I've been meaning to stay in touch, but you know how it is. Anyway, there's something I want to run by you."

Dr. Berns looked at me curiously. "Is this an official inquiry?"

"Not exactly. And I'd appreciate it if you could keep this between you and me."

Berns nodded. "Of course. Come on in. We can talk in my office."

I followed Berns through a cluttered residents' lounge, arriving at his small cubicle at the end of another hallway. I glanced around the grim eight-by-twelve office space as Berns slid in behind his desk. "When are they going to give you bigger digs, Sid?" I asked.

Berns smiled, directing me with a wave of his hand to a chair opposite his desk. "Money's tight. I'm not holding my breath on that," he said. "So what do you have for me?"

Instead of answering, I reached into my jacket and withdrew a copy of the FBI profile the task force had received. Without speaking, I placed it on his desk.

Berns's eyes widened when he saw what it was. "You're working on the sniper task force," he said, picking up the FBI profile. "And you want my opinion on this?"

I nodded. "And I want you to keep my visit today quiet."

Berns rubbed his chin. "I'm not going to ask why," he said, donning a pair of wire-rimmed reading glasses. "I've been following the sniper case in the news, and I'm sure you have your reasons."

For the next fifteen minutes I sat quietly as Berns scanned the file. Finally he removed his glasses and placed the file facedown in front of him. Opening a desk drawer, he withdrew a pack of Marlboro cigarettes and shook one loose.

"I thought you'd quit," I said, remembering that the last time I had seen Berns, he was well on his way to kicking the habit.

"I did quit," Berns said, lighting up. "Probably quit again, too. Lots of times."

I stood and cracked a window opening onto to a sterile concrete courtyard outside. "Damn, Sid. I think I read somewhere those things might be bad for you."

"Really?" Berns laughed. "What a shock." Then, turning serious, "Let's talk about your shooter."

"Fine," I said, resuming my seat. "I'm hoping you can help, because so far our investigation is coming up zeroes. Was there anything in the FBI report that made any sense to you? Anything I can use?"

"Anything you can use? Not much," Berns answered regretfully. "They're correct in their assessment that it's difficult to profile a mass murderer. Mass killers can come from all walks of life, from any race, and can be almost any age. They're also correct in saying that mass killings aren't very common, despite how it seems in the news, and because of that we just don't have enough reference points. Mass murderers usually do it only once. We have much better psychological data on serial killers, who do it lots of times. But with the exception of motive, which in serial killings often involves sexual contact with the victim, some of the serial killer data may apply to your sniper. A sort of hybrid profile, so to speak. The problem is, I don't think any of it will help you catch your guy."

"Can you give me your thoughts anyway? Get into this guy's head?"

Berns thought a moment. "All right. First, we are clearly dealing with an abnormal psyche here. He's probably not psychotic, but he is most definitely psychopathic—someone who lacks empathy and compassion and feels no guilt for his actions. There are two basic descriptors that are invariably present in people who commit these types of crimes. One, they are sad and depressed and willing to die. Second, they blame someone else for whatever has gone wrong in their lives. They feel victimized. Motivated by a bitterness and rage that transcends our everyday understanding, they want revenge. 'You pushed me too far, and now you are going to pay.' There has never been a mass killer who didn't exhibit those traits."

"Okay, so our guy isn't clinically insane," I summarized. "He can function in society without raising too many eyebrows. Neighbors might even like him, think he's a good guy," I went on. "Until he's caught, that is. He believes someone or something has ruined his life, and now he wants to get even. And he's willing to die doing it, as long as he takes as many people with him as possible. That about right?"

"Unfortunately, that's exactly right," said Berns. "Chronic depression, frustration at being victimized, rage, and finally revenge. You have men full of anger and hate who feel they have nothing to lose. They are depressed to the point that they don't care if they live or die. It's an extremely dangerous combination. By the way, revenge is a slippery motive for mass-murder or spree-type killings. Hard to pin down. In some cases revenge can be directed toward a particular person or persons; in others it might be a location, like a school or workplace. It can also be diffuse, in which someone climbs a tower and starts shooting anyone who happens to come along. In your case, because your sniper is specifically targeting cops, I think there's a strong probability your man holds the police community responsible for some misfortune, and the LAPD in particular."

"Yeah, we got that," I noted dryly.

"Another thing," Berns went on, ignoring my sarcasm. "Most mass murderers have experienced some real or imagined rejection. They feel insignificant and ignored and view their killings as a way to gain power and notoriety, even if that notoriety is based on public revulsion. To my knowledge, your sniper hasn't contacted either the police or the media yet, is that right?"

I nodded. "Not a word."

"That's unfortunate, as a desire to see their acts recounted in the headlines is how most of these killers are caught. Nevertheless, despite your shooter's lack of communication, I'm certain he's following developments in the news. Based on his silence, however, I don't think that notoriety is one of his main motivations. Or at least achieving an inflated, glorious vision of himself in the press isn't his *primary* motivation."

"Okay, so let's assume the low self-esteem factor is out," I said. "He's not feeling rejected and ignored. He's not dreaming of grabbing his fifteen minutes of fame. But if that's the case, how do we get him talking?"

Berns hesitated. "That's a tough one. Let's come back to that." Then, regarding me carefully, "I remember having a similar discussion with you several years ago. The results of our conversation back then didn't work out well for you. I'm hoping you're not considering something similar."

"I don't know what I'm considering, Sid," I sighed. "I just know that what we *are* doing isn't working. Do you have any other thoughts or insights, anything that might be helpful?"

Berns stubbed out his cigarette and lit another. "Well, there are a couple of other things to consider when you're talking about mass murderers," he said. "First, there is usually a triggering event. Something happens, some real or perceived catastrophic loss—getting fired at work, breaking up with a girlfriend, maybe even contracting a terminal illness. These men feel they've lost something precious, their lives have been ruined, and now it's time for revenge. Nevertheless, it's a common misconception that these killers simply 'snap' and head out on a killing rampage. More often there is a slow buildup involving months or even years of preparation. The Columbine killings, for example, were planned thirteen months in advance. And that's not unusual."

"Yeah, our shooter seems to have been setting this up for some time," I agreed. "The FBI profiler said a lot of the same things."

"Another factor you need to be aware of," Berns went on. "Mass murderers often kill themselves following a murder spree. There is a strong possibility your man envisions this ending with his own death."

"He's going to commit suicide? If that's the case, I wish he'd get on with it," I grumbled.

"Not like that," Berns corrected. "He's been gradually taking longer shots since the beginning, right? And he's changed his M.O., if the news reports are correct. And he recently used explosives in one of his shoots, right?"

I nodded.

"In effect, I think he's slowly revealing his abilities. From what I've seen of the case so far, I would expect some grandiose gesture at the end. Something noteworthy."

"Like what?"

Berns lifted his shoulders. He took a final drag on his cigarette and crushed the butt in an overflowing ashtray. "I don't know, Dan. Just be careful."

"Seems like everyone is telling me that these days," I said, deciding the time had come for my windup question. "So how do we push this guy into opening a dialogue? You said we'd come back to that."

Again Berns rubbed his chin. "Okay, but don't quote me on this."

"It's just you and me here, Sid."

"Right. Well, one thought presents itself. As I said, your man doesn't seem to be doing this out of a need for recognition. Otherwise he'd be taunting authorities and conversing with the press and so forth. That leaves his obvious hatred for the police as a motive, a hate specifically directed at the LAPD. You could work with that."

"How?"

"Suggest some motivation for his rage that is in direct contradiction to his actual reason for shooting cops."

I thought a moment. "You mean something like our guy has always wanted to join the LAPD, but he just couldn't make the grade?" I suggested. "He still idolizes the LAPD and wants to join our powerful ranks. He feels hurt and rejected and now he's shooting cops to prove to us he's worthy—every new killing a pathetic cry to be admitted to our exclusive club, a club that wouldn't take him. Something like that?"

Berns looked at me curiously. "Yes, that would probably do it," he said.

"Thanks, Sid." I glanced at my watch. My workday was almost over, and if I wanted to make it home before rush hour turned the freeway into a parking lot, I needed to get going. " I think I have what I came for."

Berns remained silent for a long moment. Finally he spoke. "I said it earlier, Dan, but I'll say it again. I don't know what you have in mind, but be careful."

*   *   *

Dr. Cole watched as the police detective exited the neuropsychiatric building and returned to his car. Detective Kane had been inside for almost an hour. Dr. Cole wondered what Kane had been doing in the medical building, and whom he had met. Had it had something to do with the sniper task force, or was it something else?

After Kane had started his car and exited the lot, Dr. Cole started his own vehicle and checked the dashboard display. Sure enough, there on the screen was Detective Kane's vehicle, a blue pin superimposed on an Orange County area street map. The console display showed Kane heading east on Chapman Avenue toward the freeway.

Deciding to give Kane a few minutes' head start, Dr. Cole closed his GPS iPhone tracker application and activated another app that connected him with webcams monitoring his home in Three Rivers—one watching the front door, another covering the street, a third surveying his backyard patio, a fourth inside. When he was away from home, he liked to keep an eye on things. You never knew who might be poking around. It paid to be careful, and modern technology made doing that easy.

After toggling through all four camera displays and finding nothing amiss, he switched back to his GPS tracker app. It now showed Kane's vehicle on the Santa Ana Freeway, heading north. He waited for another minute and then followed, dropping in behind Detective Kane on the freeway several miles back.

After Kane's unexpected visit to Dr. Cole's home in Three Rivers, a little online research had quickly revealed the LAPD detective's home address in Malibu. The following morning Dr. Cole had driven to Malibu, parking on a short, dead-end street high in the hills above Pacific Coast Highway. An easy hike across the brush-covered slope had provided a full view of the coastline below, including Detective Kane's house.

He had watched through binoculars as Kane returned home later that day. Kane had approached his beachfront residence cautiously, first driving past and stopping several hundred yards down the highway, then waiting on the side of the road for almost a full minute before making a U-turn and returning to his house. Seeing this, Dr. Cole had congratulated himself for not simply parking across the street to conduct his surveillance.

In his online search for Kane's address, Dr. Cole had learned a number of other things about Detective Kane. Unsettling, disturbing things. In every article he had read, Kane had come across as an unpredictable, dangerous maverick—several scrapes with LAPD Internal Affairs, six shootings (four fatal), and an unequaled reputation for closing cases. Worst of all, reading between the lines, it seemed that Kane didn't always play by the rules. Dr. Cole realized he would have to be very careful with Detective Daniel Kane.

Later that evening, when traffic on Pacific Coast Highway had dropped to a minimum, Dr. Cole crawled beneath Kane's car and duct-taped one of his Walmart prepaid cell phones and a spare battery pack to the vehicle's rear axle. With the phone's ringer and speaker muted, its screen darkened, and the Wi-Fi, Bluetooth, and vibrator circuits turned off, he estimated that the throwaway phone would continue to transmit its GPS signal for at least a week. Long enough for his purposes.

Dr. Cole had already downloaded a free GPS tracker app to his iPhone. The popular app, widely used by parents to keep track of their children, was currently set to show the real-time position of the cell phone taped to Kane's axle, as well as archiving past positions for the previous twelve hours. His own cell phone, in turn, was connected to his car's console screen via an Apple CarPlay cable, displaying everything right there on the dashboard.

Nevertheless, his surveillance of Kane hadn't turned out to be as helpful as he'd hoped. He knew where Kane lived, he knew where Kane left his car in a parking structure near the Police Administration Building, and he knew that Kane and his partner were currently investigating self-storage lots on the Westside. Now he knew that Kane had visited the UCI Neuropsychiatric Center, for whatever reason. Unfortunately, none of this explained why the troublesome detective had showed up on his doorstep. A few more days of surveillance might reveal the answer, he assured himself. He just needed to be patient.

In the meantime, maybe Kane and his partner would stumble across the storage lot where he'd left the Expedition . . . in which case Kane would cease to be a problem.

Chapter Thirty

I was up for hours that night after returning from Orange County, trying to decide what to do with Dr. Berns's information. As I'd told Berns, what the task force was doing to find the sniper wasn't working. We needed to get proactive. And in my opinion, getting the shooter to open some kind of dialogue was our best bet.

Enter the FBI profile.

With some judicious tweaking, it might just get our guy talking.

On the downside, for the LAPD to release a tailored version of the profile would in effect be lying to the media—something that didn't matter much in my book, considering that police officers were being murdered, but I suspected that others higher in the LAPD food chain might think otherwise. That left leaking the profile, in which case the task force could deny accountability for any inaccuracies, claiming it wasn't our fault if someone had leaked an erroneous report.

I considered the simple expedient of taking things into my own hands. I'd leaked material to the press in the past, with varied results—some good, some not so good. But if nothing else, it might stir things up, which was exactly what we needed.

Of course, leaking to the press involved risking my job, and it therefore required contacting someone trustworthy in the media—a contradictory requirement at best. I didn't want to use Allison, for obvious reasons. No reputable reporter would publish the profile as fact if they knew it had been modified, and I didn't want to lie to my daughter. I had other media contacts available, but still . . .

Having come to no decision by morning, I talked things over with Deluca before the task-force meeting, telling him what I'd learned during my visit to Berns. After some consideration, Deluca suggested that we once more try to get Snead to leak the profile, reasoning we should give him one more shot at doing things right. Deluca added that if Snead didn't agree, we could cross that bridge later.

And so I brought it up in the meeting.

And as expected, Snead categorically refused. "We already covered that, Kane," he snapped. "*Any* leaks will make us look bad. And if we modify the profile as you suggest, it will skew tips coming in on our hotlines, making them worthless."

"Gee, what a loss," someone quipped in the back.

Snead glared at the offender. "The subject of leaking the profile is closed."

"Let's at least hear what Kane is suggesting," said Detective Dondero. "Can't hurt to listen, right?"

Several detectives nodded.

"Yeah, what do you have, Kane?" asked Garrison, ignoring another sour look from Snead.

"Okay, here's the way I see it," I began, ignoring another scowl from Snead. "Right now every news station in the country is speculating on the case, with their own so-called profilers spouting stuff like 'We're dealing with someone whose sick psyche drives him to repeat his acts again and again, and whose arrogance and feelings of superiority have him convinced he can stay one step ahead of the police.'"

"That about covers the reporters," someone grumbled. "Now let's talk about the shooter."

After the laughter had died down, I continued. "I'm just saying there's so much misinformation out there already, throwing a little more crap into the mix by leaking a tweaked version of the FBI profile—especially if it gets our man talking—couldn't hurt. Believe me, this guy is following the case in the news, and our profile isn't doing us any good as it stands. Not to mention that it's eventually going to get leaked anyway."

"Tweaked how?" asked Dondero.

I described my proposed modifications to the FBI profile, explaining why I thought the changes could anger the shooter enough to get him talking—carefully leaving out any mention of my visit to Dr. Berns. When I'd finished, I could tell from a scan of faces that most detectives present thought it was a good idea.

"Let's do it, Lieutenant," insisted Dondero. "Like Kane said, the profile is probably gonna get leaked anyway. At least this way we can get some mileage out of it."

"I'll take it under consideration," Snead grumbled. "Let's move on."

For the next thirty minutes we reviewed a number of ongoing investigative lines, including current tip-line leads (no results), an update on new voiceprint software that had finally been installed at the Valley and Metropolitan 911 dispatch centers, the use of several military drones now on loan from the Pentagon, self-storage yard surveillance log reviews, and the status of our .50 caliber sniper rifle inquiries. So far we were still coming up dry on all fronts.

Snead usually broke our morning meeting before the hour mark, leaving plenty of time for him to prepare for his media briefing downstairs. That morning he ended even earlier. "That's it for today," he said curtly. "Everyone get to work. Kane, stick around. I want to talk to you. Now."

"What is it, Lieutenant?" I said a few minutes later. I was standing in front of Snead's desk, in an alcove off the main room. "You're pissed off about the profile? Come on, this won't be the first time the department has leaked something to kick-start a stalled investigation."

"That's not the point," Snead snapped.

"Right. So what *is* the point, Lieutenant?"

"The point is, you're not acting like a team player, Kane. I would think that after your experience on the Candlelight Killer Task Force, you would have learned a lesson."

"I don't know what you're talking about."

"You don't? Well for starters, I got a message yesterday from Captain Schwartz in Communications. He said they were unable to match a recording you submitted for a voiceprint analysis. Would you like to comment on that?"

"Not really."

"No? Well, it's clear you're striking off on your own again. Whatever it is you submitted to Captain Schwartz, I didn't authorize it. I told you I'd give you some leeway on my task force, but not like this, not going behind my back. And definitely not the way you've been challenging my authority in the meetings, as I told you when we started."

"If you're talking about my suggestion that we leak the profile—"

"I'm not referring to your *unethical* suggestion that we leak an altered version of the profile," Snead interrupted.

"Screw ethical. Our guys are getting shot."

"What I'm referring to, along with the message from Captain Schwartz, is a call I got this morning from the warden at Tehachapi State Prison. He wanted to know whether your interview with one of his inmates had proved helpful."

"Uh . . . so what did you tell him?"

"God damn it, Kane!" Snead exploded. "You think this is funny?"

"Actually, I do. Not the 'funny ha-ha' kind. What's going on here is more the 'I can't believe this shit' kind. Prior murders like the Joseph Strom case were something we should have looked at right from the beginning."

"We needed to look at *similar* prior murders," Snead corrected. "Of which there were none. Strom was killed with a .44 caliber revolver, not a rifle."

"The coroner's report originally stated that a rifle—"

"In addition," Snead interrupted again, "Albert Winslow, the prison inmate you visited, was tried and convicted for the crime, for which he is now serving time. Does that sound *similar* to you?"

"Lieutenant, I get paid to know when people are lying. When I visited Winslow, he told me he didn't shoot Strom. And I believed him."

"A prison inmate claimed he's innocent?" Snead mocked, raising his voice theatrically. "Well, why didn't you say so? That changes everything."

Despite Snead's sarcasm, I understood his skepticism. I couldn't explain how I knew Winslow was innocent, at least not to Snead. But he was.

"Assuming for a moment you're right, what do you suggest doing about it?" Snead continued angrily. "Based on your *hunch*, are you suggesting we reopen an investigation that's been closed for over a year? As it is, the task force is swamped with leads without backtracking on a dead case like that."

I remained silent, deciding not to mention my visit to Three Rivers, during which I had tried to do exactly that.

With exaggerated patience, Snead folded his hands on his desktop. "As I told you earlier, I requested your presence on this task force because of your supposed ability to think outside the box. This latest stunt of yours doesn't fall into that category. It falls into the insubordination category. Are you hearing me, Kane? Regarding the Strom case, I ordered you to drop that line of investigation. The only reason I don't have you up on charges right now is that you helped cover our asses on the Expedition leak. I suppose you can thank your daughter for the fact that you still have a job."

"I'll be sure to pass that on."

Snead glared at me from across his desk. "This is the second time you've been warned, Detective. There won't be a third."

Chapter Thirty-One

I took off work early on Friday to drive Catheryn to her medical appointment at UCLA. When I picked her up at the beach, I could tell she was nervous. So was I. Today was the two-year mark, and a lot was riding on the afternoon's results.

Catheryn's illness had showed up unexpectedly two summers back. Her condition, a blood cancer called acute myeloblastic leukemia, had proved to be an extremely aggressive form of the disease—requiring three consecutive days of total-body irradiation, followed on the fourth day by a massive dose of chemotherapy. This combined approach was designed to eliminate all white cells from Catheryn's body, normal and cancerous cells alike. The treatment, although successful, had also left her without a functioning immune system, as expected—necessitating a bone marrow graft shortly afterward.

Following the graft procedure, Catheryn had almost died.

After her subsequent recovery, she had been required to return to UCLA for regular checkups every few months. Two serious medical issues were involved. One was a possible reoccurrence of her cancer, which would have been devastating. The other centered on various complications associated with the bone marrow graft—several of which were life-threatening as well. So far all her checkups had come back normal. Today's visit, if it went as we hoped, would mark two full years of clean examinations, after which her visits would be scheduled more infrequently—possibly only once or twice each year. It would be a huge step forward, as the success of Catheryn's treatment was often measured in months, not years, and a clean two-year survival was indicative of a positive outcome for the future.

Earlier that morning it had started to rain. On the drive into town I turned on the wipers, squinting at oncoming traffic as the wiper blades began smearing weeks of accumulated highway grease on the windshield.

"Try the wiper spray," suggested Catheryn.

"Good idea," I said, giving the windshield a blast of blue, which seemed to help. "Rain's coming early this year," I noted absently.

Catheryn nodded. "I suppose we'll be dealing with mudslides before long," she observed.

Heavy winter rains routinely brought down muddy deposits from the palisades bordering Pacific Coast Highway, with some slides closing the road for days at a time. Along with brushfires, earthquakes, and storm-surf damage, mudslides were one of the hazards of living in Malibu, but they were something all of Malibu's residents grudgingly accepted for the privilege of living near the coast. Nevertheless, I knew Catheryn's mind wasn't on mudslides. And neither was mine.

"I saw on the news last night that your task force released the FBI profile," Catheryn continued, attempting to fill the silence.

"Yep," I said. To my surprise, after chewing me out Snead had held a special news conference later that day, during which he had disclosed portions of our FBI profile, complete with the tweaks I'd suggested. "We're hoping to get the guy talking."

"Do you really think the sniper wanted to be a cop, and that's why he's doing all this? That seems so sad."

"Uh, that part might not be exactly accurate," I said. "We added a few modifications to stir things up."

"Oh." Catheryn regarded me curiously, then resumed staring out the window, watching the dreary landscape slip by. Not feeling like talking either, I let the conversation die, and together we rode without speaking for the remainder of the drive to UCLA.

Twenty-five minutes later, as I turned off Le Conte Avenue into a Ronald Reagan UCLA Medical Center parking lot, Catheryn again broke the silence. "I'm worried, Dan," she confessed.

"Everything is going to be fine," I said firmly. "You're healthy, happy, and you look great. There's no way this can work out any way but well, so let's go in there and get the good news."

"I love you, Dan."

"I know that, Kate. I love you, too."

*   *   *

Dr. Cole had almost stopped trailing Kane when he realized the police detective was heading for home. Something had made him continue following, and now he was glad he had. Kane hadn't stopped at his house for long. A few minutes after arriving, Kane had reappeared, accompanied by a tall, attractive woman whom Dr. Cole assumed was Kane's wife.

Curious, he had followed Kane's vehicle to Westwood, watching as Kane pulled into a parking lot beside the UCLA Medical Center.

First a medical center in Orange County, now one in Westwood.

What was Kane up to?

Dr. Cole circled the block. On his next circuit he spotted a parking lot across the street from the hospital. The parking area apparently serviced a number of commercial businesses, including a Ralph's Market. As he drove in, he noticed a ramp leading up to additional rooftop parking. He ascended the ramp, exiting onto a nearly empty expanse of concrete overlooking the medical center. A few cars were clustered near a childcare center at the back. Otherwise the lot was deserted.

Dr. Cole pulled into a space at the far end overlooking the Medical Center. He shut off his engine and sat for a moment, surveying his surroundings. Satisfied that he wasn't being observed, he opened the glove compartment and withdrew a small pair of binoculars. Carefully, he scanned several tiers of hospital parking across the street.

Minutes later, after repeatedly checking his GPS tracker screen, he located Detective Kane's vehicle. It was parked outside the hospital entrance in an open area marked Plaza 3. Dr. Cole traded the binoculars for his laser rangefinder, another item he routinely carried in his car. Not daring to consider a plan that began forming in his mind, he ranged the distance to Kane's car.

One hundred and thirty-eight yards.

He fought to control a reckless sense of excitement growing within. That he would even contemplate so foolhardy a course was troubling. In the past his shoots had been planned months in advance and executed with machinelike precision, with nothing left to chance. At best this would be an improvised, irrational, spur-of-the-moment operation.

On the other hand, he recalled the second axiom of military theorist Helmuth von Moltke: "Strategy is a system of expedients." Would not taking advantage of this opportunity simply be following Moltke's advice?

His subsonic rifle lay in the trunk of his car, along with a box of match-grade Whisper cartridges. Although he didn't have his shooting bench with him, at 138 yards he wouldn't need it. Besides, a perimeter wall enclosing the parking lot would provide an adequate rest for his shot. He could wait in his car until the proper moment. Then, hidden by his vehicle, he could step out and quickly make the shot. With his suppressed subsonic rifle and a background of city noise, no one would even notice something had happened.

No one, that is, except Detective Kane.

As he waited in the rain for Kane to reappear, Dr. Cole painstakingly weighed the pros and cons, carefully thinking things through. It was a difficult decision, and he didn't want to make a mistake. He also didn't want to allow a singular opportunity to slip away—losing a chance to remove a dangerous adversary, an adversary whom fate had served up, as it were, on a silver platter.

In his deliberations, he reminded himself that it was Kane who had showed up on his doorstep. So far Kane was the only one who had even come close to finding him. Kane had probably been involved in making public the hideous FBI profile that had recently been released as well. Who knew what else Detective Kane had planned? No, removing him would hurt the task force, and it would hurt the LAPD as well. And that's exactly what Dr. Cole wanted to do.

But did he dare?

At last, after careful consideration, he came to a decision. All life involved risk; there was no avoiding it. One had to weigh risk against reward and decide whether something was worth doing.

Unfortunately, in this situation the risk was simply far too great . . . even considering the reward.

On the other hand, regardless of risk, maybe some things were just meant to be.

Chapter Thirty-Two

M rs. Kane? Dr. Miller will see you now."
We had been at the medical center for several hours.
During that time I had waited in a gloomy reception area while
Catheryn underwent a number of diagnostic procedures,
including giving blood and marrow samples at a hospital lab
downstairs.

Sitting beside me now, Catheryn looked up apprehensively at
the young medical assistant who had spoken. "Thank you," she
said, giving my hand a squeeze.

We followed the medical assistant down a short hallway to an
office at the far end. The office door was ajar. As we entered,
Dr. Gary Miller, Catheryn's transplant-team attending
hematologist, rose from behind his desk to greet us. "Catheryn,
Detective," he said, extending a hand to Catheryn, then to me.
"It's good to see you both again. Please take a seat."

Nervously, Catheryn and I sat across the desk from Dr.
Miller. Struck by an ominous sense of déjà vu, I again took
Catheryn's hand, thinking that we had looked across so many
physicians' desks over the past two years. Silently, I prayed that
today's news would be better than some we'd received.

Dr. Miller glanced at the medical file lying open on his
desktop. Then, with a smile, he said, "I'm going to go over the
results of your current tests, Catheryn. But before we start, I
want to reassure you both that everything basically looks good.
We do have a few areas of concern, but I'll get to those in a
minute."

I could feel Catheryn relax slightly beside me.

"The really good news is that there has been no recurrence of
your cancer," Dr. Miller continued. "Your blood and marrow
tests came back absent any sign of leukemia cells. Although we
will want to keep monitoring on an annual basis, there's now a
high probability that you will continue to be cancer free."

"Will I need to keep having marrow tests?" asked Catheryn.
"That's the only exam that bothers me."

Dr. Miller shook his head. "Only if your symptoms recur. Otherwise, routine blood tests will suffice."

"Good."

Dr. Miller referred to the file in front of him. "As we discussed prior to your marrow graft, there are a number of possible transplant side effects that we need to continue monitoring."

I thought back to the first time the marrow transplant procedure had been described to us. It had sounded simple . . . at first. Following a course of radiation and chemotherapy to eliminate all of Catheryn's white cells, her immune system would be reestablished by transplanted stem cells from a bone marrow graft. Unfortunately, the procedure had turned out to be more complicated than initially described.

For one, during the first few days following the transplant, Catheryn had almost succumbed to a condition known as graft versus host disease, or GvHD, a dangerous condition in which the transplanted marrow cells attack their new environment—in this case, Catheryn's body—recognizing it as foreign. That condition had eventually been brought under control with a combination of immunosuppressant drugs, several of which Catheryn still continued to take. The goal was to adequately suppress the GvHD response, while at the same time not incapacitating Catheryn's new immune system to the point of leaving her susceptible to life-threatening infections.

That wasn't all. Other side effects from Catheryn's treatment could continue to show up even years afterward—not only from the bone marrow transplant itself, but from the radiation and chemotherapy she'd received as well. For one, she no longer was able to conceive—not that we planned on having any more kids. At the time we'd joked that the ones we already had were plenty. But still . . .

"I'd like to go over the results of your other tests so you have a better picture of where we stand," Dr. Miller continued.

"Yes, please do," said Catheryn.

"As I said, there were no signs of a recurrence of your cancer," Dr. Miller went on. "Your immunosuppressant regime is our next biggest concern, mainly because the drugs you're taking can adversely affect your muscles, joints, and bone density. The only concern we have at present, along with keeping your regime well balanced, is with your bone density. Your scan came in a bit below normal for a woman your age, so we'll want to keep an eye on that."

Catheryn nodded.

"As we discussed, the chemotherapy and radiation you received could cause problems with your liver, lungs, kidneys, bladder, and nervous system. Fortunately, so far we see no sign of any of that, either."

We seemed to be getting good news on all fronts. I felt myself unconsciously holding my breath, waiting for whatever bad news Dr. Miller might be saving for last.

"Last, sometimes chemo and radiation can cause damage to the heart and circulatory system. Your heart is fine. We did a complete screening for other types of cancers that sometimes occur following radiation and chemotherapy. We found none."

Dr. Miller looked up from his chart and smiled. "As I noted, there are a few things we will want to watch. Your bone density, for example. We will also want to be vigilant for any signs of infection, along with any new cancers that might occur subsequent to your chemo and radiation. Cataracts might be a problem later, too. But all in all, you couldn't have had a better checkup, Catheryn."

I felt Catheryn breathe a sigh of relief beside me.

"I'll be sending your medical records to Dr. Porter, your family physician at St. John's," Dr. Miller continued, winding things up. "He will be the one seeing you for your annual visits from now on, but please feel free to stay in touch with me if anything comes up. Do you have any questions?"

Catheryn thought for a moment. "Will I need to continue my checkups, even if I feel fine?"

"Yes, for the rest of your life," Dr. Miller answered. "At a minimum, annual checkups are a must, with visits more often if any problems develop. It's a lot easier to fix something little before it becomes something big. As I said, watch for signs of infection or anything else that might be wrong, and go in right away if they occur."

"I will," said Catheryn.

"I have a question," I said. "Catheryn has been offered a new position with the LA Phil. It's a great opportunity, but it will mean more work and added responsibility. She's been waiting to give them a final answer. What do you think?"

Dr. Miller considered my question. "I think that would be fine," he said carefully. He looked at Catheryn and added, "As long as you don't push yourself too hard, get plenty of rest and exercise, take your meds, and keep yourself healthy, you have my blessing. Congratulations on your new position, Catheryn. I couldn't be more happy for you."

On the way out Catheryn seemed almost giddy with relief. I was, too. She again took my hand as we pushed through a pair of heavy glass doors and exited the hospital. "I'm so happy, Dan," she said. "We are definitely going out tonight to celebrate. Someplace really, really expensive."

"Someplace with steaks," I agreed. "Big, thick, and juicy."

"Someplace with fish," Catheryn laughed. "Fresh, mouthwatering, and delicious. And salads. I want a big salad."

"I think I know just the place," I said, remembering a new Westside restaurant I'd been meaning for us to try.

"Surprise me," said Catheryn. "When we get home I'll make a few calls and find someone to watch Nate."

"Don't you think Nate's old enough to watch himself?"

Catheryn gave me a look. "After all that's been happening, it might be wise to have some adult supervision."

I nodded. "Maybe you're right. We could see whether Christy's free," I suggested. Our son Tommy's former girlfriend, Christy White had remained a close family friend after his death, and had sometimes stayed with Nate when we couldn't find anyone else on short notice.

By then it had stopped raining. On our way in I had dropped Catheryn at the medical center entrance. Although I suggested she wait there while I retrieved the car, she wanted to accompany me. Hand in hand, we headed to the parking lot.

I'd been preoccupied with Catheryn's checkup when I parked, and hadn't paid much attention to where I'd left the car. It took us a few minutes to locate it. I accompanied her to the passenger's side, intending to make a grand show of opening her door.

What took place next seemed to happen in slow motion, unfolding like some dark, nightmarish sequence in a film.

I opened the passenger's door. Stepping back to make room, Catheryn momentarily slipped on the wet pavement, stumbling against me. As I caught her, it felt as if a giant hand had reached out and slammed us both to the ground. A massive numbness engulfed my left shoulder, quickly replaced by an explosion of pain. I lay stunned, sprawled on my back in a puddle, Catheryn on top of me.

It took a moment to figure out what had happened. I had been shot before. But not like this.

"We have to stay down, Kate," I groaned, trying to gauge the angle from which the shot had come. I thought I'd heard a pop from across the street, but I wasn't sure. "We need to stay low, between the cars."

Catheryn didn't reply.

I felt something warm soaking the front of my shirt.

Not my blood.

"Kate?"

She didn't move.

"Oh, Jesus," I said, shifting to look at Catheryn's face.

Her eyes were open, but she wasn't conscious.

"Oh, no," I cried. "Please God, no."

Catheryn wasn't breathing. I had to get her back into the hospital. And I had to do it quickly. Remaining hidden between the parked cars was no longer an option.

I quickly considered our situation. The shot must have come from across the street, from a position that gave the sniper a clear angle on us when we were standing beside the car. I needed to get around to the back before standing up, putting the vehicle between us and the shooter.

Rolling onto my side, I squirmed to the rear of the car, pulling Catheryn with me. Using my good arm for leverage against the trunk, I rose to my knees and clumsily slung Catheryn over my uninjured shoulder in a fireman's carry.

Time to move.

Taking a deep breath, I headed for the hospital doors, Catheryn's inert form bouncing on my shoulder as I ran.

I had made it about halfway to the hospital entry when a second bullet tore into my side. I felt a splintering crack as something broke.

I kept going.

A third bullet exploded a car windshield past my head, spraying me with glass.

A little farther and I would be there. Praying there wouldn't be another shot, I ran for all I was worth, stumbling under Catheryn's weight.

An instant later I slammed through the hospital's glass doors. Several people in the lobby looked up in shock as I staggered inside.

"My wife needs help," I shouted. "She's been shot. Please, get someone down here now!"

Catheryn still hadn't moved.

A woman at the reception desk was already speaking frantically into a phone.

I stood swaying a moment, dripping blood. I felt dizzy. Carefully, I knelt to lay Catheryn at my feet. I tried to position her clear of the blood spatter on the floor. Suddenly I didn't have the strength.

Several hospital attendants were rushing toward us.

Numbly, I sat on the floor beside Catheryn. I brushed a strand of hair from her face. I couldn't believe this was happening.

I felt myself growing weaker. It was all I could do to stay upright.

The men arrived. They were leaning over us.

"Please help her," I repeated. Black was creeping in on the edges of my vision. All at once I couldn't sit up.

"Please . . ."

Chapter Thirty-Three

I awoke in pain. Confused, I opened my eyes, trying to make sense of my surroundings.

Cool white sheets. Stainless steel. Fluorescent lights. Monitoring machines, plastic tubes, medicine smell.

And then it came back. All of it.

I tried to sit up. I couldn't.

My left shoulder was bandaged, my arm immobilized in some sort of sling. Another dressing covered my ribs where the second bullet had struck.

Someone pushed a button to adjust the bed, sitting me up.

Allison.

I looked up at her face. She'd been crying.

Nate and Grandma Dorothy were in the room, too.

"Catheryn . . ." I said.

Allison glanced away without answering. The look of utter, abject desolation in her eyes confirmed my worst fear. Stunned, I looked at Grandma Dorothy, then Nate, their faces swimming in my vision. I couldn't breathe. I felt like I was suffocating.

Allison took my hand. "I'm so sorry, Dad," she said softly, tears welling in her eyes.

I couldn't reply. For a moment I refused to believe that this nightmare was happening. It couldn't be real. It couldn't.

But it was. And with that realization came an overwhelming, bottomless, unspeakable wash of despair. Catheryn was gone, and nothing would ever again be the same.

"Travis is flying home," Allison said past her tears.

I nodded without answering, realizing that I was crying, too. I turned away, trying to stop.

"Mike is driving back to be here," Allison continued, still holding my hand. "Arnie and Detective Deluca and Lieutenant Long are waiting outside," she added. "Some other people are out there, too. A lot of people."

"I don't think I can see anyone right now," I mumbled.

"I'm sure they'll understand," said Allison. "I'll tell them you said thanks for coming. Do you . . . do you want us to leave?"

"No," I choked, unable now to control my tears. I closed my eyes and let them flow. "Please . . . stay."

Chapter Thirty-Four

Deluca visited me on the following day, arriving at the medical center at a little before noon.

During the night I had asked a nurse to disconnect my morphine drip, which someone had prescribed for pain. I needed to think clearly, and I didn't mind the pain. In fact, I welcomed it. It was better than thinking about Catheryn.

Deluca gazed around my hospital room, clearly uncomfortable being there. "I'm so sorry, Dan," he said quietly, shoving his hands into his pockets. "I can't believe this happened. I . . . I don't know what to say."

"Thanks for being here, Paul," I said. "That's enough. And pass that on to everybody who showed up here last night, too. Tell them I appreciate it."

"I will. Everyone at the meeting this morning said to tell you that you're in their thoughts and prayers."

"Thanks," I said numbly.

"Are you okay?"

"I'm a little shot up—a couple cracked ribs and a busted shoulder—but they tell me I'll recover."

"No, I mean, are *you* okay?"

I hesitated. "No. I'm not," I said. "Not even close."

"But you're going to be?"

I started to shrug, wincing as I lifted my injured shoulder. "I don't know, Paul," I sighed. "I'm not sure where to go from here."

"Is there anything I can do?"

I nodded grimly. "Find the asshole who did it."

Deluca brightened slightly. "We may have something new on that," he said. "We got a security log from one of the yards that you and I visited near the airport. Took the storage-yard manager a while to find it, but he finally sent it in. One of the men reviewing videos spotted a green Expedition entering the yard on the same night our patrolmen were murdered on Bundy. The time stamp on the log placed the Expedition arriving at around twenty-five minutes after the shooting."

I tried to sit up, then thought better of it. "Could be our guy," I said, groping for the bed control. Finding it, I pushed a button and brought myself to a more upright position. "Did the video show which storage unit he's in?"

"Close enough," Deluca answered. "We narrowed it down to one of two that are large enough for a vehicle. There's more. Three hours after the Expedition arrived, the log showed a guy leaving the yard on foot. He was carrying a cardboard box, just about the right size for a rifle."

"Could you see his face?"

"Not really. He was wearing shades and a ball cap. Plus he avoided looking at the cameras. We figure he had another car parked somewhere nearby, maybe at a motel. We're checking all motels in the area. We also got a search warrant and have a team visiting the storage yard as we speak."

Something was wrong. "Back up a second, Paul," I said, alarm bells beginning to sound in my mind. "You said the guy left the yard *three hours* after he drove in?"

Deluca nodded. "Approximately."

What had he been doing for those three hours?

I tried to put myself inside his head. What would I have done?

Abandoning the Expedition made sense. He knew we'd be looking for it. As careful as he had been, he must have assumed we would eventually find it, so removing any physical evidence that could tie him to the murders also made sense.

But wiping a vehicle clean of prints didn't take three hours. And anyone who has ever watched television knows that completely eliminating all trace evidence requires more than Windex and a vacuum cleaner, if it is possible at all.

Again, what had he been doing for those three hours?

I thought back to my conversation with Dr. Berns. What had he said? "From what I've seen of the case so far, I would expect some grandiose gesture at the end."

All at once I had it. "Call Snead, Paul. Have him pull our guys out of there. I think our shooter may have rigged the storage unit."

"What?"

"Think about it, Paul. He knew we'd eventually find the Expedition. And he's smart enough to know there's no way he could eliminate all trace evidence from the vehicle—not without doing something drastic. He knows how to make a bomb. We already saw him do it."

"Jesus," Deluca whispered, reaching for his cell phone. "If you're right . . ."

Deluca punched in a string of numbers. He waited impatiently for someone to pick up. Thirty seconds later he was transferred to Snead. I listened as he started to relay my suspicions. Partway through he stopped, his face turning pale. He disconnected without saying good-bye.

"What?" I asked, already knowing the answer.

"You were right," he said. "He had the car rigged. We lost four detectives in the explosion. Dondero, Garrison, Jones, and Cooper. Two FBI agents and the storage-yard manager are dead, too. They're still putting out the fire."

I stared at Deluca in shock, unable to speak. First Catheryn. Now six members of our task force. With a welling of utter, bottomless desolation, I looked away and tried to steady my breathing.

"I can't believe this is happening," I finally managed, my voice breaking.

"I can't either," Deluca replied. "I'm beginning to think that something somebody said in one of the briefings might be correct. When we do find this guy, I don't think he's making it to trial."

Chapter Thirty-Five

On the following Sunday we held a memorial for Catheryn. I had been released from the hospital two days earlier. My left arm and shoulder were still immobilized, and my ribs hurt whenever I moved, but I was on the mend.

As expected, members of the media showed up at Our Lady of Malibu Catholic Church that afternoon, bristling with microphones, cameras, and satellite hookups. Reporters were kept clear of the church by a street barrier set up and manned, at my request, by the Malibu Sheriff's Department. To the media's credit, they didn't complain.

Thirty minutes before the service began, mourners completely filled the pews of the small church. The aisles and the area in back were jammed as well. Allison and Mike, Nate, and Travis were sitting beside me in the front row. Grandma Dorothy was also with us, along with my mother, Dot, and my younger sister, Beverly—both of whom had driven from Texas to be there. As I waited for the ceremony to start, I glanced around the room, amazed that so many people had come.

Sitting near the front were Allison's friend McKenzie Wallace and her family, along with Christy White and a number of neighbors from the beach. My ex-partner Arnie sat directly behind us, joined by another close friend from the Orange County Sheriff's Department, Lou Barrello. Lauren Van Owen—there as a mourner and not as a newsperson—was sitting on the far side, accompanied by her daughter, Candice.

I recognized a number of Catheryn's associates from the Philharmonic, including cellists Arthur West and Adele Washington, the music director, and many others. Present from the LAPD, almost filling one entire section of the church's wooden benches, were Lieutenant Long and Captain Lincoln, and Deluca, and Banowski, and most of the detectives from the squad room. Lieutenant Snead and the entire sniper task force were standing somberly near the rear. I was surprised to notice Jeff and Rita Grant also standing at the back with their daughter-in-law, Julie.

Looking around the room, I felt a welling of emotion, realizing that almost everyone important in our lives was present. I wished Catheryn could have been there to see it.

The service began with a blessing by our parish priest, Father Donovan, followed by several hymns and a number of remembrance speeches. At one point the lights were dimmed. Sitting in the dark, we watched a slide show that Allison had put together on her computer—pictures of Catheryn at home, relaxing on the beach, working in the kitchen, performing onstage, laughing with our children—sometimes younger, sometimes older, sometimes joyous, sometimes pensive . . . always beautiful.

Allison had accompanied her images of Catheryn with a classical music piece, a deeply emotional composition I recognized as the Andante from Rachmaninoff's Sonata for Cello and Piano in G minor. It was a work that Catheryn and Travis had recorded years earlier, and as I watched I was filled with an ineffable sadness as memories of Catheryn dissolved one into the next, accompanied by my wife's transcendental playing.

All too soon it was over.

As the lights were raised, most of those present were caught wiping their eyes. I stood. I had told Father Donovan that I would be last to speak. That time had now arrived.

And I didn't know what I was going to say.

I wanted to speak. I needed to say something. I had attempted to prepare some comments earlier that morning, words I hoped Catheryn might have found appropriate, but nothing I could think of seemed right. When Tommy died, I had refused to speak at his memorial, immersed in my own drunken anguish and torment and grief. It was an omission I later deeply regretted, and this time I didn't want to make the same mistake. I wanted to say something from the heart. But try as I might, I didn't know how.

Feeling an inexplicable sense of déjà vu, I walked to the lectern that had been set up in front of the chancel railing. I paused when I got there, gazing out at the faces of our friends.

All of them looked silently back at me, the same question in all their eyes.

At last I spoke. "On behalf of the Kane family, I want to thank you all for coming," I began. "I know Catheryn would have been pleased and honored to see you all here today, and she would probably be disappointed about missing the party."

Several people smiled at this, and I could feel the tension in the room lessen a little. "Allison, that was a beautiful slide show," I continued, glancing at my daughter. "I think Catheryn would have loved it. I know I did. I'll definitely want to watch it again when I can do it without crying. Thank you, Ali."

A number of people were still passing tissues in the wake of Allison's slide show, and a polite round of applause for Allison traveled the room, along with laughter at my last comment.

"This is a hard day for all of us," I went on more seriously. "There are many present this afternoon who lost friends and loved ones in the explosion last week. I know Jerry Dondero's wife, Trudy, is here, and I'm touched that she found time in her own grieving to join us today. Thank you, Trudy. And to everyone else who has been hurt by the deaths of our other officers killed in that explosion—task-force Detectives George Garrison, Max Jones, Eli Cooper, and Special Agents Gene Owens and Greg Howe, as well as the eleven patrol officers murdered over past weeks—I'm truly sorry for your loss. Again, thank you all for joining us here today."

I paused, wondering where to go next. The room was silent. I looked down at the lectern, as if an answer might be found there. Not finding it, I looked up, again seeing a roomful of sympathetic faces. My children, Travis and Allison and Nate, and Grandma Dorothy and so many others were waiting to hear my words, and I wanted to make them right. I needed to make them right.

"I . . . I want to say something about Catheryn," I said unsteadily. "I tried to write a speech this morning, but it didn't work out very well. This is hard for me, and I'm not very good at this, so please bear with me if I need to stop."

I took a deep breath, trying to crystallize my thoughts. "When our son Tommy died, my world fell apart," I said quietly. "I couldn't believe that life could be so cruel. I crawled inside a bottle and stayed drunk for days. During that time I let a lot of people down. I hurt my children, and I hurt my wife, and I hurt my best friend, Arnie. And I hurt myself. I said and did things I deeply regret, things I wish I could take back. But of course the world doesn't work like that."

Several people nodded. "So here we are again today, in the same church where we said good-bye to Tommy," I continued. "And now we're saying good-bye to Catheryn. I hope that I've learned something since then, and that this time I act differently." I turned to address my children in the front row. "I'm not certain I can, but I promise I'm going to try to never let you down again."

At this last statement I noticed Nate regarding me intently. He held my gaze for a moment, then nodded slightly, as if to acknowledge that something had passed between us.

"A lot has been said here today about Kate," I went on. "It's been said she was an extraordinary cellist, a consummate artist, a wonderful teacher, a loving mother. It's been said she was kind, funny, beautiful, caring. All those things are true. I think I can add something, something that was just between Kate and me. It's this: Catheryn was a singular companion, in the truest sense of the word. She was *my* companion, someone I was meant to be with. I knew that from the first moment I met her, and I've known it every moment since. She put all the love she had into our relationship, holding nothing back. She became a part of me, probably the better part of me. And I became a part of her."

I paused, again looking out over the room. "All of us here today have lost something precious. Travis and Allison and Nate have lost their mother, and Grandma Dorothy has lost her daughter, and others have lost a fellow artist and teacher, and we've all lost the joy of Catheryn's presence. And I've lost part of myself. Things are never going to be the same for any of us, ever again."

By now the church was completely silent.

"It's a bitter truth that in this lifetime, at some point or another, we are all going to have terrible things happen to us" I pushed on. "*All* of us. We're all going to get sick, and experience pain, and worse. We're all going to lose people we love. And when that happens, when life turns on us with unimaginable cruelty, we're all going to wonder exactly what I'm wondering right now. How can this be right? Is this the way life is supposed to be? What does it all mean?"

I glanced at Father Donovan, who had married Catheryn and me, and who had baptized our children, and who had buried our son Tommy, and who was now presiding over the memorial for my wife. "No offense, Father, but sometimes I wonder if it means anything at all."

I hesitated, trying to picture Catheryn in my mind. "And then I remember a saying Kate used to have. It went something like 'Without the hard times, life wouldn't be nearly as sweet.'"

I shook my head. "I don't know whether that's true or not, but it's something I want to believe. It's something I need to believe. I hope you can believe it, too. Again, on behalf of the Kane family, thank you for coming. And thank you all for the love and sympathy and especially for all the food you've given so freely," I added with a smile, trying to end on a positive note. "But please, no more. Our fridge is packed with enough casseroles to last a month."

This engendered a number of smiles, especially from neighbors who had been delivering meals to our house unabated since the previous weekend. "In a few minutes we're going to head back to the beach for an informal reception," I added, trying to sound upbeat and almost succeeding. "We hope you can join us."

Chapter Thirty-Six

I couldn't sleep that night. After our final guest had left and we'd started straightening up, I left the kids to complete the cleanup. Numb and exhausted, I took a walk along the beach, alone with my thoughts. Although puzzled by my late-night activity, Callie abandoned her bed to accompany me, staying close to my side as we traveled the water's edge. The moon had yet to rise and most of the homes fronting the sand were dark, their occupants having long since retired. They were our friends and neighbors, and I had known most of them for years. I also knew that many of them had attended Catheryn's memorial that afternoon, then returned to their own homes secure in the knowledge that nothing like that could ever happen to them. Not to them.

For their sake, I hoped they were right.

Emotionally drained from the memorial, I tried to think of something other than Catheryn. Instead I tried to picture the man who had taken her. I realized his bullet had been meant for me, not Catheryn, but I was unable to comprehend the hate and anger that had driven him to such murderous lengths.

One thing was certain: I intended to find him.

With Callie leading the way back, I returned to the beach house sometime after 1:00 a.m. Upon arriving, I went in to check on the kids. Although Mike had delayed returning to work and was staying at his home in the Palisades, Allison had decided to remain with our family at the beach. I found her asleep in her room, as was Nate in his. After the service Travis had told me he planned to stay in Malibu for the foreseeable future, and he was asleep in Nate's room as well.

By then I had given up trying to get any rest. Instead I made a pot of coffee and retired to the kitchen table. There, for the next several hours, I drank coffee and tried to get my mind off Catheryn by thinking about the case, determined to find the man who had killed her. Since visiting Detective Montone in Three Rivers, I had been unable to shake the feeling I was missing something. But as hard as I tried, I hadn't been able to put my finger on whatever it was.

To date, the investigation had dead-ended at every turn. The Expedition lead had been our best bet, along with searching for the yard in which it was stored. Now, in a catastrophic explosion, both were gone, along with six members of our team—again leaving us nowhere.

Once more I considered backtracking on the man who I was now convinced was one of the sniper's earlier victims: ex-LAPD Officer Joseph Strom. Unfortunately, that was going to be nearly impossible, as Snead had pointed out. I just didn't know where to start.

Frustrated, I walked to my desk in the bedroom, trying not to look at the empty bed where Catheryn and I had slept together for so many years. Rummaging through my files, I retrieved the copy of Detective Silva's investigative report on Joseph Strom. I also grabbed the case notes Detective Montone had given me. Files in hand, I returned to the kitchen, poured more coffee, and began to read.

I went through the Strom file several times, seeing nothing new. Next I reread Detective Montone's notes on Dr. Luther Cole, not finding anything there, either. I was missing something.

What?

I was halfway through reading the Strom file again when I saw it. I felt a chill crawl up my spine. I have a good memory, but I grabbed Detective Montone's notes to be certain, comparing the two files. I don't know why I hadn't seen it earlier, but in my defense, everyone else had missed it, too.

Officer Joseph Strom had been murdered on June 10. According to Detective Montone's notes, Dr. Luther Cole's deceased son had been born on that very day, twenty years earlier.

I don't believe in coincidence—especially not in a murder investigation. In this particular situation, the odds were 1 in 365. Not likely. But there was still a chance. Another possibility was that someone had tried to set up Dr. Cole by picking that particular date to shoot Strom. I didn't really believe that, either. Only one thing made sense.

Dr. Luther Cole had decided to avenge his son's murder. And he had done it on his son's birthday.

Dr. Cole was our sniper.

Of course, the June 10 connection wasn't enough for an arrest or even a search warrant. Any good lawyer could argue that millions of people were born on June 10, and Joseph Strom's having been murdered on that particular day proved absolutely nothing. And that lawyer would be absolutely right.

Nevertheless, I *knew*.

The question was, where did I go from there?

Taking my information to the task force was an option, but I doubted that Snead would see things any differently than he had earlier, assuming I could even get him to listen. Albert Winslow had been convicted of Strom's murder. Who cared that it happened on June 10?

There was another possibility, another more drastic course of action. I was angry. But as satisfying as it would be to take things into my own hands, I wasn't certain I could live with myself afterward, and it wasn't something I was willing to consider.

At least not yet.

By the time the sun had risen, I still hadn't decided what to do.

I started making breakfast for the kids, then woke them at a little before seven. For the past week Allison had been spending most of her time in her room, often appearing to be on the verge of tears. Travis seemed numb, and Nate had withdrawn into a protective shell of hurt and denial. And I didn't know what to do about any of it.

Like me, Allison had eventually decided to use her job as a distraction, and after breakfast she somberly left for work in Studio City, saying she would call later. After she had departed, Travis and Nate and I spent some time together outside on the deck. Nate had little to say, and I wasn't able to coax much out of him. Travis became slightly more open than he had been at breakfast, but not much. Of all our children, Travis had probably been the closest to Catheryn. The two had formed a bond between them that was based, among other things, on their shared love of music. Like all of us, he had been wounded deeply by Catheryn's loss, and he was talking about not returning to his studies at Juilliard. Trav's dropping out of school was something I would not let happen, but I decided to put off discussing the issue for the moment. There would be time enough later.

Later that morning I left Travis and Nate at the beach and headed into town. I was still on medical leave, my left arm immobilized in a sling and for the most part useless. I probably wouldn't receive clearance to rejoin the task force for at least another week, but I wanted to keep current on the investigation. Thankful that my car had an automatic transmission, I managed to drive fairly well using only my right hand. At least I didn't hit anything on my way downtown.

After leaving my car in the parking structure on First Street, I walked the short distance to PAB and rode the elevator to the sixth floor. By the time I arrived, the morning briefing was long over and it was almost time for lunch, but I had texted Deluca that I was coming, and he was waiting for me when I walked into the room.

To my amazement, so was everyone else. Sympathetic smiles and a short round of applause welcomed me as I entered, as well as greetings from every detective in the room.

"Thanks," I said, glancing around in surprise.

"Glad you're here, Kane. Things haven't been the same without you," said Murphy. "For one, Lieutenant Snead seems much happier."

"That's for sure," someone else agreed. "I think he finally managed to unbunch his panties."

I knew that every detective present had been deeply saddened by Catheryn's murder, as well as by our team's catastrophic losses at the storage yard. The rough humor customarily bandied about in a squad room was the only way they knew how to go forward. I understood completely, although I wasn't ready to join in.

As the room began to settle back into a work routine, Deluca carefully placed an arm around my good shoulder. "Hey, Dan," he said quietly. "Great to see you back."

"I'm not actually back," I explained. "I just thought I'd drop by and see how things are going. Anything new turn up?"

Deluca had visited me repeatedly at the hospital, keeping me updated on task-force developments. After my release I'd been preoccupied with Catheryn's memorial, and we hadn't recently discussed the case.

"We haven't lost any more officers," Deluca replied. "Probably because the guy's out shopping for a new Expedition," he added bitterly.

"Was anything else recovered at the storage yard?" I asked. I knew we had traced ownership of the Expedition to a private party in Long Beach. The owner of the Expedition had sold the vehicle to someone named William Johnson, after which the alleged Mr. Johnson had failed to reregister the car. A DMV check of William Johnson had also come up empty.

Deluca shook his head. "We're still sifting the rubble. We found the remnants of a police scanner, a pair of shooting earmuffs, binoculars, a laser rangefinder, and what's left of a bench he might have been using to stabilize his shots. Unfortunately, it doesn't look promising for prints or other trace evidence. The fire pretty much took care of that. By the way, the lab pieced together the explosive device. It was a larger version of the pipe bomb he used in Santa Monica Canyon. Had it rigged next to the gas tank."

"Anything else?"

"We've been walking around pictures of the guy, shots we pulled off the surveillance video," Deluca answered. "It's hard to tell with his ball cap and glasses, but one of the managers at a Doubletree down the street thinks he recognizes the guy. Said he's been checking into the motel for the past year. Stays a few days, pays cash. He was there the night our guys were shot in Santa Monica Canyon. There was a credit card on file. William Johnson."

"You check the other dates?"

"Yep. They all matched. William Johnson, or whatever his name is, was staying there when our guys were shot in the Mount Olympus subdivision, and in the Palisades, and in Venice."

I wondered how far back the Doubletree's records went. I had a feeling that if they kept records for more than a year, I would find William Johnson's name on the register the night ex-LAPD Officer Joseph Strom had been shot in Simi Valley. "The credit card lead anywhere?" I asked.

"It was linked to a bank account in the name of William Johnson. Same deal. He opened a checking account with fake ID, deposited some money, got a credit card, and kept up on his payments. Another dead end."

I thought a moment. "Any trace evidence at the Doubletree?"

Again Deluca shook his head. "We went over the last room he rented—dusted for prints, collected hairs, the whole nine yards. Unfortunately, it had been a couple weeks since he'd been there, and the room had been repeatedly cleaned and rerented."

"Anything recovered there might come in handy when we find the guy."

"Yeah, maybe."

I looked around the conference room, not spotting Lieutenant Snead. "Snead still downstairs getting skewered by the media?"

"Yep. Couldn't happen to a nicer guy."

I thought a moment. I still hadn't decided what to do about Dr. Cole, but I wanted to bring in Deluca before coming to a decision. But first there was one more piece of the puzzle I needed to check. "Show me the storage-yard surveillance log," I said.

Deluca had the storage-yard footage I wanted to see recorded on DVD. We viewed it on one of the workstation computers. The security log, complete with a timestamp running along the bottom, showed a tall man leaving the storage lot on foot. As Deluca had said, he was wearing a ball cap and sunglasses, and he avoided giving the camera a clear shot of his face. He was carrying a long cardboard box over one shoulder. The container looked large enough to contain a rifle. Maybe several.

I watched the footage a number of times, occasionally asking Deluca to shuttle back and forth. The man might have been Dr. Cole, but I couldn't say for certain. Then I noticed something. "Paul, go back a few seconds," I instructed.

Deluca shuttled back to a point where the man was just passing the security camera. He had his face turned away, but the camera had caught a good shot of his hand holding the box. There, on his fourth finger, was a ring I had recently seen. I owned a similar ring. I had received it many years back, upon graduating from the University of Southern California.

I felt a shiver of satisfaction. The odds of Dr. Cole not being our sniper had just dropped to zero. Now I knew for certain.

"Paul, I have something to tell you," I said.

And for the next ten minutes I spoke quietly, bringing Deluca up to date—beginning with my trip to Three Rivers and ending with my connecting the shooting of Officer Strom to the birthday of Dr. Cole's son. The USC ring was the clincher.

When I finished, Deluca sat silently, regarding me with an expression I couldn't quite fathom. At last he spoke. "Damn, Kane," he said softly. "You found the guy."

"Yeah," I said. "I found him. Now what do we do? Take it to Snead?"

Deluca rubbed his chin. "It's going to be hard to get him to listen, but I don't see how he can do otherwise." Again he regarded me for a long moment. "But you're thinking of something else, aren't you? Who else knows about this?"

"Just you and me."

Deluca fell silent once more. At last he spoke. "I'm with you, Dan," he said, holding my gaze. "I'm with you all the way. Any way you want to play it."

The moment had come to make a decision.

And I did. As much as I would have liked to take justice into my own hands, as much as I would have enjoyed extracting revenge for Catheryn's murder, as much as I wanted to hurt Cole as much as he'd hurt me, deep down I had always known what that decision would be.

I took a deep breath, then slowly let it out. "Let's go talk to Snead."

Chapter Thirty-Seven

Snead glared at me from across his desk. "Go home, Kane," he ordered.

"Lieutenant, you have to listen to me on this," I insisted.

"We've already had that conversation," Snead snapped. "More than once, if I recall. I told you then, and out of respect for your recent loss, I'll tell you one more time. The Strom case is closed. We will not be reopening it."

"Listen—"

"No, you listen, Kane. Until now I've cut you some slack, and I'm cutting you some more right now. But there's a limit. I ordered you to drop the Strom investigation and concentrate on finding our sniper, and that's what I expect you to do. Anything else and I'll bring you up on charges. Is that understood?"

"I hear what you're saying," I said, trying to control my temper.

"Good," Snead said more temperately. "Look, I know you're feeling guilty about your wife's death, which is natural. Now you're trying to make things right by playing the lone wolf and catching the guy who did it. I understand that, too. Unfortunately, your half-baked theory about Strom isn't the way to go about it. Go home, Kane. Let the task force do its work, and come back when your head is on straight."

It had been a while since I'd been in a tussle, but Snead's comment about Catheryn made me see red. Years back I had broken his jaw, and at that moment I was considering breaking it again. Only one thing was stopping me.

I knew he was right.

I had tried not to think of Catheryn's death in those terms, but in the end there was no avoiding it. If I'd had a desk job like a normal person, some psycho wouldn't have taken a shot at me in a parking lot. What made things worse was that Catheryn's murder wasn't the first time my job had put our family at risk.

I took a deep breath, struggling to control myself. Punching Snead wouldn't do any good. I had to make him listen.

"Bill, I know there's bad blood between us, but right now you need to listen," I said evenly. "I know who—"

"Out of my office, Kane," Snead ordered. "This has gone on long enough. And as I told you before, it's *Lieutenant* Snead."

I placed my thick-knuckled hands on Snead's desk and leaned across. "You're going to listen to me, *Bill*—even if I have to knock that superior smirk off your face to make you do it," I growled. "Do you understand what I'm saying?"

"How dare you!" Snead sputtered.

"Do you understand me?"

Snead glanced away, unable to hold my gaze. "I understand," he said, turning pale. "You're going to regret this, Kane."

"That may be, but you're still going to listen."

Snead started to reach for his phone. Noticing something in my expression, he thought better of it. "Go ahead," he muttered. "Dig your own grave. I'll gladly throw dirt on it."

And so I talked.

And Snead listened.

At first he tried to object to almost everything I said, but I kept talking. And by the time I finished he was sitting quietly, taking in every word. When I was done, he didn't say anything for almost a minute.

Finally he spoke. "Kane, if you're right about this . . ."

"I'm right, Lieutenant," I said. "Believe me, I'm right. Now let's do something about it."

After that things began to move quickly—at least as quickly as a top-heavy, overstaffed task-force investigation can move. Snead placed a call to the Three Rivers Police Department, giving a brief summation of our situation and asking their assistance in maintaining covert surveillance on Dr. Cole's residence. Snead added that under no circumstance were they to engage Cole or reveal their presence in any way. If he left his house, they were to call us and follow at a discreet distance. Next Snead contacted the Tulare County Sheriff's Department, requesting that they take over the surveillance as soon as they could get officers on the scene.

271

Several detectives, including me, had questioned the wisdom of tasking the Three Rivers Police Department with the surveillance of Cole, even if it were only for a short time. We felt that as a small department in a sleepy mountain village, Three Rivers might be out of its depth. Nevertheless, we needed someone watching Cole's residence immediately, and the Three Rivers Police Department was the nearest agency.

Bottom line, until reinforcements arrived from the Tulare County Sheriff's Department, we didn't have much choice.

Chapter Thirty-Eight

D r. Cole glanced at his watch, surprised to see that it was nearly one o'clock. He'd been working hard all morning, which had made the time go quickly. Satisfied with his progress, he decided it was time to eat. Maybe someplace nice as a reward, he thought. There were plenty of upscale restaurants in nearby Beverly Hills that would still be open for lunch. He could drive around and simply pick one. An expensive one. After all, he'd been through a lot lately. He deserved a good meal.

Having to start from scratch for his next series of shoots was inconvenient, but he had come a long way over the past week. And to be honest, he wasn't really starting from scratch. He already knew how to procure counterfeit ID, for instance, and knowing how to do something was half the battle. He'd recently received his new California driver's license, which identified him as Adrian Duncan.

From there it had been a simple task to open a new bank account and deposit a small amount of cash. Before long he'd have a credit card as well. That very morning, paying cash and using his new ID, he had rented a large storage garage in West Hollywood—a location that provided easy access to numerous suburban neighborhoods, as well as a straight shot to the Hollywood Freeway a few miles east.

All that remained was to purchase another car. He thought that this time he might get something bigger than the Expedition. Possibly one of those Cadillac SUVs. A black one, like the government agencies used. What were they called? Navigators, Escalades, something like that.

For a moment, with the memory of his lost Expedition, his thoughts flashed back to his botched shoot at the medical center. He couldn't believe he had missed. Well, not completely missed, but this wasn't horseshoes, and "almost" didn't count. In his own defense, the woman had slipped and spoiled his aim. It was unfortunate that she had been killed instead of Kane, but collateral damage was to be expected. At any rate, we all die sometime, and it was her fault for marrying a cop.

Determined to learn from his mistakes, Dr. Cole forced his mind back to the present. The police had been lucky the last time, coming close to catching him. Too close, in fact. This next series of shoots would be different.

Anyway, time for lunch, he thought with a sigh. He started his rental car, which he'd parked on a side street near his new storage garage. Before putting the vehicle in gear, he decided to check the security cameras installed at his house. He'd been gone several days, and he liked to keep an eye on things at home in his absence.

After booting up his webcam app, he toggled through the cameras guarding his house. The inside camera showed nothing amiss. The one facing the street was a different matter.

His stomach dropped. He couldn't believe his eyes. Two black-and-white patrol cars were parked partway down the street. He could make out a pair of officers inside each vehicle. The camera facing his rear patio showed another officer hiding on the far side of his back fence.

He had been discovered. He didn't know how, but he had.

They knew.

And that changed everything.

He felt a stab of disappointment as he realized things were ending. He had hoped to continue a lot longer. The game was coming to a close, as he knew it eventually would. In a way, he was almost glad.

Dr. Cole smiled grimly, deciding to skip lunch.

He had one last thing left to do.

Chapter Thirty-Nine

Our preparations for the arrest of Dr. Luther Cole accelerated significantly when Assistant Director Shepherd was brought into the loop, adding the full weight of the FBI's considerable resources. Coordinating with the FBI's Sacramento field office and the special agent in charge at its satellite Fresno resident agency—the closest FBI presence to Three Rivers—arrangements were made for agents to meet our Los Angeles arrest team later that day. The plan was to fly selected members of the sniper task force to Visalia; from there the team would caravan to Three Rivers in FBI vehicles provided by the Fresno agency, joining representatives of the Tulare County Sheriff's Department and the Three Rivers Police upon arrival. Considering the explosion at the storage yard, a bomb squad from the Tulare County Sheriff's Department would also be present. One of the FBI's Gulfstream G-Vs was currently being gassed and readied at Santa Monica Airport, and within the hour it would be awaiting our arrest team on the tarmac.

Assembling the necessary paperwork took a bit longer. Working with the Tulare County District Attorney's office, an arrest warrant for Dr. Luther Cole was eventually issued, along with search warrants for Cole's home and vehicles. As required by law, a list of items to be seized was specifically enumerated in the warrant, including any and all of Dr. Cole's rifles, pistols, and other firearms; reloading and gunsmith equipment including cartridge cases, bullets, dies, presses, and propellant powders; rifle scopes, muzzle brakes, and sonic suppressors; galvanized pipe, fittings, detonators, and any other material appropriate for bomb construction; cell phones, sniper logs, and shooting equipment including rangefinders, earmuffs, rifle rests, and shooting stabilizers; items of clothing matching those recorded on the surveillance tape; telephone and financial records; and computers, laptops, and files. And last but not least, Dr. Cole's USC ring.

I placed a call to Special Agent Wyatt to make certain we weren't leaving anything out. After several suggestions, he assured me that our inventory of gun and shooting materials was complete.

Of course, all of our plans assumed that Dr. Cole was currently at home, an obvious weak link in our strategy. But if he wasn't at his house when we executed the arrest warrant, confidence was high that wherever he was, he would eventually return and we could pick him up then.

It had sounded good, at least on paper.

The actual arrest plan didn't sound nearly as good, at least not to me. The challenge was taking Dr. Cole into custody without giving him an opportunity to start shooting. We knew he had both the will and the firepower to do a lot of damage, and we wanted to avoid engaging him in a gunfight.

In a hastily assembled task-force meeting later that afternoon, three arrest scenarios were proposed: One: We could wait until Cole left his house and pick him up before he realized what was happening. Two: We could wait until he was asleep and execute a forced entry at night, grabbing him before he had a chance to arm himself. Three: We could call in a SWAT unit, surround Cole's house, and go from there.

Option one was rejected because it might take too long, giving Cole a chance to notice our presence and start shooting. Option three was also rejected as being too risky. In the end, a modified option two was approved. It was decided that because we would be getting to Three Rivers after dark anyway, our best course would be to quietly evacuate neighbors on all sides of Cole's residence, then enter his house with overwhelming force after he had gone to sleep. If the situation on the ground changed before then, we could work out the details as needed.

Again, it had sounded good on paper.

During this time, as the wheels turned on our arrest preparations, task-force detectives downloaded fingerprint cards that Dr. Cole had submitted when applying for his State of California controlled substance license. His prints were matched to a partial thumbprint lifted at the Doubletree Motel, giving further confirmation that Cole was our shooter. During this time we also received a callback from the Tulare County Sheriff's

Department informing us they had arrived on the scene and assumed responsibility for maintaining surveillance on Dr. Cole's residence. They added that Three Rivers' surveillance had unfortunately been "considerably less than covert." Nevertheless, Cole's silver Toyota was still parked in his driveway and his other vehicle was thought to be in his garage, so it appeared that he was still at home, none the wiser. Apparently no harm had been done.

It was eventually decided that twelve members of our task force would fly to Visalia. Of course Snead would go, accompanied by Shepherd and two of the FBI special agents who had been on the investigation since the beginning. The two remaining detectives from our Robbery-Homicide contingent—Peter Church and Evan Nolan—would make the trip, as would Brian Murphy and his partner Greg Bolton from Hollywood, Jules Jacoby from Venice, and Kevin Aguilar from Van Nuys. And Paul Deluca.

And me.

For Catheryn's sake, I needed to be there. As expected, I had a difficult time arguing my way onto the plane. Snead repeatedly pointed out that I was on medical leave and relieved of active duty. In addition, as I couldn't use my left arm, if anything went wrong I would just be in the way. Nevertheless, I was the one who had found Dr. Cole, and that counted for a lot with other members of the task force—many of whom had lost friends in the sniper attacks. In the end, bowing to pressure from other task-force members, Snead had reluctantly showed a rare streak of humanity and decided to let me go—stipulating that I would be present only as an observer, to which I agreed. Actually, my observer status was a good thing. I'm not certain I could have trusted myself around Dr. Cole with a weapon in my hand.

By the time preparations were completed, the afternoon had started to wane. As it looked like I would be staying in Tulare County overnight, I called Allison to ask her to take care of things at home in my absence. She was still at CBS Studio City when I reached her, and she sounded rushed for time.

"Sorry, Dad, can't talk," she said, picking up on the second ring.

"No problem, Ali." I told her I would probably be gone until the following afternoon, and asked her to hold down the fort until my return.

"Is this about the sniper case?" she asked.

"It is," I admitted. I considered saying more, but decided there would be time for that later. Of all the news stations, CBS had been the only one that had agreed to stop broadcasting their so-called sniper profiles. The spurious psychological analyses presented by various "experts" in the field were misleading at best, and at worst they were hurting our investigation, so we were thankful when at least one station finally eliminated that type of coverage. Allison had also been helpful in heading off an embarrassing situation with the Expedition leak, and after all she'd been through, I figured she should be first in line when the arrest announcement was made. I was going to make that happen, no matter what the repercussions.

After a slight pause, Allison said, "I don't suppose you would be able to . . ."

"Ali, you just need to wait a little more. We're looking at an arrest shortly, but keep that quiet for now. I promise when it goes down, you'll be the first to know."

"Thanks, Dad. I appreciate it. I'll see you when you get back from, uh, from wherever it is you can't tell me. And . . . please be careful."

"Don't worry. I will."

After disconnecting, I checked with Snead one last time, confirming that the FBI's G-V was scheduled to leave Santa Monica Airport at 4:30 p.m., which gave me a little under an hour to get there. By then most of the arrest-team members had already left. I took the elevator to the first floor and walked the short distance to the First Street parking structure where I had left my car. Although I still had plenty of time, I decided to be early for a change.

I had my keys out when I arrived at my car. I had just unlocked my door when a raspy voice sounded behind me.

"Hello, Detective Kane."

I froze. I knew that voice.

Slowly, I turned.

"Don't try anything heroic, Detective," said Dr. Cole. He was about eight feet away, too far for me to rush him. His right hand hung loose at his side. It was holding one of the largest handguns I had ever seen. "If you do," he added, "rest assured I won't hesitate to shoot you."

"You mean shoot me again," I corrected.

Dr. Cole smiled coldly. "Correct. Shoot you *again*. Please get in your car. Don't make any sudden movements."

"No."

"Get in the car, Detective Kane. Get in the car, or I will shoot you right where you stand."

"I think you're going to shoot me no matter what I do, Dr. Cole."

"That remains to be seen, doesn't it? Get in the car and live a few more minutes. What do you have to lose?"

I shrugged and slid behind the wheel, thinking that if Dr. Cole wanted me to drive somewhere, someplace more private, the chance to do something before we got there might present itself. Something like driving into a freeway abutment and taking him with me.

Dr. Cole levered his bulky frame into the rear seat, sitting directly behind me. "Fasten your wrist to the steering wheel," he ordered, passing me a thick plastic restraint. "Your *good* wrist," he added.

I fumbled with the restraint, my mind racing. There had to be something I could do. I had to be ready when the opportunity presented itself, if it ever did. I finally got the plastic tie looped around the steering wheel.

"Insert your hand and pull the restraint tight with your teeth," Dr. Cole instructed.

I did as he said, trying to make the tie look secure while still leaving enough room for me to break free. To my dismay, Dr. Cole abruptly leaned over the seat and finished cinching the tie. The plastic strap cut deep into my wrist.

"There," said Dr. Cole. "Two things, Detective Kane. First, I assume you are armed. I'm not going to search you for weapons. I'm simply going to shoot you if you don't remain completely still. Do you understand?"

"I understand," I said. I usually carried my service weapon in a shoulder rig under my left arm, but the medical sling had made that impossible. I still had my backup pistol in an ankle holster, but there was no way to reach it.

"Second, if someone happens by and you signal them in any way, I will shoot them, and then I will shoot you. Do you understand?"

"I understand," I repeated. "So what happens now?"

I was hoping he'd order me to drive somewhere, buying me some time. I knew he intended to kill me. Driving might give me a chance to do something—if not to escape, at least to make certain he couldn't hurt anyone else. If the opportunity presented itself, I would gladly take him with me.

"How did you find me?" he asked, ignoring my question.

"Does it matter?"

"No, I don't suppose it does. I *am* curious, though."

I decided to answer. "Your son's birthday. Same night Joseph Strom was murdered. That *was* you, wasn't it?"

"Of course. Wouldn't you have done the same?"

"I'm not sure, Doctor. Why don't we trade places and I'll let you know?"

"An interesting offer, but I think not."

"Speaking of Strom," I went on, trying to keep Dr. Cole talking. As long as he was talking, there might be a chance. "I understand why you did it. Officer Strom was scum, the kind of mutt that gives our department a bad name. Your son's death was a bad shoot, and the LAPD shouldn't have covered it up. I don't condone your murdering Strom, but I understand. But why the others? Was it losing your wife?"

"What do you think, Detective Kane? How did you feel when you lost *your* wife? Angry enough to kill? Were you angry enough to decide that some people don't deserve to live?

People like me? Were you angry enough to take things into your own hands to get even?"

"I thought about it," I answered honestly. "I thought about it a lot."

"Of course you did. We have a lot in common, you and I. We have both lost a son—mine to murder, yours to the vagaries of life. We have both lost a wife—yours to murder, mine to the vagaries of life. Interesting, no?"

"Vagaries of life? I thought your wife killed herself," I said harshly. "Probably when she discovered she was married to a monster."

"Watch yourself, Detective."

"Watch myself? Or what? What are you going to do, shoot me? Like I said, you're going to do that anyway."

"So you have nothing to lose," Dr. Cole observed. "Another interesting comparison. Now that you know you're going to die, I'll wager you're trying to think of some way to take me with you. Am I right?"

"Why don't we drive somewhere and find out?"

"I don't think so. We're not going anywhere, but don't be ashamed of your murderous intentions, Detective. I understand completely, I really do. I told you we have a lot in common." He paused a moment, then continued. "Let me ask you something. Do you want to continue to live?"

"Thanks for asking. Are you giving me the option?"

"Answer the question."

I was angry, choking on frustration and rage. The man who had murdered Catheryn and hurt so many others was sitting behind me, and I couldn't do a thing about it. With his last question, I knew we had reached a turning point. And there was nothing I could do about that, either.

"Go to hell," I said.

"Most probably," Dr. Cole said softly. "One last chance, Detective, and then our time together is up. Do you want to continue to live?"

At any moment expecting my life to end, I once more decided to reply. And to my shame, I found I wasn't certain of my answer. Something inside me had changed when Dr. Cole cinched my wrist to the steering wheel, cutting off all chance of escape. Though I couldn't admit it to myself then, still stubbornly clinging to a belief that there might be a way out, I had accepted my death.

And I hadn't much cared.

Finally I answered. "I . . . I don't really know," I said, realizing it was true.

"And why is that, Detective?"

I didn't answer.

"Is it because you've lost hope?"

Still I didn't answer.

"I've learned something from all this," Dr. Cole went on. "I suppose it might be considered my legacy," he added thoughtfully. "What I've learned is that taking a man's life is easy. Anyone can do it. What's hard is taking a man's hope. Hope is everything, Detective. *Everything.*"

I strained at my restraint. The plastic tie cut deeper into my skin. If I were to die, I wanted to do it reaching for Dr. Cole's throat.

"Have I taken your hope, Detective? Has *life* taken your hope?"

I felt blood dripping from my wrist. I strained even harder, attempting to face the man who had robbed me of so much . . . and who would now take the rest.

Silence.

This was it. This was how it would end. I could feel the tension building. Only seconds remained. I twisted my head for one last look at Dr. Cole, wondering what the next life would bring.

Dr. Cole stared back at me from the rear seat, his eyes filled with torment and despair. Tears coursed down his cheeks. He held his weapon in both hands, muzzle pressed tightly under his chin, his finger on the trigger.

"When this time comes for you . . . and it will," he said softly, "remember me."

We stared at each other for what seemed an eternity.

"Don't," I said.

With a bitter smile, Dr. Cole pulled the trigger.

Epilogue

The following Sunday after early morning Mass, I drove to the San Fernando Valley to visit Catheryn's grave. Allison, Travis, and Nate accompanied me. It was the first time we had returned to Forest Lawn Cemetery since the memorial, and I think we were all apprehensive about going, our sorrow and grief at Catheryn's loss still nearly as raw as the day she had died.

My left arm was now out of the sling, but I was a long way from being fully recovered. My ribs were healing, or so I was told. My hearing had returned as well, at least mostly, and the insistent ringing in my ears had finally abated. My burst right eardrum—the ear closest to Dr. Cole's Desert Eagle when he'd pulled the trigger—was also healing. Nevertheless, I was still on medical leave from the department, and I was uncertain about when I would return. Or, for that matter, *if* I would return.

I had a lot of thinking to do.

It was a somber ride to the valley. Partway to the cemetery I pulled off the freeway, deciding to let Travis drive the rest of the way. Allison and Nate sat in the back, both unusually quiet. Callie was making the ride with us, too. For the past weeks she had sensed that something was wrong and had become uncharacteristically timid and shy. Nate had begged to bring her, insisting she was part of our family and deserved to be with us. I agreed, with the stipulation that she remain in the car, as dogs weren't allowed on cemetery grounds.

When we arrived at Forest Lawn, Travis pulled into a deserted parking lot several hundred feet below the grassy hillside where we had buried Catheryn. With a sigh, he turned off the engine. The sun hadn't yet crested the ridge of mountains across the valley. Beneath the distant peaks, rising like monoliths, the towers of Burbank's movie studios and business parks pierced a blanket of morning mist. Except for a soft rush of traffic sound filtering up from the Ventura Freeway below, all was silent.

For a moment none of us made a move to get out. Finally I opened my door and climbed from the car. The morning air was cool and crisp, and I was struck by the realization that fall had finally arrived. "C'mon, kids," I said. "Let's go visit your mom."

With a growing sense of unreality, I headed up the slope, traversing what seemed endless lines of brass memorial plaques curving across the cemetery grounds. My children followed a few steps behind, seeming as reluctant to be there as I was.

When we arrived, I noticed that Catheryn's permanent memorial plaque had been placed since our last visit. Except for a lack of tarnish, it was almost identical to Tommy's brass plaque, set in the ground nearby. I read the inscription on Catheryn's marker, thinking the few words inscribed there a sad summary of her life.

Allison had brought a bouquet of specially ordered yellow trumpet daffodils, Catheryn's favorite flowers. Wordlessly, she laid them atop Catheryn's plaque. As an afterthought, she leaned down and withdrew a single flower from the bouquet, placing a bloom on Tommy's marker as well.

I felt I should say something. As had so often been the case these past days, I didn't know what. Instead, gripped by a heartrending sense of futility, I sat on the grass and stared out over the valley, my thoughts returning to other visits I'd made to that very spot—sometimes alone, sometimes with family—visits to Tommy's final resting place that had proved to be turning points in my life. It was here I had first learned that life could be unimaginably cruel. It was here I had first accepted my failings as a father. It was here I had discovered a truth my children had hidden after Tommy's death—a secret that had nearly torn apart our family. And it was here I had said a final good-bye to Catheryn.

And now we were here once again.

"It isn't fair," said Allison softly, sitting down beside me. "Life isn't fair."

"Nobody ever claimed it was," I agreed, attempting to rise above the black, smothering depression that had recently filled my days. Despite my despondency, I realized there was more at stake that morning than how I felt. My children had been hurt as much as I, possibly more. My family needed me, and I didn't know what to do. I wished with all my heart that Catheryn were there. She always knew the right thing to do or say, even if I didn't always listen. God, I missed her.

Nate joined me on the grass, sitting on my other side. "I miss Mom," he said, echoing my thoughts.

"We all do, Nate," said Travis, who remained standing near Catheryn's marker, hands thrust deep in his pockets. "I miss Tommy, too."

It was time that I spoke, even if I didn't know how to proceed. "I need to get something off my chest," I began. "I want you kids to listen, and we can talk things over after that if you want, okay?"

"Okay," said Allison. Travis nodded. Nate glanced away and shrugged.

I hesitated, looking out over the valley. "I'm so sorry for all of this," I said. "Ali was right. Life isn't fair, and sometimes it doesn't make sense." With a surge of guilt, I glanced at Catheryn's plaque. "Losing your mom wasn't fair, and I deeply regret bringing this tragedy into your lives. I realize if it hadn't been for my position on the police force, none of this would have happened."

"You can't blame yourself, Dad," Allison said gently. "This isn't your fault."

"I wish I could believe that," I replied. I noticed Nate regarding me with an expression I couldn't quite decipher. Distrust? Anger? I couldn't tell.

"I wish I could have protected you kids better," I went on, hoping I was getting through, especially to Nate. "But I didn't, and now I'm not certain I want to continue doing what I've been doing."

"You're going to retire from the force?" asked Travis.

"I'm considering it. It's probably like closing the barn door after the horses have escaped, but I'm thinking about it. Either way, I am so deeply sorry for the role I played in your mother's death. I hope someday you can forgive me."

"Nothing to forgive," Travis said numbly. "You were just doing your job."

"Are you going to start drinking again?" asked Nate.

"No, Nate. I'm not," I said, realizing it was the truth. No matter what else happened, that part of me was in the past. I hesitated, then pushed on. "As Ali said, life may not make sense, but I learned something from your mom about dealing with the hard parts after Tommy died. It helped me. I'm hoping it can help you."

"What?" asked Nate.

"I learned from your mother that you can't get *past* something like this," I said. I glanced at Allison and Travis and saw they were listening. "You have to get *through* it. If you try to ignore the pain, it will just make things worse. You have to embrace it, feel it all, and then somehow emerge on the other side. It won't happen all at once, but it will happen. And in the end, after all the hurt and tears and pain, it will become a part of who you are."

"I . . . I hope you're right," mumbled Allison. "I don't see how, but I hope you're right."

"There's another thing that can help," I went on, willing my words to be true. "Family."

"Kanes stand together, no matter what?" Nate said bitterly.

He was referring to the motto I had been drilling into my kids for years, and it was something in which I still firmly believed. "That's exactly right, Nate," I said. "No matter what."

Nate looked away.

"Your mother believed that, too," I said. "She would want us to be strong and help each other through this. You know that, Nate. Don't you?"

Nate still refused to answer, not meeting my gaze.

"Another thing," I added, disheartened by Nate's silence. "If any of you want to get counseling, or if you want to talk to Father Donovan, or whatever, I will support that all the way. Okay?"

When no one said anything, I went on. "I don't know what the future is going to bring," I said. "I'm sure there will be some good times again, and there will undoubtedly be more bad times, too."

"Gee, that makes me feel better," Allison mumbled.

"What I'm trying to say, Ali, is that although it may not seem like it right now, life can still be good. You have to remember that," I said, speaking to myself as well.

"So where do we go from here?" asked Travis.

"Well, Trav, at some point you'll be heading back to New York, where you *will* continue your studies," I answered. "I know you have doubts right now about returning to Juilliard, but we'll talk about that later. Just remember it's what Catheryn would have wanted. And Ali, you have a wedding to plan, not to mention that you're already off to a great start at CBS—especially with that sniper task force exclusive you somehow came up with," I added, attempting to lighten things. "And Nate, for a while it's just going to be you and me and Callie at the beach house. You okay with that?"

Still, Nate didn't answer.

"Nate?"

Instead of replying, Nate slid closer to me on the grass. Then, putting his arms around my neck, he gave me a hug. I clumsily hugged him back, feeling as if my heart were about to break. I knew there was a long road ahead for Nate and me, and there were hurts and betrayals that wouldn't be mended overnight. But this was a start.

"Well," Allison sighed, "now that we've got that settled . . ."

"There's one more thing," I said. Reaching into my pocket, I withdrew a plain white envelope and set it on the grass.

All three children stared at it. "What is it?" Allison asked.

"It's from your mother," I answered.

"From Mom? But how? I thought she—"

"She wrote it several years ago," I explained. "She wrote it when she was in the hospital, the night before starting her cancer treatments. There was a chance things might not go as planned, and she gave me this letter for you kids just in case."

"And you never opened it?" Allison asked incredulously.

"When she recovered, I sort of put it out of my mind," I answered. "I thought about it the other day and found it in my papers and . . . well, I figured this might be a good time to give it to you."

Still, no one reached for the envelope. "Read it out loud, Dad," suggested Travis.

I turned to Allison. "I think your mom would have liked you to read it, Ali."

"Me?"

I nodded. "Please."

With trembling hands, Allison picked up the envelope. She hesitated, then carefully opened the flap. Inside, in Catheryn's perfect penmanship, were three handwritten pages. Allison stared at the sheets, her eyes rapidly traveling the lines of the first page.

"Out loud, Ali," Nate insisted.

"Please, Ali," said Travis. "What did Mom say?"

Allison looked up from her reading, seeming shaken. She gazed at her brothers for a long moment, then took a breath and began reading aloud. And as she did, her voice strong and clear, I was once more struck by how much she had grown to resemble her mother. Not only in her appearance, but in the way she found strength in even the worst of situations, and in the unshakable power of her convictions. And as I listened, I could almost imagine it was Catheryn who was speaking, her words coming to us across a chasm she herself was unable to traverse.

"My dearest family," Allison began. "If you are reading this, it means I'm no longer with you. I think that's the euphemism they use in the movies, right? Anyway, I'm starting my medical treatments tomorrow, and my doctors tell me to prepare for a difficult time. Although I never thought I'd be writing something like this, it's hard to predict what life may bring, so I'm doing this now in case I don't have the strength later.

"First, I love you all, more than I can say. I have been blessed to have you as my family. You are the most important people in my life. Second, I know you are sad. You had better be (just kidding). Seriously, I don't want you to mourn me for too long. Instead I want you to remember me with love and get on with your lives. Life is precious, and in the end it will be taken from us all, so don't waste it. Ever. I've had a wonderful life, with no regrets other than not being present to watch you grow up and have families of your own, and to meet the people you will love, and to help with your weddings, and to hold your children, and to boss you around (more kidding), and to be a part of your lives. I have truly been blessed. I've had love, and music, and you. No one could ask for more."

Allison paused to take a breath, and then continued. "Trav, that you have followed me into a life in music couldn't make me more happy. Music has filled my days with joy and beauty, and my hope is that it does the same for you. It's been said that music makes us more than we are. I don't know whether that's true. But if it is, I hope that it's true for you, and that it fulfills your life as much as it has mine. You are an artist, Trav. It's not what you do; it's who you are.

"Allison, my only daughter, you are my heart. I know we haven't always seen eye-to-eye, and I know that far too often we haven't agreed on anything. But that's because we're so alike, you and I. I love you, Allison. Please remember that. I have always loved you. If I've been hard on you, it's because you have so many gifts you don't see, so much you have to offer. I know you're involved in working at the news station, but please find time for your writing as well. Your words are able to move people, Ali. Truly move them. That is a rare gift, given to a very few."

Again Allison stopped, turning to wipe her eyes. "I can't do this anymore," she said quietly.

"Please, Ali," I said. "Finish."

"Keep reading, Ali," urged Nate. "What did Mom write to me?"

Allison started to refuse. Seeing something in her younger brother's face, she instead took a moment to compose herself and began reading anew. "Dearest Nate, my youngest," she said softly. "Although I don't think of you as the baby of the family anymore, you aren't a man yet, either. You have yet to spread your wings, and I am heartbroken that I won't be there to watch you learn to fly. Listen to your heart, Nate. And listen to your father. He loves you as much as I do, and he will guide you the rest of the way. I know you have doubts about yourself, places inside where you're afraid to look. Don't be. You have so much love inside; all you have to do is let it out. Decide what kind of a man you want to be, and be it. It's all up to you."

Allison again stopped reading.

"Is that all?" I asked.

Allison shook her head. "The last part is written to you, Dad," she said, offering me the final page of Catheryn's letter.

"Read it," I said, trying to hide my surprise. I had thought Catheryn's letter had been written only to our children.

"Are you sure?" Allison asked.

It didn't seem right for Allison to stop. "I'm sure," I said.

Allison glanced again at Travis and Nate, then proceeded to the final page of Catheryn's letter. "Dan, I don't know where to start," she began, her voice once more reminding me of Catheryn's. "How do I say good-bye to someone I've loved so deeply, someone I've loved for so long? We have shared so much that sometimes I have difficulty remembering where one of us starts and the other leaves off. You're a part of me, Dan. And I'm a part of you. I know you have difficulty expressing your feelings, but I know how much you love me, and I know how much losing me is going to hurt. Please try to find joy in your life. Don't be alone. Open up to the people around you. They love you, too, and they can help. And please don't remember me with sadness. Focus on our good times together—our marriage, the love we shared, the birth of our children, our parties at the beach, our laughter, our friends, all of it—and remember me with a smile. Please take care of our family. And remember that I loved you with all my heart.

"I'm sorry that this letter is so short. I have so much to say, but I need to end this and get some sleep. Tomorrow is a big day. As I said, this letter is just in case, so with any luck you will never get to read it. Goodnight, Dan, and Travis, and Allison, and Nate. You are in my heart as I wait to see what tomorrow will bring. With all my love, Catheryn."

Allison folded the letter and placed it back into the envelope. Silently, she handed the letter to me. Overcome by emotion, I didn't trust myself to speak. Regarding the faces of my children, I knew we all felt the same. Nate scooted closer to me on one side, Allison on the other. As I circled them with my arms, Travis sat and joined us as well. And for that brief instant, for that one moment in time, no words were necessary. We were family.

No matter what.

Finally Allison broke the spell. "Dad, there's, uh, something I've been meaning to tell you," she said hesitantly.

"What is it, Ali?" I asked, wondering what else there could possibly be.

"We had hoped to tell you and Mom together," she said. "Mike and I wanted to make certain first, and then we were waiting for just the right moment, but—"

"What is it, Ali?" I asked.

"You're going to be a grandfather."

Allison's announcement was so unexpected that I once more found myself at a loss for words.

"Cool," said Nate.

"Congratulations, Ali," Travis added with a smile.

"Say something, Dad," Allison said nervously.

Instead of speaking, I took a page from Nate's book and carefully gave my daughter a hug.

"I'm not *that* pregnant," Allison said with a smile. "You can hug me harder than that. I won't break. I'm a Kane, remember?"

"I remember," I finally managed. "Allison, I'm so happy for you and Mike. Your mom would have been overjoyed. This is such wonderful news."

"I . . . I wish I'd had a chance to tell her," Allison said. "Anyway, there's one more thing. If it's a girl, and if it's all right with you . . . Mike and I would like to name her Catheryn."

As Allison spoke Catheryn's name, I suddenly realized that for the entire time we had been at the cemetery, something ominous had been prowling the periphery of my consciousness, enveloping everything I did and said and felt in numbing shades of black. Although it was a feeling that had gripped me for some time, it had grown almost overwhelming since my encounter with Dr. Cole. And although I still didn't understand why he had let me live, I now realized what that feeling was.

"Do you want to continue to live?" Dr. Cole had asked me. And to my shame, I had been unable to answer. I knew more than one police officer who had ended his life by eating his weapon, and I would be lying if I said that at a few low points I hadn't considered it myself. I had lost Tommy, and Catheryn, and at times my self-respect, and more. But had I lost hope, as Dr. Cole suggested? And if that were true, had he considered letting me live to be a fate worse than taking my life? Would I look in the mirror one day and see the same bottomless despair in my own eyes that I had seen in his?

I refused to accept that. As I'd told my children, the world sometimes didn't make sense, but it could also be beautiful, and meaningful, and filled with love. I had much to live for, more than I deserved. I wanted to believe that, and if I didn't completely embrace it at the moment, at least I felt hope for the future.

And, as Dr. Cole had also said, hope was everything.

"Dad?"

"Sorry, Ali," I said, pushing away my thoughts. "I was . . . what was your question?"

"Dad! This is important."

"I know, honey," I said gently. "I know it is. And of course it's okay. It's more than okay. Catheryn would be a perfect name for my new granddaughter. I think your mom would have been pleased beyond words."

And despite all that had happened, despite all we had lost, somehow it seemed . . . right. For wherever Catheryn had gone, wherever she was, if there were some way she could have joined us at that moment, I think she would have been as proud and moved and delighted with Allison's news as I was.

And with that realization I again fell silent, watching with my children as the sun rose slowly across the valley, lighting the distant mountains with hope for today and tomorrow and all our tomorrows to come. Determined to make the most of those tomorrows, clinging to a conviction that anything was possible, anything at all, I silently said the name that would forever live in my heart, filling me to the end of my days with the memory of love.

Catheryn.

Acknowledgments

A number of people provided their assistance when I was writing *L.A. Sniper*. For me, doing the research necessary to make my stories as real and accurate as possible always turns out to be a lot of fun, allowing me to meet and get to know plenty of interesting people as I delve into their areas of expertise and learn new things. Nevertheless, because I write fiction, I occasionally tweak things to suit the needs of my story, so any bending of facts, inaccuracies, or just plain errors in *L.A. Sniper* are attributable to me alone.

With that said, I would like to thank Brix Gustavson for his gift of time and the many helpful suggestions he offered as *L.A. Sniper* took shape. Detective Lee Kingsford had my back again with various LAPD investigative issues, preventing me from straying too far from reality. To Susan Gannon, my wife and muse with an incredible ability to spot story weaknesses (even if it takes me a while to agree), to Dr. Jack Wolfe who enlightened me on cartridge handloading and got me out on the range with a long gun, to Karen Oswalt for her early edit and Sherri Schultz for her final edit, to Karen Waters for her help on the cover, to Mike Dunning for his back-cover photo, to Chris Dunn for welcoming Kane to the Beverly Hills Hotel, to friends and family for their encouragement and support, to my core group of readers—many of whom made critical suggestions for improvements—and last to Caroline Carr and the entire gang of wonderful people at Kindle Press, my sincere thanks.

If you enjoyed *L.A. Sniper*, please leave a review on *Amazon* or your favorite retail site. A word-of-mouth recommendation is the best endorsement possible, and your review will be truly appreciated and help friends and others like you look for books. Thanks for reading!

~ Steve Gannon

About the Author

STEVE GANNON is the author of numerous bestselling novels including *A Song for the Asking*, first published by Bantam Books. Gannon divides his time between Italy and Idaho, living in two of the most beautiful places on earth. In Idaho he spends his days skiing, whitewater kayaking, and writing. In Italy Gannon also continues to write, while enjoying the Italian people, food, history, and culture, and learning the Italian language. He is married to concert pianist Susan Spelius Gannon.

To contact Steve Gannon, purchase books, check out his blog, or to receive updates on new releases, please visit Steve's website at: stevegannonauthor.com

Made in the USA
Middletown, DE
25 March 2020